I

Fictional works by Peter Meredith:

AUTHOR'S NOTE

I don't usually write notes at the beginning of my books. I prefer the reader to dive right in and let the story speak for itself. With *Generation Z*, I felt I needed to warn the fans. Not my fans mind you, because let's be honest, I have far fewer fans than an altogether made-up person with the unlikely name of Jillybean. Her fans number in the tens of thousands and they can be ravenous(not to mention nearly as mad as she is.)

It is to these individuals that this note is for. I beg that you allow the story to unfold as it was meant to. Jillybean is an integral character, but you have to have patience, because, just as in the previous ten books, she is not the only character(even if you wished she was.)

Of course, now that I've mentioned my ten book series, *The Undead World*, I should make it clear that you don't have to have read it to enjoy *Generation Z*. They are two completely different animals. The first series centers around the struggle for survival in a world that's dying *as* an apocalypse occurs. *Generation Z*, on the other hand, is a truly *post*-apocalyptic story.

The world is barren, technology is dead and the remains of our cities are being ravaged by the elements. Yes, there are zombies in the story. In fact, the zombies are for more horrific now that they average eight-feet in height and can take down a solid door with a few swings of their fists.

It's in this world that a generation of orphans have managed to scrape out a pitiful existence. I hope you enjoy their pain(insert evil grin here.)

Peter Meredith

Chapter 1
12 Years Later

Minutes before sunrise, Jenn Lockhart grabbed her two plastic buckets and hurried down to the well before the line got too long. When she arrived, there were already four people there, three teens and a tween, waiting to draw water.

"Morning," each of the four said in turn, speaking softly. She answered in the same manner. As always, they were polite, and as always, she wasn't included in their whispered conversation. Jenn stood off to the side, her pale blue eyes staring at the sunrise. It was violently red and quite spectacular. It washed right over her but she didn't think anything of it until she was heaving her two buckets of water up the stairs to her apartment.

"I'm going to need you this morning."

Slowly, so she wouldn't spill a drop, she turned to see Stu Currans standing at the foot of the stairs. Stu was tall and rangy, and the two were almost eye to eye despite the fact she was on the third step up. He had spoken so quietly that someone ten feet away wouldn't have been able to make out his words.

"We're going to Alcatraz. Be ready at the gate by nine."

At his words, the red sunrise blinked into her mind, as did its meaning: it was a warning of trouble. Hadn't he seen it? Hadn't the Coven? Of course they had, so why were they chancing a trip across the bay? It wasn't her place to ask about the omen, so she bit her tongue.

"What do we need on the island?" she asked, also in a voice barely above a whisper.

Stu hesitated, his dark eyes shifting away before answering, "The traders will be here in four days and I want to talk to Gerry the Greek about getting on the same side this time."

That made sense but, "Why do you need me?" As a rule, she was only invited to join groups venturing outside the walls if there was some annoying job to be done. She hoped she wasn't going to be asked to lug the rest of the moldy venison down to the harbor. It was rancid, but could still be used as bait. She would smell like sour rot for a week. Not that she would turn down the offer, no matter what he demanded. A trip out to Alcatraz Island was a real treat. It would be a chance to see new faces for a change and maybe talk to someone who hadn't already made up their mind about her.

"The Coven wants you to go." He hesitated again, uncharacteristically unsure of himself. "Maybe they think you deserve it, or maybe they think it's your turn. Who knows? Just be at the gate by nine."

He turned on the heels of his faded boots and left Jenn standing on the stairs in a state of confusion. It wasn't a secret that the Coven disliked her and had ever since the night of the big earthquake nine years before. They had all lived on Alcatraz back then, however after the earthquake that had sent a building falling on her father and squishing him like a grape, the Coven had decided to leave the island. They had chosen exactly seventy-seven people to come with them to the hills above Sausalito across the Golden Gate Bridge. Seventy-seven was considered a lucky number.

Jenn had trailed after the group as an uninvited, ignored, and definitely unwanted six-year-old orphan, struggling under the weight of her dead father's pack. She had been number seventy-eight—an unlucky number.

"Why would they want me to go?" she wondered as she teetered up the stairs holding the buckets just so. She worried over the question for the next half hour as she filled her bathtub, two buckets at a time, and got a good blaze going in her fireplace to heat the water. Ironically, taking a bath was a long and dirty process. Once clean, she towel-dried her auburn hair and dressed in jeans and a purple sweater, throwing a camouflage coat over both. Slinging her pack across her thin shoulders, she picked up her crossbow and headed out.

She made her way down to the one gate in the cast iron fence that surrounded the apartment complex, and was surprised to see little Aaron Altman standing in Stu's shadow. He had a school bag over his shoulder.

"What's with the shrimp?" she asked, gazing down at Aaron and noting his sickly pallor.

Stu gave her a quick up and down look. "His mom wants him to start going out more. It's about time if you ask me. It doesn't help anything to mollycoddle boys like this. Hell, I don't remember a time when I wasn't going out into the world."

Was this what the fiery red sunrise pointed to? Jenn hoped not. If something happened to Aaron, she would be blamed, like always.

"Let's get locked and loaded," Stu said, heaving back on the cable of his crossbow. Jenn did the same thing, though she had to strain with all of her ninety-two pounds to draw hers back. When they had their bolts set in place, Stu nodded at the two children sitting on the wall. The two were brothers and despite the bigger of them being only eight, they had the tired, washed-out faces of old men.

They were all like that. Stu was only twenty-one, yet he had the eyes of a man who'd seen a dozen friends die. Jenn was lucky that way. She didn't have friends to watch die.

The brothers waved, not at Jenn or Stu, but at Aaron Altman. They were jealous he was getting to leave the complex. He waved back quickly and then turned to the outside world, his eyes darting back and forth like those of a rabbit. His shoulders were hunched and he was already in a crouch as if ready to run. He was scared.

In front of him, Stu Currans stood poised, gazing down the hill, looking for the dead. He had his head cocked almost to his broad shoulder, trying to pick up what the wind was carrying. So far, there was nothing to hear except the sound of a distant screen door clapping in the gentle autumn breeze. It was a lonely sound. Stu listened for over a minute, his long dark hair blowing back and forth. Satisfied they were alone, he hitched his pack before nodding at Jenn.

Wordlessly, the three wound their way through the forest of spears surrounding the apartment complex until they reached the broken road. It was a mile from the complex to the harbor, an easy fifteen-minute walk back in the *before*. Now, Jenn figured it would take them an hour, maybe longer if the wind picked up. The wind, if it began to blow too hard or from the wrong direction, could mask the sound of the dead. If that happened, they would end up moving at a snail's pace, slipping from one hiding place to the next.

Jenn wasn't too worried if it came to that. Although she was only fifteen, she'd been out of the gates a thousand times, and Stu had been out even more than that, though what number was beyond a thousand Jenn didn't know. In truth, she had never counted to a thousand and was afraid to try. At a certain point, large numbers made her anxious. She didn't like them. They were part of the old world and the old technology and, as everyone knew, technology was what had made the dead come to life.

She put her faith in something greater than mere numbers. Signs and omens guided her, just as they did for all the Hill People, all except Stu. He had foolishly ignored the red sunrise for instance. Now, right in front of him was a fallen tree branch. To her shock, he lifted a worn boot and stepped over it instead of going around the broken end.

A few feet in front of her Aaron almost added to their bad luck. Jenn quickly closed the gap and pulled him back. As if the branch was as deadly as a snake, he jumped when he saw it. He should've known better. After all, his mother, Miss Shay, was part of the Coven. When it came to signs and omens, the seven "old" women knew everything there was to know, and it was through their interpretations that they led the Hill People.

Jenn guided Aaron around the branch—the second evil sign that morning. If there was a third, and she could feel right down into her bones that there would be, something very bad was going to happen.

She slowed, moving with extra caution as they crept along what had once been a pretty suburban street where children had played kick the can and neighbors had waved to one another, or chatted over fences. There were only ghosts living there now. The houses were like wooden skeletons, and the few cars on the street were ravaged hunks of metal sitting on tires that were not just flat but also crumbling away.

They were halfway down the block when they heard a scream of rage. As the scream echoed off the empty houses and down the tortured streets, Stu went to one knee, his eyes sharp and alert. Aaron should have done the same, instead he turned, his face a white mask of fear. He started running but Jenn snagged the back of his pack and hauled him behind a tree.

"It's okay," she whispered. "Look." It was a runty seven-footer that was missing an arm. Its face was partially torn away and one of its eyes dangled from its socket. It hadn't seen them.

She could feel Aaron's heart racing. "It's okay," she said again. "I ran the first time, too." Of course she had been six at the time and out on her own. The handouts had all but dried up during that first surprisingly cold winter on the hilltop and people were starving. Her only choice was to either go out and scrounge or die.

Stu glanced down at Aaron and raised an eyebrow at the boy's shaking hands, but said nothing. He pointed back the way they came and led them through a series of back-yards where the weeds ran as high as their belts. The next street that he chanced was very much like the first, only there were three grey-skinned beasts lurking among the ruins. They dodged again only to run into another pair of them two blocks over. The two zombies were mindlessly pulling down the garage door of a bi-level, but for what reason it was impossible to guess. Sometimes they attacked their own shadows.

"Are those locals?" Stu asked.

The three of them were crouched next to one of the empty houses. In front of Jenn, Aaron was still shivering in fright. He'd get over it. She looked over the top of his head. "I've never seen them."

"Me neither," Stu grunted, and without another word, blazed a path through more yards to where the homes began to mix with small businesses. Over the last few years Jenn had been to each, and knew them inside and out. The first was a bakery, the next a salon, the third was a florist —it was one of the few buildings with an intact front window.

As they were passing it, Aaron paused, staring at the glass and at first, Jenn thought he was staring at his own frail reflection, then she saw something move inside. Quickly, she pulled Aaron back. It was too late for Stu. He was halfway across the front of the building when a shadow took over the entire window.

He froze in mid-step.

With unbelievable calm, he turned his head slowly, inch by inch until he could see directly into the shop where a low rumbling moan had begun. A tic started to jerk Stu's left eye in a quick pulse. It was all the warning Jenn had before the window exploded outward, sending shards of flickering glass everywhere.

Stu threw himself back, firing his crossbow at the terror that came roaring out of the shop.

It was one of the dead. They were not like they had been when Jenn was little. Back then, they had been normal-sized, like everyday people. They had been scary enough, but now they were huge and horrifying beyond belief. At eight and a half feet tall and roughly six hundred pounds, the beast towered over Stu. What hair it had on its bulbous head grew in patches and hung in long greasy strands. It had sickening sores running all over its naked body, and its teeth were broken and jagged, filling its gaping mouth like the teeth of a shark.

It was so large that the crossbow bolt sticking out of its face just below its right eye looked like an over-sized toothpick. The bolt went unnoticed as it reached down with one huge hand, its yellowed fingernails like the claws of a lion.

The claws just missed as Stu dropped and rolled beneath a delivery van that had been sitting half-on the curb since Jenn had first come up the hill. When he disappeared, the creature roared and threw itself at the van, crumpling its side in and lifting it three feet into the air. It might have turned the van over, but Stu popped up on the other side and took off running for his life.

The creature dropped the van with a crash and charged after him. Not only had the dead continued to grow year after year, they were fast and getting faster all the time. In three strides it was right on Stu's heels as he turned the corner.

"What do we..." Aaron started to ask, but Jenn slammed a hand over his mouth and shoved him down into the gutter, where they landed on a bed of wet leaves next to a pile of rust and rubber that had once been a Volvo.

Jenn immediately began to burrow into the leaves and after a second, Aaron did the same. They had already passed more of the dead than Jenn would normally see in a week. She buried herself, keeping only part of her face out so she could peer under the Volvo as more of the dead appeared from whatever dark places they'd been hiding in.

She counted three sets of legs heading towards the florist shop. Quickly, Jenn scooped more leaves over herself and then froze, her muscles bunched and ready to sprint out of there. Aaron was shaking, making the leaves quiver with a rustling sound.

"Shh," she whispered, but the noise only grew as the dead came closer and closer. Jenn was worried that Aaron was on the verge of running again. This time, if he ran, she'd have no choice but to let him run—and let him die. He would never make it and neither would she if she did anything but lie still.

But he didn't run. Somehow he held it together as the three beasts came stomping around the Volvo and the van. Jenn closed her eyes and held her breath, knowing that the stench coming from the dead was sometimes enough to make a person choke.

Aaron began to gag. It was a small sound, but it brought the three right at them. Through the mesh of leaves, Jenn could see one standing right above her; from her angle it looked like a giant. It was filthy and horrid. Fresh urine ran down one scarred and mutilated thigh. There was rage in its filmed-over eyes and without warning it slammed a hand down on the hood of the Volvo, breaking one of its last windows and sending glass raining down on the leaves covering Jenn.

The rustling of leaves picked up and now she could hear Aaron's breath blowing in and out. The beast above her glared downwards and was just beginning to reach out one of its tremendous clawed hands when there came a huge crash from around the corner.

With urgent, hungry moans, the dead began drifting towards the sound. Jenn poked her head up again, watching them until they were out of sight. Only then did she start to crawl from the gutter. She stopped when she realized Aaron hadn't moved. Reaching back she dug under the leaves and pulled him up by an ear. She glared hard at him and then jerked her head for him to follow.

Like rats, they crept around the florist's shop, crossed a muddy alley and slipped down the side of another building.

"What are we going to do without Stu?" Aaron asked, his voice warbling.

"It's alright, he got away," Jenn assured him. She would have known if he hadn't. It was impossible for someone to stifle their screams as they were being eaten alive. Jenn had heard enough of those screams to know this for a fact. Her earliest memory was a hazy series of moving black and white pictures. Whenever someone said the words "Remember when…" Jenn's mind always went back to it and every time she felt the same insidious, deep fear.

It was the memory of her mom being torn to pieces by a swarm of the dead. Jenn had been twenty feet from her, hiding practically in plain sight beneath a bicycle. Her mom's screams had been so loud that even now, years later, they still echoed inside Jenn's head and as always when the memory struck her, a wave of goosebumps broke out on her arms.

She rubbed them away. "Come on," she whispered and made her way around the building. "We'll meet him at the harbor." They still had a quarter mile to go; a very dangerous quarter mile. They slunk along hedges, slipped through empty sewer pipes and crawled through gutters and by the time they got close, they were both filthy.

Stu was nowhere in sight, but she knew in her heart he would show. In the meantime they hid. Hiding was smart and it was what she did best. She was small and skinny—undernourished and underdeveloped. At fifteen she still had the hips of a boy, while her breasts were almost nonexistent.

She thought there was something wrong with her. Then again, she thought there was something wrong with all of them. The world and everything in it was dying. Everyone knew that.

After putting Aaron in a dust-filmed Chrysler and warning him not to move until she said so, she went to a Toyota whose windows were so filthy that nothing could be seen inside. There was no telling how long their wait would be, so she fished around the floorboards and came up with a magazine.

The pages made crackling sounds as she pulled them apart and gazed at the glossy pictures of a world that was nothing remotely like the world she lived in. In the magazine world, the men were strong, clean-shaven and handsome, while the women were always stunningly beautiful. Their teeth were always straight and white, their skin silky-smooth, their hair perfect.

They were all so...she didn't know the word "elegant," and had to settle for pretty.

The world these pretty people lived in was just as perfect as they were. The streets were clean enough to eat off, the cars shone and sparkled like ice, and the buildings were fantastic monuments that seemed eternal.

Everything was the opposite in Jenn's dying world. When she inched up to check on Aaron, she saw a world that was in the long process of deteriorating into nothing.

There was no flash or shine to the cars; their tires had long since deflated and their engines had seized. Even if there was gas to put in them, they would never move again. And even if they could move, twelve winters had buckled the streets, turning them craggy. Now weeds, shrubs and even trees grew right up out of the gaping pot-holes and the long, widening cracks. In some places the streets were simply gone. Flash floods had swallowed them, leaving behind mini-canyons.

She sighed as she slunk back down; she liked the magazine world better than her own world. The magazine world was magical, while hers was diseased.

One of the pictures in the magazine, that of a teenage boy on a skateboard, called to her. The boy seemed to be flying on the board, his long clean, brown hair flowing behind him, a look of joy on his grinning face. She knew what skateboards were, but like everything else, they seemed to have lost their magic. They no longer flew; they were lucky to roll anymore.

The picture went into a Ziplock bag in her pack along with a growing stack of others. She was just pulling the pack back on when the silence was broken by a long, loud, creaking noise.

It was the frightfully urgent sound of a rusted door opening. It had to be Aaron. Slowly, Jenn eased up and peeked through the dirty window of the Toyota and saw Aaron, standing half-in and half-out of the Chrysler, one arm up as if he were about to wave. Thirty feet beyond him was Stu, slunk down against the side of a building and pointing with sharp jabs to Aaron's right at one of the dead that had been standing in the shadows of a Jiffy Lube.

The beast had heard the car door and was now peering out with rage-filled eyes.

14

Aaron froze in fear, a look of utter panic on his face. He stood only fifteen paces away from it and Jenn could see, plain as day, the scream building in his throat.

Chapter 2

Stuart Currans

Stu swore when he saw Aaron getting out of the car. It wasn't as if this was Aaron's first trip out of the complex. And he had been briefed on what to do in case they ran into one of the dead, which was exactly what was practically scraping its ugly head on the eaves of the Jiffy Lube.

In Stu's mind it should have been an easy trip. A quiet one. It was only a mile from the apartment complex to the docks where the group stashed a couple of canoes and a small sailboat. Once on the water, they'd be perfectly safe…mostly. It wasn't unheard of in San Francisco for a strange squall to suddenly spring up out of nowhere, especially at this time of year.

As far as expeditions went, this should have been one of the easier ones. It was why he had allowed Aaron to come at all. Jenn was a steady girl, quick and smart. When the Coven had suggested that she go, it had been a no-brainer. It should have been the same with Aaron. He had grown up in the apocalypse, and should've known better than to make himself a target with the dead around.

Still, Aaron wasn't in the worst of positions. The creature hadn't yet spotted him. Whether out of fear, instinct or naked self-preservation, Aaron had turned to stone and now it would be a battle between his patience and the zombie's hunger. If it was hungry enough, it would start to turn in small circles, searching for whatever had made the sound.

Like all of the dead, its eyesight was terrible and its sense of smell almost nonexistent. Their hearing on the other hand was nearly perfect. It was why the group stressed the need for quiet at all times.

Stu gave Aaron a fifty-fifty chance and had he been an adult, Stu would have let the moment play out, only he knew that if something happened to Aaron he would never hear the end of it from his mother. Miss Shay would squawk and squawk, and would she take any responsibility for the fact that she had babied Aaron and coddled him too much? No. Aaron was unreliable because of her over-protective mothering.

"But does she listen to me?" he griped as he hefted his crossbow. Practically everyone who left the complex carried a crossbow. Everyone who could be trusted with one that is. Aaron didn't have one.

The bow Stu carried was a brute. It was a Ravin R15 and it could fire a steel bolt at 425 feet per second, striking with 165 pounds of kinetic energy. As impressive as that sounded, the bolt seemed small and weak compared to the beast, which was a foul, naked creature with skin like grey oatmeal, stunted nubs for fingers and jagged broken teeth set in black gums.

It wasn't the biggest zombie he had seen. No, the record-holder was a nine-and a-half-foot tall monster that was known as Frank, which was short for Frankenstein. He had received his name not just because of his great size. Frank also had a huge scar running across its forehead where he'd been shot with a .45 caliber round by a man who didn't live very long after pulling the trigger.

When Stu had come across Frank a few months back, he'd run up a tree and stayed there for four hours and although he could have taken a few shots with the Ravin, he didn't bother. If a bullet to the head couldn't kill Frank, a bolt probably wouldn't either.

Since then he had started carrying a .357 Magnum. As he only had three rounds of ammo it was his weapon in case of an utter emergency, which this was not. He also had a climber's axe. It was two and a half feet long with a deadly seven-inch spike at the end. It was strong and durable and had yet to be tested against the dead and he hoped it never would be. Getting within arm's reach of one of the beasts was a nightmare for him.

The axe hung from his belt, swinging in a cool wind. That same wind whipped his long brown hair about his face as he took aim with the Ravin and fired at the creature. Faster than the eye could follow, the bolt flew through the air and caught the beast in the cheek, snapping its head back.

The bolt did nothing but make it angry and with a scream of rage that echoed through the empty streets, the creature charged at Stu.

There was an unusual number of zombies in the town, and with them stirred up, he knew he couldn't just run again, blundering from one to the next. He had to take this one out if he could. Unfortunately, the Ravin took a good seven seconds to load and he only had three seconds before the creature was on him.

"Get back in the car," he snapped at Aaron as he sprinted around the truck twice, and then around the Toyota Jenn was hiding in, opening a bit of a lead on the moaning beast. It was fast but, like the rest, clumsy and fell a lot. When he could, Stu raced back to the truck, climbed in one side and left the truck door open, hoping that the dead thing would follow him inside.

The creature paused, staring in at Stu with its muddy eyes; its breath, all rot and horror, washed over him, making him gag. The truck seemed like a clown-car compared to the huge zombie. Stu counted on it coming in after him where it would get stuck, hopefully long enough for Stu to get his crossbow ready to fire again.

Instead, the creature stuck a long grey arm into the truck, reaching for him. Stu backed as far away as he could, scrambling for the button to unlock the door. He pressed it repeatedly, but nothing happened. The groping hand touched his left boot and passed right over it, perhaps searching for something with more of a human feel.

In the footwell was an old school bag, its many pockets unzipped and hanging open like steel-teethed mouths. Stu grabbed it and shoved it toward the hand. A second later, the bag was ripped out of sight. The beast took a bite out of it before it even knew what it was. With a bellow of rage, it tossed the bag aside, grabbed the truck's door and threw its unholy strength against it. There came a scream of metal as the door bent back further than Stu thought possible, and a moment later the hinges broke and the door swung free.

Still in a rage, the dead creature slammed the door onto the roof of the truck, crumpling it in. It then flung the door aside like it was tossing a paper plate. "Holy crap," Stu hissed, realizing that if it wanted to, the zombie could pull the truck apart with him still in it.

Using his climber's axe, he smashed out the window of the door he was pressed against and wiggled through to spill out onto the broken asphalt just as the zombie plunged into the truck after him. Stu actually grinned, knowing the beast would never get through the window. He took out a bolt for the crossbow, thinking he had plenty of time, but through some cruel trick of fate, the door popped open as the beast slammed its head against it.

With another curse, Stu scrambled to load his cross-bow. Bracing it with his feet, he heaved back on the cable until it locked in place. Next, he fitted the bolt into the groove, sliding it all the way back so he wouldn't waste any of the kinetic energy now stored in the cable.

By then, the beast was semi-stuck. It was clawing its huge frame through the back seat like some grotesque swimmer.

This gave Stu time to line up a shot. Although he was close, his target, the creature's forehead, was small, seven inches by six. Still, he should not have missed, but he did. With the creature scrambling and flailing, its head bobbing up and down as it struggled, the bolt kicked off its temple, leaving a gash that leaked black blood. A second later the beast piled onto the pavement right in front of Stu, who was cocking back the cable a second time. He managed to pull it into place but there was no time to put the bolt in the groove as the zombie struggled to its feet.

He thought that he would have to make another run around the cars, but then Jenn was there, standing on the roof of the truck, aiming her own crossbow. She was small, probably not more than ninety pounds and her bow was correspondingly smaller. He remembered the day she had come back from scrounging with it three years earlier;

she couldn't reload it by herself and after shooting it, she had to ask around for someone to pull the cable back for her.

Regardless of her strength, she was an excellent shot and when she fired, her bolt thudded home, piercing the back of the thing's head. The zombie let out a long gasping breath and turned slowly. There was no telling what was going to happen next. Sometimes the beasts ignored even these sorts of headshots, sometimes they only made them angrier. In this case, it fell face first onto the street, its skull cracking wide open, spilling a sludge of black goo onto the street.

Instead of celebrating her first zombie kill, Jenn dropped into a crouch and gazed all around, her blue eyes at sharp slits. The danger hadn't passed, and it wouldn't pass until they were safe behind the walls of Alcatraz. Anything could still happen. "Do you see any more of them?" Stu asked in a low voice.

She shook her head and slid down off the truck. They both turned to Aaron, who slowly climbed out of the Chrysler, his head hung low. "I saw you and I thought it was safe," was his excuse.

Jenn walked up and punched him in the arm hard enough to make him wince. "I told you to wait until I said it was clear. I have half a mind to leave you right here until we get back."

"He gets one screw-up, Jenn," Stu said. "The next time, the dead will take care of him for us. Let's get out of sight for a few minutes."

They hurried into the Jiffy Lube.

While Aaron watched the back, Stu and Jenn kept an eye on the street, which remained still and quiet, save for a gathering of thin, ugly crows. The birds flitted onto sagging telephone lines and sat staring at the body of the dead beast. It wouldn't be long before they began to pull strips of rancid flesh from it.

"What did they do in a Jiffy Lub-ey?" Jenn asked, glancing around at the bays and the black pits set into the concrete floor. "Something about cars, right?"

"It's pronounced *lube* and yes, they'd work on cars. I think, like repairing them or something. By the way, that was a hell of a shot. What would you've done if you missed?"

She blushed and then laughed. "I would've let him eat you." Even though it was a joke, it unnerved him a bit and their talk dried up.

Stu kept them holed up for half an hour before he chanced the street again, heading for the docks, going slower than before. He kept to the shaded side of the street and moved warily, his head constantly on a swivel. He knew the dead about as well as anyone. The local packs were predictable, lumbering from grazing point to grazing point in conjunction with the sun. Now that the days were growing colder, they spent more time in open fields, eating grass, berries and nuts. They were omnivores, and about the only thing they didn't eat were themselves.

As it was just after noon, he knew that the Langendorf Park pack would have trudged up into the open hills above Highway 444, leaving them a straight shot to the docks... unless there were more strays and of course, there were. Stu spotted two more small groups, both times before they themselves were spotted. He skirted around them and came at Pelican Harbor from the south. A block from the actual docks was a Mexican restaurant that had once been a bank. The group kept their few watercraft inside the building.

Before the apocalypse, the harbor had been home to thousands of boats, from dinghies to million-dollar yachts, but when the dead came the marinas emptied out as people looked to the oceans for safety. They left and they never came back, and where they went, no one knew. Stu liked to think there was a zombie-free island out in the middle of the Pacific where people lived happy lives.

Cautious as always, Stu entered the restaurant alone. When he found it deserted, he called the others over. Aaron looked at the sailboat sitting on its trailer almost as if it were a joke. "That's it? Really? It looks kinda small, don't you think?" It was very small, only thirteen feet long and four feet across. "*Puffer*?" Aaron asked, reading the word stenciled on the back. "Is this a toy? Or like a kiddie boat?"

"It's a real boat," Stu growled. "And it'll be fine. I've been on this thing dozens of times. It's a good boat. Just do what I say and don't do anything stupid." He walked to the front of the trailer and started pulling. Not only was the boat very small, it was also light and Stu could handle it and the trailer single-handedly.

As he hauled it down to the boat ramp, Jenn, steady as always, kept watch while Aaron just stared at the boat, his face pale. Stu clamped him on the shoulder. "It'll be fun. You'll see."

Thankfully, the winds were calm that morning and the bay was no choppier than the water in a three-year old's bath. It made for an easy time.

Aaron ended up loving the little craft and after twenty minutes was scampering around it like an old hand. Jenn had the opposite reaction. Although it wasn't her first time on board, she held onto the sides and was generally reluctant to move.

When Stu asked her what was wrong, she answered, "You saw the signs. Don't pretend you didn't. And besides, you know what happened last month, the same as me." She paused, glanced at Aaron, who was sitting at the very front of the boat with his toes skimming the cold water, and whispered, "Ralph Duggin D-R-O-W-N-D. You ever think that maybe this boat is H-U-N-T-D?"

"Hunted?"

"No, haunted by the ghost of Ralph. I know for a fact that he didn't wear a cross." She released her hold on the side of the boat long enough to fish hers out from under her camouflage coat. The cross was large, about the length and width of her palm. It glittered in the sun as if it had been recently polished.

"Maybe he wasn't a Christian."

"It doesn't matter if he had religion or not," she insisted. "He didn't wear a cross and he never paid attention to the signs. It was no wonder he..." She paused again to glance at Aaron. "It's no wonder he D-I-D."

The wind took that moment to gust heavily, tipping the boat alarmingly. Jenn sucked in a breath and grabbed the sides. Stu altered course slightly, steering into the wind, which immediately righted the boat. It also slowed them and the sail began snapping. Gradually, he eased the *Puffer* back on course, close-hauling her until the wind was nearly in their face.

Jenn's superstitions weren't out of the ordinary, especially among the middling teens and the children who were born after it all began. They'd been raised to see signs and omens in everything. Stu didn't understand why so many of the older people believed in that baloney as well.

He thought that they were superstitious because they needed to know there was more than just chance governing their lives. In their minds, vengeful spirits could be appeased and gods could be prayed to. Thankfully, no one had yet begun casting "spells." He could laugh off a goofy charm pendant or an anti-hex bag but he drew the line at anyone thinking they had real powers.

"It's D-I-E-D," he told her. "And Ralph bought the farm probably because he was reckless. You don't mess with the sea. It'll bite you in the ass if you do. At the same time, you can't live in fear of it."

Jenn cast a doubtful look at the grey water. "I'm not afraid of the water. Not really. It's the signs that got me wigged. Was it all of the Coven that said I should come with you? If it was all seven, that would be a good number, but if it was six..." She sketched a quick sign of the cross before saying, "Everyone knows six is bad, bad, bad and the worst of all is six crows all in a line. You saw the crows after we killed that zombie. There were six of them!"

"But they weren't all in a row. And it was all seven of the Coven who wanted you to come with me, so you're in luck."

"Oh, good," she said, visibly relieved. "I still don't know why they wanted me to come, anyway."

Stu hesitated and then shrugged. He was tired of lying to her and felt that silence was a better policy.

Chapter 3

Stuart Currans

He was not an expert sailor. Although he aimed the boat at the island's one docking site, the wind and current pushed him past it. Cursing, he was forced to grind the *Puffer* up against the seawall that ringed the island.

A laughing face appeared over the side of the wall. It was Mike Gunter, his long, blond braid hanging down over one shoulder, his beard coming in nicely. "Nice job, Captain Stu. Do you want to bring her around and try again, or would you like a tow?"

To try again would take another half an hour and there was no guarantee that he would do any better, which would only add to his embarrassment. "A tow would be nice. The current is running quick today."

Mike tossed down a rope saying, "Oh, it was the *current*. That explains everything." Jenn caught the rope, tied it at the prow, then sat back staring up as Mike hauled them back to the dock. The seventeen-year old was about average in height and thin as a reed. He was stronger than he looked and didn't need help pulling the boat along, still, others joined him. They would suddenly appear, grinning down at Stu. Each time Mike would say, "The 'current' got him," and each time there would be a burst of laughter.

Pretty much everyone on Alcatraz could sail better than Stu, which was to be expected since they sailed back and forth from the mainland practically every day, while Stu went out once a month or so.

By the time they made it the dock, there was a crowd of people standing around staring at the unimpressive looking boat and cracking jokes. They were a young lot. All of them were skinny and wore their hair long. Even the men had braids that hung past their shoulders. Their clothes, jeans and sweaters were mostly ripped and torn, but clean, while they themselves were not.

It was one thing to wash clothes in the cold water pulled from the bay, but to bathe in it was a painful experience. Even during the summer months, the water temperature rarely broke the sixty-degree mark. Stu's clan had forests within a hundred yards of the apartment complex and fetched wood daily with little problem. Stu took a warm bath every other day.

The island people took quick "whore's baths" and used a lot of perfume, when they could get it. It was their fashion to grow thick beards, though most of the younger men at the dock could only grow sparse and patchy scruff.

Stu was the first to come off the *Puffer,* and he did so very carefully. He knew that he would never hear the end of it if he fell in. Mike was kind enough to put out a hand and pull him onto the dock.

He helped Jenn off next and then marveled over her with a wide smile on his face. "Holy moly, Jenn Lockhart! I didn't know that was you. It's been ages. How long has it been?"

"I think about a year or two," she said. She stepped towards him and he mistook the move and gave her an awkward hug, pinning her arms to her sides. A nervous laugh escaped her. "I was just going to see how much you've grown. I used to come up to your nose and now I barely make it to your chin."

Mike's cheeks went red as people sniggered behind his back. "I-I had like a mini growth spurt." He gestured vaguely towards the top of his head.

"I wish I would get a growth spurt. At this rate, I might never crack five foot."

"You'll get there," he replied, standing straighter and lifting his head high. "What you need is some milk. We're hoping the traders have a few goats left by the time they get here. That's all Gerry has been talking about for the last week. He even has us stockpiling grass and hay and all that sort of thing. It's a pain in the butt. We have to sail all the way up to the Sacramento River to harvest it. I just hope it's worth it. What about you guys? What are you looking to get?"

26

The traders were expected on October first which was only four days away. They were the main reason Stu had made the trip to Alcatraz. "Bullets mostly."

Mike let out a grunt. "Good luck with that." Bullets had once been the unit of exchange, taking the place of the dollar bill. At one point, a single bullet could be traded for a chicken egg or ten ounces of gasoline. Now, it would take three dozen chicken eggs to purchase a bullet. Not that anyone actually had chickens. Like everything else, they had become very scarce.

"Where's Gerry?" Stu asked. "I have to talk business with him."

"Up on the water tower. The rust was getting bad." Mike shook his head, as did almost everyone around them. "Everything tasted like it. We had to drain the tower and he's been scraping at it for the last couple of days."

"How's his mood?"

Mike considered the question, his pleasant features turning plastic, which meant Stu could expect Gerry to be in a bad mood. "Hit or miss, mostly. It's been like that since Abbey. I'm sure he'll be all right with you."

Stu hoped so. He needed Gerry to be in the proper frame of mind for what he was proposing. "Hey, can you keep Jenn and Aaron company for an hour or two?"

"Can we go to the prison?" Aaron asked. "The way everyone talks makes it sound all spooky, like there are real ghosts there. Don't worry, I'm tougher now. And look, I got a knife. My mom gave it to me special for the trip." He started to pull it out; Jenn laid a hand on his arm and shook her head.

"It's not a toy, it's a tool. And don't talk about hauntings out loud." She crossed herself again. Stu rolled his eyes, wishing he could talk some sense into her. She was too fixated on omens and put too much faith in the Coven. They weren't bad people, far from it. But they were an anxious fearful lot who based their decisions with the specter of imminent death clouding their judgment and turning everything into a "sign."

The islanders were almost as superstitious while their leader Gerry the Greek was not. Stu knew that in private Gerry scoffed at their omens, while in public he used his people's fears to his advantage. Gerry Xydis or Gerry the Greek as people knew him since his last name was almost unpronounceable, was one of the few friends Stu had left.

When Stu crossed to the water tower he paused, looking up at the ladder. "Let's hope Jenn was wrong about those signs," he muttered as he began heading up. Heights weren't Stu's thing and he gripped the rungs so hard that his hands began to sweat which only made him more nervous.

Sixty feet up wasn't all that high and yet with the wind beginning to gust hard enough to sway the tower. It took all of his courage to keep going to the top where there was a gap of about a foot and a half through which he could crawl under the domed roof.

"Who the hell is that? Is that Stu-freaking-Currans?" Gerry was sitting in the exact center of the tower, which was deep and round and could hold as much water as a backyard pool. Next to him was a five-gallon bucket of what looked like silver paint and to his left was a bottle of wine.

Stu came down the rungs and shook Gerry's silvered palm. The Greek also had splats of silver all over himself, especially in his dark beard. "You know I would have come down for you, Stu."

"Naw. When I heard what you were doing, I didn't want to take any more of your time than I needed."

"Time? I got all the time in the world. There's something wrong with this stuff." He gestured to the paint bucket. "I guess it's spent too much time sitting on a shelf. It separated so badly that it took me two hours of stirring to get it to freakin' blend. That was yesterday and see that side?" He pointed to Stu's left where the silver paint glistened in an even coat. "It's still wet. I did that almost twenty hours ago."

Stu moved closer and after inspecting the silver paint he resisted the urge to touch it. "If I was you, I'd take another drink."

Gerry grinned and picked up the bottle adding yet another silver hand print to it, completely obscuring the label—not that Stu cared. He didn't have much of a head for wine and became sleepy after one glass. Gerry took a swallow and passed the bottle to Stu, who took a polite sip, and then made a face.

"Yeah," Gerry agreed. "It might have gone over. So, what's got you climbing ladders? Looking to come back to the island where you belong?"

It was always the same question and as always Stu shook his head. The only thing he missed about the island was the people. "No, I wanted to talk to you about the traders." Gerry's eyes narrowed.

When there was bad blood between the groups, it had to do with hunting rights or deals worked with the traders. Stu had been up at dawn three days before taking inventory of the group's communal stockpile. It had been a poor summer of hunting and although their winter stockpile was adequate, they had even less for trading than the year before. He had stood there imagining how the bargaining would go with the traders. They would get shredded up as always and come away cheated.

"Every year they play us," Stu said. "Every year they pit our group against yours so they can jack up their prices, while at the same time they use your goods to undercut the value of mine and vice versa."

Gerry looked confused. "What are you saying? Are you suggesting I don't bring everything I have to the table? That would be bull. We have twice your numbers and although it wasn't the best year we've had, I bet we have a lot more to offer than you hillbillies."

Stu let the hillbilly comment go. He held up his hands. "It's not what I'm suggesting. I'm saying we trade with each other fair and square ahead of time. How much fish do you have?" When Gerry hesitated, Stu said, "We have about two hundred pounds of flounder and another hundred of halibut."

"I have about three times that, plus a few hundred pounds of tuna. But I don't get how you and me trading fish will help anything."

He began to tip the bottle again. Stu wished he wouldn't since he was missing the obvious. "Every year we ask for a certain price for our fish and every year they say I can get a better price from Gerry. And I bet they say the same thing to you, don't they?"

Gerry looked a little uncertain when he nodded. Stu went on, "What happens if they couldn't come to me? They would have to take your price, am I right? And what happens to the price of salted venison if I have a monopoly on that? You see? In this way, we both win."

"Oh, hey. Ha-ha! I like it." He thumped a fist down on the bottom of the water tower before lifting the bottle a third time. "We'll seal the deal with a drink." After Stu had taken his sip, Gerry was all ready to head down to their storehouse to begin negotiations.

Stu stopped him. "There's another reason I'm here. It's about Jenn Lockhart and to a lesser extent Mary Shaw and Ginny McGee."

Gerry's eyes had been slightly out of focus, but now they zeroed in on Stu. "Oh, I see. You're looking to marry them off. And you chose those three? One not quite ready and two past their prime?"

"Thirty-five isn't past anyone's prime," he said, ignoring the fact that Ginny was forty-four. "And Jenn is a sweet kid, I mean young woman."

"Is she bleeding yet?"

Stu rolled his eyes. It was bad enough to be even having the conversation at all, but being crude only made it worse. "She's fifteen, not twelve. Look, the only reason I'm talking to you is that we really don't have anyone for her. And I'm not trying to marry her off." This was a complete lie since it was exactly what the Coven had suggested.

"Oh, sure," Gerry said with an exaggerated wink. "You're just allowing her to be exclusively courted, I get it."

"Exactly and the same is true with the two older women. Mary has her eye on Donny Price. I know he's a little younger than her, but these are odd times and maybe they can make it work. Ginny isn't nearly as picky. She's just lonely in that regard since Bill got eaten."

Gerry stroked his long beard as he peered at Stu through heavily lidded eyes. "And if we can make this work, where do you think these three couples will take up residence? I get the feeling that you're trying to weaken my group."

"I figured that we would take Jenn and you can have Ginny. We'll let Mary decide on her own. What do you say?"

"I say the same thing I always say: move back here, Stu. If you come back, then the rest will follow. I know it." Stu shook his head making Gerry curse. He walked in a circle, leaving tracks in the wet paint, which had him cursing again. Finally, he said, "Fine. This was bound to happen. Especially with Donny. That guy's a hound. You know I caught him going down to the Santas? He caught something from one of their 'service girls' and it took like three months to clear up. I thought his pecker was 'bout ready to fall off."

Stu raised an eyebrow at this little tidbit of gossip. The Santas were a wild, dangerous bunch that lived thirty-five miles away in Santa Clara. Although they claimed not to, it was common knowledge that they bought and sold slaves and had been known to waylay people coming up the 101.

"Mary will calm him down," Stu said. "Now about Jenn. I was thinking Mike Gunter."

Stu was a little shocked when Gerry didn't hesitate. "Sure. No problem."

He had spoken so quickly that Stu hesitated. "What's wrong with him? No, don't shake your head. It's bad enough being cheated by the traders."

"I'm not cheating anyone. Mike is great. He's just too much like his old man. If he lives another five years, I'll be shocked." Stu understood. Mike's father had been the bravest of the brave, but it was that fearlessness that had killed him.

Chapter 4

Jenn Lockhart

The afternoon wore away too quickly for Jenn's sake. She and Mike spent the afternoon with a gang of his friends visiting their old haunts and bringing up memories of growing up in the middle of an apocalypse.

They had been safe when so many hadn't been. Safe, but in a sense, dirt poor. Back then there had only been a few boats to support the hundreds of people crowding the island. Food had been scarce and luxuries such as toilet paper or sugar just ceased to exist. From their childish viewpoint, people seemed to die all the time. Every day there was news of this person's mother who was taken by slavers or that one whose father went out scavenging and never returned.

One by one they became orphans and as time passed, the island became less crowded.

They became hardened towards death. When the news came of each death, they would be sad for their friends and cry with them and hold them in their misery, but the next day they would be out jumping rope or playing tag. For a child, the world just kept going and these little breaks in their lives were quickly put behind them.

Of all the games they would play back then, Jenn loved hide and seek the most. With the eerie prison and all the old buildings, the island was a perfect place for hide and seek, and Jenn, due to her small size and lack of fear, had reigned supreme when it came to the game.

If she hadn't been trying to impress Mike and his friends with her newfound maturity, she would have loved to slip back into her childhood and actually play and laugh. She missed laughing. The apartment complex was fenced and gated, still a sense of quiet hung over everything.

Laughter, the proper full-throated kind attracted the zombies. The local packs would lumber down out of the hills and bang on the plywood wall that was fixed over the fence, and moan hungrily, which was always unnerving. Real laughter was rare.

Jenn was very disappointed when Stu hunted them down so early. They were sitting against the lighthouse watching Aaron try to skip stones into the bay. He failed time and again as he kept trying to use ill-shaped rocks. Worse, he couldn't get the angle of his throws down right. The stones plunked dismally, sinking one after the other. The older teens tried to demonstrate the proper technique, but growing up without a real father—his had died while Aaron was a baby and Miss Shay's next two husbands had spent more time hunting and drinking than they had trying to raise a boy who wasn't theirs—had left him "throwing like a girl," as one of the boys remarked.

"I'll show you how a girl throws," Jenn said, tempted to throw a rock right at the boy. Instead, she found a good skipper and bounced it across the water until a whitecap swallowed it. The winds had picked up as had the tide, and now the water in the bay chopped back and forth with little waves going in every direction.

Jenn thought nothing of it until Stu arrived and ordered Mike to get three days' worth of clothes together. "You're coming with us. Gerry wants you to verify what we have to trade. We're going to try something a little different this year."

"That'll take three days?" Mike asked.

"And since when does Gerry not trust you?" Jenn asked.

Stu glared. "Okay, he's a goodwill ambassador who's also going to take inventory. You have room in your apartment for him, don't you?"

"I-I do," she answered, feeling both bewildered and flushed. There were only seventy or so people living in the complex and there were over a hundred apartments. She could understand someone hosting Mike, but why wasn't Stu or one of the other men doing it? It was an obvious question, and yet she held her tongue.

Stu watched her reaction, his dark eyes appraising her. When she didn't say anything he said, "Good. I want to leave before the wind picks up any more. So, Mike, lets hop to." Mike looked just as bewildered as Jenn felt as he started off towards his quarters. "Go with him, Jenn," Stu said, giving her a push. "He might need help."

She hurried to catch up. "What kind of help do you need?"

"The hell if I know," Mike said, glancing back at Stu, who was glaring at the other teens. One of Mike's friends had made a crack about Jenn needing to pick out Mike's clothes for him. "Something weird is going on. Starting with Stu going up to the tower. He hates heights. Always has."

This wasn't news to Jenn. There were very few secrets in a group as small as theirs. "It might have to do with the traders. We didn't have a good summer. Mister Pablo got killed and Winston got giardia and was sick for like, three months."

"Yeah, our summer wasn't the best, either. Um, my room is a bit of a mess. Maybe you should wait out in the hall for a few minutes." They had entered what had once been the bachelor guard quarters of the prison. The gloomy building seemed weathered both inside and out. Paint was peeling from the walls and the handrails were dull orange with rust.

Jenn knew how messy boys could be; they were almost as bad as girls. Jenn was a rare exception. She kept her two-bedroom apartment perfectly neat, always hoping to have visitors which she almost never had. And now she was going to have a friend over for three days! It made her giddy, and as she waited in the unlit hall, she completely forgot the fishy circumstances. She was too busy worrying over what she would feed him and how much wood she had. The hills were far warmer than the island, still it was almost October and the nights were dipping into the thirties.

She had taken to sleeping in her living room where her fireplace was, but she couldn't do that with Mike over. That wouldn't be proper. In fact, she should sleep with her door closed and…

"I'm ready," Mike said, squeezing out into the hall. He hadn't opened his door more than seven inches, meaning he had to literally squeeze. In one hand he carried a plain white pillowcase with his clothes in it, and in the other hand he carried his unloaded crossbow.

There was an awkward moment between the two of them as they stared at each other. Mike then grinned, his cheeks high with color. "Do you think Stu will let me pilot the boat? He's a little sloppy when he tacks and loses a lot of momentum. Also with the wind up…" He broke off, shrugging.

"You're the expert," Jenn said, hoping she didn't sound like she was gushing.

They left the building, which was right around the corner from the dock. It was a hive of activity as the island's "fleet" was coming in. It consisted of six small sailboats and a long canoe being paddled by five men, who were straining furiously in the face of a building wind. The sailboats on the other hand went back and forth, slowly eating up the distance.

Stu stood at the railing near where the *Puffer* was bobbing up and down. Aaron was already on it, fiddling with the rope holding the boat fast to the dock. Jenn saw that he was in danger of freeing it. Sure enough the knot came loose in his hands and he began to panic.

"Chill, little dude," Mike said, grabbing a boat hook and pulling the *Puffer* back. To Stu he said, "We should cast off before the others come back. The dock gets a little clogged at this time of day with everyone fighting to come in." He turned to Jenn and whispered, "They also get a little cranky when things aren't perfectly exact. They all think they're God's gift to the Royal Navy or something."

He lowered his pillowcase to Aaron before leaping across, landing softly on the *Puffer* as if he were landing on the deck of an aircraft carrier. He turned and put a hand out to Jenn. She grinned and tried to make the same jump. Her feet slipped out from beneath her but he caught her easily.

"You did that on purpose," he said, righting her and setting her squarely on her feet. "Since when do you play the damsel in distress?"

"What are you talking about?" Like nearly everyone her age, she could barely read and didn't understand the reference but was sure that he was putting her down in some way. Her blue eyes drew down and her smile dimmed. "Damn-sel? What's that?"

He looked to one of his friends in confusion and was about to say something when Stu grunted, "It was a compliment, Jenn. Budge over."

She couldn't see how sticking the word 'damn' in anything was a compliment. With the boat bouncing beneath her, and with both hands gripping the edges, she moved to the front next to Aaron, who smiled at her, showing a wide gap in his teeth. "Boats are cool," he told her. "Do you think the Coven will let me be a captain of one?"

She agreed that they were cool. With their colorful sails flying high, there was something beautiful as well as joyous in the way the boats raced across the water. "I don't see why not," she told him. "But you know that you're going to have to learn to swim."

This doused his desire a bit. Because of his overprotective mother, Aaron had never learned to swim. He wasn't the only one, either. Only about half of the Hill People could swim and, despite living off the water, even fewer of the Islanders could. The bay was just too frigid of a place for the hours of practice needed.

Jenn could swim. She had taught herself, just like she had taught herself how to hunt and fish, to gut a deer and clean a bass. She had not taught herself to sail. Deciding to change that, she turned around on the short bench to watch what Mike was doing.

Using a thin line of rope, he ran up their single sail, while at the same time heeling the tiller all the way to the right. As simply as that, the boat spun away from the dock so that its prow pointed out into the bay. Before the turn was complete, he pulled the tiller back the other way.

"How do you know how far to pull that handle?" she asked him. "Is there a marker on it somewhere?"

He wiped a stray hair that had slipped from his braid out of his eyes and answered, "No. It's all a matter of feel and practice. You also have to know how to play the currents. Right, Stu?" He gave his friend a wink.

"Yeah, sure," he growled in answer. Jenn asked more questions and Mike was only too happy to go on and on. As they tacked right to avoid the oncoming boats she was eager to try her hand.

Stu asked, "What about your signs? Aren't you nervous?"

Her face clouded over and for just a moment doubt came over her, then Mike remarked, "Signs are never wrong though sometimes we misread them."

Stu turned away, but not so quickly that she missed his eyes rolling or his sigh which was quickly eaten up by the wind. She knew he was about to give her his usual lecture on omens and signs, when he rose up suddenly, going into a squat, his head held high.

They were two hundred yards off the island by then and only had two boats between them and the open bay. Both were tacking away from them, but would be swinging back any minute. "What's that?" he asked, pointing at the water on the *Puffer's* port side. Sixty feet away were what looked to Jenn like white seals, only they were floating and not swimming.

"Is that trash?" she asked. "Or…" Mike had checked the boat's momentum and now they all saw that it wasn't trash; they were corpses. Big ones. Dozens of them, Some, directly in their path.

Mike pushed the tiller over. "Jenn, duck!" She dropped down as the boom swung over her head. The sail filled in a second and the boat heeled with the wind, one side lifting out of the water. Stu slid easily to the high side of the boat and leaned back to keep them from tipping.

In a minute, they had worn away from the danger and were tacking upwind. Jenn watched the corpses and saw they weren't all dead. In fact, most of them would occasionally lift an arm or roll from their front to their back like logs. There were always zombies in the bay, but she had never seen so many all massed together.

"Are they really dangerous?" Aaron asked. "Could they have gotten us?"

In answer Mike grabbed the edges of the boat and shook it back and forth so that water nearly sloshed in. He laughed as Aaron held on. "What do you think, little man? And once they get a hold, they don't let go." He glanced back and the white smile on his face gradually slipped away.

There were two sailboats zipping across the water, the wind quarter-on. They were moving fast, heading towards the school of zombies at an angle. Mike immediately dropped the sheet and stood, waving his hands and pointing. "Right there, damn it! Look! Look!" Stu and Jenn took up the cry, only the wind was too strong and their words were lost.

At the last moment someone on the lead boat saw them waving and too late they slowed, but didn't turn. They plowed into the wallowing zombies who went from looking like floating garbage to looking and acting more like a school of giant piranha in a flash. The water leapt as arms and clawed hands erupted all around the boat.

The pilot tried to change course, putting the wind full at their backs. The sail filled but the boat only moved sluggishly. It had been seized by seven or eight of the waterlogged beasts and their combined weight was over three thousand pounds. The boat rocked far to port; in response, the islanders threw themselves to the other side to keep the boat from broaching and sending everyone into the water.

While this was going on, the captain of the second boat had finally woken to the danger and turned the boat towards the Golden Gate Bridge and the Pacific.

"What the hell!" Mike screamed. He hauled the tiller over and neatly flipped the *Puffer* around and, as they were up wind, charged down on the floundering boat. "Get the crossbows ready," he ordered. They had three among them and as it was customary not to walk around the island with bows locked and loaded, none were ready to fire.

As the boat bounced and crashed over the small waves, Jenn placed hers between her feet and hauled back on the cable, clicking it in place and feeding a bolt into the groove with shaking hands. It took her two tries. With every second, they came closer to the school of zombies and her fear escalated. It showed in her shaking hands and when her lower lip began to quiver.

Fighting zombies was a bad idea, fighting zombies on open water in a little boat was a terrible idea.

She couldn't see how they were going to fare any better than the boat ahead of them. Not only was it bigger, there were four grown men in it fighting for their lives and losing. And they knew how to handle themselves on the water. As sure-footed as Jenn was on land, she felt timid on the boat. And she wasn't the only one.

Stu was pale, his dark eyes larger than normal, his chest was heaving along with the boat. Aaron was making a whining noise as he struggled with Mike's bow. He was too small to load it.

"Let me," she said, taking the weapon from him. The bow had a pull that was nearly as great as Stu's. She had just managed to get it back in time and loaded it when they went crashing through the school of zombies. Her fear spiked as they rode upon the backs of three of the beasts.

Suddenly a tremendous, putrefying, grey hand reached up out of the water and gripped the side of the boat, sending Aaron sprawling in the bottom. Jenn stood to shoot the beast and a second later found herself falling as well, heading face-first at the water.

Chapter 5

Jenn Lockhart

The grey hand had checked their speed, sending Jenn lurching toward the boat's edge. She was sure she was going to be thrown in among the zombies, and in that split second when she was face down, looking into the thrashing water, she pictured herself simultaneously being ripped to pieces and drowned—her two greatest fears.

Somehow, Stu was fast enough to save her. He had been thrown forward as well, but he managed to reach out with one long arm and snag the edge of her jacket. Now Jenn was suspended over the water, staring at some pale, slagged beast as it rolled from its back and onto its side, stretching out an arm to snatch her down into the cold depths.

More of the corpses converged and arms and hands reached up for her; there were dozens of them. Her breath caught in her throat, which was the only reason she didn't scream. Luckily the beast had to let go of the boat to get at her. Without the extra five hundred pounds holding them back, the *Puffer* fairly leapt forward.

As Stu dragged Jenn back on board, Mike aimed them right at the struggling sailboat which was now thirty yards away from the main school. "You guys should probably hold on this time," he advised. Jenn, her entire body shaking now, hunkered down as Stu moved back to the center of the boat.

Before they could get to it, the other boat was finally pulled over. The sail slapped the water and covered one of the men, along with several zombies. Two of the men dove deep, while the last tried desperately to climb back onto the side-on boat.

The zombies had been churning the water before, now in their eagerness, the water frothed and splashed. A panicked scream arose from somewhere in the midst of the mess.

Stu, looking almost as dead white as a zombie, yelled to Mike, "Turn. They're done for."

Mike didn't. He set his jaw and bore down on the stricken vessel. It looked to Jenn as though he wanted to crash straight into it. She gripped the edge of the *Puffer* as tightly as she had held on to anything in her life. At the last moment, Mike dropped the sail and pulled the tiller, turning the *Puffer* so that it knifed along the edge of the other boat, cutting right across the mast, which scraped beneath them. The two boats locked together as the daggerboard struck.

With the two boats joined together, the *Puffer*, for once, felt like a sturdy platform beneath them. Jenn stood and saw a young man fighting for his life not ten feet away. He was one of the two who had dived in, but for some reason he had come up early and was now surrounded. She lined up a shot on one grey head that was the size of a jack o'lantern.

"No!" Mike cried. "It's too late for him. Aim right there." He pointed at the sail, where heads bobbed beneath.

At first Jenn didn't know which head to aim at, then one began to yell, "Son of a bitch! Son of a bitch! God!" She aimed at another. It was ghostly with dark sockets and a gaping mouth that opened and closed. She aimed between the sockets and pinned the sail to the thing's forehead.

She started to pull back on the bow's cable, but Aaron thrust Mike's crossbow at her. Mike was leaning out over the water on the other side of the *Puffer*, stomping a boot down into the face of one of the zombies while Stu was reloading his bow. She grabbed the bow out of Aaron's hands and aimed for another of the bobbing heads. She was so close that she didn't think she could miss.

When she pulled the trigger, the bow jumped and the bolt rose a little more than she expected. Thankfully the kinetic energy in the bolt was great enough to pierce the creature's frontal bone. It made a noise like a hissing tea kettle and sank beneath the water.

Although no longer surrounded, the man was still frantically trying to get out from beneath the sail.

Jenn threw down the crossbow and pulled out her hunting knife. "Aaron, grab my shirt." While he grabbed the tail of her shirt, she took a step onto the mast of the overturned boat and drove the blade into the sail, making a wide opening. She hoped the man would come through. Instead it was a zombie that came through, its face so pruney that it looked as though it was sloughing off as it breached the surface.

Its reach was shockingly long, and it had a hold of her before she even knew it. This time she knew she screamed. It went on and on. Her knife fell from her hand as she clung to the mast. Behind her, Aaron was also screaming. Desperately, he pulled back on her shirt and for just a moment, she was precariously balanced with equal forces going in opposite directions.

The greater strength of the zombie began to win out. Slowly she was pulled toward its gaping maw when suddenly Stu leaned over her and shot a bolt straight down its throat.

The point must have hit the thing's brainstem because it suddenly spazzed, going completely stiff, its muddy eyes bugged wide and its arms flung out. Jenn inched back from it like a frightened kitten with both hands on the mast. She hadn't gotten far when a man, a real living man, popped up through the hole in the sail.

"Help me!" he hissed, complete terror etched on his face.

Jenn and Stu grabbed him and heaved. He was strangely heavy and she figured he was tangled in a rope or the anchor chain. They soon found out there was a zombie hanging off his leg.

"Please, please, please," he was whispering. "Help me."

Jenn was already doing all she could. She had her legs braced and was pulling with both hands. Stu yanked his climber's axe from his belt and began thudding the pick end of the tool into the beast's arm as the man kicked.

After Stu's fourth hit, with black blood flying, the man's leg came free. Almost at the same time, Mike pulled a spluttering man from the water on the other side of the boat. He turned and saw the situation. "Lift the dagger board! We have to get off their sail. Come on, Aaron, you're sitting on it, damn it!"

Aaron jumped up onto one of the benches and lifted his feet. Jenn was the closest and grabbed the top of the board, working it back and forth. It was caught on something beneath the keel. Stu helped, gritting his fine, white teeth as he strained. Slowly, it came up. Mike already had the sail filled and with a great deal of scraping and grinding the two boats separated.

The zombies weren't done. They tried to grab hold of the boat, but Stu plied his axe, using the hammer end to break fingers until the *Puffer* was free and running across the water. There were six of them in the boat and another swimming away from the mass of zombies churning the water. Mike deftly guided the *Puffer* over to him. It took three of them to pull the exhausted man into the boat.

Except for their heavy breathing, it was quiet on the bay. The odd silence built up both tension and guilt among the people on the boat.

"I have to ask," Mike said, as he turned the *Puffer* back towards the island, "Was anyone scratched?"

The men were barely men. Now that Jenn had a chance to see them up close, one might have been twenty-five; the other two were in their late teens. They looked back and forth at each other before they started inspecting their exposed flesh. No one seemed to have been scratched, and yet someone was bleeding.

"Look there," Aaron whispered. The water in the bottom of the boat was tinged pink.

"Damn," Stu cursed. "Who is it?" With everyone wet and bedraggled, it wasn't obvious. Then one of the teens, shivering from the cold water and the shock of the attack, lifted up the cuff of his jeans. His sock was torn and stained pink. When he pulled it down, he revealed a jagged cut.

44

Jenn thought it looked like a bite wound, however the young man, an eighteen-year old named Remy who had come to the island a year after the earthquake, insisted that he had cut it when he fell in the water. "You have to believe me! Th-there's a lip on the front of the b-boat and I banged my-my-my leg on it when I fell in. Jeff, tell them. Tell them about the lip. You scraped your leg on it this morning. Tell them!"

Jeff Battaglia, the older of them, slid one leg behind the other. "There's a little lip, sure but-but the scratch wasn't bad." Like a poker player, keeping his cards close to his vest, Jeff took a peek at it beneath his covering hand. A tiny smile twitched the corner of his mouth up and down and in relief, he said, "You see? It's scabbed over."

He showed them two partially healed scrapes. Everyone in the boat leaned forward to judge and, as a group, the cuts were deemed innocuous. A second later the group turned to Remy who began shaking his head. The panicked look he had worn in the water was back. Jenn thought he was going to cry.

Just then, one of the other sailboats pulled up alongside them. In it were four people; two men and two women, all in their early twenties or late teens. One of the women stared at them unblinking, her chin going back and forth, her lips making tiny movements. It seemed as though she were counting and having a mental spasm because she kept coming up with only seven.

"Where's Ken?" she asked. Some of them glanced back to where the other sailboat was just an odd hump in the water, while others, Jenn included, glanced down at their shoes. She had known Ken Koester for most of her life and yet she hadn't recognized his frightened face as he had bobbed in the water surrounded by zombies. She replayed the moment in her mind, remembering that she had instinctively wanted to save him. Stu had stopped her from trying and maybe he had been right to.

Then again, maybe not. She had saved Remy only he had been bitten, which meant she really hadn't saved anyone.

"We need to go back," the young woman declared. "There's still time. He said he could swim. Remember? He said he had taken swim lessons back before."

This struck a chord in Jenn. She remembered him saying the same thing once years ago. It had been on the hottest day in July six or seven years before when she had been struggling to teach herself how to swim. Ken and a bunch of his friends had been watching, laughing as she shivered, her lips a purple color.

Eventually, she had snapped "You're all just jealous cuz you guys don't know how to swim."

"I had lessons when I was a kid, back before," Ken had said. "I can swim just fine." It had been a lie and Ken had taken it to his death.

"We'll send the canoe back for him," Mike said to the woman and began waving to the long canoe. Jenn spotted the half-lie easily. Yes, they would send the canoe back, but only to rescue the floundering sailboat. It was too valuable to leave behind. There would be no going back for Ken. No one could have lived through that feeding frenzy.

The woman believed the lie. She stood up in her boat and began screaming for the rowers to beat the water.

Mike watched for a moment and then, without a word, moved the boom and filled the sail. He handled the boat as if it were an extension of himself. It slid across the water, cutting straight for the dock as if the wind and current were bearing them right to it. Stu and Jenn watched him work the tiller and ducked out of the way of the boom as it swung over. They were both quiet, staring blankly. They and everyone else were purposely not looking at the doomed man who sat with them.

Remy had somewhat of the same reaction and didn't look at his ankle. One of his friends suggested letting it trail in the water in the hope that the salt water would help wash away any germs in the wound.

"It's okay," he insisted. "I scraped it on the boat."

Nearly fifty people waited for them at the dock. On an island only two hundred yards long, word had spread quickly that the fleet had run into a school. Gerry was in front. He tossed Mike a rope, asking, "Ken?" Mike nodded, his face set and pinched. Gerry read the truth from the way the look hung on Mike's face. "Who's hurt?" he asked quietly. No one looked at Remy; he was a negative space; an invisible being in a crowded boat. Gerry's face fell. "Remy, too? Damn it."

"I just scratched my ankle on the boat," Remy said, his fierce eyes daring anyone to contradict him.

A long sigh escaped Gerry. "I'm sure you're right, but you know the drill." Remy dropped his chin. The others clambered out of the boat as fast as they could, leaving the one man alone. Jenn, Stu and Aaron stood to the side on the dock, waiting for him to get out of the boat.

Remy sat on the middle bench, his head down; he had to be asked to get out of the boat by Gerry. No one offered him a hand. No one wanted to touch him.

Gerry waited in silence until Remy climbed out of the boat. "You know where to go," he told Remy. The young man slunk along the dock with his head down, watched by almost the entire population of the island. Only Gerry didn't watch. Instead, he gave Stu a long, steady look. "Do you want to wait for the outcome?" he asked. "You never know. Sometimes it doesn't take."

He meant that sometimes a small scratch or an insignificant bite wouldn't turn a person. In all of Jenn's fifteen years, she had only heard of five instances of this. Still, there was always a chance. For good luck, Jenn sketched a quick sign of the cross, finishing it with a swipe of her hands across each other to rid them of any evil taint. Almost everyone did the same. Even Gerry made the sign; only Stu did not.

"No," Stu said. "I want to get across the bay before dark. Jenn and Aaron, let's get back in the boat."

"And Mike?" Gerry asked. "Do you still want him?" He locked eyes with Stu for a ten count, which was a long time in the circumstances. Jenn didn't understand why Stu hesitated. Even though Mike was only seventeen, he was clearly an expert sailor and if anyone could get them across the bay quickly it was Mike Gunter.

And she didn't understand why Gerry had asked about Mike at all. Unless he thought Mike was bad luck. While everyone else stared at Stu, waiting for an answer, Jenn looked at Mike out of the corner of her eye, wondering if he was tainted in some way, or if he was a jinx, or under a curse, just as she was.

The curse was the reason no one ever came to her place and why she was never invited on expeditions. It was the reason she always went out alone when no one else ever did. No one talked about it, but she had been the un-lucky number from the day she tagged along to the hilltop.

Thankfully, it was Stu making the decision. He didn't care about lucky numbers or jinxes.

"Yes, we'll take him. Get on board, Mike."

Chapter 6

Jenn Lockhart

The bad luck surrounding Mike and Jenn made itself felt the moment they slid away from the dock. It was late in the afternoon and an early fog began to roll in and as they crossed in front of the Golden Gate Bridge, the fog was already wrapping itself around the base of the towers, hiding them from view. It was bearing down on them like a white wall.

Then the wind almost died. The sail sagged and they lost momentum, stranding them in the middle of the harbor. Every once in a while, a stray breeze would puff up the sail and egg them on, but for the most part they were at the mercy of the tide which bore them into the fog. As far as fog went, it wasn't the densest Jenn had ever been in. Still, visibility dropped to about twenty feet.

"This sucks," Aaron griped. He was sitting up, stretching his neck as far as possible trying to peer through the fog. "How are we gonna get home now?"

"Quiet," Mike said. He had his head cocked, listening to a rumbling sound coming from in front of them.

Aaron brightened. "Is that the shore?"

Mike didn't answer right away. He yanked the tiller all the way to the left and manhandled the boom around. Only then did he say, "No. That's either Shag or Harding Rock. If we hit it, well…let's just hope we don't." He glanced up at the sail, perhaps hoping for more wind.

Jenn did a triple sign of the cross while Stu stared around the boat. "We can use our crossbows as oars," he said, picking his up. He removed the bolt and dry-shot the weapon. "Just tell me which way to paddle." Mike pointed off the port bow. Soon the three of them were splashing away with their crossbows while Aaron held the tiller over.

Because of the power of the tides, they seemed to be drawn to the rock and the sound of the waves breaking over it got louder and louder. Beneath them the ocean pulsed. They would be dragged back and then rushed forward. Stu was paddling as hard as he could, while Mike was calling out: "Stroke, stroke, stroke," in a rhythm that Jenn picked up.

She was drenched in sweat and sea water when the fog broke around Shag Rock. One second it seemed like an insignificant stone mass poking up out of a green swell, and in the next second the water dropped revealing a huge, jagged formation that Jenn was sure would dash the *Puffer* to pieces.

"Back on the right!" Mike cried. "Back! Back! Harder, Jenn!" She dug her crossbow in the water and honestly couldn't tell if she was doing anything at all to help move the boat. Still, she swiped the bow through the water as hard as she could. It wasn't enough. No matter what they did, the *Puffer* stayed pointed straight at the rock and when the water dropped again, they skimmed across the surface shooting down the face of the wave. It felt like they were sledding out of control.

"Hold on!" Mike bellowed as they raced at the rock. Everyone crouched down as they came at the rock, passing so close to it that Jenn could have reached out to touch it if she hadn't been so frightened. Sitting on it was a gull with beady eyes. It screamed a cry at them as they drifted back into the fog.

The four of them sat in the boat for a few seconds, limp with relief. Mike let them have a breather before he said, "We still have to keep away from the mouth of the bay or we might get swept out to sea. Forward now. Stroke, stroke, stroke. Back on the left, Stu. No, you keep going forward, Jenn."

She didn't have any idea which direction they were pointing and had to trust that Mike or Stu knew. Soon, her arms were like lead and she took one stroke for every three of Mike's. When a soft zephyr puffed up the sail, everyone sat back, their chests heaving.

Eventually, Mike roused himself and corrected their course. Jenn asked him, "How do you know where we are?"

What she had mistaken for a watch was actually a compass. "You should never leave home without one," he told her. His relaxed smile was back. "Hey Stu, wasn't that a commercial back in the old days? Something about not leaving home without…something?"

Stu shrugged. "Maybe, I don't know. The only commercials I remember were for cereal and this video game *Assassins Creed*. Man, I wanted that game so bad, but my mom said I was too young."

Jenn had no recollection of TV whatsoever. She knew what they had been for, but no "show" or "commercial" that the older people talked about was ever familiar to her. To her, television like cell phones and X-rays, was just more magic from the past, lost to humanity.

As Mike and Stu talked about *Assassin's Creed*, she thought they sounded strangely young; like kids. They were animated and loud. Stu even laughed, something that was always a rarity. Their light mood was infectious, and Jenn allowed it to lull her into a false sense of security. For reasons she couldn't explain, she found herself laughing along.

"What's an assassin?" Aaron asked. "Is that like a slaver? Or…ooh, look." He pointed at a body floating in the fog. It was Ken Koester. His face had been chewed off, but they all knew it was him. Aaron crossed himself twice. Jenn did as well. As everyone knew, it was probably the worst luck ever to see the body of someone taken by zombies.

"Has it changed over?" Aaron asked, his face stricken.

"Not yet," Mike said, adjusting the sail and skirting around the body, leaving it in the fog. Seeing Ken killed their joy and the four of them were quiet for the next few minutes. It was a relief when they heard a ringing bell. Mike angled towards it. It was the Pelican Harbor buoy.

Jenn loaded her crossbow and kissed it for luck as they drifted their way through the fog, using the bell to orient themselves. They knew they were close, still it was a surprise when they nearly crashed into one of the docks. Stu fended it off to keep the boom from snapping in two.

Stu jumped up onto the dock and tied the stern, saying, "I think we should leave the boat for now. I'll come back for it in the morning." He helped Aaron out of the boat, while Jenn climbed up on her own.

Aaron was about to walk away when Stu clapped him on the back and kept his hand there. "You're going to be quiet this time, right?" Aaron opened his mouth and Stu gave him a hard squeeze. "Just nod. There you go. If we run into something, you're going to hide and you won't come out until you hear my whistle just like we talked about. Now nod again."

Aaron nodded but looked troubled. He wasn't the only one. The fog had enveloped the hill. It was very danger-ous. It hid the beasts and lulled them into a stupor so that they made only low, soft groans that were difficult to hear. If you ran into one, escaping from it could be almost as dangerous as fighting it.

They all knew the story of one of the Santas who had impaled himself on a tree branch while running in the fog. Jenn had first heard the story years before and although the details had changed over time, that didn't make it any less real.

Stu, his face glistening as the fog coated him, checked to make sure their weapons were ready. Then he gave Aaron a shake. Jenn jumped up and down twice, earning a nod from Stu. Mike just stared. "Checking for rattles," Jenn told him. She showed him how her gear was taped down so she could walk or run as noiselessly as possible.

Mike shrugged before jumping up and down a few times. Since most of his gear was stowed in the pillowcase and muffled by clothes, he didn't make much noise.

"Good enough," Stu said. "Aaron stay right on my butt. Mike will come next. Jenn, take up the rear. Everyone stay close and keep quiet."

Jenn was a little surprised at being asked to take the trail position. It suggested that either Stu trusted her a lot or didn't trust Mike at all. *How could he not trust Mike?* she wondered. Mike was older and stronger that she was.

He had proven his courage on the bay when she had been close to panicking.

Maybe he trusts me more on land. Her thin, boyish chest swelled with pride at the thought and she made sure to earn her place. She stepped lighter than ever, moving with the grace of a deer. She passed through the fog like a ghost straight out of Miss Shay's nightly tales. She swept along...

"Hey," Mike hissed. "Watch it."

She had stepped on the back of his ankle, tripping him. They stumbled together in a tangle of arms, legs and crossbows. The two were so close that her whispered, "Sorry," tickled his ear.

At the commotion, Stu turned, his bow at the ready. For a moment, anger flashed across his hard features, then strangely, he smirked and turned back. Jenn was surprised. Stu's anger was legendary when operational silence was broken outside the gates of the complex.

And yet, he only smirked? This made no sense to her and she worried over it as they made their way slowly uphill through what had once been a pretty residential neighborhood of white picket fences, flower gardens and two-car garages.

Stu stopped at each street before crossing over. Instead of looking both ways, as children were taught in the Before, he paused at the corner to listen. At Locust Street, he heard the low rumble of a zombie somewhere close in front of them. To avoid it, they turned onto Locust, leaving the zombie behind them—only to run into more of them.

Jenn thought she heard at least three. Stu held a finger to his lips and then pointed back the way they had come. In the fog he missed an aluminum can that had been sitting against the curb for the last twelve years. His boot hit it and sent it skittering away.

It was loud.

Quickly, they slunk down against a fence and froze as five zombies came lumbering down the street, groaning softly. Because of the fog Jenn could only make out their feet and lower legs and the occasional swing of a long arm. It didn't make much sense, but the fog made them more monstrous in her mind. She pictured them ten feet tall, their mouth filled with long fangs, and demonic red eyes.

Her crossbow seemed pathetic and weak compared to the monsters. She began to shiver and she wasn't the only one feeling the fear. Aaron couldn't help himself and began whimpering. One of the zombies heard.

It stopped, forming a tremendous shadow against the grey backdrop. It moaned loudly, causing the fog to swirl in front of it. Its breath had the same stench as decaying meat and when it smote them, Aaron made the smallest gagging sound.

Jenn slapped a hand over his mouth. Next to her, Mike stooped and searched around beneath the fog until he found a rock. He threw it down the street expecting it to clack against the pavement once or twice and send the zombies charging after.

Instead the rock zipped through the air and, with the worst luck imaginable, hit a white speed limit sign hidden by the fog, not even ten feet away. The crashing noise of the rock striking the metal reverberated up and down the block.

"Run!" Stu hissed. The other zombies had turned and were charging down on them. Even if the little group only appeared as misty shadows, they couldn't take the chance of being stumbled over by one of the beasts. They ran, but not quickly; the fog was too dense and there were obstacles everywhere.

Jenn leapt over a television that had no business being in the street, while Mike nearly tripped over an old bicycle that resembled a rusting pretzel. Stu kept Mike from falling and then said in an urgent whisper, "Move to your left!"

Who he was talking to, Jenn had no idea. She glanced back and saw Aaron's tiny ghostly figure. He seemed to be floating along, his feet not even touching the ground. While his face was marred by the mists, she could see the lines on his right hand and the dirt beneath his nails perfectly. He had his arm outstretched, pointing ahead of her.

Before she could turn back around, she ran full into a parked car. Because it sat on four flats, the bumper hit her just below the knees and her momentum sent her flying onto the hood, the breath knocked out of her. The pain in her knees was immediate and intense. It was so sharp she felt like vomiting. She wanted to cry out, but her diaphragm had seized up.

And that was a good thing, because her situation had gone from dangerous to deadly.

She suddenly found herself alone in the fog. Mike, Stu and Aaron had disappeared, while a shadow blocked out the feeble light of the setting sun. It was one of the zombies looming above her. It seemed mountainous. With her legs aching and her chest unable to push air in or out, she had only one choice—to freeze in plain sight and hope the creature would turn away.

Instead, it bent to peer down at her and as it did, its face became more and more solid and frightful.

Its lips had been bitten off long ago and it only had one eye, but it had plenty of teeth. With a roar, it tried to take her in one tremendous gulp. As afraid as she was, she didn't panic. She aimed her crossbow and fired, but even at a range of a foot the bolt didn't have the power to kill the beast. The bolt punctured its forehead but it didn't sink deep enough.

The shot snapped its head back. She scrambled to get off the hood before it could orient on her again, only it was too fast and pinned her down with one of its enormous claw-liked hands. Its diseased nails dug into the fabric of her jacket, squeezing, not just the breath out of her, but the life as well.

Chapter 7

Mike Gunter

Stu was on his left as they ran. Mike thought they were only just in front of Jenn and Aaron, but when he almost fell over the bike he looked back and saw nothing but the swirling fog. He slowed just as Stu said, "Move to your left." A second later, a beat-up old car materialized in front of them.

It had been sitting in the middle of the street and he would've smashed right into it if Stu hadn't warned him. He dodged left and two seconds later Jenn ran square into it.

The noise was only slightly less alarming than when he had thrown the rock.

He and Stu looked back, and both stumbled against the curb, their crossbows rattling on the pavement. Things took on a horrible nightmare quality as the zombie gazed down at Jenn with its one eye burning with hatred.

When she shot it, Mike almost cheered. Then he saw the beast slam her down with a hand that completely covered her chest. She looked like little more than a toddler compared to the monster, and he was sure it would crush her with just the one hand.

But, this zombie was in an eating mood, not a crushing one. Its teeth were only inches away from her face, when a high voice yelled: "Over here! Look at me! LOOK…AT ME…" It was Aaron. Mike couldn't see him through the fog, but he could see the zombie turn its huge head and roar. The zombie left Jenn and stormed off into the fog. A second later, there was a high piercing scream.

"Get Jenn," Stu said, jumping to his feet and shoving Mike toward the beat-up car. He then raced into the fog.

Mike went to the car where he found the girl gasping and wild-eyed. He pulled her off the hood and she sank into him, trembling, unable to hold herself up. "Hey. What's wrong? Are you hurt?"

She tried to answer only just then, Aaron screamed again. The scream got louder and louder, and it was a moment before Mike realized the boy was heading right for them.

And behind Aaron was a crowd of zombies.

Mike pulled Jenn to the ground, hiding behind the car which shook almost immediately as a zombie crashed full into it. The power and energy of the beast went through the car, lifting up the far side and breaking windows. Mike and Jenn were sent sprawling.

They got to their knees as the zombie tore at the car in rage, smashing the doors and tearing off the hood. The two were stunned by the violence and neither knew exactly what to do or where Aaron or Stu were. Mike began to help Jenn to her feet when, unbelievably, Aaron crawled out from beneath the car. There was only a gap of about four inches between the street and the undercarriage and although he was a skinny little boy, he came out bleeding, covered in rust and oil.

Mike lifted him to his feet. He was as unsteady as Jenn, and wore a shocked expression that wouldn't leave his face. Mike didn't think he'd be able to walk, so he picked him up with one hand and let Jenn hold the other.

The fog hid them as they limped up the street, keeping close to the row of houses. After a block, Aaron seemed to recover somewhat, but Jenn couldn't go any further. She stumbled and then struggled valiantly to stand. "We need Stu," she whispered before whistling like a bird.

Stu seemed to appear out of the fog like magic. "I was just drawing them off. You okay, Jenn?"

She had one arm still strung across Mike's shoulders. "My knees," she answered quietly.

He took her crossbow as well as Mike's, asking, "Can you carry her? We only have half a mile." Mike lifted her into his arms; she was very light. Stu slung their bows across his back and started once more walking down the street in complete silence.

Mike started after. Jenn was awkward and stiff. "You don't have to carry me if you don't want to," she said, her lips very close to his neck. "We're not going fast. I should be fine. I just need an arm to hold onto."

"Stu's in charge," he answered. "We should do as he says. Trust me, I'll let you know if you get too heavy." This turned out to be a lie. The streets were like all the rest in the city: cracked, rutted, strewn with trash and tree branches. Worse it was a slow, uphill march.

If it was possible, Stu was even more wary and careful than he had been. On a positive note, the fog didn't reach the top of the hill.

Mike's arms began to burn when they were only half-way to the top and soon his sweat mingled with a soft rain. Jenn raised an eyebrow when she felt the trembling. Mike said, "I'm still good."

"Okay," she said, with a touch of skepticism in her voice. A minute later he stumbled and Jenn demanded to get down. "I'm fine. It's just a couple of bruises." But it wasn't. Her right knee buckled and she drew in a sharp breath. She changed her self-diagnosis to, "Maybe it's a sprain."

"Give me a moment," he said, shaking out his arms as she leaned on him. Stu and Aaron waited just up the block. They had been pulling farther and farther away and now the two watched them, Stu with an odd look on his face. The look bothered Mike. He hefted Jenn into his arms and carried her up to them. "You okay?" he asked Stu.

Stu lifted his eyebrows, giving him a look of inno-cence. "Just a strange day. A strange, strange day." Mike would've agreed if that was what the look was all about. No, there was something else.

Once more Stu led the way. The last few hundred yards were uneventful.

Mike had been to the complex of the Hill People twice before. In both instances he had been there solely to help lug trade goods up and back.

It sat on the top of a bare hill and was surrounded by a forest of homemade spears. There were rank upon rank of them. Some were long and others short, and mixed in with them were concealed punji sticks; sharpened stakes set in small pits. Stepping on one would use a man's weight against him, driving the stake into the sole of his shoe and, more than likely, maiming him for life.

The road leading to the complex had been pulled up and it too had been riddled with spears and stakes. There was a winding path through it that went back and forth in full view of the complex. The idea was that attacking bandits would be subject to a withering crossfire.

Beyond the stakes was a heavy fence made of black iron which had a painted plywood wall attached to it. The barrier wasn't really zombie proof, but it trapped light and sound so that even up close, Mike thought the complex had a dead feel to it. Once they made their way through the maze, they found themselves in front of a set of iron gates, where a young girl was waiting for them.

She was small and thin with long blonde hair that hung loose, covering the shoulders of a faded jean jacket. She was probably no more than seven, which made Mike question whether she was the actual guard. "What happened?" she asked, her big eyes roving over Jenn and Aaron.

"It was the dead," Aaron said. "They were everywhere. They almost got me like three times and they woulda…"

"Are you going to open the gate or what, Lindy?" Stu asked, gruffly. "If you let us in, I'm sure Aaron will tell you all about our adventures."

With Stu's dark eyes on her, Lindy Smith hurried to open the gate. As she did, Jenn said, "Make sure Aaron tells you that he was a hero today. I'm pretty sure he saved my life. That's how he got all scratched up." Aaron smiled, his cheeks red as a rose petal.

The gate could only be opened wide enough for one person at a time to slip through. Jenn slid out of Mike's arms and limped through. She claimed she felt good enough to make it home without the need to be carried. Mike gave her his arm and together they walked through the complex which was as quiet on the inside as it was on the outside.

There were people about; mostly children and under-twenties. They came over and offered to help Jenn while at the same time sneaking looks up at Mike. Although most of them had seen him before, they were still just as curious about him as he was curious about them.

Compared to the Islanders, they were very clean. Clearly, they bathed daily, which was no wonder since they had easy access to both wood and fresh water. Their clothing was neat and spotless as well. Most of their garments were faded from use, but none were torn or patched as was commonly found among the Islanders. Alcatraz wasn't called "The Rock" for nothing. It was a grim, hard place with little in the way of creature comforts. Tearing a pair of jeans was a daily event and it grew tiresome searching for replacements.

Despite their hard life, the Islanders were much more outgoing compared to the Hill People. They could afford to laugh loudly and sing and be themselves. It was the byproduct of knowing that they were safe. The Hill People didn't have that luxury. Even the youngest of the children were quiet and reserved.

Although most of the older kids knew Mike from when they had lived on the island, Jenn introduced him to the people gathered around them. They treated him like a lost cousin and each shook his hand.

As the drizzle turned into a cold rain, she told them about their trip to Alcatraz and back. They *oohed* quietly when she got to the part about the fight on the bay and they marveled at her descriptions of the boats and the fog and the zombies coming up out of the water and nearly being shipwrecked by the rock.

"And he's staying with you?" Colleen White asked with a surprised look. She was easily the prettiest girl in the bay area with her shocking black hair and her deep blue eyes. Colleen glanced around at the others with a brow cocked. "Shouldn't he stay with Bill or Stu? What about Ron? He has a room."

The sun, a hidden entity giving off a grey light, had faded down below the back of the hill, and the complex was hung in shade and shadow. Still Mike thought he saw a touch of pink come over Jenn's cheeks.

Jenn didn't know what to say, and she began to stammer. Another girl came to her rescue. "What's it to you, Colleen? It's not like Dale would let him stay with you. I'm sure Stu has his reasons. Besides it'll be the Coven what has the final say. Are you going to take him to see them, Jenn?"

"I'm sure they'll call on Mike in the morning," Jenn answered. "Right now, I have to get home and get my fire going."

"I bet you do," Colleen said, giving Jenn a wink.

After that remark, Jenn wouldn't look up as Mike put out an arm. She took it and hobbled to the next building. Because she had two layers of blackout curtains on her windows, her apartment was dark as a cave. The only light was an orange glow coming from the fireplace. It wasn't enough to count fingers by and she left the door open as she looked for an oil lamp. It was nothing more than a mason jar with a hole cut in the lid through which a wick ran into murky-looking olive oil.

Twelve years before, Mike could find matches and lighters all over the place. Now they were hoarded and hard to find. Jenn took the jar to the fireplace, moved the screen away and began stirring the hot coals with a piece of kindling. She filled her cheeks and blew. The coals brightened, and she began feeding in little sticks and twigs, pulling them from a plastic bucket on the hearth.

Soon she had her fire going and used a burning stick to light the homemade lamp. "Here you go," she said handing it to him. "Make yourself at home. The bathroom is the middle door. My room is on the left and yours is on the right."

"Is there anything you need? Can I get some water or wood or, I don't know, some ice for that knee?"

She laughed uneasily. "You saw the signs, too?"

"The signs?"

"Sure, everyone knows that October fog that can't climb the hill portends snow. Then there were the pinecones, but I'm sure you saw them." She unbuttoned her jacket and only then realized that it was torn. "Ugh." She took it off, doing her best not to let it touch her. She threw it in the fire, where it almost smothered the flames.

"Say, when was the last time you had a proper bath?" she asked. "I remember when I lived on the island, we never had baths."

A bath sounded good and he agreed as long as he did most of the work. It took him seven trips to fill the tub and he didn't begrudge a second of the labor. Although they had a water tower on Alcatraz, it was completely dependent on rainfall; it was never enough.

While he luxuriated in the water, Jenn limped about and prepared a meal that would have been strange in the old world: a stew of fried crabapples, strips of venison, sweet onions and dandelion greens. Strange but good.

They talked as they ate their fill, mostly about the different people they knew. Sometimes they would bring up someone who had died, which would put a damper on their conversation and they would flounder about, looking for something positive to talk about.

"I can't wait for the traders to get here," Jenn said, grinning. "It sort of feels like my birthday when they come. If they have real chocolate, I might go crazy and trade everything I have for a single chocolate chip cookie. What do you want?"

He wanted the same thing that Stu wanted: bullets. Because Gerry felt the island was basically impervious to assault by either bandits or the dead, Gerry had been slowly trading away their arsenal.

Mike thought it was terribly shortsighted. They were safe enough on the island, that was true, but they had to come ashore sometimes and when they came up against bandits they were always outgunned. Even on the water, they weren't completely safe. What had happened that afternoon was proof enough.

But he wasn't going to get bullets, he was going to get goats and he could only hope it wasn't a huge mistake.

"Gerry is gambling everything on getting goats and I mean everything."

"So, you don't have anything to trade just for you? That's so sad. If you did want something just for you, what would it be?"

Mike just didn't think in that manner. He only thought about what was good for his people. "I don't know, a shirt? A nice one?"

"You can get a shirt anywhere. What do you really want if you could have anything?"

It took him a long time to come up with the impossible. "Batteries," he answered, honestly. "I miss music."

Chapter 8

Mike Gunter

Mike stayed the night in the guest room. It was easily the nicest room he could ever remember sleeping in. His father, as great as he had been during the apocalypse, saving his family and leading them to the safety of Alcatraz, had been a high school dropout who had worked a string of menial jobs.

They had been living in a trailer park when the zombies came. Mike's bed had been a lumpy mattress and his sheets had been bought at a garage sale for fifty cents. His first bed on Alcatraz had been in one of the prison cells, and was hard as a rock. Like the rest of the prison, it had smelled of mildew tinged with evil. His current bed consisted of three inches of padding resting on springs that creaked loudly every time he shifted.

Jenn's guest room was almost like a hotel room. There were doilies on the dresser, fake flowers and fancy oil paintings. She even had a pitcher of water next to the bed. He was so snug and the room so dark, that he slept in well past sunrise. Jenn accidentally woke him as she slunk around getting the fire going. One dropped cut of wood was all it took for him to go from sound asleep to fully awake in a heartbeat.

"Good morning," she said, as he came into the main room. "I'll have breakfast ready in a few."

"How are your knees? I don't want you going out of your way just for me."

She was dressed in a red velour warmup suit of what appeared to be soft velvet. Lifting one of the pant legs, she said, "There's barely a bruise. I'm fine. Now sit like a proper guest."

He wasn't going to sit, and he didn't ask if he could help because he knew what she would say. He brushed his teeth and then went about filling the tub for her. She made a fuss, which he ignored. In a very literal sense, Mike had been raised in a world where if you didn't work, you didn't eat.

There wasn't quite a line to use the pump, it was more of a congregation of shivering children and teens who stood around Aaron Altman, listening as he told the story of how he saved Jenn from certain death. In his version he didn't scream like a girl as the zombies chased him. The children were so engrossed in the story they didn't see Mike.

"That's exactly what happened," he said. "Only I could have sworn there were eight zombies after you, not six." Since story-telling was the dominant form of entertainment on the island it was a long-standing practice among the fisherman to spice up their anecdotes. If one of Mike's friends told him that a hundred-pound shark nearly took off his leg in a single bite, Mike knew it was more than likely a fifty-pound tuna that brushed up against him

"Oh, yeah," Aaron agreed. "You were probably right. It all happened so fast that I didn't have time to count them all. So how is Jenn? Is she laid up? Does she need anything?"

Aaron was playing the role of white knight to the hilt. This was a double-edged sword. "Actually, yes. Her poor knees have her hobbling about like a poor cripple. If you could help with her water that would be great."

Roping Aaron in was one thing, but Mike was pleasantly surprised when eight of the children and teens brought buckets of water up to Jenn's apartment until her bathtub was filled. They didn't seem to mind that she wasn't on the couch with a cast on her leg. What mattered to them was that the story was vouched for and they asked for a repeat of it before they left.

"Zombies on the high seas is an interesting story," she said to Mike over their breakfast of pears and homemade grape jelly.

"The bay isn't exactly the high seas." He spoke quietly, his mood dampened having to hear, once again, how Ken and Remy had died. In his mind, Remy was already dead. At the first sign of fever, Gerry would have had his friends come by to say their goodbyes. A bottle of Napa's finest would be sent through the bars along with a rope. Mike was sure that Remy had died alone, his face purple, the tears standing out on his cheeks like sad little diamonds.

"It's as close to the high seas as I ever want to come," Jenn said. "I can't imagine anything more frightening than the ocean."

He shrugged. "It's not that scary. It's just big and empty."

"You've been out on the ocean? Why? The bay has all the fish anyone could ever eat."

"It was just like what happened to the *Puffer*. The wind died at just the wrong time and the tide sucked us out. There was nothing we could do but wait until either the wind came back or the tide changed. It was a little freaky, but do you want to hear something weird? Both Remy and Ken were on that boat."

Jenn looked ready to say something comforting; he stopped her with a pat on the hand. "It's alright," he told her. "Well, really it's not. It'll never be alright, but you get, what's the word? Inured?"

Her pert nose wrinkled. "Inured? I'd say toughened to it."

"I think that's what the word means." Her brows came down in anger and quickly he brought the conversation back to the boat. "So, there we were stranded at sea. I don't want it to appear like I'm some tough guy, but I wasn't afraid at all. I knew that the same forces that sent us out would bring us back. And it did eleven hours later. We came ashore all the way down by Santa Cruz."

"And that's why I'll never care for boats. I should get ready. I'm sure the Coven will want to see you pretty soon about the trade business."

It turned out she was wrong. The Coven wasn't in a hurry to see him. The two spent all morning waiting to be called. After a lunch of salted cod, Stu showed up asking about Jenn's knees and acting strangely. He nosed about her apartment, sticking his head into the back bedrooms.

After making a rumbly sound that could've been one of disappointment, he said, "I like your paintings, Jenn. They real?"

"Of course they're real," she answered indignantly. "Why wouldn't they be real? I mean, how do you have fake pictures? They're either there or they're not."

He blinked at her icy tone. "I meant if they were prints or…" Her brows came down at the word. Clearly, she didn't know what a print was. Mike wasn't sure either. He guessed they were pictures that had been mass produced from an original.

Mass production wasn't a concept Jenn or the younger generation truly understood. She crossed her arms and glared. "They're pictures and they're nice ones. Why don't you leave it at that?" Stu glared right back.

"He already said he liked them," Mike said, getting between them. "I do, too. All those flowers make everything cheery." He quickly changed the subject. "So, when do I start weighing and measuring? Not that it's even needed. I trust you, Stu."

"There's no hurry. Tomorrow will do. In the meantime, maybe you could take Jenn out to do some fishing. We could use all the surplus fish we can catch."

Mike and Jenn shared a look. She shrugged, and he said, "Sure, I guess I could do that. Who else is coming?"

"Hmm? Who else? I think just the two of you. Everyone else is busy. Speaking of which, I have to get going."

"I don't know what his deal is," she said the second her front door closed. She pulled back her curtains and watched him head up the dirt path.

"He's probably under a lot of stress. I know Gerry is crazy at this time of year. So much depends on the traders, what they carry and what we can get for our stuff."

"Well, it works out for me because I get to go fishing with an expert. Let me go get my coat and crossbow." It was cool and grey out, but the snow Jenn had predicted was nowhere in sight. Thankfully, the fog had dissipated and with it went the dread of being surprised by hidden zombies. Jenn led, moving with the stealth of a cat, from one sheltered observation point to another. On their way down to the harbor they crawled under bushes, slipped through abandoned houses, and twice tiptoed across the roofs of buildings. Both times they had to dodge around gaping holes that would have sent them plunging down into dark depths.

It was better to dodge holes than zombies in Mike's opinion.

They made it down to the harbor, where Jenn showed him the Hill People's secret stash of fishing gear. He held back judgment. In the nine years since the schism, they had become hunters and gatherers, and had lost a good deal of their skill in fishing.

Jenn was an awful fisherman. As patient and quiet as she was on land, she was jittery, nervous, and talkative when they got in the *Puffer*. "The signs," she explained when he asked what was wrong, "they're not good." She kept standing with one hand on the mast, looking, not for signs but for zombies in the water.

Gently he pulled her down. "We're all alone, so try to relax. Remember, this is supposed to be fun. Now, let's talk about your bait." They spent the afternoon catching fish and chatting quietly. During the evening they smoked the fish to preserve them.

The next morning, Jenn had chores to do and, as Mike still wasn't called on, he went with her to set traps in the Marin Headlands, and then sat with her on a four-hour guard duty shift. In the late afternoon he went with her to get some firewood.

Collecting branches and stray kindling was usually a simple affair, but getting actual cord wood could be dangerous. It was why almost no one went out alone to get wood. Usually two people kept watch as two others sawed down a tree—no one ever "chopped" down a tree, it was just too loud.

When Mike asked why they were alone, a shadow crossed Jenn's face. "I'm bad luck," was all she would say. Because she normally went out alone she could only take down young trees, in this case a Maple that had a great head of red and gold leaves on it. When it came down, the crash was muted by all those leaves, still they froze, listening.

With Mike's help, they de-limbed it so that only the trunk remained and this they cut into sections and loaded onto a cart. It took three hours to fill the cart and haul it back to the complex. Stu was waiting for them at the gate. "You two make a good team," he said, right off the bat.

It was another odd statement. "We make a sweaty team," Mike said, feeling uncomfortable. "Do you want me to check your trade goods now?"

"Yeah, maybe Jenn could help you."

"Sorry, but Jenn is busy," Jenn said, pointing at the cart of wood. "I still have to cut up the larger pieces. And I have to get dinner ready. I hope fish is okay with you, Mike."

After a hard day, Mike was starving, but before he could answer, Stu clapped him on the back. "Actually, the Coven wants to have Mike over for dinner tonight. It's sort of official business, but I will make sure to send him back as soon as he's done."

For a moment, Jenn looked disappointed. She covered the look with a quick smile. "Sure. If it's official business, what can you do, right? I'll make us some dessert so don't stuff yourself."

Stu laughed and said, "He's seventeen, Jenn, he's never been full in his life." Before Mike knew it, Stu had turned him around and was marching him away. The laughter and the strange smile were gone in a blink as he asked, "Do you trust me when it comes to the weighing and measuring? Do you trust that I won't screw you guys over?"

Up until that moment Mike trusted Stu completely, but there was something so strange about him that Mike was slow to answer, "Yeah, why?"

"The Coven will tell you at dinner. First, let's get you bathed. You don't want to see them smelling like sweaty sawdust and mud."

Mike wasn't one to put on airs, but Gerry had made it a point to tell him that he was representing Alcatraz and its people. "Consider yourself an ambassador." Mike had assured Gerry that he would. When he went to his room to pack, he'd gone right to his battered Webster's dictionary to look up the word. He had been in the second grade when the zombies came and his formal education had basically ended at that point.

"I need to run over to Jenn's for a change of clothes."

Stu shook his head. "I have your bag at my place. The pants are fine, but your shirts are a touch too wrinkled. You can borrow one of mine."

They went to Stu's apartment where Mike found a full tub waiting for him. Next to it was a glass of wine. He took one look at it and asked, "What's going on here?"

"This is how we treat guests. Trust me, Gerry knows exactly what's going on and he's fine with it. Now, chop-chop, the Coven doesn't like being kept waiting." He shut the door on Mike.

At first, he looked at the tub with suspicion, but then he asked aloud, "Why am I fighting this?" He settled into the water which was agreeably warm and took up the glass. The first sip made his face blanch. He wasn't much of a drinker, but by the time the glass was half gone, he was actually enjoying the wine.

It put him in a fine, mellow mood and he washed and dressed, feeling content. Wearing a stark white button-up shirt over clean blue jeans, he and Stu went to what had once been the "clubhouse" of the complex. Now, it was a combination storehouse, seat of government and dance hall.

The seven women who made up the Coven were there waiting for Mike. They ranged from thirty-two-year-old Lois Blanchard to forty-four-year-old Donna Polston. Although he hadn't seen most of them since the schism, he recognized their faces.

Some stared down their noses at the young men while others welcomed them. Lois was one of the latter. "Come in, come in. Look at these two strapping young men." Stu and Mike exchanged glances. Neither was all that strapping as far as Mike understood the word. They were both whipcord thin with muscles like rope. "If I wasn't taken," Lois went on. "Oh my."

"But you are," Miss Shay said in a sing-song voice. "And you know the rules." She turned her sharp face from Lois and attempted to smile in Mike's direction. Her lips were so pursed it sort of looked as though she were sucking on a lemon. "There are always rules and there are good reasons for the rules. Am I right?"

Before Mike could answer, he was turned around and found himself in front of a woman whose hair was so blonde it looked white. She held him by the shoulders and looked him up and down. "Hello there, Mike. I don't know if you remember me, my name is Miss Polston, but I suppose under these circumstances you can call me Donna. I was a friend of your mother's. My, she was always such a dear."

Mike was caught off guard for a moment with the reference to his mother. As always, thinking about her brought up a flood of feelings; he had to push them aside. "Circumstances? I wasn't aware there were any circumstances."

"Let's not worry about that right now," Donna said, taking him by the arm. "We've prepared quite a spread. It's our custom to eat first and talk business later."

He wanted answers right then but with Lois on one side and Donna on the other, he was bustled to the head of a table that was lavishly spread with pheasant in an orange sauce, roasted potatoes and a loaf of bread. The bread was a prized treat, and each was given a thin slice that was savored.

Wine was also served and by the time the dinner was over, Mike had sipped away two glasses. He wore a dreamy smile on his face as the women talked about both his mother and father in words of glowing praise. Only Stu kept silent. He had eaten quietly without saying much to anyone, and for the most part was completely ignored. Only when he asked for seconds of pheasant did he receive any attention—a cold glare from Miss Shay. This he pretended not to see as he heaped more of the roasted bird onto his plate.

Finally, he cleared his throat. "I think it's time we discussed those circumstances that were brought up earlier."

"What circumstances?" Mike asked, suddenly on edge.

Lois patted his hand and said with a beaming smile, "The circumstances of your marriage to Jenn Lockhart, of course."

Chapter 9

Jenn Lockhart

Mike was gone for hours and Jenn grew sleepy waiting for him. It didn't help that she was sitting in front of the fire, wrapped in a blanket. To stay awake she walked out onto her balcony. The signs pointed to snow and yet the night was clear and crisp with an unseasonably sharp feel of ice on the air.

With her breath blooming little clouds, she stood looking up at the stars trying to find the meaning behind them.

Some people said that the stars were really suns like their own sun. Supposedly, they were so far away that their light took millions of years to get to the earth and was cold by the time it got there. That sort of information didn't mean much to Jenn. She knew there was real meaning behind the stars. The difficult part was divining that meaning.

She gazed up at the stars. There were billions in the night sky and yet, she could name only one: the North Star. To her it was the most important star because it was the only one that could show her the way home. Her father had taught her that about a week before he had been squished like a grape. It was one of the few memories of him that she had managed to hold onto.

As she was staring up looking for the North Star, something caught her attention and made her jump. There in the heavens was a blinking light, zipping quickly across the sky. It was there for all of five seconds and then it was gone.

An average person from *before* would have questioned whether they were looking at a plane or satellite or even a space station. Jenn had heard of these things, but she didn't think for a moment that the light was from any of these leftovers from before the apocalypse. That technology was dead; everyone knew that.

The question in her mind was what the speeding light meant.

"A journey," she said to herself.

"To where?"

Jenn jumped again and looked down. Mike was standing next to her garden with his hands stuffed in his pockets staring up at her. Even in the dark she saw that his face was twisted, much like Stu's had been for the greater part of the last few days.

"I don't know," she said. "Maybe back to Alcatraz?" His normally full lips drew into a thin line. "Okay, not back to Alcatraz. Then somewhere else, who knows."

"Can I come up?" he asked.

Now it was her turn to purse her lips. It was a strange question which only cemented the idea that Stu and the Coven had let him in on some sort of secret. "Of course. I said you could stay with me for as long as you were visiting."

He came up the stairs and she met him at the door. The strangeness surrounding him was worse up close. He kept licking his lips as if he wanted to say something and then when he couldn't bring himself to, he'd grow agitated.

After a few tense minutes, she said, "I have a cobbler. It's apple and cherry...unless you're too full from dinner." She had used the last of her flour to make it and the crust was dangerously thin. He eagerly said yes to the dessert, but whether he really wanted it or just wanted a break from the silence between them, she couldn't tell.

When he had scraped his plate with his fork and poked up the last crumbs with a saliva-dampened thumb, he let loose with a bear-like yawn. "That was great. I should be getting to bed." He opened his mouth, let it hang there and then shut it again. As an afterthought, he said, "Good night."

Jenn didn't go to bed right away. She wrapped herself in a blanket and went back outside, searching again for the lights. A journey was coming. That prospect excited her, however the reason for it did not. Something bad was also coming.

The next morning Mike was up before her. There were bags under his eyes and once more he was nervous. She said, "Good morning," and then waited for him to spill his secret. When he didn't, she sniffed, "I don't mean to be rude, but it's trading day and I have things to do. Help yourself to what I have in the pantry."

Her larder was well laid up for the coming winter with salted venison, smoked fish, dried kale, pickled beets and carrots, green and yellow onions, spinach and some canned preserves. When it came to fresh fruit, she only had a few brown-spotted apples and pears. It wasn't a great variety in her opinion, but she had become quite adept at spinning a meal from very little—when she wanted to, and just then she didn't feel like it.

The snow she had predicted was in the air, though it wasn't quite falling. The ghost-like flakes seemed only to swirl and eddy, and so far hadn't coated the ground, which was a good thing because she wasn't quite ready to close out her fall garden. Long ago the parking lots and streets within the gates had been torn up and the land divided among the people who were required to give a small chunk of their produce to the community as a form of tax. The rest they could keep and do with as they would. Jenn had a plot the size of an average backyard and on it she grew lettuce, beets, broccoli, and cauliflower.

The beets had to come up before the ground became too hard, while the rest had to be covered with old sheets just in case the snow got any worse. With snow lighting in her auburn hair, she laid the sheets out first before taking a five-gallon bucket down the row of beets and digging them out. These were a week too early and were runty in her eyes. Still she filled the five-gallon bucket twice over. It was nearly ten in the morning by the time she finished. She had time to either clean up properly or check her traps before joining the others on the trip to meet the traders.

Worried that Mike would still be in her apartment holding back his secret, she decided to check her traps. Although visibility was cut down, being out in a snow storm was not nearly as dangerous as being out in the fog.

Zombies didn't like snow and tended to congregate indoors or under trees, facing inward.

They didn't like intense cold either and stayed under cover in abandoned houses or stores as well. The snow made them even more dangerous than usual. It was hard to hear them, almost impossible to see them and they wouldn't hesitate to come rushing out to attack.

It wasn't cold enough for them to be hiding just yet and Jenn felt it was safe enough to venture out alone. She moved slowly, her head up, her senses on highest alert. Her knees were completely healed and she was ready to sprint away at the first sign of trouble. She went to each of the five snares she had set the day before and found two untouched, two hanging limply as if the wind or some passing animal had knocked them loose, and one that was missing altogether.

Jenn stared at the little rut in the grass where the last had been. There were rabbit droppings nearby and the grass showed no sign that a larger animal had been down the little game trail. There was blood, however, just a few drops that were quickly being hidden as the snow began to cling. She had caught a rabbit but something had taken it.

She was nervous rather than angry. This was another bad sign, one of many. After setting a new snare she went back to the complex and found Aaron sleeping on his watch. He was supposed to be on guard duty. Normally she would have given him a severe talking to and then turned him into the Coven for an appropriate punishment, but he had saved her life.

"What are you doing?" she hissed. "You know what happens to anyone caught sleeping on duty!" The first infraction was sixty hours of "service." For the older teens and young adults, this meant hard labor of some sort: re-digging the well, or fixing spears along the wall. For children it meant cleaning the Coven's quarters or weeding gardens, and always it meant worse watch times. Three in the morning was a crappy time to be sitting on the wall, especially in winter.

"I didn't mean it, I swear," he said, looking around to see if anyone else had seen him. "You're not going to turn me in, are you? Please don't. My mom would kill me."

"I won't, this time. But it better not happen again. Keeping watch is important. You never know when a team of raiders might come…are you all right? You look a little pale."

He touched the back of his hand to his forehead. "I think I'm getting sick. I haven't been feeling well. Hey, don't tell my mom that either, okay? She won't let me go to see the traders if she thinks I'm sick."

Jenn promised that she wouldn't tell. She went back to her apartment and found it empty. This was a relief and a disappointment at the same time. She went to her pantry and saw he hadn't eaten anything. He had left on an empty stomach and that was an egregious social faux pas, one that she didn't have time to correct.

She had to gather her goods for trading. Since so many people grew the same things and caught the same sort of meat and fish, it was difficult to stand out. Jenn had perfected a carrot and beet infused vinegar recipe that went well drizzled on game meat. It was earthy and sweet. She packed each of the fourteen jars into her backpack with all the care she would take if she were packing fourteen jarred hearts.

By one o'clock she was ready to go and, picking up her crossbow, she walked through the falling snow to the front gate, where the entire community was congregated, including Mike, who stood with Stu and the entire Coven. Stu waved her over.

She was ten feet away when Lois Blanchard exclaimed loudly, "My goodness, Jenn Lockhart, you are a sight. With snow in your autumnal hair and dirt on your winter cheeks you are a true and natural beauty. Don't you think so Mr. Gunter?"

Mike looked surprised that his name was spoken. "Hmm? What? Yes, you look great. Where's all your stuff? I thought you had things to trade."

Jenn opened her mouth but Donna Polston was too quick. "She's been working on something secret, or so the birdies tell me." How she knew about Jenn's secret, Jenn didn't know. It was this sort of thing that made everyone think Donna had actual powers.

"Yes, it's an infused vinegar dressing," Jenn admitted. She was more than a bit bewildered. How could they claim she looked beautiful when she had spent the morning grubbing in the dirt? And why was the entire Coven staring at her in exactly the same judging manner? Normally their judging looks ran to sour, but now they were all smiling at her. It was unsettling.

Stu saw how uncomfortable she was. "The advance team should get moving. Mike and I are going. We'll take Jenn and One Shot." Stu went on, giving the rest their marching orders. The second group would be in charge of moving the carts down to the docks with a third acting as guards. Not everyone would see the traders that first day. They couldn't afford to leave the complex completely unguarded.

Jenn couldn't believe she was being chosen for the advance team. Normally it was made up of the best fighters and as competent as she was, she wasn't the best. She was even more shocked when Orlando Otis handed her an M4. He had a sneer spread across his dim-witted face.

"Does she even know how to use a gun?" he asked. He wasn't asking Stu, he was asking the Coven.

Donna nudged Lois Blanchard who smiled, making an angry noise in her throat as she did so. "You know she does, now stop being a pain and do as you're told." The two were married, though neither much liked the other anymore. But they were stuck together. They had proclaimed themselves married and there was no taking that back, except in cases of physical abuse.

Orlando turned away, mumbling curses while his friend, One Shot Saul, a rough-cut shabby man of thirty, shook his head in disbelief. Jenn didn't think they had a right to be mad at her since she hadn't asked to be in the lead group. She kissed the gun for luck, basically claiming the gun for herself.

"Alright, that's enough," Stu said. Although he was younger than both One Shot and Orlando, he was steely-eyed and tough as leather. When he gave orders, he expected them to be followed. "I'll take point. Jenn on my left, Mike on my right. One Shot, you got the rear." Nothing more needed to be said and in silence, Stu moved out through the gate. Before going through Jenn checked the M4. She popped out the magazine and thumbed the rounds into her palm, counting them. She had nine in the magazine and one chambered.

She knew the rules: the guns were only to be used in a life and death emergency—and sometimes not even then. Three days before, Stu had not used his .357 to save any of the men in the water. He hadn't even reached for it. The gun Jenn carried was mostly for show. The traders could not be trusted. It was pretty much common knowledge that they would turn from trader to raider in a second if they thought they could get away with it. They needed to see that the group would fight to protect themselves if they had to.

Which was why it was strange that Jenn was carrying a gun and not part of the last group as she normally was.

She dwelt on this all the way down to the docks. The first group's job was to make sure the path was clear of zombies and, thankfully, it was. They made it down to Pelican Harbor without incident where Gerry Xydis waited with his small fleet moored at the docks.

There were twenty Islanders standing in the falling snow, their hoods casting shadows across their faces. Gerry leaned against a rail. He had the same odd look on his face that everyone else seemed to have.

His grin at Jenn was accompanied by a leer that made absolutely no sense. "So, how are the fortunes treating you?" The other Islanders grinned, clearly in on the secret.

Jenn didn't answer. She was certain she was the butt of some elaborate joke and she wasn't happy about it. She glared at him and then, one at a time, at the others. One

Shot was the only one who didn't smile back in that unsettling knowing way the others did. He wasn't in on the secret or the joke or whatever it was, she concluded. This little thing calmed her. Perhaps the secret had nothing to do with her after all. She shook her head, trying to clear it of the dark thoughts that had been brooding around her.

"My fortunes are good, but I should warn you, Mister Gerry the signs have not been good at all. I know Stu doesn't want to hear it, but they've been many and obvious."

Gerry's people glanced back and forth. Some crossed themselves. Gerry cast an eye at Stu, who shook his head slightly. "Well, crap," Gerry mumbled, as a sour, impatient look crossed his features. He visibly mastered himself, forcing a smile onto his face and saying, "If you ask me, I think the signs are pointing to something great. You'll see."

For a moment Jenn thought about the light in the sky, wondering if it did indeed mean a journey. Journeys were exciting, they were an adventure. They promised a break from the tedious chore of gathering wood day after day, of hauling bucket after bucket of water just to take a bath, and sitting on guard duty, bored to tears. A journey actually sounded nice…if it weren't for the other signs she had seen. There had been so many.

"No, something bad is going to happen. I can feel it in my bones. I didn't say anything before and look what happened to Remy and Ken, so I'm saying something now."

Stu rolled his eyes. "Look, nothing bad is going to happen. These signs you've been seeing, they're actually good news. Tell her, Mike."

Mike blinked, looking younger than his seventeen years. "I…I…" Just then there came a soft pop, pop, pop sound from across the bay. It was the sound of gunfire.

Chapter 10

Mike Gunter

The far-off sound of gunfire started sporadically like a kettle of popcorn just beginning to burst and then built steadily. Everyone stared, perhaps expecting the gunfire to swell into a crescendo before dying away to nothing, but it went on and on.

After a minute, the Islanders turned and looked at Jenn with the same suspicious, nervous, awed expressions. Mike, like the rest, stared at the girl, only his feelings were magnified. He had been around her for nearly four days and she had been seeing signs and reading them with unusual frequency and accuracy.

He crossed himself and a second later the twenty Islanders did the same. Some pulled crucifixes from beneath their shirts and kissed them.

"What is it?" someone asked Jenn.

"It's the dead attacking the traders," Stu snarled. "What else could it be?"

At his little outburst, they all looked from Jenn to Stu, then back again waiting for her reply. She stared across the water toward the sound of the gunfire, her face growing sad. "It's trouble and it portends more trouble. But of what sort, I don't know."

A low whispering broke out among the Islanders. They were nervous and wanted more of an answer. "Is it the dead or raiders?" Gerry the Greek asked, a whiff of gin coating his words. The Islanders began to nod at the direct question.

"It's the dead," Stu assured. He gave a Jenn a strange look then, without asking, stepped from the dock to Gerry's flagship, a twenty-three foot cutter that had the name *Calypso* painted in flaring letters across the back. It was the only boat in the small fleet with a bowsprit, allowing it to carry three sails and making it the fastest boat. "You can tell it's the dead because there isn't any answering fire."

Instead of looking to Gerry the Greek for a reply, the Islanders gazed at Jenn waiting for her to say something. She shrugged. "The signs only point to trouble and to a journey. I don't think crossing the bay counts as a journey, but I guess someone should go and see what's happening."

She took a step towards the *Calypso* but Gerry grabbed her arm. "Oh no. Don't get on my boat. Ain't no witch gonna step one foot on her. I don't know much about reading signs but that's bad luck. I'll take Mike, Stu and One Shot with me. The rest of you stay here."

He crossed himself before stepping on board. Mike crossed himself as well and was just about to board when Jeff Battaglia tapped him on the shoulder. The last time Mike had seen Jeff was after he had pulled him, shivering from the water four days before. It made him think of Remy, who wasn't among the other Islanders. *Because he's dead*, Mike thought. He thought it, but was afraid to ask.

"Hi, Jeff."

Jeff pulled him aside, glanced once at Jenn, who was standing by herself and whispered. "I have a problem. Remember those little scratches I had the other day? The day that…you know." Mike knew: the day Remy died. He nodded for Jeff to go on. "They've gotten worse. Do you think I can get your girlfriend to take a look at them?"

"She's not my girlfriend," Mike hissed. "She's… she's…I don't know what, but sure. Ask her if you want to. I have to go." What he was asking wasn't unexpected. There wasn't a doctor among either of the two groups and when medical advice was needed beyond simple and obvious remedies, people went to the Coven for answers.

Mike turned from Jeff, bent and shoved the sailboat away from the dock before leaping on board. Gerry was raising the main so Mike went to the bowsprit and hauled up the triangular staysail. One Shot and Stu did their best to keep out of the way, hunkering down near the tiny cabin.

While they worked to get the cutter underway in the light wind, no one spoke, they only listened to the gunfire which had become sporadic, coming in little bursts and then dying away for a time. It was only when they were halfway across the bay that One Shot asked. "How did she do that? It was like, 'I saw bad signs' and then *bam* we got shooting. Is she real? Really-real? I know the Coven likes to talk that crap up, but what she just did was crazy."

"She got lucky," Stu said. "There's no truth behind signs or omens. There's no science behind it."

"What do you know about science?" Gerry asked. "You were in the fifth grade when all this started, which means you don't know jack about science and neither does anyone else. Not even the Coven, no matter how old they are. Do you know why the wind blows or how a battery works? Or any of that?"

Stu stared Gerry in the eye for a few seconds before he shrugged. Gerry grunted, "That's what I thought. At a certain point, science and magic are the same. That girl knew something bad was going to happen and it did."

"And she predicted the snow," Mike said. Snow had been a rare thing in the bay area before the apocalypse. Now it occurred once or twice a year.

"I could have told you it was going to snow," Stu shot back.

"But you didn't," Mike said. "She did." Mike didn't know what to make of Jenn one way or another. He was still trying to come to grips with the fact that it had already been decided they were supposed to be married and that he was supposed to go live with the Hill People. Match-making was a common occurrence, though usually it involved people a little older than he and Jenn.

Normally, teens were given leeway to date and figure things out for themselves. Not that Mike had been doing much dating. There weren't a lot of girls his age on the island that was true, but Jenn? They had been almost brother and sister when she lived on the island. Although that had been nine years ago the familial feelings were still there. Yet, in the last few days his feeling had been getting mixed with something that might have been romance, but now that marriage was being forced down his throat, those feelings had straight-up vanished and there was only stark terror in his chest.

Marriage was such a huge and permanent step and he was still so young. He had planned on traveling, on sowing his wild oats, on…on doing something other than getting married.

"Hey Mike?" Gerry asked. "You awake in there?"

He had been staring blankly at the falling snow. "Yeah, I'm good. There's just a lot going on."

"Or not," Gerry said. "I take it you didn't pop the question yet? He knows, doesn't he, Stu?" Stu nodded without saying anything. "Then what are you waiting for? You've had four days! She's pretty and smart and she's got that second sight thing going on. I'd say you were lucky. Think about it. Who else would you be looking at, Mush-Mouth?"

A young Islander named Gretchen bore the unfortunate nickname of Mush-mouth because she'd been wearing the same braces for the last twelve years. No one knew how to remove them and gradually they had warped her teeth.

"Can we not talk about this, please?" Mike begged.

"Sure, just as long as you look me right in the eye and tell me you'll pop the question when we get back. You know what happens if you don't."

Mike knew. Like everything else since the beginning of the apocalypse, the concept of marriage had gone through an upheaval. Early strife within the group had centered on a few things: work, theft, and sex. Lazy people were belittled harshly, thieves were driven from the island and people who had sex together were instantly considered married.

There had been too many fights, too many splits and divisions. At one point, thirteen people had simply left the island because John liked Suzy and she liked Brad but he liked…

Now there was no messing around. It was cut and dried—sex equaled marriage. This led to a predictable shift in attitude in which young men and women kept to themselves. With humanity on the brink, in some ways this was a worse situation than before and thus, arranged marriages came about.

It was true that Mike or Jenn could refuse the marriage, but there would be repercussions to that. Essentially, they would be blackballed from the entire process and placed in the back of the line, so to speak. If Mike refused, he could very well end up with Mush-Mouth. This sort of thing had happened before and no one wanted to be one of the sad stories used to scare the younger generation.

"I'll talk to her but can we just deal with this for now?" There really wasn't anything to deal with yet. It was eight miles to the marina just south of the Oakland airport and from there it was another mile and a half to Interstate 880 where they traditionally met the traders coming up out of the Santas on their way to Sacramento.

The wind had picked up, and with Gerry's and Mike's skill, it was a forty-five minute trip. Somewhere along the way the firing had ceased altogether and none of them thought this was a good thing.

Slowly the opposite shore drew close. Stu and One Shot sat up and checked their M4s. They watched the docks, squinting through the snow but not seeing anything. At a hundred yards, Mike dropped the staysail and tied it off as Gerry turned up against the wind, checking their speed. When he turned again, the *Calypso* drifted right to the dock as if he were parking a Cadillac.

Mike was the first off the boat leaping up with cat-like dexterity. He tied off the boat as Stu and One Shot came off. Last was Gerry, moving reluctantly as always when he had to leave the *Calypso* unguarded.

Although Gerry was a leader of the Island people and One Shot was oldest, now that they were on land, Stu took command. He pointed Mike to his left, One Shot to his right and Gerry to the rear. They went up a street that looked as though it had been nuked. All the buildings on the left side of the street had collapsed during the great quake, while most of the buildings on the right leaned in toward the street, looking as though they could topple at any time.

The street itself looked as if it had been turned inside out. A forest of jagged and rusted rebar pointed upward. The four slipped between the rebar, and after seeing Jeff's infected scrapes, Mike took extra care. Infections had gradually been getting worse and worse over the past few years. It was blamed on "stronger" germs, though no one knew for certain.

Three blocks up they came to an industrial area where warehouses and small production facilities once vied for space. Now it was just a debris field of overturned trucks, their underbellies rusted through, pieces of shattered furniture from a Sears Outlet store, shards of glass everywhere except where pools of mud sat waiting to freeze.

Stu led them into this maze, pausing in the middle when a troop of zombies moaned and gimped their way into view. The four slunk down, hiding next to a dumpster that had once been used to recycle cardboard. There was about a foot of soggy brown mulch at the bottom.

"I don't recognize them," Stu said, indicating the zombies with his chin. "Do you guys?"

So often the dead all looked alike to Mike: giant, naked grey humanoids, their flesh running with sores, their arms and legs missing great hunks of flesh. When they had hair it grew in patches, long and greasy. Their faces were almost always mutilated in some way and it was rare to find one with both eyes, ears and lips.

Sometimes one would stand out in some way. Mike remembered seeing one that had survived a fire. It was black as a demon with red fissures running through it. Save for dark wet holes in its head where its eyes, nose and mouth had been it had no features at all. Another was missing the top of its head. From the eyebrows on up, everything was just gone. How it was still alive, no one knew.

There was nothing familiar about the ones forty yards away. Two eight-foot tall males and four females all nearly seven-feet in height. One of the females was missing both arms. It breasts were as flat and long as tube socks and when it stooped to chew the tip off a stunted pine, they hung down to the ground.

"I never seen them before. I would have recognized that female. You don't often see…" One of the males had turned abruptly and was now stomping towards them. Mike slipped back behind the dumpster. "It's coming," he hissed.

They were four armed men and yet they crawled like mice through a break in the wall of a building with One Shot frantically pushing the others out of the way to get in first. It had once been a machine shop, now it was a death maze filled with razor sharp metal, falling bricks and gaping holes in the floor.

Mike slipped in last just as the zombie came around the dumpster. It saw his feet and reached in after him. "Holy jeeze!" Mike hissed, pulling in his feet and scooting back into a table saw that had toppled over. Stu reached down and picked him up. They both stared down at the huge hand with its scrambling claws. One broke off as they watched. Mike made a face and Stu laughed in the quiet way of the Hill People.

That giant hand then gripped the edge of the hole and began tearing at it, making the hole larger. That killed Stu's laughter. He turned from the hole and gazed around at the gloom where the machines sat like hunched monsters, squatting in the dark. "Let's go."

With his M4 at his shoulder, Stu led the way through the building, stepping over fallen beams and around gaping holes. He paused every minute to listen for the groans and rumbling of zombies. "Do you hear that?" he asked Mike. The four cocked their heads and Mike did hear an odd noise that was hard to describe other than to say there was a thrumming sound filling the air.

"What is it?" Gerry asked.

One Shot brushed his long dark hair back from his right ear. "That's so weird. It reminds me of when I was a kid and my dad took me to see the Raiders play the Bears. We were late and the game had already started, and as we were walking up there was this huge sound coming from the stadium. It had an electric quality to it. Kinda like this."

"But what could be making it?" Gerry asked.

"Only one way to find out," Stu said and started on again. A side door led to a wide hall that was so dark they could only see a few feet ahead of them. Gerry lit a candle and handed it to Stu, who raised it up. The candle gave off a feeble glow and in its dim light they could see paper and trash lining the hall, while from the ceiling hung wires and broken light fixtures.

They passed doors on their left and right, each opening into dark rooms. Stu kept going until he came to what had once been a glass door. The shattered glass on the floor in front of it sparkled like ice. Beyond it was a warehouse where the industrial shelving had toppled like dominoes and leaned one against the other.

A murky light filtered over the mess. Stu blew out the candle and slipped under the lower part of the door, his crossbow getting hung up momentarily on a metal slat that divided the door in half.

The others followed him in, crunching glass under foot. The thrumming sound was louder and they proceeded slower than ever, being extra careful to look where they stepped. The light came from the very far end of the warehouse at the loading dock where a rolling door was bent in half and hanging by a chain.

Mike stole to the edge of the door and looked out to where there should have been only a wide expanse of broken cement littered by leaves and trash and the burned-out hulk of an old eighteen-wheeler. He had been through this particular industrial park a number of times.

Now, the scene was different. The burned-out truck was a little island in what looked like a sea of zombies. There had to be thousands of them, their moans thrumming the air in a chorus of white noise. "Stu," he whispered and jerked a thumb toward the door. Stu took one look and backed away from the door, hurrying back the way they had come.

Mike thought they were leaving, but Stu found a stairwell with roof access and hurried up, once more using the candle to light the way. When they came out onto the roof, the sound of the zombies was amplified. One Shot who was visibly shaking whispered, "My God, how many of them are there?"

The four crawled to the edge of the roof and lay flat in stunned silence. The sea of zombies seemed to stretch as far as the eye could see.

Chapter 11

Jenn Lockhart

The docks at Pelican Harbor were wide open, without any natural cover; not a safe place for the Islanders to await the return of the *Calypso*. The boats were made fast by their crews, who then hid in a seafood restaurant across the street. Jenn trudged back up the hill with only Jeff following her. At the complex they were greeted by the anxious Hill People who all babbled the same questions: *Was that gunfire? Who's shooting? Is it raiders?*

"Hold on now, hold on," Jenn repeated as she pushed through the crowd, wanting to get to safety before answering. "Let us through."

At the back of the crowd, bundled against the cold and the falling snow was the Coven. Jenn addressed them, "There was gunfire coming from where we usually meet the traders. Stu took Mike, Gerry and One Shot across the bay to find out what's going on. Since it'll be a few hours before they return, I offered for the Islanders to stay with us but they refused. They're down by the docks."

Miss Shay, wearing her usual pinched expression said, "That was neighborly of you and yet only one takes you up on your generous offer?" She sniffed at Jeff and if anything her expression grew even more sour. "I would have thought that…what? What's with the look, Jenn?"

Jenn touched her face, not realizing she was wearing any look in particular. "It's, um, Jeff. He wanted me to look at an injury. I'm pretty sure it's infected."

Donna's sharp eyes went from Jeff, who stood to the side with his head down, and focused on Jenn. "And he came to you? And you looked at the wound? That doesn't make much sense, no not at all." Her steely gaze pinned Jenn in place as guilt bubbled up inside of her.

"S-something else happened out by the docks," she said, her voice breaking. Everyone had crowded in close. Taking a deep breath, Jenn told the Coven about the signs she'd been seeing and about the odd timing of her statement. She didn't know how the Coven was going to react, but their looks of suspicion were what she had expected.

"I've been saying this for a year now," Miss Shay snapped. "She's got a black aura. We should have nipped this in the bud."

Lois Blanchard tutted Miss Shay, saying, "There's a time and a place and this isn't it. Now, Jenn, I want you to take this injured man to the clubhouse, but before you do, make sure he has a bite to eat. Just a nibble is all that's needed."

The Coven left, whispering among themselves. Jenn sighed, fearing she had said something wrong. The sigh stuck in her throat when she turned back to the others and found them all staring at her, some in disbelief and some in awe.

"Jeff?" she said in a wavering voice. "If you'll come with me, please." Without waiting for him, she headed for her apartment as behind her the crowd of people began whispering. When Jenn got to her place she went to the blackout curtains in her living room and pulled them back, flooding the room with light and giving her a view of the crowd. They were still milling around talking and she knew that if it wasn't for the cold, they'd be at it for hours.

Jeff stood in her doorway, his big brown puppy dog eyes looking uneasy. "Come in, Jeff," she said, heading to her pantry for a plate of salted salmon. She brought it to the table and was shocked to see that Jeff wasn't alone; Aaron Altman stood behind him, looking scared *and* pale. He was sick. "You too? Is it your scratches from the car?"

He nodded and started to take off his coat. She stopped him. "No, not in the doorway that's bad luck. Come sit down." The two went to the table while she hurried for a second plate of fish. She set it in front of Aaron and at first he turned up his nose at it. "Eat it," she commanded, thinking that if they wanted Jeff to eat before treating him, it would be the same for Aaron.

Reluctantly, Aaron ate the fish. As he ate, he glanced repeatedly at Jeff before asking, "Is it true that the zombies came from hell and that anyone scratched or bitted by them will go to hell, too?"

She had heard easily a hundred theories about where the zombies had come from and how they had been made. While a few people thought they had come from outer space, or were the result of black magic, or were hell spawn, unleashed by the devil to punish the world, most people blamed scientists.

"No one knows where they came from," Jenn answered. "But it isn't smart to dwell on the negative before seeing the Coven. Now eat your food." When he was finished, he nervously lifted his sleeve to show a scrape on his forearm that was an angry red color. Across the top of it was a yellow crust.

Jenn nodded, saying, "Yeah, it's infected. Why didn't you tell your mom? Miss Shay would have known what to do."

He shrugged, glanced at Jeff and admitted sheepishly, "She'll ask about evil spirits. She'll ask…she'll ask about everything."

The Coven reckoned things simply: good came from good and evil came from evil. They would immediately assume that Jeff and Aaron had done something to warrant their infections. They would be cured but they would also have to confess and pay reparations, usually in the form of labor or fines.

"Have you done anything wrong?" Jenn asked. The boy dropped his head, refusing to look at her. It was answer enough. "Okay, Aaron. I don't know if it's my place to judge. If I were you, I would tell your mother and…"

"No! She won't understand. You have to help me. You have the gift, too. It's even better than my mom's, I know it."

"Oh, I doubt that." The Coven's abilities were shrouded in mystery and Jenn didn't think that Aaron had any knowledge of what his mother could or could not do. On the other hand she knew precisely what she could do for him: very little. There were pills to fight infections, but in the wrong hands they could make the situation worse.

"I read a few signs," Jenn told him. "That's all. Anyone could have done it. I can't heal anyone." Aaron moaned and covered his face with both hands. She put an arm around him. "It's not going to be so bad, you'll see. Now put on a brave face and let's go see your mother."

To keep Aaron from becoming the focal point of the latest gossip, Jenn went around the back, taking the long way around the buildings. At the clubhouse doors she knocked and then stepped back, thinking that she wouldn't be invited inside.

When Miss Shay answered the door, she sucked in her breath in surprise at seeing her son standing there next to Jeff. "No! You too? What evil was awakened on that trip?"

It was a second before Jenn realized that the woman was speaking to her. Miss Shay's eyes were furious little slits that made Jenn blanche. "I-I don't know but bad signs abounded everywhere. Even before we made it to the island."

"Signs? Since when does a child know anything about signs? Come inside. You have a great deal of explaining to do." Again, she was speaking to Jenn.

Miss Shay directed the three of them to a room that was empty save for a long table and seven chairs. The Coven sat behind the table. They grew grim at the sight of Aaron, with Lois Blanchard sighing and saying, "Who will be the third?"

She was referring to the rule of three—evil always came in threes.

Donna shook her head. "Let's see what we're up against. Aaron, dear, show us what's wrong."

Aaron, shaking badly, lifted his sleeve. They quizzed him on how it had happened and after he explained how he had gotten scratched trying to rescue Jenn, his mother glared at her.

Jenn didn't believe she had done anything wrong and she glared right back. "This isn't my fault. He saved me, but I saved him earlier. Also, I tried to warn Stu. I told him about the signs but he wouldn't listen. Also, Aaron and Jeff have only normal infections. You still have the yellow pills, right?" Everyone knew the Coven had a store of big yellow pills that fought infections.

At the question, the Coven grew still except to shift their eyes towards Donna who smiled unconvincingly at Jenn. It was another one of those lying smiles that she was becoming all too accustomed to. "Of course we do," the oldest member of the Coven said. "Now let us take care of this. You go home and make a big dinner. Enough for two."

Right away she pictured Mike sitting down to dinner with her, but that wasn't going to happen. He was supposed to leave with the others after dealing with the traders…if they were going to deal with them at all. "Two? Do you actually think we'll be bunking up with the Islanders because Gerry…"

"Just do as you're told!" Miss Shay snapped.

Fuming, Jenn left and stomped straight back to her apartment, slamming the door behind her. She walked once around her little suite of rooms, peeking out of every window and not quite knowing what she was looking for. At the end of her circuit she found herself by the front door where she had set down the M4, her pack and her crossbow. "Make dinner, my butt," she snapped, grabbing her weapons and slipping outside.

By then the cold had driven everyone inside except the gate guard, Colleen White, who was pale and shivering. She perked up at the sight of Jenn, but was slow to open the gate as she stared. "How'd you do it? How'd you know what was going to happen? You don't have the third eye. I've known you since I was like seven and you never…"

"Just get out of my way," Jenn said, pushing through the small gap. She wound through the spear maze at a jog and then disappeared into the forest at the top of the hill.

Although she was angry at the way the Coven had treated her, she didn't have time to wallow in teenage angst.

Her survival depended on her ability to keep a clear head. The moment she stepped into the forest, her pent-up emotions drained out of her, leaving her senses open. Right away she became aware of a creature sixty yards off. It was loud, snapping branches and shuffling through the leaves that crinkled beneath the thin layer of snow.

Jenn shifted to her right, angling away, finding herself heading towards the Marin Headlands where she usually set out her traps in the thin scrub on the hills overlooking the Golden Gate Bridge and the entrance to the bay. On clear days she could see Alcatraz Island and all of San Francisco. From that far, the city was still pretty on warm summer days and she enjoyed watching the sailboats plying the waves.

With the snow, Jenn couldn't see the ocean pounding the rocks below her, let alone seeing the city or the *Calypso* out on the bay. The boat was the real reason she was there. First there had been the deaths of Remy and Ken, then Aaron and Jeff had infections.

"And now something bad has happened to the traders," she said to herself. There was evil in the air. In her mind's eye she had a perfect picture of the *Calypso* getting broadsided by a rogue wave and capsizing or running into another school of half-submerged zombies, or getting lost in the snow and hitting Shag Rock.

For all she knew the boat was aiming right for the headlands. Against her will, she moved to the edge of the hill, which ended at an almost vertical drop. She looked down, but could see nothing.

"I'm being silly," she told herself, trying to ignore the butterflies of fear in her belly.

To counter the fear, she decided to check her traps even though she knew full well that they hadn't been out long enough. She went to each and was happy to find she had snared a four-pound cottontail. It had strangled on the wire but was still warm. Jenn reset the snare, thinking that it would make a perfect dinner for two. "But who's the second person?"

She was dwelling on that as she went on to the next snare and found it missing completely. That was twice in two days. A part of her began to analyze what it could mean; she shut that train of thought down. There were so many signs that she began to worry she would become paralyzed by them all.

Hanging the cottontail from her belt, she slung the M4 across her back, keeping her crossbow out and at the ready. She should have gone back to her apartment to clean the rabbit and get it marinating, instead she found herself working her way northeast around the curve of the bay heading towards Pelican Harbor.

It was a twenty-minute walk and by the time she stood on the last hill overlooking the harbor the snow had died away and there was the *Calypso* tacking into a light wind. It was a half-mile out and moving slowly towards the harbor. It was in no danger now. She breathed a sigh of relief thinking that she had dodged some sort of bullet regarding the signs.

"Maybe we're in the free and clear. Nothing else is going to happ…" Her whispered words dried up as she saw some of the Islanders coming from the restaurant. One had stuck a faded pink and white table cloth on a broken table leg and was waving it as he walked down to the dock. They were trying to signal what the wind situation was close to the docks.

"What the hell?" Jenn asked. Instinctively, she backed behind a tree. Waving a flag, no matter what the reason, was an idiotic move. Zombies had bad eyesight, but they weren't blind. Jenn wished she could scream at them to put the damned thing away because, sure enough, there came a moan.

The dead had been hiding from the snow in one of the large homes that overlooked the harbor. Now that the snow was gone they were coming out to feed and they hadn't missed the flag or the people. The low moans of the beasts were being drowned out by the wind as it picked up and

Jenn saw that if she didn't do something to warn the little group of Islanders they would be trapped on the dock.

She jumped up and started waving her hands to get their attention, but they didn't turn around. In desperation, she picked up a rock and chucked it at the zombies plodding through the high grasses bordering the frontage road. Her arm wasn't the best and yet because she was up on the steep hill the rock made it to the road and bounced noisily.

Unfortunately, the rock bounced towards the dock and the zombies weren't distracted. Jenn was forced to do the unthinkable. "Hey!" she screamed at the top of her lungs just as the zombies stumbled onto the boardwalk that ran along the edge of the bay. "Hey! Up here!" Her voice cut through the wind and not only did the Islanders turn around, the zombies did as well.

They turned and charged. There were four of them coming for her. She wasn't exactly afraid. They were fifty yards away and downhill from her; she had plenty of time to get away. Turning to run away, she discovered that her arm-waving had attracted a true monster. It was the one zombie that everyone feared; the nine-foot tall Frankenstein. It took Jenn's breath away, and when it roared, her stomach turned to water and her legs to rubber.

Chapter 12

Jenn Lockhart

It wasn't just Frank's tremendous size that rooted Jenn in place. It was the fact that he looked almost prehistoric. His skin was rough and strangely sandy as if it had been dipped in cement and his huge head and wide shoulders were draped in dried seaweed making it look like he had crawled out of the primordial ooze that had formed the earth.

When it roared Jenn whimpered. She had never been so afraid in her life and hers had been a life filled with terrible moments.

Frank was uphill and when it lumbered down at her it moved faster than any zombie had ever moved. It covered twenty yards in seconds. Jenn was so petrified with fear that only at the last moment did she scream and try to dodge out of the way.

As big and ferocious as he was, Frank was still a zombie. His reactions were slow and too late he tried to stop. There was no stopping seven hundred pounds on a dime and his momentum carried him on down the hill.

The creature's arms were like those of a gorilla and even though Jenn threw herself to the ground his long fingers snagged the strap of her M4 and she found herself tumbling down the hill along with Frank. Snow flew as the sky and earth traded places so fast that everything was a white blur.

Her head struck a rotted tree stump, making her eyes cross, a rock hit her mid-thigh and her leg went immediately numb. Somehow she managed to hold onto her crossbow even as he smashed the breath out of her.

Jenn was one great bruise when the two finally rolled out onto the frontage road. She tried to roll over but discovered the strap of the M4 was spun around Frank's hand and when he stood, Jenn was lifted off the ground. If she could have breathed, she would have screamed—and she would have died.

As it was, the creature's face was covered in snow and he didn't even realize she was attached to his hand. He felt something on it and whipped his arm back and forth, sending Jenn flying. She landed with a *thwap* on the wet pavement and immediately struggled to her feet, fighting to ignore the waves of dizzying pain that wracked her.

She had to run. She had to hide. The four zombies were charging up from the docks and Frank was tearing at his face trying to clear the snow. She only had seconds to get away—six seconds to be precise—until Frank saw her and came lumbering after her with tremendous strides that ate up the distance between them. Unimaginable fear bubbled up from inside her and it came out in a blubbering whine as Frank drew closer and closer with every step.

The only cover anywhere near her was a hedge that had gone wild and was now a wall of sticks with a few straggling leaves holding on. Jenn dove into a gopher gap and crawled through it. A few feet to her side, Frank blasted through the hedge as if it were made of straw.

Jenn reversed direction, ducked back through the hedge and nearly ran into the four zombies that had come up from the dock. There was nowhere for her to go except back under the hedge as the dead attacked from both sides. The hedge was destroyed all around her and debris rained down. She curled into a ball and clamped her eyes shut, knowing she was going to die and not wanting to see it coming.

The ferocity of the attack was unimaginably loud and explosive. The bush next to her head was pulled out of the ground, roots and all. She squinted up to see Frank standing over her. He had a hold of two of the other zombies and as she watched, he drove their heads together.

They exploded like overripe melons, raining black blood down on her. The two beasts dropped, one landing on Jenn, trapping her beneath its stinking carcass. Frank charged the other two, swinging huge fists at them. Thud,

thud, thud! His fists pounded them as Jenn squirmed mightily to get out from beneath the corpse.

Frank knew only eternal hunger and rage. He never let anything get in the way of his prey, including his own kind. Right above Jenn, Frank beat the two zombies into a mush.

He was still at it when she finally pulled herself free and crawled away toward a dilapidated old house that sat behind what was left of the hedge. The pain coursing through her was terrific. She tried to get up and run, but the best she could do was a wobbling hobble.

At first Frank didn't see her escaping. He tore at the hedge in fury, uprooting the bushes one after another and flinging them aside.

Jenn might have got away, only as she opened the front door of the house, it fell on top of her. It had been hanging by a rusty hinge which chose that moment to break. Glass shattered, making enough noise to cut through Frank's fury. He turned and, seeing her struggling under the door, charged.

Terror gave her the strength to heave aside the door and she half-ran, half-crawled up the stairs that ran up from the main lower hall. Nothing about the house registered on her panicked mind. She had no idea how many floors it had or what sort of furniture was scattered about or who the smiling people were in the pictures that hung on the hall. The only thing on her mind was Frank.

The beast was a horror that completely filled the staircase behind her, cutting off the light from below. He had to duck his head as it thrust himself upward and with each rake of his claws half a dozen balusters were sheared away from beneath the bannister. He tore his way upward, coming on so quickly that his claws slipped through her long hair as she stumbled on the second-floor landing.

With her legs still threatening to give out beneath her, she held onto the railing, limping for the next set of stairs leading up, but with one swing of his huge arm, Frank tore the railing away shaking the entire house down to its foundation. She shrank against the wall, using it to hold herself up before throwing herself onto the next and last set of stairs.

The immense creature was right behind her when she made it to the third floor where there was nowhere to run or hide. She was trapped. The best she could do was rush into a bathroom and slam the door behind her like some willful teenager.

Holding in a whimper, she backed away from the door as it stomped down the hall. The sound of each step boomed throughout the house. The floor shook and the mirror rattled. A shower tile that had been on the verge of falling for months now came loose, clattering into the bathtub.

A second later, part of the door blasted inwards as Frank attacked it with one of his sledgehammer-like fists. He stuck his head to the hole he had made and peered at Jenn with one huge grey-filmed eye. Jenn was trapped, but not utterly defenseless. During all of this she had kept hold of her crossbow and now she leveled it and aimed.

She couldn't miss. The bolt went three inches deep into his forehead and had the effect of making Frank *really* mad.

His fury had been horrendous before, but it was nothing compared to what happened next. Frank turned the door to kindling with his bare hands. As he did, Jenn smashed out the screen covering the window and climbed out onto the snow-covered roof, which was slick as ice; one slip and she would shoot down the shingles to a thirty foot drop.

Once again, she was trapped.

Thankfully, there was no way Frank would be able to get through the small, slanted bathroom window. He simply couldn't, though he tried. Like a giant, hideous version of Winnie the Pooh, he got stuck.

"Ha!" Jenn hissed. She sat down on the point of the roof, braced the bow and pulled back on the cable. She loaded the bolt and shuffled along the tip of the triangular roof moving as close to Frank's one waving arm as she dared. Taking a steadying breath, she shot the thing once more in the head and now there were two bolts sticking out of it.

Still he didn't die. His rage reached a cataclysmic point and as Jenn sat down to reload once more, he strained with all of his strength. There was a cracking sound from the side of the house right before it came apart. Jenn didn't know walls could come apart. Frantically she reloaded the crossbow as two-by-fours snapped like pencils and sheetrock disintegrated.

Frank enlarged the hole and climbed through. Jenn had only one shot left and she made sure it counted. Waiting until the beast was almost on top of her, she shot it through the right eye. Dropping the crossbow, she tried to scramble back but her foot slipped. Before she knew it she was skittering down the frozen roof, a scream in her throat, her nails leaving ten perfectly even grooves in the snow.

Above her, Frank reached out one of his long arms to grab her hand. He came up just short, and with his weight too far forward, he slipped as well, sliding right at Jenn. She felt she had reached the limit of fear. Death was in front and behind, above and below. Flailing was all she had, even as she shot off the roof.

Both hands hit the lip of the gutter and held on even as the gutter split in two and let go. The screws holding it in place popped out in a long string, sounding like machine-gun fire as she swung down in an ever-increasing arc. Behind her, Frank shot past heading straight for the ground.

Just as he hit with an ugly thud, Jenn swung into the side of the house and fell ten feet down into a drift of moldering leaves. The drift had been building for twelve years and when she fell into it, other than the smell and the wet, it was no different that falling onto a feather bed.

She sank deep into the drift and for a few minutes did nothing except catch her breath and listen for Frank. Zombies, especially the big ones, could sustain a tremendous amount of damage and keep going. A fall like that wasn't going to kill Frank. And yet, she heard nothing except a steady creak of tin on tin as a length of gutter swayed back and forth.

Slowly, ever so slowly, Jenn crept out from the leaf pile, ready at the first sound to either dive back in or sprint out of there—although limp out of there might have been more accurate. The big muscle in her right thigh had a knot in it the size of her fist and no amount of massaging had yet loosened it.

She made her way around the bushes that were taking over the driveway and found Frank flat on his face, unmoving. Crouching, she watched the line of his chest for any sign of breathing. There wasn't any. It didn't make sense since his head was fully intact and his chest seemed undamaged.

"It's dead?" Suddenly weak as a kitten she collapsed in the snow as every muscle in her body began to quiver. It was some time before she got herself under control. When she could, she sat up and took stock of herself: her right leg ached as did her ribs and right shoulder. Her jaw throbbed and when she moved it around it made an unnerving clicking sound.

"But I won," she said in awe. It seemed so incredible that it took all of her waning courage to go up to the body and inspect it. Her pert nose wrinkled at the stench that came off the corpse in waves. It was so huge that she would never be able to get turned over. She settled for turning his head which was bigger than a basketball and had to weight thirty pounds.

Right away she saw what had killed the brute: her crossbow bolts. When he had landed the weight of his own head, combined with the impact had driven the three bolts deep enough to hit something vital.

"Yay me," she said, listlessly. The pain of her wounds drained away her enthusiasm and all she cared about was getting home and soaking in the bathtub. First she picked up her crossbow and reloaded it. Next, she retraced her steps until she found the M4 which had been entrusted to her; to the Coven it was more valuable than her one little life. Only then could she limp home.

"What happened to you?" Colleen asked. "Did that rabbit put up a big fight?"

"Rabbit?" Colleen pointed to the rabbit that Jenn had snared. It still hung from her pack and although it had been dead for the last four hours, it looked better off than Jenn felt. "Oh right, the rabbit. No, it was, uh, nothing. I fell." Killing Frank was a huge accomplishment that she should have crowed about; she didn't have the energy for crowing.

Colleen snorted laughter but as Jenn didn't even look up, she asked, "Do you need any help? Do you need to see the Coven?"

Jenn was quick to say, "No, no thank you. I just need to catch my breath and maybe take a bath."

Even though she liked to poke fun, Colleen had always pitied Jenn which made her the closest thing to a friend that she'd ever had. She took Jenn's weapons and pack from her and ran them up to her apartment. On the way, she yelled for a couple of staring children to fetch water.

The younger children didn't dare back-talk to their elders; even teenagers were obeyed, possibly because they were known to mete out insidious punishments that happened beyond the radar of most adults. The two seven-year olds could only manage a bucket between them per trip and grumbled about the extra chore until they saw what sort of shape Jenn was in.

One of them was Lindy Smith. "What happened?" she asked in a piping voice, her green eyes wide.

"Tussled with a zombie," Jenn said, easing down next to the fire and poking it back to life. "Actually it was five zombies." She picked up the biggest log she could handle and laid it among the glowing embers. A little kindling was added next and soon the log was blazing.

"Five zombies?" Lindy asked, shaking her head in disbelief. "No way. Not even Stu can take on five zombies."

Jenn shrugged and then winced as pain flared in her shoulder. "You're probably right. Thanks for the water. If you guys could bring up some more I'd appreciate it." Although they left, chuckling over nearly being "joshed" as Lindy put it, they spent the next ten minutes running water as Jenn heated clean river stones which she set into the slowly filling tub.

It wasn't long before she was relaxing and growing sleepy as the afternoon light faded. A knock on her front door jolted her awake. "Hello, Jenn?" It was Mike Gunter. Before she could answer, he let himself in. "Are you okay? Colleen told me that you had a fall?"

That was about a thousand times more believable than the truth, and it was a quicker explanation. "Yes, but I'm okay," she yelled, "just a little beat up. What happened to the traders?"

"There was a horde; a big one. One Shot says he's never seen one so big." His voice grew louder as he came right up to the bathroom door. For a panicked moment Jenn thought he was going to walk right in. She covered her breasts with her bruised arms, but he didn't enter. "We got as far as that Sears Outlet store. When we went up on the roof…" He broke off, swallowing loudly enough that she could hear it through the door.

"They were everywhere. There had to be a million of them. No one could have lived through that many."

There was a soft tap on her door and she could imagine his forehead touching the panel. "Maybe some of them hid," she said. With the amount of gunfire, they had heard it was wishful thinking. When he didn't answer, she asked, "So what are we going to do?"

"When the horde disperses, we'll split whatever we can salvage." He took a long breath held it, held it, held it, and then let it out without adding anything more. She knew he wanted to say more just like she knew she would have to drag it out of him.

"When do you think that will be?"

He cleared his throat. "A few days, maybe a week."

"So, what are you still doing here?"

"I-I live here now."

She sat up in the bath so quickly water splashed onto the floor. "What? Where?"

"Here…with you. We're supposed to get married."

Chapter 13

Mike Gunter

Their dinner together was so quiet he was afraid to chew. They ate rabbit which was over-cooked and potatoes which were hard and undercooked. Neither complained, because that would have meant talking and one word might have led to another, which might have led to a conversation. And there was no way they could have a conversation at the same time avoiding the sixty-ton blue whale in the room.

"We're supposed to get married," he had said, his ears burning a ripe, cherry red.

"Married?" was her stunned reply.

He had mumbled, "I think so," as if there was some ambiguity. That had been the extent of their conversation, since talking to her through the bathroom door, though at one point he had pointed in the direction of her elbow at the salt and she had said, "The salt?"

That was it. Mike even prolonged his meal, nibbling on the potatoes that tasted like wallpaper glue. As much as he disliked the silence during the meal he knew it would be nothing compared to the silence that would follow it. And he was right. Jenn went at the dishes with a will while he found himself looking for something to do.

He checked his M4 and his crossbow, cleaning both though they didn't really need it and finishing just as Jenn put the last dish up to dry. Jenn looked suddenly nervous, said, "I'm tired. I-I should get to bed," and fled to her room without looking back.

The next morning was much of the same and they both made excuses to leave the apartment. She spent the morning checking the snares, while he spent it dodging questions. With extramarital affairs and sleeping around curtailed, normal gossip on the hilltop was exceedingly dull, but that morning there were steady, unrelenting whispers and not so secretive glances everywhere Mike went.

There were three main topics: Mike and Jenn's upcoming marriage, Jenn's stunning vision, and the horde attacking the traders. In people's mind the three were linked together in some mystical fashion that made for titillating speculation and conversation.

Wishing to avoid all of this, Mike sought out one of his own, Jeff Battaglia who was staying with Stu for the next few days as he convalesced. It was Mike's hope that Stu would be gone, out doing chores or hunting or something so Mike wouldn't have to endure his flinty gaze.

Stu answered the door, and Mike had to work to hide his disappointment. "What did she say?" Stu asked right off the bat.

"Nothing," Mike admitted, unable to look Stu in the face. "She just sort of got quiet."

"Nothing? Really? What the hell, Mike? Did you ask her wrong?"

The moments before and after he had brought up marriage had the hazy feel of a distant memory, but he was pretty sure he hadn't asked her at all. He had blurted out something along the lines of *We're supposed to get married* and her reaction had been so disheartening that it had thrown him for a loop.

"I-I, look it'll be fine," Mike replied. "She didn't say no and that's something, right?"

Jeff, lying on the couch in a sheen of sweat, chuckled without putting too much effort into it. "It's something, alright. It means your marriage is in trouble before you even got to score. Don't you know anything about women?"

Mike didn't. They could be the most confounding of God's creatures. One moment happy as a clam, the next spitting nails. He had seen it before, but he had never expected to see it from Jenn Lockhart. "I know enough," he lied. Wanting to change the subject, he asked Jeff, "What's up with you? Don't get mad, but you look even worse than you did yesterday. I thought the Coven was supposed to fix you right up. You got the pills, didn't you?"

"Yeah, and they gave me that concoction of theirs. Remember when Billie Lang got sick last year? He told me it was like he was drinking something that came straight from a zeke's butthole. He wasn't wrong."

Stu murmured, "It's got to be that way. The pills aren't working like they used to. They have to supplement them with their, you know, their *craft*." He made a slightly disgusted face when he said this. "You should be fine."

"Yeah, you'll be fine," Mike agreed, even though there was a whiff of desperation and decay about Jeff. Stu must have thought the same thing because he asked Mike to come with him back across the bay to check on the horde even though they both knew there was no way it had moved on yet.

The two took M4s and crossbows. Stu also had his climber's axe while Mike had a hunting knife.

The day was grey and threatened either snow or rain. "What do you think?" Stu asked just after they left the front gate. "The weather gonna hold off for us?"

Mike looked up at the clouds before teetering his hand back and forth. "Maybe to probably not. I'm not the best at reading the signs."

"Signs? I was just looking for a weather report. If I want signs, I'd ask your wife." Mike felt his ears burn once more. His glare had Stu holding up his hands in mock surrender. "I was just kidding. Sheesh."

The need for silence as they made their way down to the harbor was a blessing for Mike. They dodged several zombies and made it almost to the harbor without saying a word, but both muttered in amazement as they came up to the partially frozen corpses of four zombies and the destroyed hedge.

"What the hell happened here?" Stu whispered.

"Looks like someone took a baseball bat to these guys. Hey, these must have been part of the group that almost got our guys yesterday. They said some guy distracted four of them. I guess he killed them, too. I wonder who it was.

Do you think Orlando could have done this? He's pretty big."

Stu only rumbled in his throat as he surveyed the ground. He went in a wide circle around the hedge before he returned to Mike, his head wagging in apparent disbelief. Mike expected an explanation, however Stu was as quiet as always and only muttered, "Let's go."

Side by side, the two walked down to the harbor to where the *Puffer* had been dry-docked a few days before. Compared to the sturdy *Calypso*, the *Puffer* felt like it belonged in someone's bathtub. It bobbed like a cork in the choppy water and kept trying to slip away from Stu as he climbed on board.

Mike had no problem stepping down from the dock. He gave the *Puffer* a slow spinning shove and before the boat had turned a hundred and eighty degrees, he had the sail up and the rudder over. Just as the day before, the wind was with them on the way there, but would be in their faces on the way back.

"I guess Gerry had the same idea," Stu said, thirty minutes into the trip. A mile back the *Calypso* had her wings furled and was practically skating across the water. The bigger boat ate up the distance in minutes. As it drew close the six man crew let the main sag, checking its speed until it was a few feet from the *Puffer*.

"Going in early to snag some swag isn't very neighborly," Gerry yelled over the wind. Stu's eyes flashed at the accusation and Mike was sure if they had been on dry land, Stu would have broken Gerry's face. "I'm kidding," Gerry laughed and then took a sip from his thermos. His cheeks were already ruddier than the cold warranted.

Stu's anger slowly boiled away and eventually he forced the ghost of a grin across his features. "I have your man with me. It's not like I was trying to be sneaky."

Gerry laughed. "What do you mean my man? Don't tell me he hasn't popped the question. Mike, tell me you've popped the question."

"I did," Mike answered, feigning indignation. "She just hasn't answered yet. She…" He broke off as the six

Islanders broke into gales of laughter. "It's not that funny. And really, I don't blame her. You guys sprung this on…"

"We don't blame her either," one of the men cried, bringing on more laughter from the boat.

Mike decided he'd said all he was going to say and calmly waited for the laughter to stop. Stu didn't have the patience. "Alright that's enough. Mike's going to get the yes, we all know it. In the meantime, I'm going to go check out the horde."

A nod in his direction was all Mike needed. He hauled up the mainsheet and in seconds, the *Puffer* was scooting ahead of the *Calypso*. Gerry was in the middle of taking a sip from his thermos and was slow to give the order to run up the main. In that time Mike opened a forty-yard lead that he knew wouldn't last unless…

"You might want to hold on," he said to Stu, who had already opened his mouth to object. "I'll be careful—more or less."

"This is an unnecessary risk," Stu growled, hunkering down lower and gripping the sides of the boat. "Didn't you just lose two men not that long ago, doing exactly this?"

Before answering, Mike glanced back to see Gerry bearing up on their starboard side. "It's the same risk every time we step on board. Think about our trip yesterday. I ran her flat out and you didn't say anything. The only difference is now there's competition. My dad used to say that testing ourselves is how we get better."

"I guess," Stu said, the tan stricken from his face as they started hitting chop. Mike had swung out to his right to cut Gerry off, causing Gerry to move even further off the wind. Mike knew he wouldn't put up with it much longer. Gerry would turn sharply and run with the wind under full sails. The *Calypso's* speed would be unbeatable.

Where the *Puffer* lacked speed, she was easier to handle and quicker to turn. Mike waited until he saw Gerry haul the boom around before he made his own turn, cutting right across the *Calypso's* bow. All six men in the *Calypso* bellowed curses as the two boats looked to be on a collision course.

"Mike, what are you doing?" Stu's voice was a frightened whisper.

He was playing chicken with a much larger boat. Fearlessly he held course, knowing that Gerry cared for the *Calypso* more than anything in the world. Sure enough, with a scream of rage, Gerry turned sharply, killing his momentum and going dead in the water.

"You can keep that son of a bitch, Stu!" Gerry raged. "I don't care what that little witch says, you can keep him!" His last words barely reached them. The *Puffer* was going her fastest.

"Was it worth it?" Stu asked.

Mike nodded. "Yeah. You can only bust my balls so much. My dad used to say that, too. He also said: 'If you mess with the bull ya get the horns.' Remember that one?"

Stu laughed easily and said that he did. The two had dreamy "remembering" looks on their faces. Stu's look changed first. It was common knowledge that he had the eyes of an eagle. He pointed at the shore and it was another few seconds before Mike saw the dead crowding the shore and the docks and the hills that swept down from the bay.

They covered the earth like locusts and like locusts they ate everything that was remotely edible.

Quickly, Mike turned away from the shore and began the laborious process of beating into the wind. The *Calypso* passed them on the port side, two hundred yards away. Stu waved them over, only Gerry kept on course as Mike knew he would. He wanted to see the situation himself. Soon he turned back and quickly caught up to the *Puffer*.

Gerry began yelling from fifty yards away and Stu yelled right back, "Shut up, Gerry! No one said you had to race. And what's the old saying? Ya mess with the bull ya get the horns."

"What do you know about anything?" Gerry snapped.

"I know that we're still on the same side. Should we meet back here at nine tomorrow morning?" Gerry agreed, without looking Mike's way. They were about to part ways when Stu added, "Your man Jeff isn't improving, by the way. He looks worse today."

This put Gerry in an even worse mood. For a few minutes Mike was glad he wasn't on the *Calypso*, then he remembered what he was going "home" to.

Three hours later he ran into Jenn as she was coming down the stairs from her apartment. She had a pot in her hands. "Soup for the sick," she said. "Oh, I have guard duty tonight, so I'll be home late. Don't wait up." It was more of a command than a friendly suggestion. She gave him a quick, uncertain smile as if she didn't know whether a smile was the right facial expression for the moment. His smile was broader, though no less forced.

The empty apartment didn't feel like home to him. The cold plate of venison she had left for him, although certainly tastier than the rabbit they had eaten the night before, could not have been more of a sign that Jenn thought he had overstayed his welcome. It sat all by itself at a table that could fit eight such plates. It looked lonely, and worse, it made him feel lonely as he sat in front of it.

With a few hours to kill before nightfall, he sat on the porch as wind swept across the hill, making a tattletale sound as it whipped through the spear forest. His view from the porch was that of the wall and forest. There weren't even zombies to keep him company. Before he was really tired, he went to bed. He slept uneasily that night and woke with a sense of doom hanging over his head. This was the third day since he had asked Jenn to marry him and he really didn't know what he would do if he didn't get an answer.

He certainly couldn't keep living in her apartment, but to scamper back to the island with his tail between his legs would be an embarrassment he didn't think he could bear. Afraid to get up and face Jenn, he lingered in his room until she left, then, like a scared child he poked his head out from his bedroom, just in case she had only faked leaving.

"This is ridiculous," he muttered at the sight of the empty apartment. Cleaning himself up, he tramped through the cold to Stu's place, thinking that he would check on Jeff. He wasn't the only one with that idea. Stu's apartment was crowded with people: the full Coven was there as were Gerry Xydis and two other Islanders.

Jenn stood in the back near the door. When she saw Mike, she sucked in a long breath. It just kept going in and in. He was beginning to wonder if she would ever release it when he heard his name called.

"Hmm, yes?" he asked, turning away from her.

It was Gerry speaking. "Mike, I'm glad you're here. I want you to represent the Islanders on the trip."

Mike's head was beginning to spin. "Trip?"

Gerry pointed toward Jeff Battaglia who sat on Stu's couch, looking as though he were fading into his sweat-stained sheets. The man seemed to be somewhere between sick and dying. "If he's not better by tomorrow we're sending a team to Sacramento for new medicine. The old stuff isn't working."

"The old stuff isn't working, *yet*," Donna Polston added.

"And when do you interfere with the decisions of the Hill People?" Lois demanded. "Mike is one of us now and not under your authority any long…" Gerry was shaking his head, a wicked smile on his face. The entire Coven turned and looked back and forth from Jenn to Mike in astonishment.

"You aren't engaged yet?" Donna demanded. "What's wrong with you, Mister Gunter?"

Gerry laughed. "There's nothing wrong with *my* guy. It's the little witch. She can't make up her mind." Jenn opened her mouth to say something but Gerry spoke right over her. "So, it's settled. I'll be sending Mike and William Trafny, and you're sending Stu and who else? One Shot?"

Stu shook his head. "No, he turned us down. I talked to him and his crew this morning and they weren't, let's just say, they weren't receptive."

He had slipped a quick look at the Coven as he said this. Donna caught it and asked, "And what's that supposed to mean? I know for a fact that Aaron is well liked by One Shot."

"Aaron?" Mike asked. "What's wrong with Aaron?"

"He has a minor infection," Miss Shay said. Her normally pinched look was unraveling revealing a frightened mom beneath. "The-the pills haven't really had a chance to begin working yet. B-But he's getting worse and no one will help. I-I don't understand."

"It's the signs," Stu sneered, waving his arms in a wide arc. "All of you with your signs and your mumbo-jumbo did this. No one wants to be the third one to die or the third to get sick. And no one wants to be tainted with bad luck. That's why no one's jumping at the chance to help."

"I'll go," Jenn said, suddenly. She stepped forward, looking absolutely tiny in the crowded apartment.

The first response was Gerry's. He groaned, "Look, you're a steady girl here on the hilltop, but Sacramento is a different story. It's not safe for women. Really, it's not safe for anyone."

"I'm sorry, Jenn but I have to agree with Gerry," Donna said. "You had a bit of an adventure the other day and one moment of precognition. This doesn't make you a warrior or a witch." She paused and looked at each of the Coven in turn, before giving her final assessment, "You're too young and too weak."

"Is that so?" Jenn snapped, her blue eyes blazing. "I volunteer while grown men cower and you call me weak? How dare you?" She spun on her heel and stormed out of the apartment. For some reason everyone turned and stared at Mike, looking at him as if Jenn's outburst was his fault.

"What?" he asked, when the stares went on and on.

Gerry the Greek laughed. "You need to get your woman in line." He then turned to Stu saying, "You're playing with fire talking that way and if you keep it up there's going to be trouble." He crossed himself which was a signal for everyone to do the same.

Stu only snorted. "Damn the signs. I'll take Jenn with me. She's stronger than she looks."

"Don't joke like that," Donna chided. "It's bad enough that the signs are against you already, there's no reason to put the girl's life at stake to spite the gods."

"Are the signs really that bad?" Jeff asked in a wavering voice. "They can't be all bad, can they?"

Donna looked up at the ceiling for a moment. There was a splatter of what looked like dried spaghetti sauce above her. "I see weakness and it doesn't bode well. A disbelieving man, an untested boy, and a girl who's more child than woman. I'm afraid to ask about William." Gerry looked steadily at her without emotion or comment—it had Mike wondering about William Trafny as well. Bill had always been a standup guy which meant there was a good chance he was coming on his own volition. Mike hoped that was the case. It wouldn't be a good sign if he was coming as some sort of punishment.

"This is pathetic," Stu griped. "Let me show you how wrong your signs are." He left the apartment in a hurry and came back fifteen minutes later out of breath and lugging a garbage bag that stank enough to make everyone groan and cover their faces. Reaching in, Stu pulled out the severed head of a zombie. It was huge, bigger than any Mike had ever seen. Stu thumped it down on his kitchen table without ceremony.

Gerry came over and peered into the hideous face; there were three crossbow bolts buried into it. Gerry asked, "Holy crow, is that Frank?"

"Yes," Stu answered. "And do you see those initials on those bolts?" Everyone peered in at the bolts. Mike saw what looked like J.L. followed by a tiny heart. "Jenn Lockhart did this, by herself."

Chapter 14

Jenn Lockhart

For the third day in a row, Jenn left to check her traps and again she carried her crossbow as her primary weapon and the M4 as a secondary one. She had yet to replace her knife which was at the bottom of the bay and she felt a little naked without it.

The day was warmer than the previous few and before she made it to the headlands, the thin snow had become puddles. It was a proper fall day in her mind, warm in the sun, cool in the shade. The breeze picked up newly fallen leaves and sent them skittering down the streets and had it been any other day she would have considered curling up on her couch with some spiced tea.

Unfortunately, her apartment was no longer the place of refuge it had once been. *He* was there, or he could show up at any time and for some reason the thought of him made her stomach go queasy. This made it all the more strange that she had volunteered to go on a trip with Mike. She blamed it on the traveling star she had seen.

The prospect of a journey called to her. She was tired of the hilltop; she had explored the Marin Headlands from the tip to Pierce Point, she knew San Francisco, Oakland and Berkley like the back of her hand. And she yearned for something more than the crumbling buildings and the buckled, weed-choked streets.

She had heard rumors about the people in Sacramento. Supposedly there were nearly a thousand of them living a rat-like existence in a complex of warehouses that had been fortified against attack from both the living and the dead. A thousand people crammed into a warehouse sounded awful, especially since they pumped their sewage into the canal that connected the land-bound city with the ocean fifty miles away. The same canal they'd be using to get to the city—if they allowed her to go.

The sewage would be the least of their problems. It was an open secret that there were slavers in Sacramento. People had a bad habit of vanishing if they weren't careful. The Hill People didn't venture within thirty miles of the city without cause. Not even men were free from the scourge of slavery, though it was unlikely anyone would try to take on Stu with his fearsome looks and cold demeanor.

Mike, on the other hand, would be fair game. "He's too pretty for his own good," Jenn decided. "Even with the beard. And that's something that's going have to go if..." She stopped in the middle of the street, her teeth clenched. "What am I saying?" she growled. "If I marry him, aren't I just as much of a slave as a Sacramento girl?"

Truthfully, the answer was: no. She was no more of a slave than Mike. A sigh escaped her. It was one filled with confusion. She knew from experience, there was one sure way to combat that sort of confusion and that was to do something besides moping.

The hike up onto the headlands kept her mind fully occupied. She walked with extra care and extra vigilance. Because of the horde across the bay there was unquestionably more danger even miles away on the headland. Hordes were never perfectly symmetrical and they didn't keep to one direction. Frequently groups would break off and there was no telling where they would end up.

She crept past a number of strays in the thin forests as they foraged on leaves and bark. As she moved to her right to skirt around them, she came close to another gang. These ones were spread out along the hillside.

Jenn would be forced to slip between the two groups. "Or I can turn around and go home," she said under her breath.

That would have been the smartest choice. She was well enough stocked for winter that a single rabbit wasn't worth the risk, but after killing Frank she had discovered that her fear of the beasts wasn't like it had been. Yes, she could feel the dread come over her whenever the beasts were near, only it was a shadow of what it usually was; her heart wasn't even racing.

There was a second reason she flitted from tree to tree and crawled through the clearings as though she were a snake hiding from a hawk: she needed to prove herself. Yes, she was weak, but that didn't make her worthless, which was the implication. Being called weak didn't make much sense because compared to the zombies, they were all weak little things that were easily hurt and broken.

Jenn made it to the headlands safely and gazed out at the bay where two boats plied the waters. The *Calypso,* fully rigged with three sails flying, drew the eyes. She was canted far to port as she caught all the wind she could.

Lagging far behind, its one sail snapping in the wind, was the *Puffer.* It looked pathetic and for a moment she was embarrassed for Mike having to pilot the little boat. For a good hour, she sat on a boulder and watched the boats until they disappeared behind the North Beach section of San Francisco. Only then did she go to check her traps; the snares hadn't been touched.

Not wishing to go back to the complex so soon, she went about collecting ten pounds of acorns, which, once the tannins were leached out of them through a laborious three-day process, would be ground into a type of flour. It wasn't anywhere as good as wheat, especially its texture, but it wasn't bad with the right recipe.

After stashing the acorns in her pack, she slipped around the east side of the headlands towards the docks. Because of the danger, she moved slowly and with more caution than ever. She avoided walking on the streets where she could be seen from far away, instead she made her way through people's backyards.

These had become an obstacle course. First there were fences that had to be climbed or jumped or wiggled beneath, then there were the overgrown yards strewn with hidden bikes, tires, rakes, just waiting to trip her up. Some had sinkholes, some had fallen telephone lines crisscrossing them and some had lurking zombies that charged out to attack her.

The first of these didn't see her until she was straddling a six-foot tall privacy fence that swayed back and forth, alarmingly. The fence had been weathered and rotted so badly that she figured the monster would tear it apart in seconds. She hopped down and ran to hide behind a small man-made jungle. It had been a neat garden a decade earlier, now it was a confusing mashup of bushes and overgrown plants.

It took the zombie all of fifteen seconds to tear down part of the wall. It fell repeatedly trying to cross the section of wood and if Jenn had been ready, she could have zipped to the next fence before it had the chance to right itself. Her attention was on the jungle in front of her. She recognized some of the leaves and fading sprouts.

Excitedly, she shoved her hand into the loose soil and found something that looked like a large rock. It was a sweet potato bigger than her foot. Pulling off the shoots growing from it, she set it aside and dug for more. She found four altogether and quietly slipped them into her pack as the zombie trudged around the yard, its fury slowly abating.

She needed it gone and when it turned her back to her, she threw a rock at the house next door. It charged back through the broken fence and when it did, she went back to the garden and poked around through the mess, finding a handful of extremely ugly carrots and some sage. She harvested what she could before heading to the opposite fence and making a run at it.

Before she could get over, the top part of two boards snapped off with the sound of bones breaking, spilling her into the grass. She was up at once as the zombie came charging to see what the sound was. It again tripped over the downed fenced, giving Jenn time to get over.

When she dropped down on the other side, she found herself squatting in the shadow of another of the grey-skinned beasts. It spun around with its long arms out, its hands so close she could have kissed the wiggling nubs where its fingers had once been. Shock and fear froze a scream in her throat.

The creature took a step closer and now she was a foot from its sagging man parts, which in truth were easily the least frightening part of the creature. It was an eight-footer and so foul-smelling only Jenn's paralysis kept her from gagging. It had tremendous scars all over its body, demonstrating that the man it had once been had suffered a horrible death.

There was a scrabbling sound as it reached out and ran what was left of its hands over the wood, feeling it, going up and down, and side to side. A second later, the zombie in the first yard hit the fence with the strength of a bull, splintering wood and causing the entire thing to shake back and forth.

Above her, the zombie turned aggressively, accidentally smacking Jenn on the side of the head with one of its heavy hands and knocking her to the ground. She lay there, too stunned by the blow to do anything except stare up as the zombie on her side of the fence went to where the first zombie was tearing a hole in the wood. The two roared and clawed at each other for a few seconds and then separated.

Although her head was still spinning, Jenn knew she had to move. She had to try to get out of there and with an effort, she pushed herself to her feet and as she did, her backpack shifted, causing the acorns to rattle.

The chewed-up zombie turned at the sound, its head cocked to one side. Only then did Jenn notice one side of its face was a gaping, moldy hole rimmed with pale bone. The other side of its face was untouched except for the eye which had a stick jutting out of it.

It was blind! Her fear vanished as the zombie grabbed empty air. She slipped away, heading for the house, pausing near the sliding back door. It had once been made of glass. Now that glass covered the ground. She tiptoed through the shards and made her way into the darkened house.

Out of habit, she went to the kitchen first and saw without surprise that the place had been ransacked and looted down to the last grain of salt and the last ketchup packet. Ketchup was one of those flavors that hung just on the edge of her memory. She'd never forget it and yet she couldn't quite remember the taste.

After going through the cupboards she poked around through the bedrooms and then made her way to the garage. Again, out of habit, she went to the shelves where the average American dad kept his tools and his tackle box and his rarely used camping supplies. These had been pawed through, probably numerous times, but that didn't stop Jenn.

She was rewarded for her efforts, finding salt and pepper shakers that had never been opened in with the fishing supplies. She also found a small bottle of Wesson Oil, but after eleven and a half years it was strangely dark and smelled rancid when she opened it. Lastly, she found a machete sitting on one of the shelves. It probably hadn't belonged to the homeowner as there was a film of dried black blood on it.

Someone had set it aside to search and hadn't picked it up again. "Or they died." Jenn crossed herself. Chances were she was right. Lots of people died every day.

Sticking the machete into her belt, she left, deciding to call it a day. Because of the many zombies, it was late afternoon by the time she opened her front door. She was nervous because she didn't want a confrontation with Mike which was strange since Mike was a nice guy who never yelled, was easy to talk to and even easier to look at and who...

"Stop it," she snapped, as she went to the kitchen table to unload her finds. For the next hour she was kept too busy building up her fire, drying out the acorns, and filling the tub in case Mike wanted a bath, to even think about marriage or any of that garbage.

It wasn't until Mike and Stu arrived that it went back to being front and center in her mind.

After Jenn greeted them, the air in the room seemed to stiffen. Movement became awkward and words dried up. Stu made a few attempts at smiling while Mike's expression was so decidedly plastic, he looked like a manikin. Jenn just sat in front of her pile of acorns not knowing what to do.

It was up to the normally taciturn Stu to begin the conversation that none of them wanted to have. "So," he said, waited a few seconds and added, "Bad news: Aaron and Jeff aren't improving."

"That's too bad," Jenn said. "Am I going with you guys to Sacramento?"

He nodded. "Yes, but first we should work things out, don't you think?" She cleared her throat, opened her mouth but only ended up nodding as well. "Good, that's very good. I think the trip will work out for the best. You like signs, right? Look at what we caught on the way back. Show her, Mike."

Mike opened a bag and produced a fifteen-pound trout. She stared it right in its black eye for a few moments before smiling and saying, "Sorry, but it's not a sign if you go fishing and you catch a fish."

"No, you don't get it," Stu said, pointing at the trout. "That's a lake trout but we caught it in the bay. You see?"

"I see a fish," she replied, with all the warmth of the trout.

"Fine," Stu growled. "Forget the fish. Let's talk marriage." He cleared his throat and saw Mike suddenly very interested in the acorns and Jenn twisting her hands together. "The Coven wants this, I want this and for some strange reason Gerry the Greek wants this. Oh, and Mike wants this, right Mike?"

Mike nodded, then looked stricken. "I only want it if she wants it." A pained expression swept across Stu's face and Mike quickly added, "But I do want it."

"Why?" Jenn demanded. "Why now and why me?" Neither Stu nor Mike had an answer. "That's what I thought. You know what? I'm angry and you should be as well."

"Why do I need to be angry?" Mike demanded. "I'm doing my duty to my people. That's what this is all about. It doesn't have to be more."

Jenn glared. "Maybe I want it to be more." He leaned back in shock and she backpedaled. "I mean when some-one asks me to marry them I want it for a better reason than just duty."

"What about the signs?" Stu asked. "You practically live your life based on signs."

"What signs exactly?" she asked, cocking an eyebrow.

Stu glanced to Mike who was blinking like an owl. Stu was on his own. "You know, the signs. Like the, uh…like the stars or something? And everyone thinks it's a good idea. And there's the fish." He gestured at the trout.

Jenn snorted. "Do you actually think a fish symbolizes love?" Stu shrugged and even that wasn't very convincing. "If anything, the trout represents a trip which I already knew about it." She had no idea if that was true. She hadn't been looking for signs, afraid to see love in the signs and terrified not to. Love was a rare thing and ever since her father had died, she'd been loved by no one and had loved no one.

She desired love greatly, but she didn't want a false love foisted on her.

Chapter 15

Stu Currans

Unlike Jenn, Stu wasn't looking forward to the trip. He had been to Sacramento twice and each time he was left with a bad taste in his mouth. They were an ugly, filthy lot who lived what they proudly called a Darwinian existence. Survival was all that counted to them, even above family and friends.

Although there were a few fishermen among them who pulled trout, sturgeon, and striper from the Sacramento and the American Rivers, most of the people survived by endlessly scrounging among the ruins of the city. Of course, thievery was so commonplace that it was practically an accepted profession in itself.

They owned slaves; they kidnapped and raped the unwary; they allowed sadists and murderers free rein and just about the only law they recognized was that might made right. This would suggest that any trip to Sacramento would be a trip into a lion's den. Yet, unlikely as it seemed, Stu could expect to be treated with some respect.

The people of Sacramento were many things but they weren't self-delusional. They knew they were uncivilized savages. It was a sad fact that they reveled in their own debauchery. Still, as clear-eyed as they were when looking in the mirror, they tended to view outsiders as paragons of virtue and bravery. They also exaggerated, in their own minds, the strength and resolution of both the Hill People and the Islanders.

Although individuals sometimes disappeared if they wandered too close, any official visit to the city was treated with all the politeness and diplomacy a gang of criminals could muster. So far the yearly trading trips had come off without incident, though it had been close at times. The wrong word could be taken as disrespect and even though there wasn't a thing respectable about the petty crime lords who ran Sacramento, they demanded the deference one would pay to…well, crime lords.

"When we arrive, let me do the talking," Stu told the group sitting huddled in the *Puffer* as a cold wind pushed them up the Sacramento.

Jenn snorted at this. "You want to do *all* the talking? You've said like, five words since we left. I was just about to check to see if you had frozen to death."

They had left at six that morning after Jenn had checked on both Aaron and Jeff and found them worse off than the day before. It was now nearing noon. Behind them was the remains of the Carquinez Bridge: two towers with stubby bits of highway jutting a few yards out, while looming in front of them was the still intact Benicia Bridge.

Stu knew his reputation as a quiet man, but it was precisely this which would keep the group safe. The less the criminals of Sacramento knew about the Islanders and the Hill People, the better. And they would pry; they always did.

Ignoring Jenn's completely factual remark, Stu said, "If, or rather when, they ask how many people we have, the answer is always the same. You tell them 'we have enough.' They'll tell you that's no kind of answer, but no matter what, it's the only one you give. Understood?"

They all nodded as once more silence fell among them. Stu hadn't been the only one who was quiet. Jenn, at the front of the boat hadn't said much more than Stu and when she did speak it was either to Stu or William Trafny. There was still a wall between her and Mike, who sat at the back of the boat, one hand on the tiller and the other on a rope holding the boom in place.

William, who wasn't known to be exactly chatty, either, had spoken the most. He had sensed things weren't going well between Jenn and Mike and when the silence had become uncomfortable, he had just started talking.

"This has to be the most gossiped about expedition in the history of the apocalypse. Everyone is yakking back and forth, running their gums. My dad used to say 'flapping' your gums, but that never made much sense. I think he meant to say 'flapping your lips,' but who knows? All those sayings from before are getting a little turned around, I bet."

"Maybe this isn't something we should talk about," Jenn said, her eyes flicking towards Mike quickly and then away again even faster.

William had broad shoulders set upon a thin frame and when he shrugged, he looked like a puppet being controlled by hidden strings. "They're talking about me," he said, ignoring her. "I had that damned fool, Winston ask me if I had got caught stealing. Can you believe that?"

When no one answered, William barked laughter. "No, it wasn't anything like that. Jeff...Jeff has saved my bacon from the dead three different times. And they weren't simple, easy distractions, either. Each time he put his butt on the line."

"Was it one of those times when he killed one with a baseball bat?" Mike asked.

William nodded. "We were in this house that we had no business being in. I mean, the floors were like this." He held up a hand canted at a steep angle. "The beast was trapped in the basement and we didn't hear him until I fell through the floor. Man that was bad. I was crawling around with a busted leg...it was really bad. I was a goner and then out of nowhere there's Jeff. He put himself in front of me and just goes to town on this huge zeke. That's why I'm here. What about you, Mike? You could have turned Gerry down."

Now it was Mike's turn to flick his eyes in Jenn's direction. "I don't know, maybe it was the right thing to do."

Stu guessed that was only half the answer. He had been put on the spot with the girl he was supposed to marry standing right next to him. To make matters worse, she had volunteered. There was no backing out then, even if he had wanted to. Stu didn't think he would've backed out no matter what. Mike had guts.

"And what about you?" William asked Jenn. She opened her mouth to answer what she thought was the same question, but he added, "You really killed Frankenstein?"

Her mouth hung open for a few seconds and then, as if embarrassed, she shrugged and said, "Yeah, I guess."

"Wow!" William cried, slapping a hand across his knee. "You have to tell us what happened. I mean that thing was a nightmare. I saw him once next to this house. I kid you not, he banged his head on the eaves. That's how big he was."

"How did the other four zombies die?" Stu asked.

Hesitantly, she told the story of what had happened. The three men sat there spellbound by her words. None of them had ever heard a story quite like it. When she was done, Stu and William peppered her with questions, while Mike just sat, gazing off into the distance.

When the questions had been answered, Mike finally spoke. "That's an awesome story. Wait, I didn't mean to call it a story. I meant like a tale….or…"

"I know what you meant," she said, and for the first time, gave him a genuine smile.

That lightened the mood and while the wind continued to blow they had an easy time of it. The breeze generally came out of the northwest which made their eastward trip a quick one, however when they were forced to turn almost due north their speed slowed to a crawl.

They were making so little headway that Stu ordered them to break out the oars. They had brought them along for just such a moment as this. Normally, they would have putted along at two miles an hour and thought nothing of it, but with two people in the process of dying they took turns at the oars. They weren't easy to handle with ropes strung everywhere and the sail overhead. Using the oars doubled their speed to that of a purposeful walk.

This went on for two hours and they were all quite tired when they came to a wide open manmade lake: *Prospect Slough*. It was part of the canal system and was wide enough to allow them to sail properly. Compared to the rowing, they positively raced up the slough. Unfortunately it only went so far and when it ended they had fifteen miles still to go up a much narrower canal, the builtup walls of which channeled the wind almost directly into their faces.

"Back to rowing," Stu said and took up the oar on the port side while William sat down on his right. The wind picked up and brought with it a change in the weather for the worse. Everyone bent forward as sloppy wet flakes plastered against them.

Hoods were drawn, gloves were pulled on and scarves wrapped around their faces though it did little good and they were soon soaked, all save Jenn who pulled a yellow slicker from her pack. Stu gave it a look. "What?" she asked snapping the last of the buttons. "I would have warned you but you don't believe in signs."

"You could have warned me," William muttered. "I believe the signs." He crossed himself and then knocked on the oar three times.

"As do I," Mike said, "especially after what you did at the dock." She smiled briefly and then covered her face. This was the last smile of the day for any of them. The cold, the wet, and the endless labor robbed them of any mirth and joy. Hours went by as they worked against the wind and the current. When Jenn was on the oar, they slowed, taking a snaking course. Mike was too strong and when he gritted his teeth and heaved, the boat swung to port.

He had to take it easy without making it look like he was taking it easy. He was the freshest of them when they came to the end of the canal and saw the dead city of Sacramento outlined in the gloom. Unlike San Francisco, the buildings of Sacramento were untouched by the ravages of earthquakes and yet to Stu they looked like nothing more than giant tombstones.

They rose up on the east side of the canal and at their base were the dead, moving slowly, confused by the snow, their low moans echoing along the canyon-like streets. Other than the quiet flick of snow touching down on their hoods, it was all that could be heard. On the west side was farmland choked with weeds and brambles.

Trash and bloated bodies floated in the canal. These weren't the bodies of the undead. These were the rotting corpses of people. Like all the rest of their trash, the dead had been flung into the canal.

Jenn's oar struck one, causing it to roll over. As it did, the putrid flesh of its face slid off like hot cheese. A shudder racked her, and she gagged, trying to keep from vomiting. She looked away until it floated past then she dipped her oar in the water once more.

Now the scenery changed on the west side of the canal: piers and docks and warehouses that were rusting at an incredible rate. "They live in one of those?" Jenn asked.

"It's coming up," William said. "It's the big one; you'll see it." He had his rifle in his hand as did Stu who was squinting into the wet snow. Ahead, was another dock sitting in front of a warehouse that was as long as a football field. "That's the one." From here and there across the vast, flat expanse of roof, several thin trails of dark smoke disappeared up into the snow. "Remember, let me do the talking. When we go in, I need you to face outward without making it look like you're facing outward."

William agreed. "When I came with Gerry, we would pretend to be interested in different things so that it didn't look like we didn't trust them. It should be fine. We've never had trouble with them before."

They rowed to the dock where the *Puffer* was chained and locked in place. Stu led the diamond formation with Jenn a few feet behind his left shoulder, Mike behind and to his right, and William taking up the trailing position. Each of them carried M4s with fully-loaded magazines, but they did so as casually as they could.

They hadn't gone thirty feet before they found the first dead body. Stu angled towards it and saw that it had been a woman, rail-thin with sunken eyes, and a blue tinge to her flesh. She wore only a rag of a sundress which made no sense since the body was relatively fresh. He toed the woman's abdomen and found it soft. As she had no wounds or obvious injury, it was a mystery as to how she had died.

"Probably not dead even a day," he said, pulling his eyes from the corpse and staring around. There were five more bodies scattered about the rear parking lot. "Maybe less since the birds haven't got to her."

"What do you think, Jenn?" Mike asked. "What do the signs say?"

"Signs?" Stu growled. "We're standing over a dead body and you're asking about signs? I don't think we need to read any signs to know things aren't exactly hunky-dory around here. Then again, things are never hunky-dory around here. Keep your eyes peeled and your mouths shut."

Once more he moved off, and although there were other bodies he didn't bother to inspect them. It was growing dark. He wanted to get the pills and get back on the boat as fast as possible. With the wind coming from the northwest, they'd be able to zip down to Rio Vista, twenty miles south and spend the night there.

He hurried to the one partially open bay door. From it came an outrageous stench. The warehouse always stank, however these fumes were dizzying. Stu wrapped his scarf around his face and ducked under the partially closed door, almost stepping on another body, this one much like the first, except it was a boy of maybe eight or nine.

"Hello?" he called out, moving wide around the body and squinting into the dark. The only windows were dingy squares set high up on the walls. It took a minute for Stu's eyes to adjust and in that time the only sounds were whispers in the dark and the slap of bare feet running towards them.

"Hello? I'm Stu Currans. We're from the Hill and Alcatraz." He paused, wishing he had a working flashlight. Flashlights were a dime a dozen; they could be found anywhere, but batteries were a completely different story. Even if there were any to be had, the best batteries had a shelf life of between seven and ten years and were long dead.

Still no answer. "We'd like to talk to someone concerning a trade." This time he raised his voice so that his words echoed throughout the warehouse. There was no true leader among the people living there, rather they had a confusing array of factions that were constantly on the verge of war with one another. They fought and bickered over everything, including trade, much to their detriment.

"What do you gots?" a hesitant voice asked from the darkness.

"Bullets, grape seed oil, cocoa powder, fresh oregano, smoked salmon, and infused vinegar."

Mike broke their only rule by adding, "It's carrot and beet infused vinegar. It's very good."

Stu glared at Mike who replied with an apologetic shrug. Before he could turn back, Jenn gasped and William raised his rifle. Stu jerked around and stared. A crowd of people were slinking from the dark. Sweat dripped from their greasy heads and they peered out of sallow faces from eyes that were sunk back in their sockets. They weren't just a little sick, they were diseased.

Chapter 16

Jenn Lockhart

The stench of sour feces coming off the crowd filtered past Jenn's wet scarf, making her gag. Even fighting the urge to vomit, she didn't dare take her eyes from the vile creatures. They were a desperate and dangerous lot who looked ready to rush at the four of them any second.

Behind her, William cleared his throat and she assumed he was having trouble with the smell as well. Then he stepped forward and hissed, "Eyes left."

She was supposed to be watching their left flank. When she turned she saw a fresh horror: four little children were creeping out from behind a pyramid of hot water heaters. The four, three boys and a girl, didn't look or move like normal children. They were small for their age, standing on legs that were so bowed they resembled scuttling crabs as they came forward.

She swung her M4 in their direction, stopping them. Two of them had that same sweaty, sick look as the adults.

"Take it easy," Mike said. He hadn't been facing where he was supposed to be either; now he turned and scanned down the barrel of his rifle.

The warehouse opened up in front of them. It was tremendous in size with row upon row of sturdy, industrial grade shelves that towered forty feet above their heads. The hundred-foot long shelves were divided into ten-foot long sections that were just about five feet high and another five wide. Almost all of them had sheets or blankets hanging from them. It was in these odd spaces that the people lived and slept like bees in a hive.

Jenn was still marveling over this when she checked the left flank again and saw that the children had disappeared behind the water heaters and were peeking out with fever-bright eyes.

Ahead of them, someone in the crowd asked, "What do you want for all of that? My left nut?" This brought on a tittering from those with the strength to laugh.

"Medicine," Stu answered.

This caused even greater laughter. "Do we look like we have medicine to spare?" the same man asked.

"Shut up, Frankie," a tall man said, passing a hand across his damp brow. "We have stuff, Islander. We have stuff, come see." He pushed a woman out of the way and shooed more aside so that there was a path between the hundred or so people.

The four moved forward, making no effort to hide the fact that they were afraid. Their guns were held tightly, not quite at their shoulders, but they could get there in a blink.

Among the crowd were women who wore rusting iron collars and from the collars hung chains. Some had weights dangling from them and others had bells that jingled. They were slaves. Jenn didn't know why they would have to lug weights around, but the reason for the bells was obvious: they kept them from running away. Zombies would be on them in a blink. Like the others, they were almost all sick.

"This way, this way," the man wheezed pointing down one of the rows.

Stu hesitated and for good reason. The cement floor was littered with trash and wet with urine and excrement. "Why don't you fetch what medicine you have and we'll make a deal here?"

"Fetch?" the man suddenly shouted. "I am Willis Firam! Do I look like the kind of man who fetches? It's almost like you're calling me a dog. Is that what you're doing? You calling me a dog?"

For a long tense moment Stu stared at him with eyes like ice. "I'm just asking you to bring what you have here. We've come fifty miles in driving snow. The least you could do is meet us here. We can call it a compromise. If not…and if you can't be more polite to guests, then maybe I'll be trading my bullets for your blood."

Stu brought up his M4 and sighted it on the man. Jenn, Mike and William brought up their rifles as well aiming at the few armed men among the crowd. Jenn was surprisingly calm. Death hung like a specter over the entire city and the warehouse could have doubled as a morgue but she wasn't afraid.

There hadn't been a single omen of death on the trip. They weren't going to die in Sacramento; she was sure of it.

She was so sure of it that she canted her rifle to point over the head of the crowd. "I know you don't want to die today," she told Willis. "You can still get better. What's wrong with you guys, anyway?"

"TB, I think," he answered, his shoulders drooping. Just like that, the tension spilled from the crowd. "You guys got anything for TB?"

"Sorry, I don't know what cures TB," she answered. In truth, she didn't even know what TB stood for. "What about you guys? You have any pills? We're looking for the yellow ones."

Stu was the last to lower his rifle. "We need antibiotics. We're willing to trade for any you have. Unless they're…" His words faltered as Willis started shaking his head. He wasn't the only one either. Half the people shook theirs while the other half looked glum.

"Everett Baron and eight of his boys took all the pills and medicine we had and ran away, the damned cowards!" Willis cried, his voice rising so that his words echoed. This brief explosion of sound took the last of his energy and he sagged against a brace holding up one of the shelves.

"And do you know where they are now?" Stu asked. "We can pay you something. Jenn, can I have one of the jars of that vinegar?" She had brought six of them to trade, though she had secretly hoped it wouldn't come down to it. Each jar had taken days of work on her part. Still, she didn't hesitate.

She stepped forward and handed the man the jar. "It's my own recipe. It's really good with venison."

"We don't have any venison," he answered, clearly hoping to be offered some.

"Neither do we," she shot back. "Now tell us where this Baron guy is."

He held up the jar to the feeble light and squinted at it. Next, he unscrewed the lid and stuck a finger in it and tasted it. A look of disgust passed over Jenn's face. There was no taking the jar back after that. Fortunately, his brows shot upwards and he dipped the diseased finger a second time.

"Well?" Stu demanded, pulling Jenn back.

Willis lifted a shoulder as he screwed the lid back on. "I don't know. They took everything a week back and straight-up disappeared. If I knew where they went, I would have gone after them myself."

Jenn started sputtering angrily. Mike spoke over her, asking, "A week ago? Interesting timing. Where do you meet the traders?"

"Out front, but the traders are two days late."

"And where do they come from?" Mike asked. "Which direction? I-5 or 80?" The man nodded at the latter. "That's where these guys are. Somewhere along I-80. When do the traders usually show up?"

Willis' glistening brows came down. "It's always high noon. But, but if you find them, you can't have our stuff. You can't have it." He took a dangerous step forward.

Stu pulled Jenn back behind him, saying, "We don't want all your stuff, just the antibiotics, but if we can get a fair price for the rest, I promise we'll come back and work something out."

"What's there to work out?" someone called out from the crowd. "They crossed the line. Kill them and we'll give you half."

"He meant a quarter," Willis added, quickly. "Don't listen to him, he's got the delirium going."

Stu shared a surprised look with William before saying, "We're here to trade. We're not mercenaries. But like I said, we'll do what we can." The crowd buzzed with whispers as the four hurried back out into the snowy evening where the wind drove the flakes sideways.

"I feel disgusting," Jenn said, pulling off her scarf and tossing it into the water. She contemplated throwing her gloves in as well, then decided to keep them on a little longer. Almost immediately a crow flew across the canal. She waited for a second—she hoped for a second. When it came to counting crows, one crow was bad luck, two was good luck, three meant health, four told of wealth, five meant sickness and six meant a death was coming. Six in a row was the ultimate; death came quickly.

"We aren't going to fight anyone, are we?" she asked, getting into the boat last.

Mike and William had been looking off in the direction the crow had taken. Mike crossed himself, which had Stu rolling his eyes. "I hope not," Stu said as he and William began to paddle. "Getting mixed up in another group's affairs is a sure-fire way to start trouble. I say we let them work it out. We have our mission."

"But it would be the right thing to do," Mike said. "You saw how many people were sick back there. Hundreds. We should help."

Stu pulled his oar out of the water and the *Puffer* drifted, gradually losing headway. "We'll see," was all he would commit to. He and William went back to heaving on the oars. They didn't have to heave far before they came to a long, narrow lake on their left.

They pulled the *Puffer* ashore at the north end of it and crept up the embankment, each of them clutching their crossbows. "Anyone have a map?" Stu asked, an embarrassed note to his voice. No one did. "Damn. I've never explored Sacramento and I don't know where I-80 is."

"Me neither," William said. "We always just stuck to the canal when we come up here. It's poor form to scavenge in someone else's backyard."

They were surrounded by industrial facilities which had only one redeeming quality: there were plenty of big rigs and it was a guarantee that most would have maps in their glove compartments. Stu climbed up into one and searched around for all of three seconds before he pulled out a folded map.

"How's this for a sign?" he asked, grinning. "I-80 is right on the other side of this building." He gestured with the map at a low rectangle of a structure that was such a drab shade of grey that the driving snow improved its appearance. Once more he studied the map. "If I had to guess, I'd bet that Everett and his friends are shacking up someplace right up the road waiting on the traders."

Right up the road turned out to be a five-mile walk in the wet snow. Soaked and shivering, they stopped after a few miles as they came to a dreary farm house set a little ways off the highway. It would have been miraculous if the home hadn't been ransacked and, as expected, it was a terrific mess. The four didn't care as long as the place was zombie-free and relatively dry.

With the others hiding behind an old Ford pickup, Stu went to front door and listened for a minute while snow built up on his shoulders. "Hey!" he called out softly through the crack of the door. When that didn't elicit a response, he called louder, "Wake up! Anyone home?"

Nothing budged inside, so the four trooped in. "Mike and I will get a fire going, William will get the windows covered. Jenn, if you will find us some warm clothes that would be great."

She went to the bedrooms and poked around in open drawers and in closets. Without any light, it was impossible to read sizes and so she used herself as a measuring stick—and stick she was. Everything she found seemed not just tall but shockingly wide. She found a dress that could have been stitched into a sleeping bag for two. On the nightstand was a belt that, when stretched to the floor, came up to the notch in her throat.

She had seen such things before and as always, she couldn't help but wonder at the wealth of food that had to have existed back in the past. How had they had so much? Where did it all come from? Supposedly, back in the past there had been uncountable numbers of people, like sand on the beach, and yet they had all been, not just fed, but fed to such an extent that everyone had to worry about overeating.

Overeating was a concept that boggled her mind. And overeating as a bad thing made no sense at all. If there was still food around like she saw in her magazines, what they called "feasts" she would happily accept round cheeks and a little bulge of a belly.

Sighing, she tossed aside the belt. The men didn't have an ounce of body fat on them and the belt would have to loop twice around their thin hips to work. A length of rope would work better.

Embarrassingly enough, the only things that came close to fitting her were found in a ten-year-old boy's room. It was embarrassing but she was too cold to care. Stripping down to nothing, she put on layers of clothing: two pairs of socks, thin pajama bottoms that she wore under jeans that were too wide around the waist and too short at the ankle, and finally, a t-shirt, a turtleneck and a hoodie. In the boy's closet she found a winter coat that had a grey cast to it from layers of dust.

Warmer now, she went on but didn't find anything that would fit the three men. Their only choice was the triple-extra large clothes that had belonged to the man of the house. She piled pants and shirts, socks and underwear in her arms and came back to the living room where a fire was burning.

"Hey little boy, what did you do with Jenn?" William joked at the sight of her, He elbowed Mike who kept a very neutral face.

"Ha-ha," Jenn said. "Let's see how you like your clothes." If anything, the three looked even more ridiculous. They used appliance cords to cinch the ballooning pants around their waists, while they wrapped duct tape around their ankles to keep the cloth from swishing as they walked. The over-large shirts made them look as though they were boys themselves, ones wearing "Daddy's" clothes.

Stu allowed them to rest and warm up for only an hour. They fed pieces of a broken kitchen chair into the fire and nibbled on smoked cod that they heated up on the ends of straightened coat hangers.

Jenn found a stack of magazines. The ones on top she had seen before and in deference to the next person to come by she set them aside. Beneath were some from 2012 and earlier. She poked through them, staring at the beautiful people. Although there was an abundance of food, the people in the magazines were always tall and thin. "I think we're shrinking," she said, suddenly. "I mean as a group. You never see people who look like this." She showed them the picture of a runway model.

William, the tallest at just about six feet, nodded. "When I was a kid, they used to say the Chinese were short but they were getting bigger because their diet was getting better." He was twenty-five and knew a lot about things from before.

Jenn didn't even know what he meant by Chinese, exactly. They were a people, like the Islanders were a people, but what characteristics they had, she didn't know. She had seen Asian people, but assumed that they were separate from Chinese people.

Now, she had to wonder if she was part Chinese. She didn't ask, however. William was a nice enough guy, but he tended to make rude comments and then exclaim, "I'm kidding."

"Did you see those kids back there?" Mike asked. "What was the deal with their legs? They looked like they had been broken and not set properly."

"They've been like that since I first went on a trade mission," William said. "It's some sort of disease and it's getting worse."

After seeing the horrors in the warehouse, Jenn didn't want to go back, and she was sure her desire for traveling was good and dead. She tried to take her mind off the odd bowlegged children by going back to her magazines. For the most part it was all the same and somewhat depressing. She then turned to a picture of a true monster and a gasp escaped her.

The picture was of a tyrannosaurus rex standing in between two cars and letting out a roar. She tried to read the caption however there were too many words that didn't make sense, *tyrannosaurus rex* being two of them, *Jurassic* being another. "Are these real?" she asked.

"They were," Stu answered, standing and stretching. "It was a long, long time ago. Okay, everyone, I think it's time we got moving."

Jenn quickly pulled the page from the magazine and stuck it away with the other pictures she had collected. In her mind a long, long time ago included the day her mother died. Thirty minutes later, she was still fretting about running into a tyrannosaurus rex when she caught the scent of a wood fire and cooking meat.

She wasn't the only one. All three men smelled the fire, as did ten or eleven zombies. They were milling around in the dark in confused circles. Strong smells got the dead excited and perhaps more hungry than usual, but with their limited brain capacity, they couldn't orient on the smell. They tried, however. Even with the snow blinding them, they searched for the fire.

"What do we do?" William asked, fumbling his M4 from his back, fear stamped on his face. He was an Islander. Severe weather kept them huddling indoors and it was rare they left their island at night. He was holding the rifle with fingers that looked like the long legs of an albino spider.

"No guns," Stu said. "They'll only attract more of them. No, we keep quiet, we keep low and slow. We move from cover to cover. If we get spotted, I'll attract them to me. Only run if you have to and if you do run, always run for cover and always make quick cuts. But don't worry, it'll be fine."

It didn't sound fine and Jenn was very worried. The flying crow haunted her; every time she closed her eyes it was there, winging silently by. It was the only omen she had seen. Something bad was going to happen, she could feel it in her cold bones. She wanted to suggest going back to the house or maybe all the way back to the boat, but before she could open her mouth, Stu was slipping away into the snow.

He headed across six lanes of highway where wrecks and stalled-out cars littered the landscape and in between them giant shadows roamed. At first the dead were easy to dodge, their moans giving them away, but as they closed in on the smell of the fire, the zombies grew more excited and would suddenly lurch along faster, going in random directions.

Stu moved in quick dashes with everyone hurrying after. He went from car to car as if they were little islands of safety or base in a child's game of tag. But there was little safety to be found anywhere that night. Twice they were nearly run over by charging zombies and they only escaped being mauled because the zombies were nearly blinded by the snow and couldn't tell what was what even from five feet away.

It seemed like forever that they were out in the open where death was a second away, but somehow Stu got them to the relative safety of a little community. It had a high fence that couldn't be climbed. They slunk along it until they found a gully that had been dug by long-ago rains. They crawled through the gully on their bellies.

"We're close," Stu whispered. The smell of the fire was heavier now. They started south, but after a block the smell seemed to fade. Sounding like bloodhounds trying to sneak up on their quarry, the four sniffed their way back the way they had come. After crossing though a few yards, climbing a smaller fence and hiding while three immense creatures lumbered by, they soon were huddled on the porch of a two-story home, eager to get inside, eager for the warmth of the fire they could hear snapping and crack-ling on the other side of the door. Jenn was particularly eager. She couldn't feel her fingers and her feet were like bricks strapped to her ankles.

Stu knocked softly on the door. He heard what sound-ed like a panicked scramble from inside as Everett and his friends grabbed their weapons. Then only silence. Stu cleared his throat. "We're from the Bay Area and looking to trade," he whispered. "We have bullets, grape seed oil, cocoa powder, fresh oregano, smoked salmon, and infused vinegar. We're looking for medicine."

A spear of light shone out from one window. Stu faced the light, holding up his empty hands; his crossbow sat against the door.

The light blinked out of existence. "I don't know 'em," they heard from inside. "There's three of them and a girl."

Jenn was too grounded in reality to be insulted, she knew her sex and her size made them more likely to view her and the group as less dangerous and if that got them inside then she wouldn't say boo about it.

The door opened and a scruffy, scarred face peeked out at them. The man wasn't sick which was an immediate relief. He gave them each a quick once-over before saying, "Come in, Islanders. Come in. How did you find us? Was it Willis? If so, I wouldn't believe the lies he spun if I were you. He's a self-serving little git."

They were ushered into a little open area just inside the door. To their right was a sitting room that was covered in sleeping bags and backpacks. A small fire was crackling in the fireplace. To their immediate left was a staircase which curled up the wall to the second floor. A little ahead was a formal dining room that was covered in splinters and spears of wood. Everett and his men were getting their wood from in there and there wasn't much left.

Jenn had expected to find nine of them in total, however there were only seven and two were sweating through their shirts. The other five, Everett included, had a hungry, feral look that she didn't trust. Neither did the others; they kept their crossbows ready.

"What went on between you and Willis isn't our concern," Stu said. "We're here to trade and we heard you had medicine. We need antibiotics."

"Well damn," Everett said, turning. Now, with the fire behind him, he was only a shadow of a man, his features hidden. He brought a hand to his face and scratched at the scruff growing there, saying, "That's the only kinda medicine we don't have. You can blame Willis for that. He tried to treat that TB crap with antibiotics and it didn't work, but he kept going and going. It's why we left. He was wasting everything we had."

"No antibiotics? None at all?" Stu asked. Everett shook his head.

"We have other stuff. Do you need insulin? We got lots of that. And we got lots of other pills. Morphine and codeine and tramadol. We got stuff that'll keep your heart going and, hey Rick, grab the big box. You'll see we got all sorts of…"

Stu grimaced, cutting him off. "No. We need antibiotics and nothing else. If you don't have them we'll go somewhere else, sorry. Thanks for your time." Stu turned, as did the others. Jenn was closest to the door and she had it half open when Everett pulled out a big black pistol.

"Where do you think you're going?" he asked, in a quiet, deadly voice. "You wanted to make a trade and we're going to, one way or another. You got stuff we want and…" He lifted a single shoulder. "And you don't want to die. Sounds like a fair trade to me."

Chapter 17

Jenn Lockhart

Everyone, including Everett's own men, was caught off guard by the appearance of the gun. There was a moment of stunned silence as the room became very still. Both the silence and the stillness were broken by Mike, who started to lift his crossbow.

Everett shifted the gun his way, saying, "Don't even think about it."

Mike openly scoffed. "Please. We both know you're not going to fire that thing. Do you know how many zombies are crawling all over this neighborhood? A couple dozen, easy. If you shoot, it'll bring them running."

"Maybe, maybe not," Everett said, an evil smile playing on his lips. "I'm willing to risk it. They probably won't orient on one shot."

"Do you think it'll only take one shot to kill me?" Mike asked. He shook his head, slowly lifted the working end of the crossbow, aiming it from the hip.

William, his eyes huge and round, his hands shaking as he held his crossbow, hissed, "Everyone needs to calm down. No one's getting shot and no one's robbing anyone. This isn't how civilized people work. If we want to make a trade, we will, if…"

"Who says we're civilized?" Everett asked. "Who says anyone is anymore? We're almost out of food, and you have plenty. We're running out of ammo and you got some. I tried, right boys? You heard me. I tried to make a deal that would help us both, only you guys threw that back in my face. What am I supposed to do? Let my guys starve? Let them get eaten by the dead? No way. I take care of my own."

"And you'll just let us go once you take our stuff?" Mike asked.

Everett's eyes flicked toward Jenn and his weren't the only ones. She suddenly felt like everyone was looking at her. Even the two infected men turned her way. The moment stretched out long enough for her to find her voice. "I'm walking out this door and nobody better even think about stopping me."

"I'm gonna do more than just think about it," Everett said, swinging his pistol in her direction. Jenn froze while everyone else seemed to leap into action. Mike fired his crossbow hitting Everett dead center in the chest—Everett grimaced and fired his pistol three times; the first shot splitting the air between Mike and William, the second punched a hole high up in William's chest and the third passed so close under Jenn's little chin that it actually tickled her.

She was too horrified to laugh and too shocked to move; the crossbow sat uselessly in her hands. She had to actively will herself to aim it. Before she could, Stu's hand went to his hip in a flash. He drew his .357 and fired his only three rounds. Compared to Everett's gun, the .357 sounded like a cannon. The dim foyer lit up with the flashes of his gun. It was like a strobe light and within the pulses of yellow, Jenn saw three men go down, one screaming and holding his face.

Somewhere in between those flashes someone had fired a feathered bolt at Stu. It seemed to magically appear sticking out of his chest.

Another bolt sailed through the air and stabbed the door next to her face—this finally got her moving. She dropped into a crouch, bringing her crossbow to bear. The foyer was a tiny battlefield with the combatants not ten paces from each other. As she was at one end, she had an excellent view. On one side Mike was dragging William up the stairs, while Stu, ignoring the bolt sticking out of his chest, was trying to pull his M4 from his back only it was hung up on his pack.

On the other side, four men were down, two were scrambling into the sitting room and the last had flung aside his spent crossbow and was digging a gun from a hip holster. Their eyes met as Jenn centered her sights on his chest. He dove away just as she fired. Her bolt transfixed his shoulder, knocking him back, but not killing him. With a scream of rage, he pulled the gun.

Jenn dropped her crossbow and scrambled out the door, where the cold sucked away her heat. She didn't feel it. She was too frightened although now she wasn't afraid for herself. Stu was almost a sitting duck. He would never get the rifle off his back or escape up the stairs before the man she had hit in the shoulder killed him.

Her own rifle was tightly strapped and had to be ignored at least for the moment. Looking around, she saw Stu's crossbow, cocked and ready to go. Next to it was a planter with a few brown stems poking up out of the dry dirt. She grabbed it and hurled it through the sitting room window with a great crash of glass. The man fired three booming shots at the window, punching little holes through the blankets they had been using as blackout curtains.

"Missed me, jerk!" she yelled at the crack of the door before kicking it all the way open. She ducked away as he fired twice more, this time out into the night. Jenn was just about to say something else when she heard a roar from behind her. She turned to see monsters converging out of the snow, stomping towards her from three directions.

She was essentially trapped, with her only option being to step back into the house where she would most certainly be shot. For a fleeting moment, she wondered if the man would be a good enough shot to kill her right off the bat. Perhaps a head shot where she would feel an instant of pain and then be gone forever.

With her bad luck she would be gut shot before being eaten alive. Still, she had no choice but to go through the front door—the timing had to be perfect. She grabbed the doorjamb to keep herself from flying inside too early as the first zombie hit the porch stairs. It fell, but it fell forward, reaching for Jenn with a stump that ended in shards of bone jutting like a pair of spears from its forearm.

Jenn counted to three and then shot through the doorway keeping so low that she could, and did, use her hands to keep her balance and propel herself along as a monkey would. A bullet scorched the air above her head and she couldn't tell if it was aimed at her or at the zombie charging after. The thing was huge, even bent over it took up the entire doorway and then some. Its shoulders were so wide that grey diseased flesh tore off as it heedlessly came after her.

More bullets flew past Jenn, thudding into the dead meat of the monster's flesh. She could hear the wet slap as each struck home. The power in those slugs would have killed a man, but the zombie didn't even slow down. The only things that affected the creature were the flashes of light and the explosions coming from the gun.

To the zombie, the girl, small to begin with, was a blur in the darkness, while the gun blossomed great yellow flowers. It turned to charge the man with the gun, but it tripped on the sprawled bodies of Everett and the others. This only slowed it for a second and it crawled ravenously onward on all fours.

The man fired once more before the beast was on him. Jenn reached Stu at the same time. He had been simultaneously kicking backwards and struggling to get the M4 off his back. Jenn grabbed him and held him in a crushing hug, pinning his arms just as a second zombie rushed inside.

The two, looking like a dark hump in a murky hall, were overlooked by that second zombie and by the third, both of which went to feast on the screaming man. The next one to enter, did not. The screams were now little more than grunts of pain. Most of his throat had been torn out and he was seconds from death.

On some strange level, the last zombie to come into the house seemed to know this. It turned away and stared around at the bodies. Zombies didn't like to eat the dead. No one knew why, but they preferred their meat hot and bloody, preferably still screaming.

The beast reached down, picked up Everett and gave him a shake. When the corpse just hung, rag-like, the zombie tossed it aside and reached for another.

"Now," Stu whispered. Jenn jumped up, hauling him to his feet and then was running down the hall towards the kitchen as fast as she could. There was a doorway on her left which led to a study and one on her right which was so dark she had no idea what was in there.

She barely gave it a glance and didn't see the man charging out of it until it was too late. The two slammed into each other, the force sending them both sprawling. A second man wearing a look of sheer horror on his sweaty face appeared in the doorway, hesitated, and then tried to clamber over Jenn to get away from the zombie that was now lunging down the hall. In the dark it looked and sounded like a demon and Jenn was sure it was going to eat her and drag her soul to hell.

Desperately, she tried to get up, only to have her leg kicked out from under her by the man she had run into. He was flailing like mad to get away, as was his friend. Jenn would be left behind. It was survival of the fittest and she was small and weak.

Stu didn't live by that credo He was in the very back of the pileup and with the zombie bearing down, he grabbed one of the men by his jacket and heaved him around and flung him bodily at the creature. The two came together with a screech and a roar, and right before their eyes, the man was torn limb from limb.

The zombie's strength was so shocking that the three people were slow to take flight. They backed up, untwining themselves, panting high in their throats. It was only when the beast flung aside a still bleeding arm that they turned and rushed into the kitchen where they were trapped. There was a back door but was it locked? Were there zombies beyond it attracted by the screams and gunshots?

All three looked at it, hesitated and then passed. Jenn and Stu ran to a pantry. The man tried to get in with them, but Stu shoved him out. "Find somewhere else," he hissed, pulling the .357 out and shoving it in the man's face. It was empty, but the man didn't know that. He only saw the huge bore and smelled the spent powder. He fled into a laundry room just as the zombie pushed open the swinging door that led to the hall, leaving a bloody hand print.

Stu had been struggling the M4 from his back and now stopped with the strap across his forehead. The two of them froze in place and too late saw that the pantry door had somehow swung open half a foot. Stu reached out for it only to have Jenn grab his hand. The door would have to stay open. They couldn't chance it. Movement and sound attracted the beasts.

Jenn couldn't even chance pulling her M4 from her back. The only thing they could do was ease Stu's rifle from the odd position it was in.

Through the gap in the door they saw the zombie plod slowly through the kitchen, walking into the counters, bumping off the table and jingling the chandelier as it knocked it with its head. Jenn found it strange that this dull, vacant-eyed creature was the same rage-filled monster of only a few seconds before.

Moaning softly, it turned slow racetracks around the room as if looking for the way out. It went in circles for ten minutes before it stopped, staring at the kitchen sink with all the intelligence of a phone booth.

It was going to be a long wait, hours maybe.

Jenn helped Stu get his pack off and then turned to allow him to help her with her gun and pack. Then they settled down, their backs to the dusty pantry shelves, their legs splayed out in front of them.

Their wait wasn't as long as they thought it would be. From above, there came the sound of soft steps and a creak of wood. This woke the zombie up and once more it began to walk in circles. The sound of the steps continued and now they could hear the beasts in the front of the house stirring.

Then all at once there was a loud scraping from above them. Someone was moving furniture! Jenn and Stu leapt to their feet as the zombie stormed out of the room. They followed it to the swinging door and peeked out as something crashed in the front of the house. It was a dresser being heaved down the front stairs.

The dull-eyed zombies were in full rage and charged the stairs but the dresser, caught halfway down, stopped them. The beast in front tore at the piece of furniture, ripping off chunks of wood with its bare hands. It was in full roar when it suddenly dropped, turning from a monster to a soft pile of grey flesh, a crossbow bolt sticking out of its eye.

It was pulled aside by the next beast, who mindlessly attacked the dresser. It took three shots to kill this one. When it died, the dresser slid into the next zombie. Now there were only two left.

"Cover me," Stu said, pulling his climber's axe from his belt. With Jenn right behind him, he crept up on the last beast and whammed the pick right into the back of its head. It jerked around so quickly that the axe was yanked from Stu's grip. He jumped back, banging into Jenn. The two would have been in trouble if the beast attacked. It only stood there, blinking slowly as black blood dribbled down its back, forming a puddle beneath it.

Stu and Jenn didn't know what to do about it and were still standing there when a bolt sunk four inches deep into its temple. They both jumped a little as it crumpled to the floor.

"Help me with William!" Mike demanded from midway up the stairs. His coat was smeared with blood; in the dark it looked black and oily.

Jenn started forward only to be stopped by Stu. "Go get that last guy. Don't let him close on you. Shoot him first."

She hefted her rifle to her shoulder and stalked down the hall, stepping over bodies and leaving a trail in the blood. The last of Everett's men hadn't budged from the laundry room. She could hear his breathing. He sounded like an over-worked poodle.

"Get on out of there," she ordered, standing behind the counter, her elbows resting on the granite countertop. "They're all dead, including all your friends."

"They weren't my friends."

She found that hard to believe. "Whatever. Get your butt out here now! With your hands up, too." She had never held a gun on a criminal before. It was a strange feeling. As self-righteous as she felt, she didn't know if she could pull the trigger.

"Hi," he said, with a boyish wave of one of his lifted hands. "My name's Kevin. I-I didn't do anything wrong. You gotta understand, I only went along with them because I was sick and they were saying they were going to take all the medicine."

"That doesn't give you the right to steal from everyone." He started to reply; she cut him off, snapping, "Shut up and get moving." She walked him out into the hallway where he gaped at the blood and the bodies. He was still staring when Stu and Mike carried William down the stairs.

"Clear a spot by the fire!" Stu yelled.

Jenn jabbed the M4 into Kevin's spine. He might have been sick, but he was still much bigger than Jenn. When he had cleared a spot, she ordered him to haul the medicine over to where William was lying. For the most part this consisted of four cardboard boxes of various pills.

Stu began reading the labels, one after another, while Mike knelt next to William with a frightened look on his young face. Jenn found it strange that eight-foot tall zombies and a room full of thieves didn't seem to scare him, but a little hole in a man had him sweating and nervously licking his lips.

"Anyone know what to do?" he asked.

"You put pressure on the wound," Kevin said, pointing at the bleeding hole high up on William's chest.

Mike and Stu glanced at each other, each shrugging. Mike leaned over William and pressed down with both hands locked. Seconds later William opened his eyes and Mike looked hopeful.

"Can't...breathe," William whispered.

Mike leapt back. "Oh, man, I'm so sorry. What can I do? How can we make this better?" William shook his head, closing his eyes again. This seemed like a bad thing to Mike. "Hey, Will. Look at me. Stay with me." William cracked his eyes and nodded.

"I have some pain meds," Stu said, handing Mike a white bottle. "Have him take two of them." It was such an effort to get William into a sitting position and for him to swallow the pills that it didn't seem worth it, especially as he could barely summon the energy to open his eyes after.

They had a thousand different pills, but really nothing that would help someone who'd been shot. "We need a doctor," Stu said.

To Jenn, doctors weren't a real thing. She knew they had existed before, but now, if she had known the word extinct, she would have placed both doctors and dinosaurs in that same category. The closest thing to a doctor that she had ever heard of was the dentist who used to travel with the traders years before—he had become fabulously wealthy and was stabbed in his sleep by a slave girl who had made off with his riches.

Jenn believed it was more likely she would run into a tyrannosaurus rex than a doctor, but it did remind her. "Weren't you shot?" She pointed at the bolt sticking out of Stu's coat.

They all stared. Even William opened his eyes as Stu looked down at himself with sudden worry.

Chapter 18

Stu Currans

He hadn't noticed it before in all the action, but now he felt a sting across his chest. Having never been shot by a bullet or a bolt before, he expected the pain to be worse. Slowly he unzipped and unbuttoned the layers he had put on to keep warm until he came to the last and saw the blood.

There was very little. He let out a shaky laugh. "I got shot right in the coat. It's only a scratch." He pulled the bolt out and was about to toss it aside, then thought better of it. They needed every bit of ammo they could lay their hands on. William was still alive but he wouldn't be for long if they couldn't get him in capable hands—the closest being the Coven.

But what could they do? Probably nothing.

"Jenn, keep an eye on that guy. Mike, watch over William. Check his, uh pulse or something. I'm going to see if these guys had anything besides meds."

"We had a few guns and some bullets," Kevin said, wearing a miserable smile, perhaps hoping to appear pleasing in some way. It made Stu want to punch him in the face. He deserved it; that and more. At a minimum, Kevin had been part of thievery on a grand scale, armed robbery and attempted murder. For all Stu knew he had been more than just a "part" of it. He might have masterminded the theft. Not that the sniveling hunk of crap looked like much of a mastermind.

Stu went through the packs and found very little that was useful: a pound of dried jerky, some rope, a few bullets, two handguns, three bottles of wine and a box of matches in a crinkled Ziplock. The rest of their possessions consisted of clothing and spank magazines.

He gathered what they were going to take by the door. "So, any idea how to move him?"

"We have a little cart out front," Kevin said, with that same warped smile. "It won't carry your friend but it'll carry everything else."

"Move him? Are we really going to leave tonight?" Mike asked, jerking his head toward William and then giving Stu a significant look. Clearly Mike thought that moving William would kill him and he was probably right. "Maybe we should wait until morning."

While it was usually more dangerous traveling at night, Stu couldn't imagine trying to make it back to the boat in daylight while hauling a cart and carrying William. They would need flat, unbroken ground and that meant walking straight down the highway where there wasn't a lick of cover, and *when* they were spotted by zombies, they would have no choice but to leave William behind when they ran for safety.

Their only real choice was to travel at night where the snow and the cold of the night could kill him.

It was a decision he wished he didn't have to make. Thankfully, Jenn said, "It's bad luck to stay in the house of the dead."

That was all it took to get them all on board to leave as soon as possible. Even Kevin happily agreed. Stu glared at him. "I don't know why you're so chirpy. You're coming with us. You have to face up to what you did."

He went white. "But…but they'll kill me. If I go back they'll kill me. Don't you see that? H-How about this? I'll help you lug your stuff. You brought a boat, right? I'll help you lug your stuff to your boat and then you let me go. That's punishment right there if you ask me. All alone with nothing. Don't you think that's punishment enough? It'll be the same as banishment."

Stu started to shake his head, but Mike held up a hand. "It's not a terrible idea. It saves everyone the headache of a trial and we can keep all the meds."

Jenn looked shocked at the idea. "Take all the meds? That's not right. Those poor people back at the warehouse need them more than we do."

"They need them right now," Mike answered, "but what about tomorrow? What about next month? Maybe we get the TB, then what do we do? Doing the right thing is good, but doing the right thing for your people is even better. Besides, they owe us." He gestured toward William.

"But they didn't hurt William," Jenn answered. "Kevin and his friends did. He should pay, not the others."

"That's just it. They're all the same. He's one of them. You could say *they* made him like this. We've heard all the rumors about them; the stealing, the slaves, the filth. This guy right here is who they are." Jenn and Mike bristled at each other and then, unexpectedly turned to Stu demanding his input.

He didn't know what to say since they both had good points. "Maybe we can do both. We can keep some of the meds as payment for William and give the rest back. And I think we should let Kevin go once we get back to the warehouse. Chances are he'll die out there. Dying alone is about the worst thing I can think of."

Kevin's smile bent. "Or I can come back with you guys. I learned my lesson. You have to believe me. I can…"

"No one believes you," Stu said. "Your only choices are to accept this punishment or be turned over to your people."

Kevin pushed the desperate smile back into place. "What if I told you I knew where you can find a doctor?"

"And you haven't mentioned it yet?" Mike asked. "Then I'd say you were even more of a lowlife scum than I thought. A man's life hangs in the balance and you want to play games."

"My life hangs in the balance!" Kevin shot back.

Jenn stepped between the two. "You better tell us what you know," she whispered. "Tell us and trust us to treat you right."

He nodded and started, "There's a girl doctor up north who is…" Stu groaned and Mike cursed.

"What?" Jenn asked. "What's wrong with a girl doctor?"

Since Mike looked ready to hurt Kevin, Stu told her, "There's no girl doctor. It was just a rumor that was going around. Supposedly she was in Portland, but two years ago traders went up that way looking for her and came away with nothing. If traders couldn't find her she doesn't exist." The true story was that slavers had been searching for this mystical girl for years but Stu didn't think it was a good time to bring that up.

"Watch him closely," Stu told Jenn. "Shoot him if he even blinks." Despite his tough talk, Stu was in a much better mood now that a decision had been made. He hurried through the dark house looking for something to use as a stretcher.

There was precious little save for the runners of a bed. These were heavy but sturdy. Using rope and bedsheets he created a stretcher which he and Kevin used to carry William out into the night. To keep Kevin from running away at the first chance, Stu tied a noose around his neck. He tied the other end of the rope around William's waist as an anchor.

Then they were ready to go. Mike hauled the cart with their belongings and Jenn led the way. The dead were still out in force in the neighborhood. Their enormous shapes could be seen outlined in the swirling snow, going here and there. Twice they came too close and Jenn was forced to run out into the darkness waving her hands to distract the beasts.

Both times Stu waited for her to return, huddled down against the cold, his heart in his throat. Jenn proved sure-footed in the snow and both times came back winded but unhurt.

The danger grew less when they escaped from the neighborhood and got to the highway. Then it became more of a physical ordeal as they slogged along hauling William's dead weight. It was back-breaking and after an hour Stu and Kevin could barely go on. Mike switched places with Stu while Jenn went to help Kevin. Even rotating like this, it was a struggle. They would go for a hundred yards, stop, and kneel in place with their heads bowed, their muscles burning. After a minute they would force themselves on again.

It took them almost two hours to cover the distance back to Sacramento and by then they were all numb from the cold and completely exhausted. But there was no quit in them. Except for Kevin that is. He had to be kicked to his feet after every break during the last half a mile. When they got to the *Puffer* he ran away the moment he was untied.

They watched him reeling through the snow like a drunk and none of them had the energy to go after him even though he fell after fifty yards and could only crawl away. "Good riddance," Mike mumbled. There was nothing good about it. Without Kevin's help, the three of them struggled mightily to get William onto the boat.

Without a word, Mike untied the mooring ropes and raised the sail. He started for the middle of the channel, but Stu shook his head. "Head for their warehouse." Mike was too tired to complain. A dark look was all he could muster and that too disappeared as a sudden gust of wind slapped him with a fresh wave of snow.

Mike had reached the limits of exhaustion and was groggy by the time they reached the dock. Jenn had covered her and William with a blanket and was asleep with her head resting on his chest, despite his gurgling breath. It was up to Stu to haul the boxes to the warehouse. Forty yards had never felt so far.

Dropping the boxes, he hammered on the door and turned away. "What is this?" Willis demanded. He and a few others stood in the doorway, wrapped in coats and blankets. They made no move for the two boxes. "Where's the rest?"

"Don't you mean, thank you?"

"No, I mean where's the rest of our stuff? And where are Everett and those other turds?"

Just then, telling the truth seemed like too much work. "Dead, and you're welcome for that, too."

Willis looked startled by the bleak answer. Swallowing noisily, he said, "That still doesn't explain why all you brought…" Stu turned his back on the man in midsentence and didn't react when he started cursing. He was simply too drained to care what the man thought.

It wasn't just physical exhaustion weighing him down either. He had failed in his mission. It had been a complete fiasco. William sounded like he was drowning on his own blood and now Jeff and Aaron had no chance. They were doomed.

"Move over," he said to Mike as he got to the *Puffer*. Mike was slumped at the tiller, his hood drooped over his face. "I'll take us home." Mike's exhaustion was such that he didn't argue.

Sailing at night in a snowstorm was the height of stupidity; but he had no choice. Luckily, with the wind almost blowing straight down the canal it took very little skill to keep the boat centered far from danger, except for the occasional body. When he hit these there would be a thump or a shudder along the keel. At one point he hit a living corpse. It swept under the boat and got caught up on the daggerboard.

The beast acted like a forward rudder and they slewed right. Stu was too tired to panic. With a heavy sigh, he hauled the rudder to center and then crab-walked to the daggerboard and hefted it out. Immediately the boat swung back.

This was about the only bit of excitement on the three-hour trip. While the snow turned to biting rain, the wind stayed strong right through the bay. They fairly shot across the water to Pelican Harbor, where the wind slackened enough to make mooring the boat a piece of cake.

"Is he still alive?" Stu asked. William was eerily white, his face swimming up out of the dark like a ghost. Jenn nodded, the lines crossing her forehead telling Stu that she didn't think he would be alive for much longer. "Go ahead of us and get help," he ordered her. She took her crossbow and left at a jog.

He and Mike heaved the homemade stretcher onto the dock and then began the laborious process of hefting William up the hill. It had never felt so steep.

Halfway up, they were met by Winston and One Shot. They each grabbed a corner of the stretcher. A few minutes later, more men and women joined them, allowing Mike and Stu a chance to rest their arms. When others arrived, Stu asked some of them to go back to the harbor to get their packs and the medicine.

No questions were asked and they wouldn't be as long as they were outside the gates. No, the questions and the judgments would come only once everyone was safe inside. Then they would come hot and heavy and he knew the one that would be chief of these: Why didn't he go in with M4s at the ready? He had his excuses, the cold being chief of these, but right behind it had been the fact that they had never been attacked by the people of Sacramento before.

When the solemn, silent parade of people reached the gates of the complex, William was hustled away to the clubhouse, with Stu, Mike and Jenn following behind. They were stopped at the doors by Miss Shay who watched without emotion as William was carried in.

"Do you have the medicine?" she asked, showing that her main...her *only* concern was for her child.

Miss Shay's face went rigid as Stu shook his head. "We will call for you and when you we do, you had better be prepared to answer to the Coven."

Stu dropped his chin and wouldn't look up as she stormed inside. Mike put a hand on his shoulder. "You didn't do anything wrong."

"I didn't do anything right, either."

Chapter 19

Jenn Lockhart

Since they were the ultimate authority, facing the Coven in their official capacity would normally have kept Jenn from sleeping. The seven governed through a fair amount of native wisdom that could be utterly overthrown by the capricious nature of the omens, the gods and the fates.

Although Jenn had done nothing wrong, it didn't mean that her life couldn't be turned on its head if the wrong Tarot card came up. Still, she had been up for nearly twenty-three very hard hours and, fully clothed, she slipped into sleep the second her head hit the pillow.

A steady thumping on her front door woke her seven hours later. It took a moment to blink herself awake; it took no time for her stomach to swirl with guilt and worry. The thumping continued. "Jenn? Are you in there?" It was Colleen White, her voice pitched nervously high. "Jenn? The Coven is asking to see you."

Jenn slid out of bed, went to the door, only to pause before answering. She was still wearing the "boy" clothes from the day before—they were stained with dried blood.

"Can you tell them I'll be right down?" she whispered through the door. Colleen said she would and Jenn heard her take a step away. "Hey? How's William?"

"Still alive, barely."

Jenn put her forehead against the door; it was cold, the entire apartment was cold. She had banked the remains of the fire the morning before and now the embers were no longer hot and only ash remained. It was an ill-omen, but how to read it? Did it portend death? Likely, but there were other interpretations: a cold hearth could also mean a journey or change of residence. None of which sounded good to Jenn. She'd had her fill of journeys and a change of residence could only mean banishment, though this was highly unlikely since she had done nothing wrong to warrant such a terrible punishment.

She was still kneeling in front of the fireplace when Mike left his room. She could feel him staring at her. "We should get ready," he said. "It'll only be worse if we keep them waiting."

There was no time to get the fire going and heat water. They used cold well water to clean themselves up. Mike wore jeans and a plaid shirt which he buttoned nearly to the top, while Jenn wore a floral dress and, in the odd fashion of the Hill People, wore a pair of jeans under it to keep out the chill.

Together they went to the clubhouse where a crowd of people were gathered. At the sight of the two, they stopped gossiping and the children stopped playing. A few people waved and a few said hi. The rest only stared.

Stu and Colleen waited for them in the open front room. Stu's face was like granite, hard and unsmiling. His eyes were bloodshot as if he hadn't slept at all. Colleen, wearing a dress with black slacks beneath, flashed a sad smile, showing a single dimple.

"I'm witnessing today," she told them. It would be her job to watch the proceedings, write down what was said and then tell the rest of the Hill People. She led them to the audience chamber where the Coven waited. Sitting to the side was Gerry the Greek. He shook his head at them.

"Start at the beginning," Donna Polston ordered.

Standing stiffly, his hands at his sides, his eyes staring past the women and at the wall behind them, Stu told them the entire story. When he explained his reasoning for going into the house where Everett and his friends had holed up without their guns ready, Gerry muttered, "Pathetic."

"We've never had problems with them before," Mike said, coming to Stu's defense. "And it wasn't like we had a lot of time to discuss things right there on the porch, the place was crawling with the dead."

"Enough," Donna said. Although she had a quiet way of speaking she had power to her voice and Gerry bit back a retort. Stu finished his story.

Other than the lapse of judgment in trusting Everett Baron, Jenn thought the three of them came across as brave and determined, which made Lois Blanchard's pursed lips hard to comprehend.

Lois sighed and said, "A sad tale all around."

"We should send someone to the Santas and ask them for antibiotics." Miss Shay sounded close to begging.

"We will," Donna replied, with a look of sympathy.

Gerry the Greek snorted, "Don't bother. I sent a couple of the boys down there yesterday. They don't have nothing." He scratched at his black hair, causing it to stick up in a rooster's comb.

Miss Shay began blinking rapidly to keep the tears from falling down her stern face. She was as unsympathetic of a person as Jenn had ever met but even she wanted to give the woman a hug. "There's always the girl doctor that everyone talks about," Jenn said. "We could try to find…"

In a blink of her watery eyes, Miss Shay picked up a pencil and hurled it at Jenn, missing high. "Girl doctor? Shut up! This is your fault. Yours and his!" Surprisingly, she was pointing at Mike. "You two did this."

"What the hell did I do?" he demanded, furiously.

Donna tried to calm Miss Shay while Lois answered, "You're both bad luck, especially together. It was a mistake to try to connect you two. We know that you asked her Mike, but did she answer yet? Tell me she didn't."

Mike shared a look with Jenn. She turned away first, unable to meet his eye as she felt the stirrings of panic well up inside of her. Not only was she being publicly labeled as "bad luck," she was being blamed for what was likely going to be three deaths. On top of all of that, having her marriage proposal taken from her would put her on the bottom of the list.

She hated the very idea of being on any list, but to be on the bottom of the list was even more awful. They would try to stick her with one of the widowers who were all at least twenty years older, which was gross. The thought had her belly twisting. And yet if she turned down whoever they tried to stick her with, she could very well end up alone forever.

To an orphaned fifteen-year-old, the idea was frightening. The words, "Yes. I said yes," just came blurting out of her mouth. She grabbed Mike's arm with both hands digging into the plaid shirt.

He looked surprised at first, but this faded into disappointment which he hid behind a smile. "She said yes. We, uh we're going to get married."

"Good for you," Gerry the Greek said, getting to his feet to clap Mike on the shoulder. Up close, his dark eyes bored into Jenn's face, searching for the truth. She couldn't take this and, still clinging to Mike, she took a step behind him. "Good for you," he repeated before turning to the Coven. "You guys got something, now I need what's coming to me. I need a little compensation. I lost two perfectly sound men, three if you include Mike."

"They're not dead yet," Lois answered, softly, fooling no one. She didn't believe they would live, either.

"Sure," the Greek said. "I'm just saying we had a deal, and now it's only fair if both Hilly and Ginny come to the Island."

Donna released Miss Shay and stood. "Our agreement is not open for public discussion. We're here to decide on what to do about them." She pointed at Mike and Jenn. "The signs couldn't be any clearer. They were a mistake. Have you consummated your marriage?" Their blanks looks told her they didn't understand the question.

Gerry turned and with a wink, asked, "Have you guys done *it*, yet?"

Jenn flushed so violently she could feel the blood pulsing in the tips of her ears. It was through that thrumming that she heard Mike say in a strangled voice, "Yes, of course." Somehow this lie was even more embarrassing for her. She was sure that everyone in the room was imagining her lying naked with Mike. She couldn't look up from the floor.

"It's a done deal," Gerry said. "My boy Mike gave it to her good."

"That's enough, Gerry," Donna said. "Well, I guess there's nothing that can be done."

Stu, who had been standing stiffly this entire time, the hard planes of his face unmoving, spoke suddenly. "Is this really what you called us here for? Just to talk about these two and if they've had sex? We have three people dying in the next room and this is what you want to talk about?" His fury cut through Jenn's embarrassment and she was able to stare at him in disbelief. No one talked to the Coven like that.

"What would you have us do?" Donna answered. "Operate on them? None of us are surgeons, and even if we were, we don't have any equipment, we don't have the right drugs and when was the last time anything was sterile? No, our only chance is to put out trust in the gods."

Stu spat, "The gods?"

"Or fate or whatever it is out there guiding us," Donna said. "They try to help by sending us omens: the horde which is still across the bay, the sickness, the deaths, all of this started with those two." She pointed an accusing finger at Mike and Jenn. "I blame myself. When I looked on them I only saw who their fathers were and I ignored the signs."

Lois spoke up. "Don't blame yourself, we all wanted them together, even you, Stu."

"I didn't want to do it to appease some 'gods.' I thought Mike would be a good addition to our group."

"So did we all," Donna returned, "but we were wrong. It's okay to be wrong except when you continue to make the same mistakes. You won't ever go into a meeting with thieves without a gun in your hand and we…we have to do something about these two. I think the simplest thing to do is allow them to split up or banish them."

Miss Shay quit crying long enough to say, "I think we should banish them."

Donna patted her arm. "Not in public, please. If you three would step out? And you as well, Colleen." Jenn was numb from the roots of her hair down to her feet. "I can't be banished," she said as they left the room. "I didn't do anything wrong."

"Neither of you did," Stu grumbled. "This is all my fault. I thought Everett would see reason about not using guns. Why even flash a gun with so many of the dead all around us? It didn't make sense. It was completely *senseless*, just like all this omen crap. These are grown women who lived in the before, damn it! They should know better."

Colleen crossed herself at the heresy. Stu sneered, "If you don't like what you're hearing you can take a walk. Go on. You don't want bad mojo to get you." He pointed at the front door and snapped his fingers. She left and his anger deflated into sullenness. "They're going to try to ruin you two. Hell, they already have. The whispers are out there."

"What whispers?" Jenn asked. "What are they saying?"

Stu looked as though he regretted saying anything. "You know. That you're bad luck…that you're marked." He meant marked by the devil or some evil spirit. There wasn't anything worse than being marked. Even though he didn't believe in it, Stu mumbled, "I'm sorry."

"It's not your fault," Mike said.

"Yeah, it is! I'm the one who did this. I went into that house without a gun in my hands. But no one will ever say anything about me. They need me. They need me to provide and protect. But I failed." He crossed the room to a door marked *Gymnasium*.

It had never been much of one. In its heyday it had boasted a few stationary bikes, a treadmill and a garish multi-station Nautilus machine that looked to Jenn like a giant mechanical puzzle. Now the room was the hilltop's hospital. Stu cracked the door.

Inside were three beds. Aaron was closest to the door. The blackout curtains had been pulled back and in the light he was pale and sweating but still awake. Next to him was Jeff, his right leg bandaged, his eyes closed, a yellow tinge to his face. Furthest away was William. He was unconscious, a wheezing sound coming from his throat.

Stu shut the door, looking visibly shaken. "I wish the Coven had powers like they say they do. Then they would have seen all this coming. All they have is perfect hindsight."

"Jenn saw it coming," Mike remarked.

"She had a lucky guess." Stu looked at her sharply, almost accusingly. "Unless you want to make a prediction now? We'll see if it comes true."

Put on the spot, she didn't know what to say. The only signs she had seen were for a journey. But banishment wasn't a journey. The idea of being alone out there was horrifying to her. A death sentence would be less cruel than banishment.

She didn't want to believe it let alone admit it aloud. "No," she said. "I don't see anything."

Stu eyed her closely "You sure?" he asked, a little less confidence in his voice. "Because I…"

Just then Lois opened the door to the inner chamber. "We're ready to see you now." They followed her in. The faces of the Coven were grim. Jenn began shaking. The epicenter of the tremor started down in the pit of her stomach and radiated out until she had to pull her hands into her chest to hide her fear. The hilltop was her home and the people living there were the only family she had.

Donna Polston took a deep breath before saying, "From the day we first considered your union there hasn't just been bad luck swirling around you, but terrible luck. There's even a rumor going around that you're marked. I personally don't believe it, but sometimes the truth doesn't matter."

Jenn knew she was right. The rumor was out there, and now anything bad that happened would be laid at her and Mike's feet.

"There are two solutions and neither one is very palatable," Donna said, looking down at her folded hands. "There is banishment for the two of you or you can have

166

your marriage annulled. We're going to leave it up to you to decide. Personally, I would choose the annulment."

And be put on the bottom of the list, Jenn thought. Although there wasn't an actual written list, there certainly was a mental one which created a pecking order of sorts. Jenn had always ranged somewhere in the middle of that order. On one hand she was pretty and had a talent for reading signs. This was offset by the fact that she had always been considered bad luck.

Now, even if she and Mike were forced to separate, she would always have the "mark" hanging over her head. Her name on everyone's list would always be followed by the word "but." *She's nice, but—She's pretty, but*.

"We'll meet back here at nine tomorrow to hear your final decision," Donna went on. "If you can't decide, the Coven will make the decision for you. That will be all."

Stu, Jenn and Mike left the clubhouse, walking through the crowd. Stu glared at anyone who would meet his gaze; Mike stared straight ahead with his head held high. Shame kept Jenn from looking up. She wanted to go home and sit in front of the fire. She wanted to be alone, however both Mike and Stu preceded her right to her door and walked in.

"So, what do you want to do?" Mike asked right off the bat. Jenn shrugged as she pushed past him, going to the fireplace and piling kindling in something that looked like a sloppy cone. She didn't want to think about it just then. Her answer should have been easy. As much as she liked Mike, and she really did, despite her reaction to his feeble marriage proposal, she would never choose banishment.

The only groups she knew of were the *Santas* out of Santa Cruz, they were known slavers; the diseased people in Sacramento who probably wouldn't last the winter, and the *Guardians*, a bizarre group who still worshipped the old Christian god; they were about the only ones who still did. They made Jenn nervous whenever they came north in their tall-masted cutters. The Guardians always referred to the Hill People as "heathens," which Jenn thought meant something close to barbarians.

She didn't belong with any of these people; she belonged with her family. And yet she had seen the signs for a journey over and over again. Did a day trip to Sacramento count as a journey? She didn't think so.

As she was mulling over her answer, Stu went into her kitchen and inspected her pantry. "You'll split up," he said. "It's the only smart thing to do." He looked around the corner, holding a five-pound wrap of venison jerky. "I need some supplies. Can I have this?"

He was the best hunter on the hilltop which meant he should have plenty of food, which begged the question, "Why?"

"Because my place is right across from the clubhouse. I'm going on a little journey tonight and I don't want the hens to get wind of it before I leave." Jenn's hands slipped when she heard the word journey and her pile of kindling fell to the side.

"Where are you going?" Mike asked.

Stu hesitated before saying, "I have business to attend to. That's it. Leave it alone, alright? And don't say anything to anyone." He took the jerky, stuffed it in his jacket and headed for the door.

"What the hell?" Mike groused after he left.

Jenn was quiet for a moment, her eyes roving over the pile of kindling. It spoke to her as much as the lights in the sky had the other night. The pile had fallen to the right...to the north. "He's going to Portland," she said. There was only one reason for his journey. Without looking up from the pile of kindling, she added, "He's going to find the girl doctor. And I'm going with him."

Chapter 20

Jenn Lockhart

Mike stared at the back of her head for a long time. She could feel his eyes and sense the unease radiating from him. "How do you know?" he asked. No answer would suffice, she just knew. She shrugged and he breathed out, "But isn't this girl only a myth? That's what everyone says. Even Stu said so."

"Maybe he's desperate," she answered, pulling her head from the fireplace. "He blames himself for what happened to William."

Mike turned away and then turned back again quickly, his Adam's apple bobbing up and down. "And you're going with him? Are you saying you're accepting banishment? Are you saying…are you saying you want to marry me? For real?" He suddenly looked young, even younger than Jenn, as if the question had robbed him of years and left him a nervous boy.

The question had certainly momentarily robbed her of the ability to speak. "Uh—uh, that isn't what I meant say. I don't think." When it came to marriage, the signs had deserted her.

"Well, they're going to banish us if we go without permission. And they'll never give it to us, not in a million years."

"You don't know that. Okay, maybe they won't let Stu go, but I don't see why they won't let us try. What do they have to lose?"

Mike smiled rakishly. "They're going to lose a boat. What? Did you think Stu would walk all the way to Portland? It's five hundred miles away. Jeff and William will be long dead by the time he gets back."

Jenn had been feeling a strange level of confidence concerning the journey. The signs all pointed her towards making the trip. At the mention of the boat, she felt that confidence pulled out from under her leaving her stomach in a free fall. "The *Puffer* won't make it that far on open ocean. What if there's a storm?"

"We won't be taking the *Puffer*. We'll be taking the *Calypso*, and Gerry is going to be more than just angry. *If* we make it back I'll be banished no ifs, ands, or buts. Chances are you will be, too. So..." He was suddenly nervous again.

"So? So what?" Mike lifted a shoulder. Jenn's eyes flashed daggers. "Oh, don't tell me this is your way of asking me to marry you? Before, you asked me out of a sense of duty and now what? You're asking me because once we're banished you'll be stuck with me no matter what? Do you expect me to swoon?"

Mike's mouth dropped open. "I-I was just, you know. That's not what I meant. I meant, I meant. I don't know what I meant, exactly. I just..."

Without warning she walked away from him and grabbed her pack. It was sitting on the table along with the M4 and her crossbow. "The answer is no. I don't settle." She threw some more food into her pack and stormed out, hurrying for the gates. Although she wasn't supposed to leave with a rifle unless given permission by the Coven, little Lindy Smith took one look at the storm of anger brewing on Jenn's face and didn't say a word as she opened the gate.

"Gonna go check my traps," Jenn said, by way of explanation. It wasn't a lie. Of course she was also going to deposit the extra food and rifle close to the docks. She walked in a figurative fog and it was strictly luck that she made it to the headlands without being attacked by the dead. They were near, hidden by the forests with only their ghostly moans reaching her ears.

The first four traps were empty. The fifth held a red fox, caught by the throat and strangled to death. The mental haze she had been trapped in blinked away at the sight of it. Instinctively she dropped into a crouch with her bow trained outward. Catching a fox had to be a sign. They were rare, elusive and harder to catch than steam in a fist.

Jenn removed the snare and stroked the pelt. It was beautiful and soft. She knelt there running her fingers through the fur, waiting for the reason behind the sign to come to her. When none came, she ascribed luck to the fox and tied it to her pack. It might have been lucky, but it didn't smell good.

The musky scent was heavy on the nostrils and Jenn joked to herself, "Maybe this will keep Mike away." Her smile was brief. In truth, she didn't want Mike to stay away, she wanted him to act like a proper man. She wanted him to get down on one knee and ask her to marry him the right away. Even then, she didn't know what her answer would be. Everything felt rushed. Everything felt out of kilter. Everything…

"Nice fox," Stu Currans said, making her jump. He seemed to have appeared out of nowhere as she passed the trunk of an elm.

"Thanks. It's lucky. I think."

His smile dimmed at this. "Where was its luck?" She didn't have an answer to this. He waved a hand, dismissing the question. "I talked to Mike. He says you two are coming with me. You know that we probably won't make it back alive?"

Normally, death wouldn't have crossed her mind. Death was all around them. It was a threat she lived with every second of every day. But the specter of drowning was something new and something awful in a way that left her second-guessing herself. She knew Mike probably hadn't even blinked at the question, so she forced a grin onto her face. "I know."

"Even if we do make it back with a doctor and antibiotics, they won't let us stay. Banishment is the sentence for theft. We all know it. I worry that you won't do well in banishment. I know it's not fair to say, but you're a girl. Some people will look on you like you're a thing to be bought and sold, and not a person. You need the protection of the community."

This wasn't exactly news to her, and it was exactly why she knew she couldn't be banished. But the signs all pointed to a journey and as frightened as she was of the Coven and the idea of banishment, she was more afraid to piss off the fates or the gods or whatever it was controlling her life.

"I'm going because it's the right thing."

"It is. We'll meet behind building four at eleven sharp. Dress warm."

Jenn left her gun and food in a house overlooking Pelican Harbor. She then went back for more. Anything could happen on an ocean trip. They could be blown out of sight of land; it could mean days at sea. They would need to be prepared. She and Mike took three trips each hauling items.

At five minutes of eleven that night, the two picked up their packs and snuck out of her apartment like the thieves they were. The complex was quiet and dark. Chances were that everyone except the gate guard was sound asleep.

They stole to the meeting place and found Stu in the shadows. "I've dug a trench," he whispered. It was a muddy little rut and, more like worms than snakes, they inched beneath the fence. From there they crawled past a hundred spears until they were free of the complex.

Jenn didn't feel free. She faced the world, picturing it as an immense prison that she would never be able to escape from. She hesitated, afraid to go on. Stu and Mike were already a fair distance away, disappearing into the night. It was a warm wind plucking at her sleeve that got her moving. A warm wind was always a good sign.

Her first steps on a real journey were to the east to Pelican Harbor.

The night was very dark and that too was a good sign. The dead, with their filmed-over eyes could barely see a thing at night. They could still hear perfectly well, and they would charge anything that sounded even remotely human. Stu moved slowly along, taking his time and the three only had to dodge a few of the dead as they gathered their hidden supplies and made their way down to the docks where the *Puffer* sat ready.

172

Here it was Mike's turn to take the lead. In the dark he could set a sail, luff and tack better than Stu or any of the Hill People could on the brightest day. He piloted the little boat, glancing up at the position of the stars every other minute and he used the sound of the buoys in the bay to keep out of reach of Shag and Harding Rocks.

At one in the morning the *Puffer* approached Alcatraz, moving soundlessly out of the north. The three were keyed up and nervous. They had to pass beneath the guard tower which was always manned. If they were spotted, their journey would end before it got started.

Mike assured them that everyone slept on guard duty. They even brought their own blankets.

Still, they didn't sleep soundly and getting a boat underway wasn't exactly a quiet endeavor. Mike hauled down the *Puffer's* sail fifty feet from the side of the *Calypso* and guided the boat using only the rudder and their forward momentum. They slid in alongside of it nice and easy. With the rubber fenders absorbing the impact, there was only a light thump as the two boats came together.

Stu threw a leg over the edge of the *Calypso,* straddling both boats and holding them together as Jenn crawled across and squatted down in the doorway of the boat's cabin. Mike, who was the most surefooted, began handing packs and weapons and bags of food to Stu, who handed them to Jenn. She laid them down as quietly as she could in the cabin.

"Hurry up," Stu hissed at her. She tried to hurry, but the cabin was pitch black and she ended up tripping over a crossbow.

"Hello?" The word filtered down, soft and nervous, from the guard tower. "Who is that? I have a gun."

Mike and Stu both put a finger to their lips as if Jenn was about to blurt out their mission. "It's me," Mike said as he handed a bundle of blankets to Stu.

"Who is me? And what are you doing?"

Another bundle was handed over. "Oh sorry. It's Mike Gunter. Who is that, Phil? What did you do to get guard duty at one in the morning?"

Phil ignored the question. "Mike? Jeeze, what the hell are you doing here?"

Another bundle was pushed into Jenn's hands as Mike answered, "I really should talk to Gerry first."

"Gerry? Hold on." There was a new sound from the guard tower; it was the unmistakable muffled thud of boots hitting the rungs of a ladder.

"The mooring lines," Mike whispered, urgently. Stu went to the aft line while Jenn hurried to the bow and pulled on the free end of the mooring hitch and the knot came loose. Stu and Jenn pushed away from the dock and there was a hollow thump as the two boats came together. This was followed by more thumps as Mike began chucking their gear across as fast as he could.

"What's going on?" Phil asked as he came off the ladder and began hurrying down the dock. "Is it about Jeff or William? Did one of them die? I just want…what the hell?"

Stu had his .357 out. Despite the dark, it gleamed. Phil stared at it with round eyes. "We need her," Stu explained. "And we're going to take her, so be cool."

Phil took a step back and began shaking his head in disbelief. "No. You, you won't shoot me. I know you Stu Currans. I know you wouldn't shoot me."

"Keep telling yourself that."

Jenn heard Phil's breath begin to quicken and she knew he was about to shout a second before he did. "Help! I need help at the docks!" Stu cursed and lowered the gun. Phil had been right. Stu wasn't going to shoot any of the islanders. "Help!" Phil cried, louder now.

"Switch!" Mike cried, leaping across to the *Calypso,* where he immediately attacked the lines wrapped around the sail. Stu was much less steady as he went to the *Puffer.* He reached a long arm across the space and hauled the small boat to them. Jenn scrambled to help. She grabbed the edge of the *Puffer* and held on tightly while Stu threw the rest of the gear across.

Phil continued to yell and in seconds the sound of racing feet could be heard thudding along the dock. By then,

174

Mike had the mainsail up and was coaxing the *Calypso* away. Within half a minute, Stu had tossed over all their gear and climbed across. He pushed away the *Puffer* and then began to help Jenn clear the deck.

"It's Mike and Stu Currans," Phil yelled, as men came up. "They're stealing *Calypso*."

"Stop right there, Mike," growled a voice. It was Rocky Duckworth, the head guard. "Bring her back in, damn it. What the hell do you think you're doing?"

They were only some thirty feet from the dock and Mike was in the process of worrying at a knot that was holding the foresail down. "I'm just borrowing her for a spell. Don't worry, Gerry knows what I'm up to."

"We both know that's a lie," Rocky said. "Now bring her back or else." When Mike made no move to bring her back in, Rocky asked, "Do I have to declare this a theft? Is that what you want?" Normal theft could be punishable by banishment, but this wasn't only Gerry's most prized possession, it was the community's as well and Gerry could implement the death penalty.

"It's not theft if I'm only borrowing it," Mike said, and then cursing, brought out a knife and cut the knot. In seconds, he had the sail raised.

"If that's the way you want to play this," Rocky said before barking out orders to get the next fastest boat ready. With a dozen experienced seamen working as a single unit, they had the *Sea Sprite* going inside of a minute.

That minute was enough for Mike to open a hundred-yard lead. To Jenn's amazement, he didn't point the *Calypso* straight out to sea. "The wind would be right in our face and a crew like theirs will be able to eat into this lead pretty quickly." He took a north-northeast heading, aiming for Angel Island two miles away. Their lead was three hundred yards by the time he rounded its tip.

When the *Sea Sprite* followed the *Calypso*, Mike laughed, "They should have cut under and blocked our way out of the bay. We would have been trapped." With the wind at their backs, their lead grew to half a mile and Mike was all smiles.

Five minutes later the smile dimmed on his handsome face. The Islanders had more than one boat. A quarter mile away, its sail grey and murky, was the *Scalawag*, looking like a ghost ship out of a storybook. It was rushing to trap them in the mouth of a side bay.

Even Jenn knew that if they cut back, they would lose both time and speed, which would allow the *Sea Sprite* to catch up. The captain of the *Scalawag* knew it as well. He trimmed his sail back and turned to the western coast of the bay. He was in the perfect position to pin the *Calypso* against the shore.

Mike turned as well, only he did so at full speed, causing the windward side of the boat to lift out of the water. When Stu and Jenn only grabbed something to hold onto, Mike snapped, "Get over there!" He meant the side of the boat that was pitched high in the air. The two crawled to the high side, their weight helping to keep the boat from flipping.

Gradually the *Calypso* pulled ahead and if there had been more room it would have swung to the left, ahead of the *Scalawag* before making its run out of the bay—there was no room for such a maneuver.

Jenn figured that Mike would turn the boat to the right and attempt to circle around, hoping to get between the other two boats. With what he'd said about the sailing qualities of the other crews, she didn't think they would make it.

Mike had no intention of swinging around.

"Wait. What are you doing?" Stu asked. The question was rhetorical. It was obvious Mike was going to try to cut in front of the *Scalawag* with only a hundred yards to spare before they hit the shore. "You'll never make it. Mike, please."

To their left and slightly behind them, the crew of the *Scalawag* were screaming the same thing as the two ships raced at the shore. They were so close it looked as though Mike was going to run the *Calypso* right up onto the beach.

With a final curse, the captain of the *Scalawag* hauled hard on the rudder pulling his boat sharply to port. A quarter of a second later Mike did as well so that both boats turned as one. They were so close to shore that Jenn felt, as well as heard, a rasping sound coming from beneath them, they were in such shallow waters that they were running over sand.

"Jeeze," Stu whispered, his face pale.

Mike let the boom swing to the left to catch the full wind, sending them cutting at a sharper angle. "Just a sand bar," he said, as a shudder went through the keel. Of course, where there was sand there was rock.

They ran along the beach for a few more precarious seconds before the wind pushed them away and hurled them south under full sail and there was nothing the Islanders could do to stop them as they crossed beneath the Golden Gate Bridge and shot out to sea.

Chapter 21

Stu Currans

The sun was setting in long bands of pink and blue. Stu ran a hand across his cheek, listening to the rasp of the stubble as he watched. It reminded him of the sound of the sand beneath the keel of the *Calypso*. Stu didn't think he would ever forget that particular sound. He'd had a case of the shakes for a good five minutes after that.

In the five days since that close call, they'd had a rather boring time of it. All they had done was sail. Really, all they had done was tack from one end of the ocean to another, zigzagging up the coast, day and night, fighting both the current and the light breezes that always seemed to be in their faces.

It was dull, dull work. The days had stretched out one by one, each seeming longer than the last, and while the days passed, the scenery never changed. It felt like they were crisscrossing the same patch of ocean every day and worse, they were crossing it very slowly. They knew they had to get to Portland as fast as the wind could take them if they had any chance to save their friends, only the wind absolutely refused to help.

They had made landfall only once and that had been two days before. Despite strict rationing they had run out of fresh water and headed east until they came to *Gold Beach* and the *Rogue River*.

Mike found a map in their quick scavenge and when he saw how far they had come he cursed savagely. They were just over halfway to Portland and far off their schedule. They had all agreed that if they didn't make it back in two weeks it would be better not to go back at all.

"Time for me to freeze," Jenn said, ducking from the tiny V-shaped berth and zipping up a faded blue parka that draped on her small body like a heavy curtain. It hung to her knees while the sleeves would have extended past her fingertips if she hadn't pinned them back.

"You're early," Stu said, gesturing to the sun.

"By ten minutes. I didn't want your dinner to get cold." It was a joke and he had smiled. Although the weather had been mild for October it was still October on the open ocean which meant that it was chilly even with the sun shining down at high noon. At night, the temperature hoverd around the freezing mark. The three of them had been perpetually cold from the moment they had slipped beneath the Golden Gate.

Mike came out after her and gazed toward the sunset. "What do you think? Pink is close enough to red, right?" He was as superstitious as Jenn and sailed with the old adage: *Red skies at night, sailors' delight, red sky in the morning, sailors take warning,* as a guide. Mike checked the horizon every day, morning and night.

Dutifully, Jenn turned to face west. The shoulders of her parka lifted slightly indicating she might have shrugged. "I don't think pink counts. It is pretty, though." He agreed that it was. When it came to Jenn, Mike was very agreeable. It seemed the more she shot down his pathetic attempts at marriage proposals, the more he wanted her.

He tried to hide it, but they were thrown together on a tiny boat out in the middle of the ocean. There were no secrets and each of them, Mike included, worried he would attempt another inept proposal.

While the sun set, Jenn turned in a full circle, a habit just as ingrained as Mike's saying. She had an eye out for signs. These seemed to have deserted her from the moment they had set foot on the *Calypso*. The evening sky was as empty as the ocean.

"Let's come about," Mike said. He was the captain on board and when it came to all aspects of the boat and their course he was the ultimate authority, though in this case Stu had known the order was coming and could have made it himself. Every night at sunset, when it was Jenn's turn to take the helm, they came about to take a northwesterly course. As it pointed them away from land, it was the safest course.

Jenn would be the first to admit that she wasn't much of a sailor, though she was quite a bit better than she had been. Stu had gained in knowledge as well and he was beginning to get a real feel for the various forces at work: the wind, the current, the waves, the sails and the rudder. It was a dance of sorts. Mike was the master of this and when they came about he usually took the helm. This had changed the day before when he had said to Stu, "You get the next couple."

The *Calypso* being so much bigger than the *Puffer*, Stu was too slow bringing the boom around, stalling the boat. "That's okay," Mike had said. "Just haul us around. Use the wind. It's your engine." Stu had tried again on six different occasions, getting better with each. Then it was Jenn's turn. She had learned from Stu's mistakes and had done a halfway decent job, but didn't feel the need to try more than once.

"If there's ever a need for me to pilot the boat, for real, I think it might be best for everyone to tie anchors to their feet and jump overboard." She went back to sharpening her machete, which was finally getting an edge on it.

Now, with the last light, they came around, Mike making it look effortless. Then as usual, they sat staring up at the sky as the stars began to come out of hiding. Stu stuck his long legs out and pitched his head back, not really seeing the stars; they were only a backdrop as he thought about what they would find in Portland.

For Jenn, the stars were the focal point of her world; she was oblivious to the many quick peeks that Mike sent her way. Stu knew she was looking for a sign, just like he knew she would find one, eventually.

It came two hours later, a moment after Stu started a chain yawn. Jenn was just stretching when she jumped up knocking the tiller out of position and turning the boat side on to the wind. She didn't seem to notice. "Do you see that?" She pointed into the sky with a gloved hand. "Right there! The lights!"

Stu's first thought was that the boat was tipping alarmingly as the wind struck the sail flat. The winds were too light to capsize the *Calypso* and after the moment of alarm, he squinted up at the night sky and for all of two seconds he saw what looked like a blinking light moving in the darkness. Then it crossed the Milky Way and he lost sight of it against the bright background.

"What direction is that?" Jenn asked.

"North, mostly," Mike said.

"Then that's the way we go," she said self-assuredly, a little smile playing on her lips.

Mike looked embarrassed as he said, "That's already the way we want to go, and we're going there. We just can't go directly in that direction. You know, because of the winds."

She only nodded, the smile still in place. Stu didn't say anything. What was the point? She'd seen her sign and that's what counted. Any logical argument to the contrary would be a waste of time. "I'm going to bed. Wake me at four."

Stu took off his jacket but left the rest of his clothes on as he went into the little cabin where they had laid out their blankets to form a nest in which two people could sleep at once. Once bundled up, the bed was surprisingly comfy and with the rocking of the *Calypso*, he was quickly out.

He woke with the boat pitching up and down and the mast creaking against the strain of a much heavier wind than that which had rocked him to sleep. When he stood, he almost fell over backwards as the bow pointed suddenly into the air.

It was safest to crawl out of the cabin. When he did, the first thing he saw was a mountain of water behind them. It towered three times higher than the mast. He was sure they would be crushed by the wave, but it seemed to slide beneath them and then lift them into the air higher and higher so that when he turned, the boat was pointed down a slope that would have made a black diamond skier crap himself.

"Stu!" Mike cried. "Don't just stand there, help me shorten the sail." The teenage boy was at the very tip of the boat, tying down the foresail.

Before he could move, the boat slid down the embankment of water. Stu held onto the cabin door with both hands, his knuckles white. The ride was shorter than expected and they were already being lifted up again even before they got to the bottom.

Moving as carefully as he could, Stu leaned out onto the roof of the cabin and began shortening the sail. They would lose speed by this while gaining greater control… supposedly. Even with the shortened sail the boat was buffeted by crazy gusts that would hit them whenever they mounted the peaks of the waves. Sometimes the winds would be so strong that the *Calypso* would heel almost all the way over before Mike could get her pointed into the wind.

The wind was a struggle but it was the waves that continued to terrify Stu. When they were lined up in a row behind them he could stomach that, barely. It was when waves also came from the sides that Stu was sure they would sink. The power released when these monsters collided was immense, sometimes making the *Calypso* leap and spin. There'd be a huge eruption of water which frequently rushed over the deck.

"What are we doing?" he called out to Mike. "Are we heading to shore?" In the dark with the clouds pressing down on them, Stu couldn't tell north from west. Mike shot Jenn a look and that was all it took for Stu to know they weren't heading to the safety of land, and judging by the sail and the neutral rudder position, they were heading north just as Jenn's sign had directed.

At least for that night he gave up his skepticism of the supernatural. It didn't seem to matter what he believed. They were likely going to die out there. All three of them tied ropes around their waists, a precaution that saved Jenn twice. She was the lightest and whenever a heavy wave broke over the boat she would be swept around like a piece of styrofoam.

The first time she went overboard, Mike left his station at the helm and Stu had to shove him back toward the rudder. The boat couldn't be allowed to flounder. Stu hauled Jenn out of the water. She was soaked to the bone and freezing, then again they all were. Heavy rains swept them in grey sheets and sleet pelted them so that whenever Stu looked into the wind it felt like thousands of stinging bees were chipping away at the frozen flesh of his face.

The second time Jenn went overboard, Stu was too weak to haul her back in. The cold had sapped his strength, turning his hands numb and making his arms feel heavy and useless. With her many layers, her parka and her heavy boots flooded with water, she seemed to have gained a hundred pounds. The rope, like an oiled serpent, kept slipping from his fingers while Jenn slapped at the churning waters with just enough strength to keep herself afloat.

She managed to stay alive long enough to be picked up by a lucky wave and thrown back onto the boat as the wave crashed over them. Stu knew they couldn't count on that sort of luck a second time, and begged them to turn to land.

Mike refused. He stayed at the helm all night and kept them pointed north even as nature did its best to pound them and the *Calypso* into pieces. At daybreak the seas were as high and as rough as ever and yet the murky light gave them hope. It made everything from tying knots to ducking waves just a little easier.

They took turns sleeping. They ate, and they lived.

By three that afternoon, they didn't so much as break free of the storm as they were spat out of it. In the light airs north of the storm the waters were choppy and hard, but compared to what they had gone through it seemed like a vacation. Somehow Mike still had energy enough to take a run along the coast to find out where they were.

There were very few towns of any size along that stretch of the Pacific shore. They found only miles of empty beaches until they came to an inlet which everyone assumed was the mouth of a significant river. Carefully Mike piloted them into the mile wide opening and toward a series of jutting piers, all of which were crumbling into ruin.

He picked out the sturdiest-looking dock and slid in next to it. Five minutes later, Jenn threw herself down on a small hill at the end of the dock, where the tall grass swished back and forth with the breeze. "Does anyone mind if I just lie here for a bit?"

"No," Mike said. "Stu and I will explore." The only exploring they did was in a single house down the beach. They went with crossbows at the ready, but the place was deserted, even by the dead. All the seaward-facing windows had been blown in long before and the two walked on a fine carpet of glass and sand. The place had been ransacked and stripped of anything of immediate value. Still, there were dry clothes to be had and they quickly tossed aside their old soggy, rank outfits and redressed in sweaters and jeans. There were no coats left in the house so the two settled for blazers found in the master closet. Shaggy and dirty, the two looked like bums who were playing dress-up for the day.

As Mike looked for clothes that would fit Jenn, Stu went to the garage in search of a map. He found one sitting stuffed down between the driver's seat and the console. When he opened it and realized where they were, he stared for such a long time that Mike came looking for him. He had two shirts in his hands, one blue and one green.

"What are you doing?" Mike asked, forgetting the shirts.

"I'm…I'm just trying to figure something out. We overshot the Columbia. We're ten miles north of the mouth of the river."

Mike shrugged. "That's not a problem. The wind is straight out of the west. It should be smooth sailing back. Which one do you think Jenn will like?" He held up the two shirts.

"Sailing isn't the problem. I just…I just don't know how Jenn knew, you know, how she knew to keep going north into that storm. We could have ended up anywhere, but we ended up almost exactly where we needed to go."

"She has a gift," was Mike's simple reply. "She knew about the journey, she knew about that horde back in Oakland. Face it, Stu, the signs are real and so is she."

Chapter 22

Stu Currans

They boarded the *Calypso* and with the storm they had escaped from swinging inland, they had plenty of wind to shoot them down the coast to the mouth of the Columbia River and from there the gale swept them inland along what had once been some of the most beautiful land in the world. Now, the north bank of the river was a wasteland of ash and fallen trees. There was nothing left standing. A fire greater than Stu had ever heard of had swept over the land turning it into a desert where nothing lived, not even the dead.

There was some life on the south bank only it wasn't what Stu would call normal life. He could only describe the land there as "infected" but by what he didn't know.

"Look at that," Jenn said, pointing at a seagull struggling to lift off. Feathers dripped off of it as it flapped its misshapen wings. Beneath it hung stumps instead of webbed feet. It flew overhead and they could hear its breath wheezing in and out.

Even the dead were affected by the disease. The few they saw in the light of the setting sun were a horror of running pus and slagged flesh. They seemed to be melting into the earth as they walked and their moans were so filled with despair that for a moment Stu forgot they were evil monsters and felt bad for them.

"People actually live here?" Jenn asked, sniffing the air and wrinkling her nose. It smelled of metal in a way none of them had ever experienced before.

"Oh, yeah," Stu said. "That's what the traders say. Though they never actually go to Portland. They meet somewhere south of it at a place called Salem." This was a normal practice, even the Hill People met the traders across the bay to keep them from knowing the exact location of their complex.

"Maybe they did this on purpose," Mike mused. "You know, to keep people away."

Stu didn't think so. It might have started out as part of someone's plan, but clearly the fire had gotten out of hand. The tortured landscape went on for miles and when the sun set, the darkness couldn't hide the destruction; even the shadows were bent.

Sailing in the dark on an unknown river was exceedingly dangerous, but they pressed on and not because of the urgency of their mission. They braved the water out of fear of the land.

The further inland they went, the worse the destruction and the sharper the smell. They wrapped damp scarves around their heads as a protection against the stench and whatever germs lingered on the air. It was a forty-mile trip up the Columbia to Portland, but after only an hour, the wide river branched left and right around an island a mile wide and several miles long.

A fifteen-foot high wall made from what looked like the scraps from a junkyard had been built around the island. There were stacks of old cars, refrigerators lined up like rusting teeth, ovens piled on dishwashers, lamp posts and tree trunks wrapped in cables, cargo containers set end to end, farm tractors and cranes interlocked in complex puzzles. Oddest of all was the back half of a naval destroyer half-in and half-out of the water.

As they sailed up the west side of the island the rain came back in a deluge, soaking them again. Mike ordered the sail shortened as a precaution, while next to them the crazy wall went on and on without a break or a gate. At the far end of the island, Mike swung the boat around and turned down river to inspect the long south side. Midway down, they discovered a canal that that led through an arch in the wall. The canal was all of twenty feet across; too narrow for a sailing vessel. Mike looped around and let out the anchor just upstream from the arch.

There they waited to be hailed or even noticed. "Hello?" Stu called when they grew tired of waiting. There was no reply and the only noise was the patter of rain and a metallic grinding coming from the wall as the wind blew against it. Stu turned to Jenn. "Um, what do you think? Any signs?" He couldn't believe those words had come from his mouth, but he had a bad feeling about this island.

She glanced up, squinting into the rain at the dark clouds blanketing the sky from one end to the other. "I don't see any, sorry."

It was just as well. He wouldn't have believed a good sign and things looked sketchy enough that he really didn't need a bad one. "I want you to stay with the boat," he told her. "Keep hunkered down and if there's any shooting move down to the far side of the island and anchor as close as you can to the shore. Don't wait more than fifteen minutes for us. If we don't make it by then, just…just head back home."

"But it'll be okay," Mike said. "We're on a trading mission. People respect that." It was a fine lie that calmed Jenn's sense of rising panic. Generally, people didn't respect strangers coming unannounced through their gates after sunset.

Slow and carefully, Mike maneuvered the *Calypso* almost to the edge of the island near the canal. They were only a few feet away when there came that soft rasping sound as the keel ground on the riverbed. With M4s in hand and crossbows across their backs, the two men leapt out of the boat.

The icy water came to their chests, turning them numb from the nipples down. Together they pushed the *Calypso* away from the bank and out a little further into the river. It floated past them. "Good luck," Jenn said.

Stu worried they needed all the luck they could get. It was one thing showing up uninvited in Sacramento—they were neighbors, after a sort—but these island people were utter strangers. And strange strangers at that. He couldn't help wonder what sort of weirdos would live in a wasteland like this.

They ducked under the arch and found a muddy trail with muddy prints, fresh and human. They were the only things fresh. There was a strong scent of urine and feces coming from the canal which was a stagnant stew that had their stomachs rolling. They hurried through the wall to a little slope leading to someone's backyard. The canal was lined with houses, some which had been there from before and others of the mobile sort which had been dragged up the banks sometime in the last twelve years.

They all looked utterly miserable. Whatever paint had been on the houses wasn't just faded, it was gone, turning everything into a uniform grey color. This included the shingled roofs. These weren't just weathered, they had been eaten away exposing the roof itself. In places this had been eaten away, too and there were tarps held down by bricks or cinderblocks.

"What do you think?" Mike asked. "Do we just pick one and knock?"

"Would a doctor actually live here? In all this? Maybe we should look around. Maybe there's a nice area that…" He was cut off by a high, piercing cackle. It was a woman, though Stu pictured a crone with warts and yellowed teeth.

"I get the feeling there isn't a nice part," Mike whispered. "Let's get away from this canal. It's awful."

Stu was all for the idea. They trudged up the hill which was covered in dead grass. Passing between two mobile homes, both of which leaked light through cracks in the walls, they came to a trash-lined road that paralleled the canal. There were more mobile homes lined up along the other side of the road. Beyond these were empty fields where nothing grew.

Everything was crap as far as the eye could see.

"Let's go with that house," Stu said, pointing at the largest home in sight. In the before, it had probably been worth close to a million dollars. Now he wouldn't trade a bullet for it. They were passing another of the shoddy little homes when someone coughed not ten feet away. It was a lung-scraping cough that sounded like it was pulling up something big.

They both jumped, pointing their rifles at a shadow of a man. He cocked an ear. "Someone dere?" he asked, in a quavering voice. "Who dat? Middie?"

"No," Stu said softly, stepping closer. "We're just looking to do some trading."

"Hmmm," the man said and then coughed again. This time he spat. "Trading or stealing? Hmm? Traders don't noways come out at night. Only raiders come in the night. Dats in the bible. You can look it up."

Stu nodded. "Most of the time you'd be right, but we're not here to take anything. We're looking for medicine and we're willing to trade for it. We have..."

The man let out a bark of laughter that turned into one of his awful wet coughs. After spitting out something that sounded like it had the size and consistency of a crushed frog, he said, "Medicine? Dere's no medicine what'll cure us. You knows dat as well as any, so why pretend?"

He was sick, that was obvious even in the dark, but with what, Stu couldn't tell just by a cough. "We're not normal traders. We came up out of San Francisco looking for medicine and a doctor." Any doctor would do and if the girl doctor was just a myth or a joke, he didn't need to be laughed at.

"Y'all gots problems, too? I guess the fallout got 'round just like I knew it would. Well, if so, ain't no doctor gonna clear up what you got a-coming." He struck a match to a homemade cigarette. Mike drew in a sharp breath. The man had wet black holes where his eyes should've been and there were several odd bulges the size of golf balls pressing up under the skin of his grey face.

"Wh-what's wrong with you?" Mike asked, leaning back.

The man, who wasn't nearly as old as his voice made him seem, snorted bringing up something green. "The fallout from the bombs got me same as ever-body else." Mike looked to Stu who shrugged; he didn't know what fallout was either. Somehow the man sensed their ignorance. "Y'all came up the river, didn't y'all? Y'all saw what them bombs did to the land, right? Well, it's doing the same to us, only slower."

"I'm sorry to hear that," Stu said. "I take it you tried antibiotics."

"Thems for germs. Ever-body knows that." The man paused, shrugged and grinned, showing only a few isolated teeth growing up out of red gums. "But yeah, we all did. Ya gotta try sometin, right? Ya just don't lay down and die. Hell, I fought the dead all the way up from Mobile an' I'll fight all the way into the ground."

"That's brave," Stu said. "Say, could you maybe talk to whoever's in charge for us? We have three very sick people who are desperately in need of antibiotics and a doctor."

At the question, the man went into what Stu thought was a fit that seemed to be a prelude to his death. He shook and made a gurgling sound deep in his chest. One of his hands went up and down smacking his own knee. Gradually, Stu came to realize the man was laughing.

When he could speak, he told them, "The pills are all worthless. Like all of us, dere falling apart. Dere just little bits of powder now. An' dere ain't no doctor here. Dere ain't no doctor anywheres."

At this, Stu felt gutted. His entire body sagged, drained by the disappointment. Mike wasn't ready to give up just yet. "What about the *girl doctor*? We heard she was up here."

Stu expected more laughter from the man, however he made a growly noise as a prelude to another hacking cough. "Dat's nothin' but a scam. When the fallout came a few years back and people got sick, we went to see dat girl. We went all the way to Seattle and ya know what she said? Dere ain't nothing what could be done, sorry."

He hacked up something big and spat it angrily to the ground, where the rain began to disintegrate it. "Sorry! Dat's what she says. Well, we was like you, you know desperate, an' so we's start begging but she only stares at us like we was bugs or sometin'. I gets really mad an' I start a-yellin', tellin' her 'bout the pain our folk were in, an' you know what she says to dat? *If the pain gets too bad, I suggest you kill yo-self.* Tell me that's not fuc…"

Someone in the mobile home a few feet away yanked open a window and said, "Will you shut the hell up Kyle Taylor? I swear you're always running your gums and I always have to hear it. Who are you talking to anyways?"

Stu was about to answer when Kyle held a finger to his lips. "Never you mind who it is," he said. "Go back to scratchin' your ass, Bob. It's what y'all do best." Bob grumbled and shut the window. Kyle waited a few seconds with his misshapen head cocked, before whispering, "Y'all should git gone while you can."

"Why?" Stu asked. "We haven't done anything wrong." Despite the "fallout" in the air, Stu wanted to ask at least one other person about the girl doctor. There was a good chance that Kyle was not quite right in the head. If he had lumps growing outward, he could have some growing inward as well.

"It don't matter what you done," Kyle whispered. He was now so quiet that Stu had to lean in to hear. "All dat matters is dat y'all is fresh meat. Y'all ain't tainted yet."

A cold shiver went right down Stu's back. In the post-apocalyptic world, cannibals were a reality. They weren't a story to scare the kiddies around a campfire and they weren't some far-off threat that could be easily dismissed.

"We have to get back to Jenn, now!" Mike hissed, grabbing Stu's arm and pulling him away from the mobile home.

"Y'all have a girl?" Kyle asked, a look of longing on his tortured face. "Is she young?"

There was a rusting creaking noise as Bob stepped out into the rain. He was wearing a wide-brimmed cowboy hat that cast dark shadows across his face. The poncho he wore draped over sloped shoulders made him shapeless.

"Who has a girl?" he asked, his voice couched low. "Who is that?"

He stepped closer, but stopped and did a little jump when he saw Mike's M4 pointed at him. "Get your hands up," Mike demanded.

"It's not my hands you have to be worried about," the man said, lifting them to shoulder height nonetheless. "It's my voice that should make you nervous. If I say the word you'll be surrounded by a hundred men, so be cool with that gun."

"He's cool. We all are, except you," Stu said, speaking quietly. "Now, hush up so we can work this out."

"I'll hush up when I'm good and ready," Bob said, even louder than he had been and if anything, he sounded as off-kilter as Kyle. "Do you think you scare me? Do you think a gun can possibly scare me now? Take a good look and tell me what you think." Stepping closer, he pulled off the cowboy hat.

Like the seagull they had seen earlier, his hair grew in little patches. Where he was hairless, his scalp as well as his face was covered in sores and more of the same lumps that plagued Kyle.

"Take a good long look at the freak." It was hard not to stare and Mike gaped, his lips drawn back in a look of disgust. Stu pulled his eyes away just in time to see that Bob had an ulterior motive for showing off the horror that his face had become. While his left hand held the cowboy hat out, his right had stolen into a slit cut into the side of the poncho. He had a Glock halfway out before Stu even saw it.

"Don't you…" Stu started to say but by then the gun was free and coming up. He fired his M4 from five feet away. Bob's poncho seemed to inflate as the bullet blasted through it and Bob. The gunshot was shockingly loud and the echoes from it carried on and on. Bob fell flat on his back, let out a final gurgle and died with rainwater collecting in little pools in his open eyes.

Kyle had his hands out and was waving them around. "Bob? Was that you? Who was shot?"

Stu dropped down and snatched the Glock out of Bob's stiffening fingers. "It was Bob. He's dead." That was all the explanation he had time for. Doors were opening up and down the street and people were asking: *What was that?* Or: *Hey, did someone get shot?*

It wasn't going to be long before someone noticed Bob. Stu grabbed a stunned Mike and started towards Kyle's backyard, which led to the dead field. It would have been better to head straight back to the canal only that way was filling up with curious people.

They had just gone around the side of the mobile home when someone walked over to the body and said, "Is that Bob? You do this, Kyle?"

"It weren't me. It was strangers what done it." At this Mike and Stu began to run, not in a wild sprint, but in a ground-eating jog. They moved parallel to the canal, keeping to the backyards, where they ran through a strange desolation of dead shrubbery, crumbling swings sets and above-ground pools which were now little more than giant vats of algae, mold and frequently, human excrement.

Stu glanced at Mike and saw that if the young man was afraid, he wasn't wearing it on his face. Stu wasn't afraid. Things were far from great, but he had been in far worse positions. Here they had the advantage of the dark and the rain, combined with the confusion they had left in their wake. Unless they got terribly unlucky they'd make it to the south side of the island where only a decrepit wall stood between them and safety.

The thought had just entered his mind when a bell started ringing behind them. Seconds later it was taken up by more bells all around them. Doors banged open, lanterns flared and guns were loaded. The bells were a call to arms.

"Keep your head," Stu warned, then turned back to the street that ran along the canal. People were streaming from their houses and heading in all directions. A dozen headed for a small footbridge that crossed the canal. Taking a deep breath, Stu followed them. Each had the same question on their lips: *Is this for real?*

For the most part they didn't think so. They thought it was either a drill or a false alarm.

One man joked, "Maybe Todd shot himself in his other foot." He laughed so long at his own joke that he broke into a coughing fit reminiscent of Kyle. His fit stopped him near the end of the bridge where he hung over the rail, spitting into the foul water.

His friends left him behind. Stu and Mike slowed, hoping the man would finish with his coughing and leave. Mike bent and fiddled with his bootlaces, while Stu squinted back the way they had come. There were more people coming up from behind.

"Come on," he whispered. They walked with their heads bowed, their hoods flung over their faces. When they were a few spaces from the coughing man he looked up. The cough caught in his throat as he stared, not at their faces, but at their rifles.

"Where'd you get those?" he asked in a croaking voice. Stu pushed past and the man went on, "No one's got…it's you!"

Stu looked back and saw the man had a hand on Mike's coat and was staring into his face. At almost that exact instant, there came a thud of more boots on the bridge.

With a whisper of fabric, Stu pulled his climber's axe from his belt loop. He had to kill quickly and silently, and strange as the weapon was, it was perfect for murder.

Chapter 23

Jenn Lockhart

The sound of the M4 going off came as no surprise to Jenn. She hadn't needed any signs to know trouble was coming. Nothing good or pure would ever live in such desolation. Only the weak of heart or mind would allow this to be their home.

She had been sitting in the back of the *Calypso* with her feet braced, two hands on the rope, ready to lift the anchor. Her secret fear was that it would be too heavy to lift. This proved true. She heaved on the rope which bit into her palms, burning them as the *Calypso* slid toward the arch. Jenn thought she was lifting the anchor, but she was only taking up the slack in the rope.

When the stern was directly over the anchor and the rope sank straight down into the river, Jenn fought the rope, her rangy muscles straining to heave the anchor up out of the mud. It wouldn't budge and as the precious seconds ticked away, her anxiety began to redline. She gave up.

Out swept her machete. With one swing, she split the rope and splintered the wood beneath. Immediately, the *Calypso* swung out into the stream and before she knew it, she was forty yards from the edge of the island. She wasn't used to steering with just the tiller though when she got the hang of it, she found it easier than expected and quickly got the boat back near the wall where she felt the keel sliding over submerged logs and dinging off hidden rocks.

As she moved slightly away, someone on the island rattled off a half a dozen rounds. The reply was a furious barrage.

"Oh no," she whispered, desperately afraid for Mike and Stu. She pictured them running for their lives chased by hundreds of crazy-eyed people. Fearing that she was going too slowly, she raised the mainsail only to send the boat into a spin as she misjudged the wind.

She was close to panicking now. Everything seemed to be going against her, the wind, the rain, the dark, the current and the terrible urgency of the situation that was punctuated by more gunshots.

She dropped the sail and sent the *Calypso* so close to the bank that she ran aground on a sandbar. It didn't matter. The boat was more or less where it needed to be and without an anchor, the sandbar was the best she could do. Now came the wait. She checked her watch and saw that it was ten minutes after nine. At twenty-five after the hour she was supposed to leave, only she knew she never would.

In fact, she did the opposite. She grabbed her M4 and slid out of the boat and into the icy water; she didn't even blink at the cold. Her mind was fixated on the wall and the constant thunder of gun fire. It seemed to be heading in her general direction. Still, this end of the island was a quarter mile wide and there was no time for the men to be searching around in the dark for the *Calypso*.

"Stuuuuuu!" she screamed as she slogged up to the wall. This section of the wall had been created from broken slabs of old concrete upon which newer concrete had been poured, clearly by someone inept. Sloppy didn't quite describe the work. Bizarre would be more accurate. It looked as though Salvador Dali had been consulted. Everything dripped and flowed so that the base of the wall was thicker than the top.

With rebar jutting out here and there and deep cracks in the cement, Jenn found plenty of handholds to the top where she had a good view of the southern part of the island. It had been cut up into fields, all of which were long dead. Within those fields was a running gun battle. It was almost all one-sided.

She let out another scream: "Miiiiiiiiiike!"

This shifted the angle of the battle and it started flowing towards her. Two ghostly shadows ran, stopped and shot, then ran again. Chasing them were dozens more shadows. These sprouted little flashes of fire. Even with the danger so great, she was so conscious of wasting bullets that she waited until Mike and Stu were within thirty yards of the wall and their pursuers fifty yards back before she fired three times, taking her time to re-aim between each shot.

She had no idea if she hit anything, but once the people realized they were targets, they dropped to the ground or hid behind cover.

They sent a torrent of bullets her way. Some of the bullets missed by twenty yards, sending chips of concrete flying far to her left, others passed so close that they sent chills up her spine.

Despite the near misses, she fired again and again until the return fire came so close and hot that she was covered in dust and cement chips. It seemed to take forever before Stu hissed, "We're clear." Mike was already halfway down the wall while Stu was only just swinging a leg over the wall and starting down. Even though he was only an amorphous shadow, Jenn knew right away that something had gone wrong. He seemed to be climbing using only his hands.

It was time for her to go and she started down, but with the rain turning everything slick, she lost a handhold and before she knew it she wasn't falling exactly, but sliding down the sloping wall. At the bottom, she went into a tumble that sent her into the river next to the *Calypso*.

She came up spluttering with Mike standing over her. As though she were nothing but a half-drowned cat, he picked her up and tossed into the boat. "Get the mainsail up!" he ordered, before running back to help Stu who was limping along in the shallows of the river.

It took her a second to find the right rope, but before she could haul the sheet up, she heard a scraping sound on the other side of the wall

Dropping the rope, she pulled the M4 from her back just as someone climbed over the top of the wall. She had no idea whether it was a man or woman, all she saw was a silhouette against the backdrop of the clouds. She shot it down with one pull of the trigger. It landed with an ugly thump.

"Who's next?" she yelled. "Show yourself and I'll put a bullet right between your eyes!" No one tested her, though there was a good deal of name-calling and cursing from the other side of the wall. Gradually, she lowered the rifle and pulled up the sail as Mike helped Stu into the boat. Stu was bleeding from a pair of holes in his thigh.

"Tend to him," Mike said. "I got the boat." He heaved them off the sandbar and climbed onboard. As he worked the boat away from the wall, using the wind to send them to the deepest part of the river where the current was fastest, Jenn crawled to where Stu sat, gripping his leg with both hands.

"A b-belt or a rope," he said in a quavering voice. "W-we need to t-tie it off." She had never heard him sound so weak. There was even a hint of fear in his voice that was matched by the look in his eyes. This was completely un-nerving. He had always carried himself with such quiet maturity that Jenn tended to forget he was only twenty-one. Just then he looked like a little boy.

She yanked her own belt off and was about to wrap it around his leg when she realized he was bleeding too much for a belt alone to be much use. She tore off her jacket and the sweater beneath to get to the blouse she wore under that. Without considering anything but his wound, she exposed herself to the lashing rain. Using her pocket knife, she cut the shirt in half. She then folded both pieces and pressed one to the entrance wound and the other to the exit, before wrapping both with the belt and cinching it tight.

Only then did she put her soaking wet clothes back on. When she zipped the jacket, she found Mike staring at her. He started in a guilty little spasm. Recovering, he said, "Get him into the cabin. He shouldn't be out in the cold."

Stu tried to help her by pushing with his good leg, only he was too weak, his white face swimming up out of the gloom. Straining with all her might, she managed to get him into the cabin. She shut the door against the rain and wind, but it didn't seem to help Stu who began to shiver uncontrollably in a way that didn't seem natural.

For a moment her wits left her and she was on the verge of panic. She was about to call to Mike to beg his help but was afraid the people of the island would be coming after them with boats of their own. Mike had to get them out of there as fast as possible.

"I-I can do this by myself," she whispered. Taking a deep breath, she assessed the situation. "He's just cold." The first step to getting him warm was to get him out of the clothes plastered to his shivering body. The very thought sent a new fear through her.

Because of the ease of marriage, both the Hill People and the Islanders lived a prudish existence—Jenn had never seen a grown man naked. "We have to dry you off," she told Stu and with shaking hands went to work unbuttoning his jacket and peeling away the layers he wore under it. When he was half-naked, she toweled his head, chest and shoulders.

When she went for his pants, she hesitated and used his injury as an excuse. "I'm going to cut your pants so I don't disturb the tourniquet. Is that okay?" His eyes were glazed over; he was beyond caring about modesty. She ended up using a knife to cut him out of his bloody pants, stripping him down to his underwear. "Close enough," she said, as she layered him in blankets and lit their four candles, hoping to give the cabin a little heat.

Gradually, he stopped shaking and fell into a light doze. She went out to see Mike, who was tacking back and forth on the wide river, coaxing every bit of speed out of the headwind and the current.

"What happened?" she asked. He told her the story that ended in a mad chase down the western end of the island. "Is he going to make it?" She had no idea. Her knowledge of first aid was very basic: apply pressure to the wound and clean it with alcohol.

"So, what do we do?" Jenn asked.

Mike sighed, saying, "I don't think we have a choice. The girl doctor was a fake. We can only go home and hope they take us back. And hope Stu makes it. If we get lucky with the winds we can be back in three days."

Jenn felt an utter blank at the word "home." She had no home and she had no hope. Her bad luck had only grown worse, and Stu was the latest victim of it. "We should go north," she said. "There may be no girl doctor, but there are people. Maybe they'll take us in. Maybe they're nice."

Mike slammed the rudder over. "If you had seen these people, Jenn you'd know there aren't any nice people left in the world. You're the last one. So no, I don't think we can take a chance going north." She had never seen him so angry.

"I should keep an eye on Stu," she told him. "Let me know if you need anything." She went into the cabin and found Stu unconscious, blood leaking from the makeshift bandages. They were both sopping and red. Once she had replaced them, she yanked even harder on the belt, waking Stu up briefly.

"Go back to sleep," she told him. It was all she could do. They had nothing to clean the wound with and nothing to stitch it together even if she knew how.

Stu fell back to sleep. Jenn stayed with him until the boat started rocking badly and the wind made a howling sound around the foresail. They had slipped down the Columbia River faster than she had thought possible and now they were toiling through the chop, heading out into the storm-swept Pacific.

She figured Mike would need her help, but he had already shortened sail, cleared the deck and tied himself down. She did the same as they turned south out of the mouth of the river and began mounting huge white-capped waves.

Everything was the same as it had been the night before: the cold, the dark, the rain, the howling wind and the crashing waves that threatened to sweep them out to sea every other minute. The only difference between then and now was the feeling of doom hanging over their heads. The one thing that had kept her going the night before had been the certainty that they were heading in the right direction. Now, she was afraid there was no right direction, or if there was, south wasn't it.

Every twenty minutes, she would crawl along the streaming deck to the cabin door to check on Stu, and every twenty minutes her heart crumbled just a little bit more. He wouldn't stop bleeding. Each time she went in, she changed his bandages and tied the belt a little tighter.

She had just ducked in for a third time when she heard Mike cry: "Jenn! Get out here!" Afraid that a wave had knocked him over, she rushed out and was promptly plowed over by a wave that sent her crashing into the low rail. She grabbed a rope and looped it around her waist with one hand while she held on with the other.

"Look!" Mike cried as he pushed the boom around. He pointed off the port side in the direction they had been traveling. He was coming around as fast as the *Calypso* could manage without broaching. Scattered here and there were lights on the water. It was fire.

"What are they?" she yelled over the wind.

"It's the Corsairs!"

Even though she was cold and wet, she felt the brigades of goosebumps crawl over her flesh. She squinted into the wind and saw the vague outlines of sails and prows. The Corsairs were running north, heading right at them. The fires were burning in hanging pots in an effort to keep the fleet together.

"Let go the foresail," Mike ordered when they had turned. He left the tiller and went to work on the main, letting out more of the sail. In a storm such as this, letting out more sail was close to suicide. They'd be flying by the seat of their pants on a lee shore without anyway to properly navigate. All it would take to sink them was a rogue wave or a confused gust of wind.

Still, Jenn didn't hesitate or question the order. She knew what would happen if the Corsairs caught up to them. They would take Mike as a slave, while Stu would simply be tossed overboard. Jenn could expect to be raped, passed around from man to man until she either went crazy or they made port and she was sold to some slaver.

She figured if they were caught, she would jump overboard with Stu. It would be a quick end compared to the torture they would inflict on her.

Chapter 24

Jenn Lockhart

Ignoring the danger of the elements, she went to the foresail and worked the knots with numb fingers until the sail billowed out. Seconds later, the mainsail snapped like a whip and filled.

The Corsairs had much larger boats, and if they had wished, they could have charged down on the *Calypso* and gobbled it up. Thankfully, it seemed that the Corsairs were more interested in preserving their ships than in pursuing one not very large boat.

Mike ran north with the wind. Sometimes it was like riding on a rollercoaster and if Jenn hadn't been so busy trying to stay alive, she likely would have puked her guts out a dozen times. Along with helping Mike keep the boat afloat, she also had to check on Stu who was in a bad way.

Not only was he suffering from shock due to blood loss, he was also being battered senseless by the fantastic punishment the boat was taking. When Jenn was able to look in on him, she found him crumpled in a corner with blood leaking from both holes in his leg. She changed the bandages again, afraid that the next time she came back Stu would have run out of blood.

When she came out on deck again, she looked past Mike and saw nothing but black clouds hanging over a black ocean with a fury of wind and rain flying between. The Corsairs were nowhere to be seen. "They might have doused their fires!" Mike yelled over the howling wind. "They're probably hoping we shorten sail. They'll be able to catch up if we do."

Jenn didn't think for a moment the Corsairs were out there lurking in the storm. From everything she had heard about the pirates, she knew they weren't so desperate that they would risk one of their ships in a storm like this. But if thinking they were out there kept Mike going at full speed, Jenn wasn't going to disabuse him of the idea.

Stu didn't have three days. All night long she worried over him, changing his bandages and begging him to drink water when he was lucid. He seemed to be fading when, suddenly, they slid out of the storm almost as though they had sailed into another ocean.

"He's not going to last a day," Jenn told Mike when she left him once more.

"We'll go to Seattle," he said. "Though it would help if I knew where we were." He gazed around at the ocean. It was three hours before sunrise and without landmarks or stars he had no idea where on the vast Pacific they were. Ten minutes later, they heard the distant crash of waves. Mike looked at his compass in confusion. "That's coming from the north. How is that poss…" He dug out the map Stu had handed him the day before. "I know where we are. Well, I think so. The only thing north of us is Canada. That's probably Vancouver."

He turned east, heading down the canyon-like strait that cut toward Puget Sound and Seattle. It was still windy and the gusts were almost as dangerous as they had been. What was more dangerous, was zipping along an unfamiliar waterway without a single nautical map. Mike was forced to pilot strictly by sound.

When they crept too far north, they heard the familiar thunder of waves breaking, and when they went too far south where the waves didn't amount to much more than a splash, there was only a sighing sound as water passed over sand and shells.

Once they came so close to the shore that they ran across something that made the *Calypso* shudder and they heard what sounded like a dry stick snapping. Still, Mike didn't shorten sail. Stu was fading.

They were both nervously scanning the horizons as they followed the waterway south, thinking they would be lucky to catch sight of an early morning cooking fire. The one thing they didn't expect, however was to see a sudden, magnificent blaze of lights. An entire ten-mile long island was lit up, ringed with hundreds of searchlights all pointing outward. The interior of the island also sported lights, though these were smaller.

Jenn stared open-mouthed. On a certain level, she understood that these were lights that worked through electricity, just like in the old days. This should have been a good thing. It meant the people here were living like real people, and for some reason the idea completely unnerved her.

Would they be like the people in the before that she saw in her magazines? Would they be perfect and pretty? And what would they think of her? She looked down at herself: blood-stained jeans that were tied at the waist with a length of rope. Over this she wore layers of mismatching boys shirts that had been wet for days and smelled like unwashed dog. Her deep brown hair, that was normally clean and always brushed, looked like a ragged mop sitting on her dirty brow.

The perfect people on their perfect island would look at her with disgust and she wouldn't blame them. She didn't even have a hairbrush and there was no time to stop for clean clothes or to bathe. An intense sense of shame stole over her and she slunk down, not even realizing she was squatting in a foot of water. She was already so wet and cold that a little more water went unnoticed.

As Mike piloted the *Calypso* down the length of the island, he seemed dazed. "Those are porch lights. Can you believe it?"

She couldn't remember a time when everyone had porch lights; in fact the very concept wasn't just foreign to her, it was foolish. Lights at night attracted the dead. Everyone knew that. If she lived on the island she would never use porch lights.

Not that the people there had much to fear. They had built a wall a few feet back from the water's edge. Unlike the island of cannibals, where the wall had been thrown together piecemeal, this wall had been built by a master builder. It was thirty feet tall and five feet wide. There was a walkway set three feet from the top from which people could shoot, and every fifty yards were towers made of reinforced concrete placed to allow for converging fields of fire.

The island was impregnable. No horde that Jenn had ever heard of could take it, and no human force, not even if all the Corsairs were gathered together could hope to defeat the wall.

When the search lights pinpointed them, she felt exposed and tiny. "I should check on Stu," she said, and fled into the cabin. She found him unconscious and no matter what she did, she couldn't wake up him up. His heart rate was thready and weak.

They needed more speed, but the wind was sketchy and it seemed to take forever to find a break in the wall. By the time they did, the sun was over the horizon and they could see dozens of people watching them from the walls. Most looked like ordinary people, however there were soldiers with scoped rifles among them and, every once in a while, one would put his weapon to his shoulder and use the scope to inspect them. This was very unnerving, and Jenn did her best not to cringe when it happened.

At about eight in the morning they finally made it to a tiny harbor. Across the mouth of it were a series of towers rising out of the water and between the towers was a stout chain, the links of which must have weighed twenty pounds apiece. There was also a double wall of fencing that hung above and below the waterline. A gate was opened between two of the towers and Mike steered them through and toward a dock where a few small sailboats were moored. None of them were even as large as the *Puffer*.

On the dock was a squad of soldiers, waiting with weapons at the ready.

Since a fight would have been suicide, Jenn had already unloaded their weapons and set them aside. "We need a doctor!" she yelled to the soldiers when they were fifty yards out. "We have a man who's been shot!"

Two men darted away but they didn't go far and they didn't get a doctor. They came hurrying back with a stretcher just as Mike slid the *Calypso* along the dock. He tossed lines to the soldiers and the boat was made fast.

Just as Jenn figured, the people on the island were very much like the people from before. Everyone wore clean clothes and unscuffed shoes. The men wore their hair short and almost all were newly-shaven. Those who had beards kept them neat and trim. The women wore makeup, had styled hair and long, sharp fingernails. For the most part, they wore dresses and when they did wear jeans or slacks they looked practically brand new.

Jenn felt utterly shabby compared to them. She was helped off the boat by a stern-faced soldier who then frisked her. He pulled her aside as Mike received the same treatment.

Two of the bigger soldiers, and all of them seemed very big and strong to Jenn, went on board with the stretcher and hauled Stu out. "Was it the Corsairs?" the soldier next to Jenn asked. At the sight of Stu, the stern look had receded. He was a young man of twenty-two or so, handsome with ruddy cheeks and a cleft chin. He was so handsome and clean that Jenn had trouble looking him in the eye.

"No," she answered after a touch of hesitation. "It was cannibals up the Columbia River. Can I ask a question? Is it true you have a doctor here?"

His jaw clenched briefly. "We have something." It was such a cryptic reply that Jenn had no idea what he meant. Did he mean they had a witchdoctor who would cast bones and offer sacrifices? Or was it a saw-bones like the one the Santas had; he only did amputations and more often than not, his patients died from gangrene.

There was no time for a followup question. Stu was being rushed away. Mike, Jenn and their guards followed along, heading inland. Even though it was October, the island was robustly green and everywhere Jenn looked there were gardens and makeshift farms. There were people tending those gardens, and there were others walking here and there. In the fifteen minutes it took them to walk to what had once been an urgent care facility, Jenn saw many, many hundreds of people. Not since the early years on Alcatraz had Jenn seen so many people.

It was bewildering, especially how they were acting. It was as if they didn't have a care in the world. No one carried weapons of any sort, no one cared about noise protocols and no one worried about how much smoke was belching from their chimneys. They seemed unaware of just how dangerous the world was.

They were pleasant, too and many waved to Jenn. When they entered the urgent care facility, there were two men in blue scrubs waiting for them, one of whom took a look at Stu and said, "Oh, the poor dear," in a voice that was more like a woman's than a man's.

The stretcher bearers took Stu to a back bay and set him down on one of a dozen empty beds. While one of the men stuck a needle in his arm and hooked it to a bag of murky-looking yellow fluid, the other addressed the gunshot wound, saying, "This is bad. It might have just nicked the femoral artery. Barry, you better run that full bore."

Biting his lip, Mike tried to get closer. "Is he going to make it?"

The soft-spoken one named Barry answered with a shrug. "It depends."

That was hardly a satisfactory answer to Jenn, who asked, "On what?"

The two men shared a look; Barry swallowed loudly before answering, "It depends on what sort of mood the doctor is in. If she's in a good mood, I think he might make it, so make sure you smile and act polite when she comes in."

"We will," Jenn replied. "We're very grateful for anything you guys can do for us. And we do have…" She broke off as a side door banged open and a teenage girl walked into the clinic. She wasn't much taller than Jenn, though she looked it because of her hair. Her brown hair wasn't messy or mussed, it was in a wild state, as if she had never used a brush in her life.

Her Converse high-tops, her tight jeans, her t-shirt and leather jacket were all deep black. Where Jenn was pale, the girl was purest white, as if she had been carved out of a single piece of alabaster. Set in this white face were huge blue eyes that stared at Jenn with unsettling intensity. If it weren't for that intensity, Jenn would have considered her eyes beautiful. Instead, she was frightened of them and dropped her chin after only a second.

Without looking at Stu, the girl stepped lightly around the room, taking in each of them, the two men in the blue scrubs and the guards included. No one except Mike could hold her gaze any longer than Jenn had. Mike stared straight back at her as seconds passed. As far as Jenn knew, these could have been Stu's last seconds.

"Excuse me?" Jenn asked in a whisper. "Are you the 'girl' doctor?" The blue eyes shot back to Jenn and she did her best not to look away even though she began shaking. She had no idea why she was shaking and she had no idea why she was afraid of this girl who was maybe eighteen. "W-We don't have much, but we'll give you everything we have if you can save him."

"And if I can't save him I get nothing?" the girl asked. "Not even a base hourly wage? Even a menial laborer should be able to look forward to compensation of some sort, otherwise I'd be acting the part of a thrall, don't you think?"

Jenn began to blink in confusion. She didn't understand the words: base, wages, compensation or thrall. The only thing she understood was that she was likely ruining any chance for Stu. "You can have everything we have, right now. It's yours, just please help."

For a moment, the girl looked as confused as Jenn felt, then a smile spread across her face. "Oh, don't listen to her," she said. "That's just Eve being mean again. We don't need your belongings, I'm sure. Unless, of course you brought a multi-point NIR system with you? I could really use one."

Jenn couldn't seem to stop blinking. None of what this girl was saying made any sense. "I-I don't think we did."

"Don't worry about it," the girl said, turning from Jenn and finally looking at Stu. "It was a joke." After glancing at the hole in Stu's leg and saying, *Hmmm*, she produced a stethoscope and listened briefly to his heart and lungs. "Barry, get a second line in him, normal saline. Ricardo, why don't I have sterile gloves? Didn't I teach you to always have gloves ready?"

Before Ricardo could say anything, the girl said, "Maybe he didn't have time. You're being too hard on him, Jillybean."

The girl who might have been named either Jillybean or Eve looked back at the stretcher bearers and answered herself, "Yes. Their respirations are still at an elevated rate. I shouldn't have missed that. I blame the girl and her handsome friends. So, which one do you like?"

There was a long pause before the man who was acting as a guard nudged Jenn and said in a low tone, "*Jillybean* asked you a question."

"Which one do I like? Do you mean which one of my friends do I like?" She cast a quick glance up at Mike but before she could answer Ricardo slid back into the room with a tray on which were latex gloves and a variety of surgical tools, none of which Jenn had ever seen before.

Eve or Jillybean, or whatever the girl's name was, seemed to forget all about Jenn. She stripped off her coat and pulled on the gloves. "Let's go, Ricardo. Let's have the retractors." The girl bent over Stu's leg, thankfully blocking the surgical process from view. Jenn didn't think she could handle seeing much more blood. A pool of it had collected beneath the gurney.

"Here we go," the girl said, after ten minutes. "You see that, Sadie. It got the femoral just like we thought. This guy's lucky he's cute."

Jenn had no idea what being cute had to do with whatever a "femoral" was. And there was no way for her to know who Sadie was.

"You never did answer my question," the girl said, without looking back. "Though I suppose you didn't need to. You're from San Francisco. That much is obvious and so is the fact that you're engaged to that handsome statue next to you. That guilty look you two shared told me that.

What's not as obvious is why you're here." Now, she turned to look back at Jenn who wilted under the intensity of the gaze.

To Jenn's relief, the girl only stared for a few seconds before turning back to Stu.

The relief was short-lived as the girl went on. "You aren't related. None of you are. Which makes banishment an unlikely reason for you to be this far north. You care for this man, though, that was easy enough to read. You think of him as a brother and…oh wait, I get it now. Of course. I must be slipping in my old age. You're here because of the signs."

She threw back her head and laughed wildly, making everyone uncomfortable. "Oh, those foolish signs. This world has become an anthropologist's wet dream. So much madness disguised as rational thought. Religious zealots on one hand, telepaths on the other. Warlords and pirates and race wars and everything in between. So much madness! And they call me crazy! And they're right too. I don't hide my insanity. You see it, don't you?" She paused long enough for Jenn to swallow loudly. "Why do you always hesitate when I ask you questions? What's your name?"

Jenn always hesitated because she never knew who the girl was talking to and what she was talking about. "Jenn Lockhart."

"Okay, Jenn, so what do you think? Am I crazy or has the world come apart so terribly that you can't tell one way or the other?"

The girl had stopped working and Jenn was sure her answer would be the deciding factor whether she would start again or not. The girl *was* crazy, but Jenn didn't think it was something she could say; nor would a lie do. The girl would see right through it.

Jenn ended up not saying anything which caused the girl to grow angry. It was as though the temperature in the room dropped twenty degrees. "Why aren't you answering? Is it because you really do think I'm crazy? Is it? IS IT!" She turned now, and in her red-stained hands was a bloody scalpel. Frightened almost out of her wits, Jenn sketched a sign of the cross which only made the girl angrier. "God won't help you unless you tell me right now. Tell me or else! And Jillybean won't be able to stop me. Tell me…"

"Eve," a soft voice said. A small, thin man had entered the room from behind them. He had pretty, baby-blue eyes, while the rest of his face was a ruin of craggy scars. Along with two fingers on his left hand, he was missing an eyebrow and half of one ear. The scars looked like they had been made by one of the dead, but that wasn't possible. The man would have become one of *them* if he had been bitten.

"Leave her alone, Eve," the man said, his voice still soft. With his penny-loafers, khaki pants and a blue sweater vest, he looked like someone's dad, except for his face, that is.

The girl ground her teeth, gripping the scalpel until her fist shook. The man ignored this. He limped to Stu's bedside and glanced at the mess. "Tell me, *Jillybean*, what are the twelve cranial nerves?"

"There are thirteen, Neil," the girl replied in a snarl.

"Okay there are thirteen," Neil said. "What is the seventh?"

The girl's mouth opened, hung there for a moment before she blinked and answered, "That's the easiest of all. It's the facial nerve. Next time go with the ninth. It's the glossopharyngeal. Even if Eve looked it up she would never remember it."

"If she can't remember that, how am I supposed to?" Neil asked giving her a warped smile. "Now, why don't you do what you can for this man while I look after our guests." He turned to Jenn and Mike. "We should leave. Unplanned surgery can be stressful and she doesn't handle stress very well. Though this wasn't bad."

Chapter 25

Jenn Lockhart

That wasn't bad? As the three of them walked out of the clinic and into bright sunshine, the words bounced around Jenn's head without finding purchase. She had never heard anything so ridiculous in her life. The girl was out and out crazy.

"I don't know if anyone's welcomed you officially to Bainbridge. If not, welcome," the scarred man said, putting out his hand. "My name is Neil Martin. I'm an advisor to the governor…"

Mike had ignored the hand and now he interrupted Neil, "What's wrong with her?"

Neil didn't answer right away. He gazed at the two of them, judging them. This went on for long seconds before he said, "Okay, I usually save the Jillybean exhibit for last, but I guess it's a little late for that. Most people would say she is schizophrenic." When Mike and Jenn only shrugged in unison, Neil tried to explain, saying, "She has multiple personality disorder."

Mike's face clouded over with doubt. "I don't think we have that where we're from. Is it catchy?"

"Catchy?" Neil laughed easily. "No. The problem is all up here." He tapped his forehead. "When this all started, she was six. Her dad got scratched and died, and her mom, well, she just gave up. She went to bed that night and never left it again. She slowly withered to nothing. She's still in the bed. I've seen her body."

Neil's smile had faded and for a few moments, he stared off at nothing. Presently, he shook his head and the smile came back. "Either way, Jillybean was alone for a year surrounded by the dead. Every time I think about that,

214

I seriously get the chills. I don't know how she survived. I don't know how she didn't starve to death. What I do know is that her mind fractured. It's broken into pieces. There are personalities or 'people' living up there."

"Are they real people?" Mike asked. "Like ghosts or something?"

"I suppose it's best to think of them as real people. If for some reason you find yourself talking to Eve try to be very polite and agree with everything she says."

Mike's eyes narrowed. "Why, what will happen? Something bad?" He didn't wait for Neil to answer. "Of course it's bad. Those were grown men afraid of a girl. Hell, you're afraid of her."

"I am," Neil replied honestly.

"Is Stu in danger?" Jenn asked. She had been afraid of Jillybean from the second she walked into the clinic. It had been a gut reaction and now that same gut was churning. Neil hesitated and that was answer enough for Mike who turned around and began stalking back to the front doors.

Neil grabbed him. "He'll be in more danger if you go in there. I told you that surgery is stressful for her. Operating on someone isn't like it was before. She doesn't have a trained staff, she doesn't have access to real drugs, and she doesn't have the proper equipment. People die…a lot, and she blames herself and what's worse other people blame her, too. It's completely unfair, but they do."

"So, what are you saying?" Mike asked. "Stu is going to die?"

"I'm saying that from what I saw, your friend's only hope is Jillybean. Let her do her job and pray for the best."

Mike, looking exhausted, hung his head, while Jenn did the opposite. She gazed out, looking for a sign. A crow winged by, flared and landed on the gutter of a church across the road. Jenn drew in a sharp breath because, as everyone knew, a single crow meant bad luck. Before she could release the breath, however a second crow joined the first.

In that split second her fears dissolved, leaving her with a feeling of shaky relief. She grinned at the birds before turning to Mike. "It'll be okay. The signs are with us." When he hesitated, she said, "The same signs that guided us here are telling me this now."

The lines around Mike's eyes eased. "Really? If you say so." His shoulders slumped as the tension which had been with them all night drained out of him. "That girl is just sort of…" He paused, glancing at Neil. "Sort of odd. How did she become a doctor? Did the old doctor teach her?"

"I think it's best to show you." Neil started walking along a west-bound road. "I have to check on some things before I take you to see the governor anyway." Unlike all the other roads Jenn had walked on in the last five years, this one was smooth. Where the asphalt had cracked, it had been filled in with tar. On either side were young fruit trees growing among the stumps of old conifers.

Although the road was wide, they kept to one side to allow bicycles to zip by. Everyone slowed to say good morning to Neil and to stare at Jenn and Mike, making Jenn acutely aware that she still had a dirty, vagabond look about her. Neil saw her discomfort.

"We'll get you cleaned up in a bit. First, we have to go to the school. Well, it's not *the* school. Are there a lot of children where you're from?"

"Twenty-four," Mike answered before his breath hitched slightly. Jenn understood: if the populations of both Alcatraz and the hilltop were counted there were twenty-four children but that was only if Aaron was still alive. She found herself trying to count how many days they had been gone, but their time on the *Calypso* felt like one great blur and the best she could manage was between five and seven.

The number seemed to surprise Neil. "Only twenty-four? We have over two hundred children. About a third go to a school about two miles north of here. The rest go to a school down by the harbor, but…okay here we are."

In front of them was a small complex of brick buildings; the sign out front read: *Woodward Middle School*. It wasn't a normal school. The windows had heavy bars set across them, while most of the doors were welded shut. "Who goes here?" Jenn asked.

"This is where Jillybean goes to school," Neil said, going to the front doors and unlocking a heavy chain. He had to key two more locks to open the door. He didn't hurry inside; he paused, listening to low moans echoing throughout the building.

"Why do you have zombies in there?" Mike demanded, his green eyes flashing. "Is this some sort of trick?"

Neil shook his head. "If we wanted you dead, we could have killed you before you docked. No, this is no trick. You asked how Jillybean became a doctor and I'm showing you." He went inside and flipped on a switch, filling the halls with light. He paused again. "Hello?" he called out. "Yoo-hoo!"

"We're good," he said, and began limping down the hall. As he went, he checked the doors to the classrooms to see if they were locked. At the fifth door, he glanced first at a chart hanging on the wall, then into a small peephole drilled through the door. Only then did he unlock it.

The rich rotting smell of the dead struck Jenn, causing her nose to wrinkle. Nervously, she poked her head into the doorway and saw an eight-footer chained to a steel table. The zombie strained against the heavy chains.

"She had one that tore its own hand off once," Neil said, mildly. He walked into the room unconcerned about the creature. "This is how she became a surgeon. When she was eight-years old she taught herself using the living dead. Since then she practices on them at least once a week to keep her skills sharp." Now that Neil had pointed this out, Jenn saw that the hundreds of scars covering the zombie were almost all perfectly straight.

Jenn was floored by the very idea that a child would or could learn to be a surgeon on their own. Mike was less impressed. "You say her skills are sharp but you also said a lot of people die when she operates on them. Which is it?"

"It's both," Neil said, turning off the light and locking the door behind him. "I also said things aren't like they were before. She doesn't have access to MRI machines or

CAT scanners or any of that. The best she has is a portable X-ray machine that's always in need of one part or another. It's been almost twelve years since the apocalypse began. Things break down. Still, for the simple surgeries like removing a gall bladder or repairing a gunshot wound to the leg, she's excellent."

"What about a gunshot wound to the chest?" Mike asked quietly, as if afraid of the answer.

Neil grimaced. "Oh, boy. I've seen her operate on two people with gunshot wounds to the chest and both were successful, however, both those surgeries occurred very quickly after the incident. I'm no expert, but it's pretty safe to say that the longer the delay, the less chance of success."

"What about antibiotics?" Jenn asked. "Do yours still work?"

"They do, only I can't just give you any without talking to the governor. Let's go get you cleaned up so I can take you down to city hall." Before they left, he went to the gym locker room where three of the dead were chained to the wall. Two of them were normal-sized, about seven and a half feet each, however the third was the biggest zombie Jenn had ever seen.

It was even larger than Frankenstein. It stood almost ten feet tall with shoulders as broad as a kitchen table. It was also whole. No one had torn chunks from it or bitten off its fingers or parts of its face. It had huge rolling muscles and an expansive gut. The chains on its wrists and neck could have held back a Humvee.

"Is she going to practice on these ones?" Jenn asked, in a whisper. She had never been this close to the dead before and not been in mortal peril. Her breath fluttered in her chest and she couldn't feel her feet.

Neil picked up a push broom and gestured at the smaller two. "Those ones, yeah, but not Igor. She's had him since we came to Bainbridge. It was her theory even back then, back when the dead were normal-sized, that under optimum conditions the dead would continue to grow. She doesn't see an upper limit."

"They'll get even bigger than that?" Mike asked.

"Yep," Neil said, using the broom to shovel piles of grass, beans, and leftovers at the dead. The beasts were so intent on getting to the three humans and tearing them to pieces that they ignored the food. "The rate of growth on that one has slowed but he's grown every year since she carted him over from the city."

Jenn wondered if she had heard Neil correctly. "She brought them over? And people let her? There would've been a riot back on the hilltop if I tried anything like that."

Neil strained to keep his grin in place as he pushed the last of the food over. "It's really not the best subject to talk about. Why don't you tell me where you're from?"

Mike immediately stiffened, and Jenn's lips pressed together. Neither of them knew Neil well enough to divulge that sort of information. "Originally?" Jenn asked, playing stupid. "I was born in Ogden. I don't know where that is or if it's still a place. Probably not. Mike was born…where? Oma-who?"

"Omaha," he corrected. Quickly changing the subject, he asked, "Weren't we going to get cleaned up before we saw your governor?"

Neil didn't pester them with any more questions. He locked up the school and the three of them walked back towards the harbor, stopping twice. The first time, was at a little bungalow of a house. It was painted lime green with clashing red shutters.

An older man of about thirty with flaming red hair and a spattering of freckles, answered Neil's knock. He was very close to Mike's size and build and much to Mike's embarrassment, Neil asked the man for a set of clothes. "Something nice, if you don't mind, Eddie. They just got in this morning after what must have been a harrowing journey, and I'm going to take them to see the governor."

"Of course," Eddie said. "Come in, come in. Gina! We have guests!"

"I'm not really in a proper state to receive guests," a woman called down from an upstairs room.

Eddie turned a slightly deeper shade of his natural pink color. "It's Neil Martin and he has two newcomers to the island. I think they'd be fine if you came down wearing nothing but a pillowcase."

"We really don't want to be any trouble," Mike said. This fell on deaf ears as Eddie pulled them into his living room and pushed them down onto a sofa. He said something about tea and dashed out of the room. A moment later Gina hurried down the stairs. She was as dark as Eddie was light. She was skinny as a rail but had a wide set of hips made seemingly wider by the toddler she held. The baby, with his curly hair, his freckles and his soft brown color looked as though he had gotten an exact genetic split from mother and father.

"Hi, hi. I'm Gina and this is Bobby. Have you eaten? Did Eddie offer you anything to eat? Wait, of course he didn't. Eddie!" she cried as she rushed out of the room, Bobby bouncing on her hip. Somewhat out of breath, she was back in blink. She held out her hand to them.

Jenn, who was reeling from the commotion, was suddenly shy and it was up to Mike to introduce them.

Gina was about to shake Jenn's hand when she noticed the dried blood. "Neil, what's wrong with you?" she demanded. "They can't see the governor in this condition." She thrust Bobby at Neil before pulling Jenn and Mike to the stairs. "We'll get you fixed right up with showers straight away. By then I'll have some decent clothes for you both."

Jenn felt as though she was being held hostage by the woman's enthusiasm and energy. She was shown to a hall bathroom where the tub was filled with brightly colored plastic toys. As Gina began picking them out, Jenn said, "I don't want to be a burden. I can draw water if you show me where the well is."

Gina looked lost for a moment before a wide smile lit up her face. "Oh no, dear. We don't have well water. We get ours from the tap." She pointed at the faucet jutting from the wall above the bathtub. "Use the shampoo and conditioner. Whatever you need."

She handed Jenn a towel and breezed out of the room. The towel wasn't just soft, it smelled...well, Jenn couldn't describe the scent, except for perhaps perfumed. Putting it to her nose, she breathed it in. It was a wonderful, clean smell and she set it aside with great reluctance.

She faced the tub as if she had never seen one before. She had been told that in the old days people got their water from the faucets, but where that water came from no one seemed to know. She assumed the water would be cold and as Gina and Eddie were already going to so much trouble, Jenn figured she would grit her teeth and bear it.

Turning one of the knobs confirmed this. A rush of cold water came from the faucet. Jenn collected some in the palm of her hand and tasted it. "Oh, wow." It was the cleanest water she had ever tasted. The water back on the hilltop always had a slight earthen tang to it. This was so clean that she stuck to her mouth to the faucet and drank until her belly gurgled.

All that running water reminded her that she had to pee. She lifted the lid on the toilet tank and saw there was water there as well. Grinning like a child, she used the bathroom and when she flushed, she marveled as the water filled back up. It was sort of like magic.

In fact, it was so close to magic that she had to test one more thing before she got in the tub. The light switch on the wall drew her. The rumor was that a weak form of lightning made the lights work. Using just the tip of one finger, she flicked the switch up. Just like that, the room was bathed in a stark white light. She turned the light on and off a few times before reaching up to touch the bulb. It was hot enough to burn.

Stripping out of her dirt and blood-stained clothes she eased into the cold water of the tub. Although there were only a few inches of water she began shivering in seconds. She washed up quickly and was about to get out when she saw the word "Cold" on one of the handles.

Her eyes went to the other which read "Hot." Turning the handle brought out a rush of hot water. "Definitely magic," she said, swishing the water about to even the temperature. It was good magic, at least. She lulled in the sudden warmth and would have fallen asleep in the tub if Gina hadn't knocked on the door.

"I have clothes for you out here."

This got Jenn moving. Gina was nearly a foot taller than Jenn and the only thing she had that came close to fitting her were a black cocktail dress and a pair of pink flipflops. As ridiculous as the outfit was, it was still better than the filthy "boy" clothes she'd been wearing.

Eddie made omelets for breakfast with real chicken eggs, strips of fried pork meat and real cheese. Jenn was as famished as a wolf and had to force herself to stop after two servings. Mike, dressed in jeans and green woolen sweater, his clean blonde hair pulled back in a simple braid, couldn't say no to a third helping.

They ate and ate, which helped to deflect questions. Eddie and Gina were filled with curiosity. They wanted to hear all about Mike and Jenn's journey, from the ocean to the Corsairs, and they wanted to know where the two were from, how old they were, if they had brothers and sisters or if their parents were still alive.

Mike did a good job of deflecting the questions and near the end of the meal brought it around to Jillybean at which point Gina and Eddie plastered fake smiles across their lips and Neil abruptly said, "I'm afraid we have to go."

Very quickly they were back on the road heading south towards the harbor. Neil remarked, "We could go into any house on the island and receive the same welcome. Is that how it is where you're from?"

"Sort of," Mike said. "We don't have all the stuff that you have. Like the eggs and cheese and the hot wall water. But the people are generous to strangers…proper strangers that is. Not everyone where we're from is nice. There are slavers nearby. Do you have slavers here?"

"Not on Bainbridge. The Corsairs are the worst, but they don't give us any trouble. This is probably the safest place in the world."

And yet everyone's afraid of a girl named Jillybean, Jenn thought. The place was perfection except for that one little problem. As if the thought of the girl had summoned her, Jillybean came out of the woods to their left. At first, the girl in black didn't see the three of them as her lion's mane of hair hid everything in her periphery. She was deep in conversation—with herself. When she did notice them, her eyes went right to Jenn and her smile was almost angelic; a far cry from the frightening madness she had displayed earlier.

"I take it the surgery went well?" Neil asked as the girl came up and began walking beside Jenn.

Jillybean shrugged. "Yes, he's sedated and sleeping. He's lucky, the wound track was remarkably small. If the bullet hadn't nicked the femoral, I would have been done an hour ago. Laparoscopic suturing is a such a pain in the ass." This last she said to Jenn.

"Right, I guess it probably is," Jenn said. She had no idea.

"She guesses, my ass," Jillybean replied, speaking out of the side of her mouth. She then started as if the words had been a surprise to her. "Um, I mean that would be a good guess if we had to guess, ha-ha. But we didn't, so that's good, right?"

"Maybe you should go decompress," Neil suggested, gently. "Or take another pill."

She shook her head. "My liver function tests haven't been good. It wouldn't be safe. And you know I can't take any of the other pills when I have a patient." She turned to Jenn again. "They make me all jittery. Your friend might still need me if there are complications."

"Do you think there will be?" Jenn asked, nervously. "The signs say he's going to be okay, but sometimes I read them wrong."

"The signs," Jillybean scoffed out of the side of her mouth. "What an idiot." Jill's eyes went wide before she turned away and started whispering angrily to herself.

Perhaps as a distraction, Neil gestured to a large building surrounded by narrow strips of rolling farmland. It had been the clubhouse to a swanky golf course. Now it was the City Hall. With Jillybean trailing, still in a heated conversation with herself, they went inside where they were shown into a room where the walls were of polished wood and the carpets were soft and deep.

Three women were in the room. Neil introduced them, but Jenn was so overwhelmed she didn't catch any of their names. Although older, the women looked like they belonged in one of her magazines. They were all tall and pretty and their clothes seemed to have been tailored to their bodies.

And yet they were nothing compared to the governor.

Jenn had expected it to be a man, but it was a woman with long blonde hair. She was even prettier than the other three. She almost looked like an angel. "Hi there. My name is Deanna Grey. How can the people of Bainbridge help you?"

In her silly dress and even sillier flip flops, Jenn wanted to hide. She even took a step behind Mike, who seemed nearly as tongue-tied as Jenn. He started to stutter when Jillybean spoke for them. "They're here for me. They want me to go with them."

Chapter 26

Jenn Lockhart

Although there was a large polished desk with a comfortable leather-bound chair behind it taking up a good chunk of the room, Deanna didn't retreat behind it. She leaned against the front of the desk, her long legs canted out in front of her as she nodded her head, considering Jillybean's words.

"They want you to go with them? Did they tell you this?"

"They didn't need to. The *signs* all pointed at it." Jillybean gave Jenn a wink as she said this. Jenn didn't know if this was a joke at her expense or an attempt to be friendly. She gave the girl a weak smile just in case it was the latter.

The smile Deanna gave to Jillybean was much more practiced. It was a confident, reassuring smile. "The signs? Since when do you look for signs? I thought you were all about observation and deductive reasoning."

"That hasn't changed. I only reference 'signs' because of our new friend. She's undoubtedly from San Francisco where the occult holds sway over monotheism, science and common sense."

Deanna turned to Mike and Jenn. "Is this true? Are you from San Francisco?" They both hesitated, their ingrained instinct to protect their group was too strong. Deanna didn't get upset. She said to Jillybean, "I'm sure you won't mind laying out your conclusions for us." This caused one of the women to smirk.

Jillybean's blue eyes flashed at the smirk, but only for a second. She swallowed loudly as if gulping down Eve, the strange creature inside of her. "I don't know what you're smiling about, Joslyn. Hasn't your tongue taught us that observations are always preferable to a verbal statement?"

Joslyn looked as though she wanted to say something, but kept her lips pressed together, a touch of fear shading her eyes.

Satisfied, Jillybean said, "That they're from San Francisco is obvious. Aside from their pagan beliefs, this one's rope belt," she gestured at Mike, "was tied with what looked like an *Alpine Butterfly Bend* rather than a granny knot or a simple bow suggesting he's a practiced mariner. Yet he lacks the facial tattoos of a Corsair and the religious paraphernalia of the Guardians, the two dominant seafaring people along the west coast. They could be from further south, but judging by my patient's facial hair and the accumulation of sea salt on his body I would say they've been traveling for approximately five days. That puts their starting point within the vicinity of San Fran."

She glanced at Jenn who nodded slowly. "She's right. We're from San Francisco. But we didn't lie."

Jillybean laughed suddenly and pushed Jenn's shoulder, playfully. "I don't think you could lie if you tried, Jenn Lockhart. You're an open book, which is very delightful, but no I can't go with you."

"We haven't asked you to," Mike said, warily, eyeing her as though she were a street performer who might take his wallet if he blinked.

"You didn't need to. I saw your reaction when Eve mentioned 'signs.' You both looked petrified. Kind of like you do right now. You're afraid that I can look into your soul, and maybe I can. Someone is hurt. And I don't mean your friend, either. He was shot yesterday, but something drove you from your home days ago. You looked for signs to guide you, but why? What happened? No one gazes up at the stars one day and decides to cross a pirate-filled ocean in a rinky-dink little boat. There was a reason you needed guidance."

She stepped closer to Jenn, their eyes locking. Jenn couldn't seem to break away as Jillybean went on, "Was it a diplomatic mission? No, you're all too young. Was it to trade? No, your boat is too small to carry much of anything. Was it because someone got hurt?" This time she didn't answer her own question right away. Time seemed to draw out further and further as her huge blue eyes drilled into Jenn.

Finally, Jillybean said, "Yes, someone got hurt. It was an accident, wasn't it? It wasn't your fault."

Jenn began to nod, her eyes still locked on Jillybean's. Next to Jenn, Mike's fists were clenched. "How is she doing this?" he demanded.

"That's enough, Jillybean," Neil said. As though she were waking from a dream, Jillybean blinked and smiled. Now that she was released from the girl's stare, Jenn took a wobbly step back.

"Sorry about that," Deanna said. "I hope you understand. In times like these, if you have a human lie detector it's best to use her. Now, why don't you tell us your story?" With Jillybean right there, her large eyes taking in every facial tic and her ears catching every stuttered word, Jenn didn't even think about lying. Not that she had anything to lie about. She was brutally honest and included in her narrative the humiliating fiasco surrounding her and Mike's engagement as well as her deep-seated fear that she was "marked" something the Hill People and the Islanders took very seriously.

She finished the story of their journey and the reason for it, begging, "Can you help us?"

As she spoke, Jillybean became less and less of a "human lie detector" and more and more like a real girl with actual feelings. She even had tears welling in her eyes. That's why it was a bit of a shock when she shook her head. "I'm sorry, but I'm afraid I won't be able to save your friends. *If* they're still alive, their infections will have become systemic by now. Do you understand what that means?"

Mike guessed, "It'll be in their whole body?"

"Exactly. The longer an infection goes untreated or in this case partially treated, the greater the chance that the bacterium causing the infection will begin to flow throughout the body, where it will multiply unchecked until the patient becomes septic at which point his or her organs will begin to shut down. Death follows quickly after."

"What about Aaron?" Mike asked. "What if we amputated his arm? Would that stop…" Jillybean shook her head. Mike glared at her. Raising his voice, he asked, "Okay, what about William? He didn't even have an infection. Can you help him?"

Getting angry at Jillybean was a mistake. Her eyes grew cold and she stared at Mike through drooping lids; contempt radiating out of her. "I know your true motivation. You're drowning in guilt. That's why you want me to drag my ass five hundred miles away to fix your mistake. Oh, yeah. This one's on you, Mikey. You got your friend shot. You…"

"Jillybean," Neil warned.

"Don't 'Jillybean' me," she snapped. "He did this. He got his friend killed. If he hadn't been so chicken, he would have fired his crossbow while the slaver's gun was pointed at himself. But he hesitated just long enough to get his friend killed."

Mike's face froze in a grimace, his eyes blurred, losing their focus. He was looking into the past. Jillybean smiled and Jenn could swear it was the same cold, deathless smile of a bleached skull.

"Jillybean," Neil said again. "Look at me." The smile dimmed as the girl turned to look at Neil's craggy face. "Have you finished machining the molds for the 9mm casings?"

She jumped and the smile vanished altogether. "Oh, right. Sorry about that. Um, speaking of the mold, can I show them the plating process I invented?" She turned to Jenn. "It's standard zinc plating but with an aluminum oxide twist. Would you like to see?"

Neil patted her on the arm. "Not just yet. There are some things we have to discuss with our new friends. Perhaps you can see them before dinner."

He started to shoo her out of the room when Mike asked, "What about antibiotics? Do you have any? There's something wrong with our pills. They don't work anymore. Or they work hit and miss. Do you know what I mean?"

She turned and stared into his eyes. The stare lingered, and Jenn was shocked to feel the poison of jealousy begin to work its way into her bones. It spiked when Jillybean put her hand on his chest and said, "Of course I know what you mean. My doctoral thesis in chemical engineering was entitled: *The Anatomic, Physical and Mechanical Properties of Naturally Occurring Reverse Chemical Synthesis.* I'm still waiting for it to be peer-reviewed."

She finally took her eyes from Mike and shifted them toward Neil who threw up his hands. "I said I would get to it and I will. You know I've been busy. Either way, the subject at hand is antibiotics. I think the entire idea of trying to run them back to San Francisco is a little dicey. I can only imagine that you were extremely lucky to get here when there were three of you. I can't imagine you making it back when it's just the two of you. Unless you think your patient will be able to travel in the next day or two?"

Jillybean only laughed in answer. Mike stiffened at the sound. "I'll go by myself if I have to."

"I'll go, too," Jenn said. "We'll pay any price you ask."

"I know what I want," Jillybean purred, stroking Mike's chest.

Neil rolled his eyes as he took her by the elbow and escorted her to the door. "Stop it, Eve. Have Jillybean get the pills ready and tell her I expect to see those molds by dinner. Now, off you go." He shut the door and waited, listening to the sound of her retreating steps. When she was out of earshot, he nodded to Deanna.

The governor had her fingers steepled beneath her chin in contemplation. "I agree with Neil. A trip back south is foolhardy. Very brave, yes, but foolhardy nonetheless. Still, I can't stop you or at least I can't stop all of you. As payment for the antibiotics, I require that one of you stay behind. Not as a guest and not as a slave, but as an active and equal member of our community. Your friend Stu seems to be the ideal candidate."

Stu was being taken from them. Jenn was thunderstruck, while Mike could only open and close his mouth like a fish lying on a dock. Deanna gave them a curt nod and a sympathetic smile. "I have a meeting I can't miss. Neil, if you'll explain things."

Neil nodded and then bustled them out the door. "Stu is going to be your prisoner, isn't he?" Jenn blurted the moment they stepped outside.

"First off, no. There's only one prisoner on this island. Everyone else is free to come and go as they please. Your friend included. By the way, the offer to stay permanently extends to you two as well. From what I see in you and from Jillybean's reaction, I think you would make ideal additions to our island."

Mike looked pained as he mentioned, "We have a home, but thank you."

"Really?" Neil asked. Without waiting for an answer, he walked down to the road they had taken to get there. "Even if you make it back with antibiotics, how many of your friends do you think you'll save? You'd be lucky if one lives. And his life will be offset by the loss of your friend Stu, who, by your own admission, was the biggest, the bravest and the strongest. Do you really think your people will take you back?"

Mike turned his eyes down to his worn and saltstained boots, leaving Jenn to answer, "Probably not, but we have to try. And if they kick us out maybe we'll come back here."

"Five hundred miles on foot? With winter approaching? No. One way or the other if you two leave this island, you'll die. I don't want that to happen."

He was right, chances were they would die— it made her angry. She lashed out, "You don't even know us. Why would you care?"

Neil absorbed the anger, his scarred face remaining infuriatingly calm. "About six or seven years ago, Jillybean wrote a thesis paper entitled *Minimum Viable Popu-*

lation in a Post-Apocalyptic World." At Jenn's blank look he laughed. "That's what I thought when she gave it to me. Like all the rest of her papers, I put it aside and made excuses. But she insisted that I read it. She was so adamant that I relented and waded through mathematical population models, R versus K selection theories and more. Thankfully, she had summed up her thesis at the end of the paper, which was basically the idea that humans aren't going to survive much longer as a species."

"I don't understand," Jenn said. "Are you saying we're going to die? All of us?"

"It's Jillybean's theory that the zombie apocalypse is an extinction-level event. You know what dinosaurs were, right?"

At the question, Jenn's chest constricted. She had no idea what Neil was talking about and was afraid to look stupid. Mike answered for her. "Yes, they were the big monster lizards that all died out." He turned to Jenn. "Extinction is when a whole group of animals gets, like wiped out."

Neil nodded. "And that's going to be our fate. Every year there are fewer and fewer of us. We're spread out, we're weak, and we're dying off. This island is our only hope. We can be safe here. We can grow as a species. That's what I care about, and that's why I care about you."

That helped Jenn a little. "But you don't really know us. We could be slavers or bandits or something."

This brought a soft laugh from Neil. "It's obvious that you're neither. I'm a pretty good judge of character. Now, if you're nervous about us, give us a trial run. See what you think. We need people who know boats. You can captain the *Calypso* for us. There's great fishing on the Sound."

The offer sounded wonderful. The little Jenn had seen of the island had been fantastic compared to the relatively primitive standards of the hilltop and she could see humanity flourishing here.

"But my family is back there," she said in a whisper. "Well, not my real family. They're all dead, but the people who adopted me and took me in when I was just a kid are back there and they need me. I'm sorry, but I can't." Mike shook his head as well.

Neil snapped his fingers at his bad luck. "I guess I can't get them all. Hey, you two look dead on your feet. I have a couple of extra beds if you want to sleep."

Mike had blue rings under his eyes and Jenn felt suddenly lethargic. "Sure," she said, biting back a yawn. They walked north for a few minutes, Jenn growing more and more sleepy. To keep from falling asleep as she walked, she asked a question that was bothering her. "Your prisoner, is it Jillybean?"

He chuckled. "Noooo. The last thing anyone would want to do is try to put her behind bars. No, I'm the prisoner. I can't leave because of Jillybean. She needs me. She…she's special."

"Yes," Jenn admitted, softly. "I guess I don't understand her very much. And I don't know what you mean by thesis papers and all the rest. I don't mean to be stupid but I never went to school."

Despite his face, which was hard to look at, Neil had a fatherly way about him as if he was always on the verge of telling a bad dad joke or suggesting a game of catch. "Just because you don't know something doesn't make you stupid. Jillybean is a genius. Maybe even more than a genius, whatever that designation may be. At the same time, like I said before, she has a fractured mind. My main job on the island is to keep her safe and keep her busy. Those research papers are one way to keep her busy. Tinkering is another."

He pointed at a cloud on the other side of the island. It was so low that Jenn had thought it was from a fire, and yet it was the purest white. "Our electricity used to be solar-powered, but gradually the panels lost their oomph while at same time more people came to the island. Jillybean drew up plans for a coal-powered generator. She had to teach herself the basics of architecture, engineering, plumbing and general construction. That took her a few weeks."

232

When neither Mike or Jenn reacted beyond a simple nodding of their heads, Neil laughed. "You don't get it. What she taught herself would have taken a normal person years to learn."

Jenn was impressed to the point of feeling small, while Mike seemed a little lost in the conversation. He asked, "You said you had to keep her safe, but from what? Everyone is, uh nervous around her."

"Let's just say she can be dangerous. There are dark parts to her past that haunt her. Things that happened when she was little. But that really shouldn't worry you. Your friend Stu will be just fine and you two are leaving, right?" He smiled, but there was something beyond the smile that didn't feel right to Jenn. She couldn't put her finger on it, mainly because she couldn't read Neil.

"Here we are. This is my house. Jillybean lives here as well, but she'll be busy going back and forth from the clinic to the school for most of the day."

"We don't want to sleep too long," Mike said, as they were led upstairs. "Just a few hours."

"Of course," Neil replied, wearing his warped smile. It was eight hours later, just as the sun was beginning to set, when he came for them.

Chapter 27

Stu Currans

When Stu woke, the first thing he saw was a girl of about seventeen standing over him. She had a heart-shaped face, huge blue eyes and a wild mass of brown hair. In her hand was a straight razor; there was blood on it.

"Don't move," she warned, bringing the knife to his throat. "I don't want to cut you, but I will if you don't listen to me."

In his groggy state, he had no idea where he was or what was happening. He did know that he was powerless against this girl. There was nothing stopping her from slashing his throat wide open. The razor moved upwards along his throat and as it did, he sucked in his breath.

"Don't be such a chicken," she said, holding up the knife. There was now white foam on the edge.

"Oh," he said, realizing that she was shaving him. He sagged in relief. "I thought you were with the Corsairs," he said in a rasp. The last thing he remembered was Mike yelling something about the Corsairs. But that was when they were on the boat and they were most certainly not on the boat. They were in… "A hospital? I got shot, didn't I?"

"You did."

He looked down and saw his leg was covered in a hard white bandage. "Wait, that's a cast. Why do I have a cast?"

"To keep your leg immobilized. I don't want to have to open you back up to fix a ruptured artery. Now lie back. I didn't think you'd want to go to a formal dinner all rough and tumble. A sponge bath and a shave were called for. You're welcome."

A bath? He blinked and looked down at himself once more. He was very much naked. The fog he'd been in cleared in a snap. "Where are my clothes?"

"Don't you think it's a little late to be modest? Besides, I've seen my share of genitals in my time." He stared in shock at this admission. "I meant as a doctor, you pervert. It comes with the territory."

"I'm sure, but could you…you know, hand me a towel or something?"

She shrugged and handed him a sheet from a stack. "I have all the pictures I need anyway." As his eyes widened again, she squealed with laughter. "Your face is priceless! I don't have a camera, silly. Now that you're covered let's do this correctly. I'm Jillybean Martin." She stuck out a small hand.

He expected the hand to be soft, but it was rough, her grip was surprisingly strong. "I'm Stuart Currans. Are you the girl doctor people talk about?"

"Luckily for you, I am."

"And did my friends ask you about…"

She interrupted with a simple, "Yes." The *but* that followed was expected. He read it in her eyes. "But there's a problem. More than one, actually." She put a hand on his shoulder and left it there. He glanced down at it as she went on. "You're one of us now. You were bought for a handful of pills."

"I'm a slave?"

She laughed again, high and sweet. Having lived so long in a world throttled by fearful silence, he found himself smiling at her despite his situation, and despite the hand that wouldn't leave. "No, you're not a slave. You are a free citizen of Bainbridge Island. You may come and go as you please…"

"But?"

"Hold on, I wasn't going to say 'but' I was going to say that there are stipulations, the chief of which is that when you leave you can't take community property with you. Your friends were honest concerning the circumstances in which you fled San Francisco. Thievery will not be tolerated."

Stu glared. "We *borrowed* the boat, there's a difference, and we did it to save lives. Besides, if we have the pills, we don't really need to steal anything else."

"Except for me, of course. You came for the 'girl doctor' right? Antibiotics alone won't save your friends. The only chance they have is me. Would you steal me?" The hand on his shoulder squeezed hard, her fingernails sharp against his skin. At the same time, her eyes bored into his with unusual intensity.

He stared right back. "No. We're not slavers. I won't steal you, but I would beg you to come with us."

Her hand squeezed hard enough to leave marks and then she released her grip. She took the bowl of water and the razor and walked to a sink. "He's exactly like we thought he'd be. He's just like Grey."

She seemed to be talking to herself, something that would have been disconcerting, except she then turned on the water faucet. Stu's body jerked at the sight. Running water? He blinked up at the neon lights, only just realizing they were on and actually working. Next, he looked down at his cast in a growing sense of amazement. It was real. He touched it lightly, running the tips of his fingers over it. It wasn't just real, it was perfect. When he had been eight, years before the dead had come, he had broken his wrist. The cast he wore for weeks on end was just like the one on his leg.

"W-where am I, exactly?" He had almost asked *When am I?*

"Bainbridge Island, across from Seattle. You were shot by those miserable mutants from Cathlamet. Do you remember that? Do you remember your friends bringing you north?" He remembered the ride; he'd been in endless, miserable pain. "They brought you here and I saved you, but if you're like Grey, then I saved you for nothing. Are you like him?"

"I don't know anyone named Grey," he answered. She was still holding the razor and for some reason, he felt a note of worry deep inside his chest.

"It doesn't matter if you know him or not. You're still like him." Something about her had changed. Her voice was now filled with sadness. "That's what I say. But we can find out easily enough." She stared hard at him, saying in a monotone, "I'm almost certain that if you leave Bainbridge, you'll die. You'll get an infection or your stitches will pop and you'll bleed to death. What do you say to that?"

"I would have to take that chance," he told her. "I would walk back…well, crawl back to my people if I had to."

She briefly glanced away. "That's what we thought. Neil did as well." When she saw his look, she said, "He's my father and he knows people. It's his strong suit you might say. He likes your friends. He thinks they have heart and while they were sleeping, he made arrangements to keep all of you here."

"So, I am a prisoner." Forgetting his leg, Stu tried to get up. She gently pushed him back. He was so weak, he couldn't resist.

"He did it for your own good. Bainbridge is practically a paradise and what's more, the *Calypso* really did have a number of leaks. Bad ones. It's one thing to splash around in the Sound, but if you had taken her back on the open ocean she would have sunk. He has her dry-docked. The repairs could take up to a week."

They didn't have a week. She seemed to read this on his face. "Yes, if you wait a week, your friends will die. I won't be able to save them."

Stu shook his head in confusion. "Wait, I don't understand. Are you saying you're coming with us? Do you have a boat?"

The hand on his bare shoulder squeezed him again before she turned away. She went to the sink and touched the straight razor. It was a gentle touch, like she was stroking a baby's cheek. "I can get a boat, but I don't know if I should let you have it or if I should go with you at all. If we're around each other too much, I'm afraid you'll start looking at me like everyone else does."

"I don't know what you're talking about. I'm sorry, I must have missed something. How do people look at you?"

"They look at me like I'm crazy. They look at me like that because I am crazy." With an angry flick, she threw the razor into the sink. "When you were first brought in, I didn't know if I would like you. Normally, I like new people right away. I like them until they become like the rest. I like them until they start looking at me out of the corners of their eyes, but you didn't do that. You just lay there, sleeping and I liked that. I liked it a lot, but I also worried that it would change when you woke up."

She turned back suddenly, as if she wanted to catch him looking at her funny. He shrugged. "A lot of people are crazy, if you ask me. Some are bad and some are good. Which are you?"

"Both, I think, but I haven't been really bad in years… well, I guess Eve's been bad a few times and I did tell a small lie to your friends earlier. I think Jenn and I could be good friends and I was hoping to get her to stay, so I told them that your friends back home were going to die no matter what. The truth is that they'll only *probably* die no matter what."

"And you can help them?"

"Maybe, if we get there quickly. But, but if I go, you have to promise that you won't look at me funny. Not ever."

He grinned. "You saved my life. This is the least I can do." He held up his hand, palm facing her. "I promise not to look at you funny. Now where's that boat?"

"It's close by in a secret place. You also have to promise not to tell Neil. There's no way he would ever let me go with you." Stu nodded in agreement, but that wasn't good enough for her. She picked up his hand and lifted it, palm out.

"Okay, I promise not to tell anyone."

He was about to drop his hand, but she hooked his pinky with hers. "Now pinky swear."

"I pinky-swear not to tell anyone."

This came out sounding like a question, but it was good enough for her. "Good, let's get you dressed." To his shock and embarrassment, she ripped the sheet off him. For some reason, she seemed just as shocked at what she had done. "Sorry, that was Eve. She thinks you're cute."

Stu covered himself with his hands. "That was who?" He could feel his face beginning to slip into what could easily be described as a "funny" look. He forced himself to adopt a bland expression.

"N-no one," she stuttered, her pale cheeks going red. "It was a joke. Sorry. But, but you're going to need my help anyway." She withheld the sheet and picked up a pair of pants. When she straightened, her eyes seemed to be drawn right to his crotch. With a deep breath, she swallowed her embarrassment and went to work. He quickly discovered he was weaker than he thought; there was no way he could've gotten dressed without her. Once he had on a pair of jeans that had the right leg cut up the seam and a long-sleeved shirt, she maneuvered him into a wheelchair.

"Ricardo?" she called. An older man with little glints of silver in his dark hair, hurried through the door and looked at her expectantly. "Can you take him up to the governor's house?"

As Ricardo came around the wheelchair, Stu asked, "Couldn't he have helped me get dressed?"

The red color came back into her cheeks as she remarked, "Eve isn't the only one who thinks you're cute." As he sat there, dumbfounded, she gave him a wave and walked out.

"She thinks you're cute?" Ricardo asked, his one eyebrow pipped upwards. "Good luck with that." Stu's first reaction was to demand to know what he meant. It was pretty obvious, however and he didn't ask.

Ricardo was quiet as he huffed and puffed Stu across the island. Stu wasn't in the mood for conversation. He was too much in awe of all the lights and all the people casually strolling around. Once again, he had that strange sensation of having slipped backwards in time. This was how things were when he'd been a kid. It was how things were supposed to be.

When they drew near a stately home that appeared to have every light in it burning away, Ricardo broke in on his thoughts. "This is it. Hey, a little advice: be careful with Jillybean. She's killed at least two of her patients and when I say killed, I mean…" He drew his thumb across his throat.

Stu leaned back in his chair, not quite believing the man. "Then how come she's not in jail or banished?"

Ricardo leaned in closer. "Her dad's Neil Martin. The dude may be little but he's scary. Some of the things I heard he done? Messed up is what it is. And wait till you see his face." Ricardo let out a little whistle. "That's messed up, too."

"You make it sound like he's famous or something."

"You've never heard of Neil Martin? What about the Azael? He's the guy who took them down. And it was Jillybean who blew up the River King's bridge. She killed like five hundred people and she did that when she was just six years old. Everyone knows she's got a thing for fire. They say she's got all sorts of bombs in that school of hers."

Stu had heard of the Azael. They had been slavers who had somehow been able to control the dead. Supposedly they had an entire army of them and had used them to create a kingdom, but that had been years and years before.

"Wasn't that out east?"

Ricardo grunted, "Yup. In Colorado, the same place where like half the people were gassed to death. They say it *wasn't* Jillybean, but it's not just bombs she plays with, it's germs too. All I'm saying is be careful around her and whatever you do, don't get her mad."

Jillybean was certainly strange, but she was also kind, kind enough to have saved Stu's life. That wasn't something he took lightly, and he felt the immediate desire to defend her. "You make her sound like some sort of monster, and yet you work with her? She couldn't be that bad."

They were on the driveway now and Ricardo had to strain to get him up the hill. "It beats farming any day. 'Sides, she thinks I'm dumb. She kinda has a soft spot for stupid people. She feels sorry for them. It's like she thinks that anyone without a college degree is a retard or something."

She certainly isn't going to be impressed with my sixth-grade diploma, Stu thought to himself.

Ricardo wheeled him to the door, but before he could ring the doorbell, a sound Stu secretly wanted to hear, the door opened revealing a tall blonde woman in a deeply blue knee-length dress. She was in that thirty-something range that was hard to pin down. "I'll take him from here, Ricardo," she said. "If you'll be back at eight for him I would appreciate it."

"Of course, Governor," Ricardo answered, bowing at the waist before leaving.

Governor? Stu took a closer look at the woman, seeing the wrinkles around her eyes and the worry lines across her forehead. Leadership was taking its toll. Feeling young and awkward in her presence, he put out a hand. "Stuart Currans. Thanks for the hospitality, and thanks for, I guess you can call it an invitation to join your group."

They shook, and her hand, like Jillybean's, was stronger than it appeared. "You've heard? I take it you've also heard about the damage to the *Calypso?*" He nodded, then shifted his eyes away. Talking about boats was the last thing he wanted. Keeping secrets felt a lot like lying and he was a poor liar at best.

Deanna let out a sigh. "The boat just wasn't seaworthy. Hopefully you understand that what Neil did was in your friends' best interests."

"He didn't have the right to touch our boat," Stu answered. "It's really as simple as that."

"Seeing as you stole the boat in the first place that's a debatable point, but it's not a debate I want to have, especially when your friends need your help. Mike and Jenn are threatening to walk back to San Francisco. We can't stop them of course, but we're hoping you might be able talk some sense into them. You do realize they'll never make it, right?"

Mike and Jenn had proven to be made of sterner stuff than even Stu had guessed. Still, their chance of making it on foot were terrible. *Thank goodness we have a boat,* he thought. "I'll talk to them."

"They're out back about to eat dinner. They refused to come in, but no one can refuse my cooking. I'll have a plate brought out for you." She pushed him through the house to a set of glass doors that led to a deck. Standing just beside it was a small man in brown corduroy pants and a checkered sweater vest. His face was an ugly mass of scars.

"You must be Neil Martin," Stu said, trying to look past his mutilated face and into the man's eyes as he stuck out a hand.

Unlike Jillybean's and Deanna's grips, Neil's was rather soft. "I am. I see Jillybean did a hell of a job on you. You were practically dead not so long ago. It's a good thing she saved you, because now you have a chance to save your friends. You can ask anyone on the island and they'll all tell you the same thing. Trying to make it to San Francisco on foot is suicide. Even the traders don't try to make it through anymore."

"I'll talk to them, I promise." Neil came around behind his chair, but Stu waved him off. "I better go out alone. I'm sure you understand." He wheeled himself out onto the deck where a table was set, a single candle flickering between Mike and Jenn.

Mike jumped up quickly to help him. "Stu! My goodness, you look good. I didn't think I'd see you up and about." He then lowered his voice to a growl, "Did you hear what that weasel did?"

Stu nodded. "He took our boat, but I have a replacement. The girl doctor has one and what's more, she's coming with us."

Neither Mike nor Jenn looked excited at the prospect. "You know she's insane, right?" Jenn asked. "Everyone,

242

including her father, thinks she's dangerous. I don't know if she should come."

"I don't think you have a choice." All three jumped as Jillybean emerged from the darkness next to the deck. "We want to leave and you're going to take us whether you want to or not." In her hand was a pistol. She brought it to her nose and sniffed at the barrel, a queer smile playing on her face.

Chapter 28

Jenn Lockhart

Neither the gun nor the girl scared Mike. "We're not going anywhere with you if you threaten us. Put the gun away and we'll talk."

"Maybe I don't want to talk," she shot back in a hissing whisper, "and maybe I don't want you to come with *me*. I'm the one with the boat, remember? Do you think I need your help to find my way to San Francisco? Not hardly. The way I see it, you guys are along for the ride."

Mike may not have been afraid, but Jenn was so nervous her stomach began to hurt. Jillybean was dangerous. She was like a volcano that could erupt at any second. Jenn reached under the table and squeezed Mike's knee saying, "He didn't mean it and neither did I. We were just nervous. Right, Mike?" She made overly large nodding motions until Mike began nodding along. "See? We're just not used to being deceptive like this."

Jillybean sneered. "Oh, I doubt that. Did you think I forgot about you three stealing the *Calypso* in the first place? Well, I didn't. What I…" She was interrupted by Deanna pulling open the kitchen door. Jillybean disappeared in a blink, somewhere out of sight along the edge of the deck.

"Here's your dinner, Stu. I don't know if Jillybean has placed any restrictions on your diet, but I would take it slowly if I were you."

When she went back inside, Jillybean reappeared, creeping along the edge of the deck. She pointed at Mike and Jenn. "You two meet me at the school at eleven. I'll make sure Stu gets there. Don't be late or I'll leave you behind." With that she faded into the dark. There was no telling if she had really left and Jenn simply couldn't relax knowing Jillybean was out there carrying a gun.

She ate what was arguably the best meal any of them had ever eaten in a stiff silence.

It wasn't until after they were served rhubarb pie by a teenage girl who was the spitting image of the governor, that Stu said, "I'm supposed to be talking you...you..." His mouth stretched into a long O as he yawned for what seemed like a minute. "Sorry. I'm supposed to be talking you into staying. I think it might look fishy if you guys change your minds too quickly."

"We can tell them we'll think on it tonight and decide in the morning," Mike said, around a mouthful of pie. "Boy, I hate the idea of lying."

"I hate that they touched our boat," Stu remarked before forking a huge chunk of pie into his mouth. "But I love this pie. Do you think there's real sugar in it? And the crust is so buttery." They were quiet for a few minutes before he jokingly asked, "Is this their way of bribing us into staying?"

Jenn was so stuffed that her belly bulged out like a ball. She couldn't even finish her piece of pie and slid it to Mike who devoured it in two bites. As if she had been watching from inside, the girl came out to clear their plates the moment he put down his fork.

"I like your hair," she said. Jenn was about to thank her when she realized the girl was talking to Mike and once more she felt that sharp jab of jealousy. "Men around here wear their hair too short. You sort of look like a Viking."

Jenn had no idea what a Viking was, but she was sure it was a brazen compliment. "We should get going. We should rest. We have a big day tomorrow."

"Are you really leaving on foot?" the girl asked. "I don't want to be rude, but that's insane. Do you know about the fallout region just north of Portland? It's impassable. You'll have to swing way out to the east. I'm talking about going as far out as Yakima or Kennewick. That's days out of your way. I have a map if you want to see."

"What's fallout?" Mike asked.

Stu stifled another yawn. "It's probably what made those people on that river island so sick. I'm sorry but I need to lie down. Young lady can you see if Ricardo is available?"

"Don't," Mike told her. "I can take you back."

The three of them re-entered the brightly-lit house where they were greeted by the governor sitting alone at her kitchen table. "Have you made a decision?"

"They're going to sleep on it," Stu said. "We'll let you know in the morning."

"That's fair enough, but I have to warn you, I'll be making my famous double ham and cheese omelets. Once you've had them, you won't be able to leave. It just won't be possible. Right, Emily?"

Emily agreed and added, "They should stay here with us. We have like, a gazillion rooms, and no offense to Uncle Neil, but his place is too crammed with Jillybean's books. Not to mention it always smells like chemicals, like there's a bomb in the basement or something." Her eyes suddenly shot wide. "Not that she'd have a bomb in the house, of course."

Jenn didn't like the idea of being anywhere near Emily. She couldn't seem to take her eyes off Mike and Jenn told herself that it would make sneaking out difficult.

"I think we'd rather stay at the clinic itself," Mike said. "They have extra beds there. We think it's best to stay with Stu tonight to make sure he's going to be okay. Besides, I'd hate to impose on anyone."

"Yes," agreed Jenn, "we'd hate to impose." This was a much better plan.

They said their goodbyes and trundled Stu back to the clinic. His face, normally chiseled and strong, looked soft and his voice was somewhat slurry as he said, "Can you imagine this place at Christmas? Think about all the lights." For the most part, Christmas had died with the apocalypse. Jenn had never celebrated Christmas as far as she could remember and it wasn't a big deal to her. "It would be just like before," Stu went on. "Just like it used to be."

"I bet," Mike said, giving Jenn a worried look. "Maybe you should stay behind, Stu. Maybe it would be smart, considering your leg. I have Jenn. She's really coming along as a sailor. Not to mention, you know who."

"It's because of her that I have to go. If she's as dangerous as people think, you'll need an extra set of eyes on her. Besides, I think she likes me."

"I'm more worried about you than I am about her," Jenn said. "If we hit another storm or if something happens to the boat, you won't be able to swim. We don't even know what sort of boat we're talking about. The ones down at the harbor were even smaller than the *Puffer*. None of them are meant for ocean travel."

Stu only grunted in reply. He seemed too tired for anything more. The three were quiet until the clinic came into view. By then Stu was lolling in the chair, barely able to keep awake.

Mike whispered, "What do the signs say about the trip, Jenn? They steered us here, what about getting back?"

She stopped and looked up at the stars, expecting to see the usual uncountable splash across the sky. It was a clear night, yet there were far fewer stars visible than ever before. They were just gone and in their place, was only darkness. For a person who relied on the intangible nature of stars, it was like a kick in the stomach. She gazed all around her, trying to find other signs, but there were no birds or flies or dropping acorns or anything.

"I think something's wrong," she whispered so quietly that he could barely hear her. She was afraid that if she spoke too loudly, Jillybean would suddenly show up out of the dark, either with her crazy eyes or her way-too-friendly grin. "I don't know why, but it feels like the signs have deserted me."

"Do you think that means we should all leave? Even Stu?"

Although he didn't believe in the signs and omens, Jenn didn't like the idea of leaving Stu in a land that was dead to her natural senses. Instinctively, she blamed Jillybean. She had brought technology back almost single-handedly. Sure, it seemed good now. Hot baths were wonderful and lights that just blinked on without effort were fantastic, and the food was so plentiful as to feel unreal, but where would it all lead?

Already, the dead were like pets to Jillybean. That alone told Jenn that in the long run, nothing good could come of it.

"He should come with us," she decided. "We have a few hours to kill, let's get him to bed and let him rest." They rolled him into the clinic and with Ricardo's help, got him onto a bed. He was asleep before Jenn could even get the covers over him. "We'll watch him," she told Ricardo.

He was happy to leave. "I'll be in the back if you need anything."

They both breathed a sigh of relief once they were alone. Jenn had been afraid Ricardo would start to ask questions. She really was so new to deception that she had worn a strained smile as if the secret she had bottled up within her was about to burst out at any moment.

Mike and Jenn made up a pair of beds just in case Neil dropped by to check on them, but he didn't. The clinic was quiet until eleven when Jillybean came sneaking in. She had added a gun in a hip holster, a thigh-length black coat and a black ski cap to her usual all-black attire.

"Okay, we're ready to roll," she said. She asked Jenn, "Can you handle the cripple? I'm going to need Mikey's muscles." She gave Mike's arm a squeeze and left her hand there. This wasn't Jillybean or even Sadie, this was Eve.

Jenn hoped her disappointment didn't show. "I can push him in his wheelchair if that's what you mean."

"I wasn't asking if you could handle his junk."

"Junk?"

Eve groaned. "Of course, I meant his wheelchair. Come on, let's go. We don't have a lot of time." She waited with building impatience as they woke Stu and helped him into his chair. He was heavier than expected and it took everything Jenn had to push him along the night roads heading north.

Mike struggled as well, pushing a strange cart along. It looked somewhat like a shopping cart except it was longer and wider, and it had bicycle tires instead of the little rubber ones. It had been handmade, but that didn't make it any less sound. It was loaded down with weapons, ammo, crates of food, gallons of water, medical supplies, rope, an axe, boxes of what looked like junk and amazingly enough, two car batteries.

"These still work?" Mike asked.

Eve rolled her eyes. "Why don't you lick the posts and find out?" He glared and she glared right back. "Let's hold all of the truly idiotic questions until we're off the island."

Jenn clamped her mouth shut. She had been about to ask how they were going to get off the island since they were walking away from the only break in the wall. She also wanted to know how they were going to get away without being seen. The towers were all manned and the searchlights swept back and forth continuously.

It was a two-and-a-half mile walk to the very tip of the island to an old and neglected cemetery that once had a waterfront view for the grievers and the corpses. Now the headstones ran right up to the wall.

On the edge of the cemetery was a building where wakes and services had once been conducted. It was boarded over and padlocked, used only when a cremation was called for. Eve had the key and let them in.

They took an elevator down to a low-ceilinged basement where a large oven sat encased in brick, its heavy steel door hanging open. The place smelled like a mixture of a campfire and bleach. It wasn't pleasant, and Jenn kept her chin turned away. There was only one other door and it, too was locked. It opened into a room filled with old machines, most of them disconnected from anything and covered in dust.

Eve led them through this room to a final door. This one was squat and curved. She checked her watch. "We have ten minutes left." The door opened onto a tunnel that slanted away into darkness, in the direction of the Sound.

"What is this place?" Jenn asked, making sure not to touch the walls which were slimy with algae. She was secretly afraid the other end of the tunnel was underwater.

"The way out," Eve answered shortly. She took a flashlight from her belt and lit up the dark.

"How's that thing still working?" Mike asked. "I haven't seen a real flashlight since I was a kid. Can I see it?"

She pulled the light away. "No, you can't see it. Jillybean makes the batteries herself, and before you get all in awe, they suck compared to the old ones from before. Speaking of Jillybean, um, do you guys know what *Pi* is? You know, the number *Pi*? It's 3.14, something."

All three of them shook their heads, each looking as lost as the next. A number pie wasn't something Jenn had ever heard of.

"It's 3.14 something," Eve said again. "I want to say one or seven or…damn it. What are you guys waiting for? Come on." She shone the light ahead of her where the sound of water lapping against rock echoed. Soon they came to a boat sitting in the tunnel. It was a tiny thing, all of three feet wide and about ten feet long. It had no sail, only a single oar and a tiny outboard engine with a cartoon snail painted on the side.

Mike looked at it in shock. "What is that? A skiff? Is that even a skiff? I guess your smarts don't extend beyond medicine and chemicals. This boat *will* sink if you try to take it out onto the ocean. There's no question about it."

"Oh really?" Eve smacked her forehead with the palm of her hand. "I guess I am dumb because I thought it was a freaking battleship. Of course, it's a skiff. Now shut up and get the stuff loaded." When no one moved, she knotted her hands into fists and growled, "The tide is coming in. We have a five-minute window to get the boat out of this tunnel before it floods, so move!"

Even as she spoke, Jenn noticed the water was slowly creeping along the edge of the boat. She pointed to it and hissed, "She's right. We have to hurry."

"I'm right?" Eve asked sarcastically. "No duh. It's a concept you guys need to wrap your head around. I'm always right. Now, get the stuff loaded. I gotta check something out." She left them in a semi-darkness as she splashed toward a gate that hung over the entrance of the tunnel.

"How are we going to get everything on board?" Mike asked, grabbing a dozen or so fenders from the boat and chucking them away. They were made of plastic-covered foam and were used to keep boats from damaging themselves when they docked, which wasn't their biggest issue at the moment.

"There's not going to be any room for us," Mike decided. The cart, which was practically filled, was almost as big as the boat and what was worse, the boat was extremely shallow. They couldn't pile the goods very high and expect them not to topple into the sound at the first wave they hit. Even a small wave would be trouble.

Mike and Jenn, with Stu doing his best to direct, tried to get all the items on board, shifting them constantly, only it was like a puzzle with no answer. No configuration worked, especially as they had to account for four people taking up most of the room on the skiff.

"How the hell are we supposed to do this?" Mike asked.

Eve turned the light towards them and the skiff. "How should I know? Just get it all in there and be quiet about it. There's a tower like fifty feet away."

A muttered curse escaped Mike. "This is impossible. We're going to have to leave some stuff behind. What do you think? The water? The batteries and the engine? I could paddle if I had to."

"No," Stu said, gazing at everything. "If Jillybean packed it all, then she did so for a reason. She wouldn't have brought any of this stuff just to leave it behind. Too bad she's schizo, and too bad that other 'her' isn't as smart. Really, it's too bad none of us are."

Jenn sniffed at this. If being smart made you crazy, it wasn't worth it. Besides, she was dumb and she did just fine, as long as she had her signs and omens to guide her, that is. Out of habit she stared around her looking for meaning in the way the foam fenders were scattered or the streaks in the algae or the silly cartoon snail. It was streaking across cartoon water, leaving behind white waves.

As far as she knew snails couldn't swim, though in truth the only thing she really knew about them was that they carried their homes on their backs. Sort of like turtles. "And sort of like us if we can figure a way how to float all this stuff across…" In midsentence she realized she'd been looking at a sign all along.

"I know what to do," she whispered, excitedly.

Chapter 29

Jenn Lockhart

"Put everything back in the cart and hurry," she cried. The water level in the tunnel was rising quickly and they not only had to get the cart filled, they had to get Stu into the skiff and somehow get the gate open. They didn't have long, already the skiff was floating.

"The cart will just sink, Jenn," Mike said. He held up a length of rope. "Do you think we can drag it across the bottom?"

She pointed at the fenders. "Why would Jillybean have *all* of those? We only have two or three on the *Puffer*, and ours are much smaller. Do you get it now? If we tie all of those off under the cart, it'll float."

"That's pretty smart, Jenn," Stu said as he locked the brakes on his wheelchair. Before Jenn could say anything, he leaned far over and purposely spilled onto the floor of the tunnel. She jumped towards him, but he waved her away. "I can get into the skiff by myself. Help Mike."

Mike waved her away, too. "I'm good. This is really a one-person job. What we need is someone to get that gate open." Eve was still standing at the gate, shining the flashlight at something on the wall. The water was up to her waist. Jenn climbed into the skiff, crawled over Stu and then used the single oar to propel them to where the girl was hissing and whining to herself.

"What's pi?" Eve demanded right away, blinding Jenn with the light. "It's 3.14 something, something, something! But what? It's a sort of math. Do you guys know it?"

Stu was older by six years and knew all sorts of things that Jenn didn't, however he could only shrug his broad shoulders. Eve made a fresh whining noise and turned to a little board attached to the wall which had ten glowing numbers. She pressed the three, the one and the four and then hesitated.

"I need three more numbers," she said. "What do you think? An eight?" She hit the eight, but nothing happened. "Okay, how about five and a two?" When again nothing happened, she cursed worse than any Corsair.

"Maybe you should ask Jillybean?" Jenn suggested. Eve glared. "I'm guessing she put that doo-dad up and I bet that means she knows all of the pie."

Eve scoffed. "No one knows the full number. It's infinite, doorknob." Jenn didn't know what she meant by infinite or doorknob, though she figured the latter was a put-down of some sort. Eve tried to explain, "Pi is a number. It's like, how do I put this to a doorknob like you? It's like the size of a circle and the line that runs through it…"

"The diameter," Eve said, in the middle of her own explanation. She didn't even notice.

"Right the diameter." Eve held up her hands forming a circle between her curved fingers. "That diameter thing cuts it in half and you can find the, uh, the, uh…"

Again, she filled in her own word, only now she did with a softer tone, "The ratio of the circle's circumference…" Eve began to blink and sway, still holding her hands up. "The circle's circumference to its diameter using pi which is commonly shortened to 3.14159 or simply 3.14."

She grinned and said, "Excellent, Jenn. You brought me back just in time. As always, Eve would have ruined everything."

"Jillybean?" Jenn asked, searching her eyes.

"Who else would I be?"

Jenn's head began to feel spinny. "Eve maybe, or that other girl you mentioned before, Sally, I think."

The light in Jillybean's eyes dimmed somewhat. "It's Sadie, but she's not here. No, it's just me. Eve can't handle irrational numbers, perhaps because she's irrational, herself. I use pi as a pass code to keep her from escaping. It wouldn't be good to let her loose on the world. But enough about her. How are we doing? Almost ready to go, I hope?"

She looked past Stu, who had quietly watched the strange conversation and the even stranger transformation, to Mike, who was hauling the now filled cart towards them. "Good, we're almost all set. I'll need those batteries in the boat, Mike."

Jillybean climbed into the skiff, tilting it crazily, and pulled a couple of plastic-coated cables from the little engine. The water was up to Mike's waist as he brought over the first of the heavy batteries. Using an adjustable wrench, Jillybean connected it to the engine and then linked the next.

"Do you remember the numbers?" she asked Jenn after Mike had tied the cart to the back of the skiff and climbed in.

"Yes: 3.14159, but what about the lights in the watchtowers? The guards will see us."

Jillybean chuckled, "Oh ye of little faith. I designed not only this gate, but also the wall, the towers, the lights and the electrical system that feeds them. When you punch in the numbers, not only will the gate open, there will also be a five-minute interruption in the power supplying the towers on this side of the island. Five minutes will be plenty of time to get away."

Nervous about the electricity flowing behind the buttons, Jenn used just the tip of her finger to press each in turn. There was a tinny sound, like a spoon striking a can and then the heavy metal gate opened.

"Everyone duck," Jillybean whispered as she flicked on the electric motor, which purred as the blades began to spin. They were cutting things very close. Jenn had to hug the prow as they scraped through the opening, while Mike and Jillybean threw themselves over one another to keep from being torn out of the boat.

Once free of the tunnel, Jillybean surprised them by steering them straight east towards the dark and ugly city instead of going north, which was, as far as Jenn knew, the only way back to the Pacific. She glanced at Mike, who shrugged. Neither said anything and for five minutes they slipped through the cold water of the Sound at the boat's full speed, which was about three and a half miles an hour.

When the tower lights clicked back on, they still seemed very close and everyone held their breath as the beams swept the water. To Jenn they made the island look alive, like a many-eyed monster searching for its next victim. Luckily the guards were mostly concerned with anything that might have gotten in close during the interruption and their lights ran along the shallows near the island before methodically moving further and further out.

By the time the lights turned towards the skiff and its trailing cart, they were nearly a half a mile away.

"I think we're good," Jillybean said and turned the boat south, again confusing Mike and Jenn, who shared another look. Jillybean saw it and sighed. "I suppose I should come clean with you now before we get too far into our adventure. I don't actually have a boat. We're going to have to steal one."

"From who?" Mike demanded. "And why do you say 'we?' We're not thieves. Like I said before, we 'borrowed' the *Calypso* and I'll bring her back one way or another."

Jillybean patted his arm. "I believe you. I don't plan on giving back the boat we're going to take. It belongs to the Corsairs."

Mike jumped as if pinched. "We're going to steal a boat from the Corsairs? Are you kidding? How?"

"I don't know yet."

Jenn stared back to see if Jillybean's fractured mind had fractured again. She seemed like her 'normal' friendly self. "Maybe we should talk about this," Jenn said. "If I had known this was the plan, I don't think I would have come along, and I know I wouldn't have let Stu come. We don't stand a chance against the Corsairs. There's like a million of them and only four of us."

Jillybean frowned. "A million? Jenn, hyperbole isn't helpful. We need to discuss this logically. I agree, the chances seem slim as we sit here in this little boat. If we allow our imaginations to run wild we can easily picture the Corsairs to be an immense, monolithic horde, hypervigilant and armed to the teeth. But is that how they truly are?"

Once more Jenn was lost in Jillybean's words. "What are you saying? That they're really weak? Maybe you don't know them like we know them. No one is stronger than the Corsairs."

"Is this conjecture on your part or do you have proof?" The word conjecture threw that sentence so far out of whack that Jenn was afraid to open her mouth.

Stu coughed, soft and weak before saying, "The proof is that no one's ever defeated them. That's a fact. They come and go as they please and they take what they please. For ten years the rule has always been: if you see the black flag, you run. I think we should look at another option."

"Mike?" Jillybean asked. "What do you think?"

He answered in a whisper, "I don't know. What do the signs say?"

Jenn was just craning her head back when Jillybean said, "The signs?" She wore a wide grin, looking like she was holding in laughter. "Normally, I'd say go for it, but the signs aren't going to help now. I've looked at all the options and this is the only viable one. Yes, it's dangerous, but just a few hours ago you three were threatening to walk to San Francisco, which is even more dangerous as well as useless. Even if you lived through the journey, your friends would be long dead."

They were quiet as the skiff purred south. Somewhere off to their left there was a splash and a bubbly moan. The sound was faint, still Jillybean steered them away from it. Eventually, she said, "I can take us back easily enough. I have a transmitter that will duplicate the power shortage. We can go back and no one will know."

The desire to give in was so strong in Jenn that she was afraid to look back at Mike and Stu. They would see the fear rising in her. She looked up and jerked in surprise. The missing stars had returned and the sky was full once again.

"We should go," she said. "To the Corsairs, I mean. The stars are back. They came back to guide us."

Mike and Stu looked up in a synchronized move. Jillybean only gazed fondly at Jenn. "You are simply adorable, Jenn Lockhart!" Jenn was pretty sure being adorable was a good thing and stuttered out a thank you, which only made Jillybean grin that much wider. "You say the stars are back? Did they go somewhere?"

"When we were on your island, the stars were…I don't know if they were missing or if they went anywhere, I just couldn't see them. It was like they were hidden from me."

"It's true," Mike agreed. "It really was strange. I didn't want to say anything because I didn't want to spook anyone." Jenn could tell he meant that he didn't want to spook her.

Jillybean nodded, perhaps thinking she looked wise, however the cat's grin was condescending. "That's so interesting. Primitive men might have thought the same thing when they stood around their fires at night. It's sort of sad that you don't get that small luxury, you know, sitting next to a fire and gazing up at the stars."

On the hilltop, having fires out in the open was too dangerous, while on Alcatraz, the idea of hauling wood all the way from the mainland just to let the light and heat go to waste would never happen. "I don't know if it's all that sad," Jenn replied, her tone cold. The cat's grin was bad enough but to be called primitive on top of it was out of bounds. "When my father was crushed by a building and I became an orphan, that was sad. Not having a fire outside isn't sad."

Jillybean was crestfallen. "No, I didn't mean it that way. I was referring to the effects of ambient light on our perspective…" Jenn groaned, interrupting Jillybean, who drooped. "Sorry. I'm sorry. I didn't mean it. The science stuff just sort of comes out and you have to know I don't mean anything by it. I'm not trying to make anyone feel bad."

She was so apologetic that Jenn reluctantly said, "It's okay."

"Good, good," Jillybean said, eagerly. "I'm glad you guys are letting me come with you. I use this little boat to go into the city whenever I need something, you know, something Neil wouldn't approve of, but it still feels like I've been cooped up for so long that it's driving me a little crazy."

A little crazy? Jenn thought.

Mike must have been thinking the same thing, because he coughed suddenly and turned away to hide the startled look on his face. After a moment he pulled himself together. "Yeah, we're glad, too. Just a question. Are you sure you know where you're going? I have a map of Washington if you want to see it. There's no way to get to the ocean in this direction."

Jenn cast a dubious eye down at the skiff. "We don't want the ocean, do we?"

"Not in this thing," Jillybean answered. "We'd be swamped by the first wave that hit us. No, the ocean would be bad and it would take us a hundred and eighty miles out of our way. This way is a shortcut."

"A shortcut to where?" Stu asked. "You know where the Corsairs actually live?"

They were nearing a point of land that rose like a turtle's back out of the water. Jillybean steered them to the right of the dark mass. "Yes, we've known for quite some time. Four years ago, a couple of slaves escaped from the Corsairs. They were able to give us a detailed layout of what I like to call their *lair*, for want of a better word. The pirates are holed up in the town of Hoquiam in Grays Harbor."

She was interrupted by Mike who began unfolding his map with a great deal of crinkling. "Can I borrow your flashlight?" After she handed it over he scanned the map, tracing the craggy, maze-like Sound inland all the way to Olympia. With one finger pressed on the city, he went in search of the Corsairs' lair. "Here it is, Grays Harbor. Hold on. We can't get there from Olympia. There's nothing connecting them."

"That's true enough, but it gets us close. As you can see, the Sound runs for about forty miles to Olympia. From there it's a quick ten-mile walk across to the Chehalis River which we'll ride right down to the harbor. If we press on hard enough, we should be there by two in the afternoon. After resting, I propose we attempt to cut out one of their ships around midnight."

"There's one problem in this plan," Stu said, "Me. We left the wheelchair back in that tunnel and you probably should have left me behind with it. Now, we'll have to find a clinic or a hospital in Olympia. It'll eat up time we don't have."

A side wind swept Jillybean's hair in front of her face. She laughed and turned her face into it. "Don't be silly, Stu. I would never have left you behind. You are special. You'll ride in the cart."

"And the boat?" Jenn asked. "You said we're going to take it down a river. How are we going to get the boat across to the river? Ten miles is kind of far for me and you to carry it, and if we're carrying it and Mike is pushing the cart *and* Stu, who will provide security? Someone has to scout ahead or who knows what we're going to run into?" Jenn was secretly happy to have thought of this before anyone else, anyone but Jillybean, that is.

"You'll see," she said, in that infuriatingly cryptic manner of hers.

Chapter 30

Mike Gunter

Jillybean steadfastly refused to answer their questions concerning how they were going to cross from the very southern end of the Sound to the Chehalis River. Her response was a somewhat nerve-wracking: "It's a surprise."

Mike wasn't just unnerved, he was more than a bit angry. "Out in the wilds is no time for a surprise."

His tone couldn't be missed and Jenn had done the smart thing, locking eyes with him and saying, "It's okay, Mike. We *trust* Jillybean, right?" She nodded until he started nodding as well. "She got us this fine, uh skiff-thing. And it's got a motor. I'm sure she's doing the right thing."

This was the end of the discussion until they finally made it to Olympia, a city that was slowly being engulfed in plant life. Even in the dark, the buildings weren't starkly defined as in many other cities. Their edges, covered in snaking vines, looked soft. The roads, or what there was left of them, were worse. With the tens of thousands of trees sprouting through every crack and seam, they were barely passable.

They putt-putted along an inlet that ran right down the gullet of the city to the farthest reaches of Puget Sound where many of the docks were rotted away.

Jillybean picked her way through the mess until she found a dock that was both intact and had a pulley system in place. "First thing, let's get everything hoisted up onto the dock," she whispered.

The dead were sending up moans that echoed throughout the city. It was an eerie sound that had all of them keeping one eye constantly on the far end of the dock as they worked. If one of the dead came, their only choice would be to jump into the water, pulling Stu along with them.

Luckily, it was so dark that the dead didn't see them working to raise both the skiff and the cart. Stu climbed into the cart once it was on the dock and Jillybean had them place the skiff over the top of it.

"I'll go first," Jillybean said. "You two follow along with the cart." Weaponless, she set off down the dock which creaked and swayed beneath her.

"Does this feel crazy to you?" Jenn asked, as she picked up the rope attached to the front of the cart.

Mike nodded. "Still, a part of me trusts her. It's like she's thinking three steps ahead which is way better than me. All I know is that we gotta get Stu and everything out of here before one of them comes."

"So, get moving," Stu hissed from the cart. "I don't trust this at all." If something happened, he would be a sitting duck unable to do anything but shoot his M4 which would only attract more of the beasts.

Mike went behind Jenn, grabbed a part of the rope and took almost all of the weight of the cart. Jenn was left holding a slack line. She held it up as he pulled. "Show-off," she whispered. In the dark, her teeth seemed whiter than ever. He found himself staring at that smile instead of watching where he was going and nearly walked off the side of the dock.

He was sure his face was red as a beet, and even though she couldn't see it, he stared down, watching his boots and placing each one squarely in the middle of the dock. It wasn't a very long dock, which was a good thing since Stu and the skiff added enormously to the weight of the cart. Mike was out of breath by the time they came to a low, grey building that had once been a yacht club; now it was nothing more than a fire hazard. At some point in the last dozen years, a pickup truck had blasted through the front doors. It was now on a set of stairs, canted danger-ously to one side.

Jillybean was standing in the lobby among a spray of twinkling glass and spears of wood. "In here." She waved them inside and helped to take the skiff off the cart. "You're like a pearl," she said to Stu.

"Sure, I guess," he said tiredly. His young face was worn and his eyes were dim.

"Sorry to say, Stu, but you look like crap," Mike said. "Do you have any pain meds, Jillybean? Like aspirin or something?"

She snorted. "Do I have pain meds? Of course, I do. I'll just need a little light. Jenn, if you'll be a lamb and keep watch. Grab one of the guns. Oh, except for that one." Jenn had pulled out an odd weapon that looked like a cross between an M4 and a shotgun. "That one's special."

As if the "special" gun would go off if it was looked at with crossed eyes, Jenn placed it back in the crate very gently, taking an M4 instead. Jillybean took out her flashlight and beamed it into her opened med bag.

"Jeeze!" Mike hissed. "Are you crazy? The dead will see the light. Turn it off."

"Give me a moment." It was more like two minutes, though it felt like ten as the seconds dragged out. She handed the flashlight to Mike. "Keep it pointed at the crook of his arm." Moving with practiced dexterity, Jillybean got an IV going and then sank a needle into a port in the line, giving Stu some sort of liquid pain medicine. In seconds, he lay back, his constricted features relaxing.

Mike turned off the light as fast as he could. The four of them sat in the dark listening for the dead and only Jillybean was disappointed when none came sniffing around. "It'll mean we'll have to go to them." Mike gaped in astonishment. "You'll see, it'll be okay," she said. "Let's get you ready. Have you ever used a low-light scope before? Just click it on. Go ahead, give it a try."

He put his eye to the scope and then backed away again, but only for a moment. "Holy cow, I can see everything. It's a weird grey color but I can see you and Jenn and, and this is just crazy!" Jenn was looking back at him with strange ghostly eyes. He saw her make the sign of the cross, almost as plain as day.

"Yes," Jillybean said. "Don't waste the battery."

"How do you have batteries when no one else does?" he asked. "That, uh, *other* girl said you make them. How?"

He expected her to give another of her unfathomable answers, however she said, simply, "Reading. Pick up a science textbook the next time you go to a high school. You'll be amazed how simple some things are. Speaking of which, where's the box with my books?"

She dug around in the cart, growing ever more agitated until she turned on the flashlight again. In her hand were old comic books. "What the hell is this? Where are my books? Son of a…it was Eve! Eve damnit! I need those books." She was talking to the air—loudly.

Stu roused himself and took her hand. "Hey, calm down. We can get you new books."

"Oh really? Do you really think I can find a copy of Autumn Dempsey's evaluation of the pharmacological effect of the test compound D2-009 just anywhere? This is Eve's doing. She wants out. I can feel her."

Mike wasn't comfortable with all of this "fractured mind" business. He didn't quite understand it, but he did understand that Eve was trouble, not that he was truly afraid of her. Jillybean/Eve was small, barely bigger than Jenn. "And this book would keep her inside you?" he asked. "Does the book distract her?"

Jillybean turned off the flashlight and gave a slump-shouldered sigh. "No. I'm trying to replicate certain drugs and it's not easy. It took me over a year to design broad-range antibiotics, but my attempts at creating psychotropics have been abysmal. And if I can't replace the ones I have…" she shrugged again. "I'll go mad, or rather, more so."

"Do you want to turn back?" Stu asked. "I think we'd all understand if you did."

"You need the skiff and your friends need me." She smiled suddenly. "And you need me as well, Stu Currans. Don't think you're going to get rid of me so easily." She hefted out the box of comics and set it on the floor. "Now, let's get ourselves a motor."

She picked up the odd gun and checked the chamber. Next, she loaded her backpack with a length of chain, a padlock, a hand-axe, a circle of rope and what looked like

264

a CB antenna whip that was broken down into three pieces. "An engine?" Mike asked. "What's rope got to do with an engine and is there really a working engine left in the world?"

Putting her finger to her lips, she whispered, "Just do what I say and it'll be okay. Jenn stay here and guard Stu. We won't be gone long." She paused on the edge of the ragged hole in the wall and brought her weapon to her shoulder. Mike did the same, using the low-light scope to scan the edge of the city next to the inlet. It seemed clear of the dead.

Jillybean started slinking forward. A parking lot, littered by a few dead cars surrounded the building. Normally they would have been an afterthought to Mike, just a part of the background. Now, he gave them a closer look and even with the scope they seemed altogether useless. The windows were caved in and the doors hung open, exposing their faded innards. A few of them had their hoods banked open wide, while all had their gas caps exposed.

The gas in them had long ago evaporated, leaving behind a foul-smelling sludge, a mixture of rain water, rust and toxic chemicals.

Jillybean scampered from car to car, staying low, frequently pausing to scan with her scope. When Mike was slow to follow, she patted her own bottom and then pointed straight down. *Stay on my ass*, she meant by the move.

He had figured she would check out the cars, but despite her stated desire to find an engine, she ignored the cars and slunk across the street to where a couple of office buildings blocked what had once been a pretty view of a lake with the Washington State Capitol Building rising behind it.

There were more cars in front of the taller of the two buildings. They were just like every other car in the world: useless. She ignored these as well and went to the front of the building, her feet crunching through glass. It had once been a building of steel and glass. Now, without the glass, it looked like a dark cage.

"What sort of engine are you thinking about getting?" he whispered. The only engine he knew of in an office building was the type that ran the elevators. As far as he knew they were called motors, although what the difference was, he didn't know.

"One that will get us over those hills." She pointed to the dark swells that cut off the stars to the southwest. "I don't think we're going to find one here."

Then why did we come here? He bit back the question, happy that she couldn't see his face.

She went around the building, moving so quietly that Mike felt like a blundering giant compared to her. Unlike Stu, who would have given him a glare, Jillybean didn't react even though he was sure she heard every kicked rock and every crunch of glass.

Crossing another street, she led him in the worst possible direction: *towards* the sound of a zombie. It was letting out a mournful wail that echoed along the empty streets. Gripping his M4 harder, he followed her as they got closer and closer until finally he couldn't take it.

"You can hear that, right?"

"Are you talking about the zombie or all the racket you're making? B.T.W. Mr. Magoo, it's a yes to both answers."

Mr. Magoo? B.T.W? What the hell did that mean? Mike leaned back away from her, suspecting that she had changed again. There was a new, slightly nasal quality to her voice.

She went on. "We're here for one of *them*. Your one and only job is to pop it in the head, but only if I tell you to." She flashed a grin. "It'll be a piece of cake, am I right?"

"I guess."

"Not quite the spirit I was looking for, but since you're cute, you'll get a pass. Okay, time to zip the lip." She took a deep breath and began to wind through the saplings until she reached a bank. It had the only intact windows on the block. She eased around to the front and found that the zombie wasn't in the bank, but in a parking garage next to it.

Since it was almost completely empty, it was basically an echo chamber. Jillybean, with a very nervous Mike following after, went slowly up along the ramps. It was so dark that when Mike wasn't using his scope, he had to actually hold her hand to keep from walking into her.

Her hand was small, cool and dry; his felt damp as a dishcloth. He was scared and would freely admit it. This was a first for him. He had never stalked a zombie; it helped that he had a full magazine, but what if there were more than one? What if a dozen came up the ramp, drawn by the noise of whatever Jillybean was planning? The bullets would go fast.

They finally spotted the zombie between the second and third floors. It had been scraping its way along the wall, only it had run into a truck. Through his scope, Mike watched the creature pawing at the truck's door, the top of which came to midway on its chest, while its head nearly scraped the ceiling.

Mike had to grit his teeth and force his feet from racing out of there.

The *only* reason he stayed was because the dark had rendered the creature completely blind. As long as they kept quiet and still, they would be safe. Jillybean had no intention of doing either.

"Yoo-hoo?" she called softly. Mike took a step back. She yanked hard on his hand. "Don't you leave me!"

The creature spun around and came lumbering at them. Mike was just about to start shooting when she said, with stone-cold nerves, "Not yet." She produced a small device which caused a brilliant red dot to appear on the concrete ten feet to their right.

The zombie charged, not at them, but at the dot. With a little flick of her wrist, the dot shot to the wall of the garage. The beast raced after it and basically ran face first into the wall with an ungodly slapping thud. Had Mike run into the wall like that he'd be down for the count, but the dead were rarely hurt by such things.

It popped up with a hideous screech and went after the dot again. Jillybean moved it back forth in short twitches, confounding the beast, who scraped its fingernails right off as it tried to get at it.

"Here," she whispered, handing her odd weapon to Mike. "Don't miss." He raised it to his shoulder, but she put her hand on it. "No, get closer. I'll keep it occupied."

Once more, it had turned at the sound of her voice and was coming at them. She shone the light at the truck and seconds later there was another tremendous collision. As the beast picked itself up, Mike moved in for the shot.

Just as he was about to shoot, she said, plain as day, "Aim for the throat." The beast spun around, towering over Mike. He shot, thinking that he would miss low, but this was no ordinary gun and what came out of it wasn't a bullet.

The sound it made wasn't natural either. *Thoomp!*

Mike was sure the gun had misfired. Jillybean pivoted the light and the beast turned, took two steps and then pitched forward onto its face.

"For a Magoo, that wasn't half bad," Jillybean said, flicking on her flashlight. "Help me roll him over." It took both of them to roll the beast; there was a big dart stabbed up into its throat. As a question formed on Mike's lips, Jillybean pulled out a pocket knife and stabbed its eyes out.

"What…?"

She turned the knife side-on and jabbed it first into one ear and then the next. "Let's have that hatchet," she said, turning her back so he could fish it from her pack. Mike's hands were numb as he handed it over. Without a blink, she hacked off its fingers and toes.

"Okay, what the hell?"

"Oh, you know Jillybean, she's got another hare-brained scheme. Right, right, 'hypothesis.' You know it's just a fancy word for wild-ass guess, right?" She wasn't talking to Mike, which was good because he didn't have an idea what she was talking about. "Let's get the chain on it," she said, this time looking right at Mike. They crisscrossed the chain over the beast's shoulders and chest. She then tied the rope off in back like a leash.

"This is the engine you wanted?"

"I didn't want it, Jillybean did. She just doesn't like this part of the deal." She held up the axe and then casually tossed it aside. "Blood bothers her, but I don't mind. It's why she has me. My name is Sadie. Me and Jilly go way back…" Just then the beast stirred. "That was fast. Now let's see if this works."

Mike backed away from both the dead and from Jillybean. "You don't know if this is going to work?"

"What part of 'wild-assed guess' didn't you understand?" she asked as she pulled out the CB antennae and began screwing it together. "Keep the light on me, will ya?" By the time the beast got to its feet, she had it assembled. Using it like a ten-foot long pointer, she touched the creature's chest.

It pawed at the tip with its mutilated hands, while at the same time staggering forward, bellowing in rage. Jillybean backed up, tapping it to keep it coming. The two went up the ramp, the beast raging and trying to get at the annoying pointer, and Jillybean staying just out of reach of its swinging arms. At the top, she casually stepped to the side, letting the creature pass within inches of her.

Mike cringed and she laughed. "It's perfectly safe." She tapped it on the back with the pointer. "Touch is the only real sense it has left. Now let's practice with the rope to get it accustomed to the weight."

She took the flashlight from him and had him grab the rope trailing behind it. "Now pull back, gently." The beast reacted to the new strain on its shoulders by smacking its bloody hands against the chain and Jillybean had to poke it in the face several times to get it focused. They went up the ramp again, only this time with Mike pulling hard on the rope.

The strength of the creature was fantastic and he was yanked along. They practiced for a while until Jillybean was satisfied. They then went back to the dock: the girl in front, poking the beast and Mike trailing behind seeing a fatal flaw in the plan. Someone would always have to walk ahead where they would be exposed and vulnerable.

Chapter 31

Jenn Lockhart

The two seemed to have been gone for ages. Jenn desperately wanted to look for them, but she couldn't leave Stu. Not that he would have noticed. Whatever shot Jillybean had given him had initially put a smile on his face; now he was lolling back in the cart like a limp noodle.

She wished she was that relaxed. The moans of the dead, like a wind blowing straight from hell, could be heard all around them. She shivered in fright as well as from the cold. The shivering only got worse as she heard one of the dead getting closer.

"Stu?" she whispered. In the dark, he looked dead himself. Normally, she wouldn't have been so nervous. Then again, normally she would've been able to run away if she had to. Now, she couldn't run because of Stu and she really couldn't hide because of him, either. If she hid, he'd be eaten.

She would have to fight. "If only I had one of them scope thingies," she grumbled. Without it, the beast lumbering through the parking lot towards her was just a dark shape against a dark background. She would have to wait until it was right on top of her before she fired—the thought was enough to make her sick.

Crouching behind her rifle, she watched as the creature began going in circles. Then she heard a short whistle. "What the hell?" Jenn slunk forward until she realized that there were actually three dark shapes, two much smaller than the giant beast.

Unbelievably they had captured one of the dead! It moved slower and slower until it finally stopped. When it did, Mike came jogging towards her. "Help me with Stu and the boat, k?"

"How…"

"I'll tell you later. Let's get the stuff. We have to hurry." Together they laid the skiff over Stu, who just went right on snoring. Next, they pushed the cart out into the parking lot and towards the beast. Jenn dragged her feet. The closer they got to the creature, the more she leaned further back from the cart. She wanted to run away very badly.

Mike angled the cart behind the creature, where the stench of it was eye-watering. *Why was it just standing there? How did they get it to move? Why wasn't it trying to eat them?* These and a million other questions spun through her head, but she knew better than to ask them when they were right out in the open.

Jillybean slipped over to the cart. She handed what looked like a long metal whip to Mike. "Don't touch it unless you have to." He nodded, then went in a wide circle around to the front of the creature. Mike looked awful twitchy and she didn't blame him. In fact, she jumped when Jillybean tapped her on the shoulder. "Help me with this." She had pulled back the skiff and had hold of a box. "Keep the boat from falling."

Jenn steadied the boat as Jillybean pulled the box out. Inside it was a fisherman's net that had thousands of strips of green and brown cloth attached to it. Together they un-folded it and laid it out on the ground. "We're going to lay this over the cart," Jillybean whispered.

They draped it over the cart, making it look like, well, Jenn couldn't say what it looked like except it no longer looked like a cart and that seemed to be the point. Next, Jillybean pulled out smaller versions of the net. She slipped one over Jenn's head.

"There you are. Now you're a bush."

"Wow," Jenn said, looking down at herself. She had worn camouflage before, but this was exceptional.

Jillybean flashed white teeth in the dark. "If one of the dead get too close just freeze and they'll never see you. Come on, I want you to meet George." Jenn had to be dragged in front of the creature. "This is George. Have you ever been this close to such a monster?"

272

The memory of killing Frank played itself through her mind. "Yes. What…what did you do to it?" Jillybean explained the purpose behind blinding and deafening it. "But why its hands and feet?" Jenn asked. She was relaxing by degrees. Not only did the homemade ghillie suit comfort her, it was obvious that the creature was almost harmless.

"Simple. Without fingers, it can't grab us and without toes, it can't really run. Something we don't want when it's pulling the cart with Stu inside. You got to hand it to Jillybean, she may be crazy as a loon, but the girl's got a thinker like no one I've ever known."

"Jilly…" Jenn began, her brows hanging low over her eyes.

Mike interrupted, "This is Sadie. Uh, I think she's Jillybean friend. You know, her *friend*." He cocked an eyebrow that was so obvious that Sadie rolled Jillybean's big blue eyes.

"Right, I'm her 'special' friend. Damn, Magoo, why don't you make cuckoo noises while you're at it?"

"I didn't mean anything by it," Mike protested. "I just, uh, I'm just interested to know when she's coming back. You did say she could think three steps ahead. Can you do that? Do you know what's going to happen?"

Sadie chuckled, shaking her head in disbelief. "Oh, so you're one of them? You're going to sit back and let her do your thinking for you. I should have seen it coming."

The girl was growing loud. Mike looked as though he was about to shush her, which Jenn thought would have been a mistake. Quickly, she added, "No, Mike's not like that at all. We appreciate the help, but I can still guide us using the signs sent to me. That hasn't changed at all. We're on the right track."

"Oh yeah, the signs," Sadie said, basically giving Jenn the same sort of look that Mike had given her a minute earlier. "They're pretty good, but I'd listen to Jillybean when she comes back, and sorry about getting heated there. It's just I've seen her be used a hundred times. I understand it a little. When you have a genius in your midst,

why not use her? If only you knew what it's like in here."
She tapped her head.

Jenn thought she was going to explain herself but
Sadie only looked sad. After a few seconds, Mike said,
"We should get moving." There wasn't much need for a
conversation after that. Once the three of them were in
ghillie suits, they picked out the simplest route across the
hills: they'd take Highway 101 until Highway 8 branched
off it going west.

Their order of march was simple as well. Although
Jenn could move like a soft breeze and was clearly the better scout, Mike insisted that he lead. She demanded, "Do
you really think you're better on land than I am?"

"That's not really the point," he said, as if that was any
sort of explanation. He took Sadie's strange weapon as
well as her laser pointer with him. They gave him a hundred-yard head start before following along with Jillybean
or Sadie, Jenn had no idea what to call her from one
minute to the next, using the CB antenna to goad the beast.

Although the cart weighed hundreds of pounds the
beast didn't seem to notice and stumped steadily along. In
fact, once it got moving in a direction it just kept going.
Sadie only touched him to maneuver him around trees and
junked out cars, and in one case, the charred remains of a
helicopter.

They went steadily up into the hills, where the trees
crowded in on the road and the darkness gathered. At first,
Jenn was nervous and couldn't stop looking over her
shoulder at the creature, afraid that it would suddenly re-
grow its eyes and toes and attack.

"Why don't you go check on Stu?" Sadie said, trying
to calm her. "I got this."

Stu was zonked out, but she was alarmed to find that
his IV had run dry and now blood was going back up the
line. It sent Jenn into a worse panic than before and she ran
to tell Sadie.

"That's nothing. Here, take over for a bit." Before Jenn
knew it, she was holding the antenna and nearly wetting
herself as George came at her, its arms flailing.

She crossed herself and then practically fled from the thing. She just couldn't walk as calmly as Sadie had in its shadow. If the thing tripped, she would be crushed. She kept at least twenty feet between her and it and even that seemed too close. With the dark and her attention divided, she tripped even more than George.

When Sadie came back, Jenn pushed the antenna into her hand and began to babble in relief, "How's Stu? He isn't going to bleed to death, is he? I just pictured him filling up that bag with his blood and then it popping and…"

"He's fine. How about you?"

"Me? I'm, I'm, I don't know how I am. It's been a tough couple of days, that's for certain and now…" She paused to look back at George and lost her train of thought. It was just so horrible. Normally, the dead look in the eyes of the dead made her skin crawl, but the gaping holes in George's face were even worse. In the dark, the holes looked like they went straight into its skull, yet it still walked.

It reminded Jenn of what Sadie had said earlier. "What is it like in her head?" she asked.

Sadie sucked in a breath. "It's like a nuclear reactor. It's hot all the time unless she's sleeping, and she doesn't sleep like a normal person. At the most she gets five hours a night and when she's up, she's always, always thinking. It doesn't look like it, but her mind is always racing."

Jenn's mind never raced like that. "Are you as smart as her?"

"You would think so since we share the same brain and all, but no, I'm just me, the same as I was back when I was alive."

"Back when you were alive?"

Sadie sighed; it was the sound of ultimate exhaustion. "Oh yeah. I died ten years ago. I got shot by some jerk but I stayed because Jillybean needed me. I just hang around keeping an eye on her, but when she's stressed I try to step in."

"S-so are you saying you're a ghost?" Jenn snuck a peek at the older girl, but her wild hair hung over her face casting it in shadows. It was like she didn't have a face at all. A shiver went right through Jenn.

"I think so. Either that or a spirit. But don't be afraid. I would never hurt a friend of Jillybean's. She needs friends. Hey, let's not talk about me anymore. What's going on with you and Mike?"

Jenn and Mike had been studiously avoiding the issue of "Jenn and Mike." There was definitely an attraction on her part and yet, if they made it back to San Francisco there could be no "Jenn and Mike." It was why she was constantly squashing her feelings for him down deep.

"Nothing. He's just a friend," she lied.

Sadie stopped and with George blindly stomping at them, she inspected Jenn. After a moment, she laughed softly. "Please. You like him and he likes you. That's why he's taking point, to keep you safe. I know you two have a screwed-up deal but don't make it worse by lying to each other."

George was now right on top of them. Jenn grabbed Sadie and pulled her along. "We shouldn't even be talking about this, especially now, out here. You and uh, Jillybean are too loud. There could be more of the dead around."

"Unlikely. They don't like hills and need a reason to climb them and to stay in them. They tend to flow like water, always collecting in low places." No sooner had she said this, than Mike began flashing the laser pointer at them. Sadie quickly stopped George by tapping it on the head. It turned its blind eyes upward and swiped at nothing with its stumpy hands.

Mike came hurrying back. "The road is blocked. There's like twenty zombies down there." He looked up at the wooded hills on either side of the highway. "We'll never be able to get the cart up there. We'll have to go back and find a way around."

"Back to where, Magoo? The only road we passed was three miles back and not only was it much smaller than this, it went south instead of west. No, we aren't going back. We'll go through them. We'll ghost through them."

She tipped Jenn an intimate wink. Jenn let out a tepid, "Ha-ha."

Mike didn't see anything funny at all. "First of all, stop calling me Magoo and second, going through them is a terrible idea. Sure, going around may take some time, but…"

"But nothing," Sadie snapped. "The road was much smaller and if you're afraid of a couple of dozen dead-heads on four lanes, you're going to piss your pants if we run into three on a dink county road like that was, *Magoo*."

Before Mike could spit out a curse, Jenn put up her hands. "Everyone calm down. Maybe, uh, maybe we should talk to Jillybean. I don't want to upset you Sadie, but you did say she was smarter than you. Maybe she'll have a better plan than either of the ones we've heard. How, uh, how do we get her back?"

"I'm not mad," Sadie said, lifting one shoulder in a half-shrug. "But I really doubt you'll like what she has to say. And you know how to get her back. Just ask her a question."

"What sort of question?" Mike asked.

Jenn knew. "What is the first cranial nerve?"

A grin crossed Sadie's face and she lifted that same shoulder again. "That one's easy. Do you know how often Neil asks these? It's the smelling nerve."

"That's not what it's called." Jenn had no idea what it was called, but was sure there was no such thing as a "smelling nerve."

"Of course, it is. It's called the 'old' something. Wait, it's the old factory nerve." Jenn shook her head and Sadie, who looked both confused and angry, began to mutter, her eyes as slits.

After a moment she smirked. "It's the olfactory nerve." Jenn began to shake her head again. "It's okay. It really is the olfactory nerve. Where are we?" She spun slowly, paused when she came to George standing, grey and still, like a stone statue. She looked around him at the cart. "And how is my patient? Have you looked in on him recently?"

"We have," Jenn answered, leaning closer, trying to see if this was really Jillybean. "He's sleeping. We have a bit of a problem." She explained what was going on.

"Sadie was right. We'll go through them. I brought the ghillie suits for exactly this reason. If you'd like, I can demonstrate the effectiveness of them." Jenn had no intention of walking through a pack of the dead, ghillie suit or no ghillie suit. Jillybean read her expression. "Follow me."

Without waiting, she walked straight down the road. Just after a turn, the highway dipped and there in a low point were thirty-two zombies. Most were sleeping on their feet, while a few were on their hands and knees on the side of the road eating the remains of a deer, chewing endlessly on its bloody hide or gnawing its bones down to nothing.

"Pay close attention," Jillybean said, before pulling the ghillie suit over her head. The net hung down, hiding her completely. Very slowly, she walked straight towards the dead.

Jenn crossed herself and Mike muttered, "Holy crap," as she walked through the group, turned around and walked back.

Jillybean grinned when she saw their expressions. "Hopefully you're not chalking what you just saw to supernatural entities. It's really very simple. What do we know of the dead? They eat, they sleep, they kill. But what do they kill? Do they kill trees or rocks or buildings? No. They kill people. As long as you don't look or sound like a person, they ignore you. The Russians knew precisely what they were doing."

"The Russians?" Jenn asked. She had heard of the "The Russians" but didn't know anything about them other than they had been "our" enemies at one time. They were like the Corsairs in her mind.

"Oh yes. It was the Russians who created the virus in the first place. They called it the *Super Soldier* serum. They wanted a way to make their soldiers bigger, stronger, tougher. They wanted them impervious to pain and immune to the elements. They got zombies instead."

278

Mike glanced back down the road, squinting as if he could see the beasts. "How do you know?"

"I almost killed the guy who made all this happen. His name was Yuri Petrovich. He's one that got away." She sighed and then smiled. "That's water under the bridge. Let's concentrate on getting past these guys."

Jillybean gave them a very brief tutorial on how to act when walking through a bunch of zombies, which boiled down to go slow and keep quiet. She had Mike lead the way and the only thing she let him carry was the laser pointer. He looked like he wanted to walk through the crowd of dead about as much as a cat wants a bubble bath.

One dreadfully slow step at a time, he went forward until he was within ten paces of the first beast, then he slowed down even more, going so slowly that Jenn caught up to him. She wanted to go faster. In fact, she wanted to race out of there. Being close to George was one thing, being close to so many had her right on the edge of panicking. There were so many of them that they could literally tear her to bits in seconds and eat her, bones and all, in less than a minute.

There was a horrible finality to the thought that had her heart beating frantically. She could feel her pulse in her fingertips and in her ears. She was so scared that she couldn't help herself; she reached out to touch Mike. She needed to feel something real.

He jumped and his breath hitched in his throat. The closest of the beasts, an eight-footer had been sleeping, now it woke with a breathy growl. It was a hideous thing with only half a face. The rest had been eaten off and was now a crag of ugly scars and exposed bone. It turned its one glaring eye on Jenn and reached out a long-clawed hand.

Too late Jenn realized she might actually look too much like a shrub. The dead ate plants after all, when they couldn't get small girls that is.

Chapter 32

Jenn Lockhart

Giving up the entire useless charade, Jenn wanted to sprint away only panic had her in its grip and she couldn't move. As the hand came closer and closer she found herself petrified with fear.

She was staring death right in its one eye when suddenly that eye blazed red. Mike had used the laser pointer. With a roar, the beast stabbed its fingers into its own eye, its elbow hitting Jenn's shoulder with the force of a ram, knocking her to the ground.

The beast, blinking its one eye, reached for her again, only Mike used the laser pointer, casting a red dot onto the ground to her right. The beast chased after it, turning from them. The other dead things glanced over with expressionless eyes not having seen the dot when Mike flicked it on and off quickly.

Jenn lay on her side, breathing in shallow ragged gasps until the beast moved away, then, with shaking hands she slowly pushed herself up. Mike stood still as a statue until she was on her feet. Even then, he didn't move. He let her walk out of what felt like a death trap, first.

When she was safe, he waited for Jillybean who had the toughest job of all: moving George through the group. She made it look easy, though a few of the dead meandered close to gawp at the strange, moving bush.

"So, will you trust me from now on?" Jillybean asked when they were a quarter mile away, the sweat cooling down their backs.

Mike didn't hesitate to say that he would. Jenn was slower to agree. She had nearly died. That was the complete truth. She had been within an inch of being killed. As always, Jillybean seemed to be able to look right through her. "You set yourself on this course and it's a dangerous one. We could have gone back to Bainbridge. We still can if you want to. But if we go forward, you have to trust me."

A nod with downcast eyes was all Jenn could give. Jillybean clapped her hands. "Good enough. Now let's get moving. We have a lot of ground to cover before daylight."

The three of them, and George, fell into the march. Mike in front, Jillybean with the antenna, poking the creature every fifteen minutes and Jenn walking next to the cart. She claimed it was to keep an eye on Stu, however, the real reason was because she had embarrassed herself in front of Mike and was frankly afraid of Jillybean.

She believed wholeheartedly that Jillybean was haunted or possessed or whatever the right word was. And when the Coven found out, there would be trouble.

Her fear continued mile after mile until Jillybean called a halt and checked on Stu herself. He woke up for a few minutes, his eyes slipping in and out of focus. "Okay, let's cut you off," Jillybean said. "Too much of Mama Jillybean's poppy concoction can be a bad thing."

At Jenn's look of alarm, Jillybean shook her head. "Nothing a couple of hours of sleep won't cure. I'll be right back. I have got to wee." She stopped them near an old farm house and ran inside.

While she was gone, Jenn poked her head under the skiff. "You okay? Do you need anything?"

A spasm of pain crossed his face as Stu tried to re-arrange himself among the boxes. "No, I'm good. Don't worry about me."

He had always been so tough that she didn't see just how much pain he was in. Jillybean saw it all. She came out of the house with her arms loaded down with dusty-smelling blankets and three pillows. She made a bed for Stu in the cart and when he laid back down, he was asleep in a blink.

"I wish I had thought of that," Jenn said.

"You're too hard on yourself. You're just fifteen years old and despite that, you've shown remarkable courage. Why don't you move George along the rest of the way? It's only another mile or so and the more you're around the dead the more you'll come to realize they aren't all that scary."

Jenn didn't think she would ever come to realize this "fact," not if she lived a million years. Still, by the time they made it to the town of Elma and the Chehalis River, she was far more relaxed around the creature. "What are we going to do with him?" she asked when George had dragged the cart down to the river's edge.

"He's served his purpose. I say we let him go," Mike said. "He's basically harmless."

"No," Jillybean said, quietly. "We kill it. Always kill them when you can safely do so." It seemed cold, but neither Jenn nor Mike argued. After unhooking the rope, Jillybean tapped the beast until it fell in a little washed-out gully. While it was trying to right itself, Mike dropped a heavy rock on its head.

Jillybean was suddenly all smiles again. "Let's get this boat in the water." Even though it wasn't much more than a fast-running stream, it was a wet and cold job getting the skiff and Stu into the water. Then they just let gravity take them away. With the water so shallow, the cart shuddered and banged along in their wake sometimes floating and sometimes running on its bicycle wheels.

Eventually, as smaller streams emptied into the Chehalis, the water grew deep enough to float the cart. It was an easy trip at that point but slower than Jillybean had expected. It was four in the morning when they came to Gray's Harbor and found a long rambling town hugging the northern shore.

Running the batteries low, Jillybean purred the skiff along until they smelled smoke. Stu was finally roused. "That's coal smoke. Do you know if they have a coal-fired generator? If so, they might have spotlights just like Bainbridge."

Jillybean didn't know and decided to err on the side of caution, slipping the skiff in among the trees crowding the bank. "Mike, stay with Stu," she said. "Pull the boat and the cart out of the water. Jenn and I will get the lay of the land. No, no arguing. Jenn is the quietest and right now that's what we need."

Jenn took an M4 with a night scope while Jillybean took her funny dart shooter. The two made their way through the town, following the coal smell. Being stealthy in Hoquiam wasn't easy. A battle had been fought there and not a battle between man and zombies.

Men had fought each other with guns and tanks and bombs of all sorts. The eastern portion of the town was in ruins. Where the streets weren't clogged with the burned-out husks of Humvees and armored personnel carriers, there were either craters the size of swimming pools gaping the streets or their way was blocked by toppled buildings.

Jenn was both awed and disgusted by the destruction. Here and there were heaps of bones taller than herself, as if bodies had been bulldozed into piles and left to rot.

"I don't like this," Jillybean whispered as they came to one of the piles. There was a strangled quality to the words and Jenn looked at the young woman through her scope. Even accounting for the greyscale, Jillybean didn't look like herself. Her eyes, always very large, were popped wide open. She didn't blink as she stared at the bones.

"Hey, it's going to be okay," Jenn said, putting her arm around the girl's shoulders and squeezing her in a hug. "We need you to stay with us, Jillybean. Eve and Sadie can't help us, we need you. Stu needs you. Come on. Let's get away from all this."

Jenn pulled Jillybean past the bones and across the front of a roller rink. She thought about going inside but, she didn't have the foggiest notion what a roller rink was and because the word "roller" sounded like there would be things that would trip them up in the dark, she pushed on. Beyond that was a small engine repair shop that stank of oil even after so long. She could only imagine how filthy it would be inside.

She kept going and simply moving seemed to be what Jillybean needed; she grew less shaky and her eyes began to clear. Jillybean was herself again by the time they came to a river. "This is it," Jillybean said, as she scoped the far side. Across the water was a hedge of tangled wire. A little beyond that was a wall of cinderblocks ten feet high and then there was another wall, this one twenty feet high. Stationed every hundred yards or so was a guard, their heads just visible above the second wall.

Jillybean looked both ways, asking in a whisper. "Where are the boats? What do you think, upstream?"

"Maybe."

"There's no maybe. They're upstream. See that coil of rope?" She pointed her rifle at the base of what had once been a bridge. "One end is attached to the base and the other to a buoy. The sailors use these to pull themselves against the current. You can see another one at the bend in the river."

"If you knew which way to go, why'd you ask me?"

Jillybean put a serious hand on her shoulder. "Not to show off, if that's what you think. I want you to start actively using your eyes. Right now, you're a passive observer, missing so much the world has to tell us. Come on, the sun's almost up."

Jenn glanced east where the stars were already fading. All save one: Venus. It was the wandering star, never in the same place from night to night. Seeing it singled out against a black sky was extremely good luck for travelers. She wanted to tell Jillybean that she had missed a very obvious sign instead, she kept the secret to herself.

They crawled back a block and then angled north for a quarter mile, keeping well away from the river. When they approached it once more, they saw boats lined up one after another along a series of floating docks. Almost all of them were sailboats, ranging in size from dinky twelve-footers to a gorgeous sixty-foot cruising boat. There were other boats as well including long canoes that could hold twenty people.

Set on the wall overlooking the docks was a huge machine gun. The good feeling Jenn had at seeing Venus was crushed at the sight of it, especially as it was manned.

Even without the night scopes, they could see the orange ember of a cigarette.

It looked as though their mission was over but Jillybean wouldn't leave, not even when the sun came up. She studied every detail, from the way the boats were positioned, to the time of the guard shift, to the way the shadows played along the water.

Finally, she crawled backwards, but instead of heading to where Mike and Stu were, she went downriver to where it washed out into the harbor. "Look," she whispered. Stretched across the mouth of the river was a chain that sat three feet above the water line.

On their side of the river, the chain was hooked around a tree. On the far side the chain ran through the wall and disappeared.

Again, Jillybean stared for what seems like ages. They were still there when a man walked up to the building, unlocked the door and went inside. Soon the chain went from taut to bowed and then gradually it disappeared beneath the water. It wasn't long before eight sailing boats, under shortened sails, and one of the long canoes came down the river.

"Which one will suit our purpose the best?" she asked, gesturing at the boats.

"I'm not an expert, but I guess the biggest one. Mike knows more than I do." Without another word, the two hurried back to where they had left Mike and Stu.

The cart had left muddy tracks and the two girls followed them right to a house across a service road. "Jenn, tell them the situation," Jillybean ordered. Jenn hadn't expected this but was able to rattle off everything she had seen and including seeing Venus.

The lines on Mike's face had been deepening until she mentioned the planet. They cleared immediately. "Okay. I can pilot any of those ships, but the bigger the better. We should go for the biggest we can."

Jenn shook her head. "The biggest ones are right below the main guard. Sound carries at night. I think we should go for a thirty-footer that's moored midway down the line. We'll have to be extremely quiet, but I think we can get it. The biggest problem is going to be the chain. It looked like it was half a foot thick, we'll never be able to cut it."

"The chain is that thick, but there's only a bike lock holding it to the tree. A good pair of bolt cutters will do the trick. Once we get the chain down, the three of us will cut out the ship while Stu waits for us in the cart out in the harbor."

"Is that the whole plan?" Jenn asked, expecting more.

"Sometimes simplicity is the best plan. I would have liked to have brought along a few surprises for our friends, but," she paused to tap her head. "It wouldn't have been good for any of us."

While they were getting some badly needed sleep, sprawled on mattresses dragged into the living room, Jillybean disappeared out into the town. Jenn woke near midday with the smell of motor oil in her nostrils. "Go back to sleep," Jillybean said. "I decided a few surprises wouldn't hurt me too badly."

"What sort of surprises?"

Jillybean held up her hand, palm out. It was covered in dirt and grease. "No explosions, I promise. Sadie was adamant about that. It's just a little fire, nothing too crazy."

A little fire was okay with Jenn. She went back to sleep and didn't wake again until the sun was beginning to sink. Stu had woken her by trying to crawl out of the room, dragging his leg behind him. "Sorry, but I've got to take a leak, *badly*."

Mike hopped up and helped him. While they were gone, Jenn inspected what Jillybean had brought inside. There were fifteen dresser drawers, piled high with paper and kindling. They had been tied together with three-foot long pieces of rope.

"I don't get it," Jenn said to Jillybean, who was taking small stacks of paper and using tape to turn them into tubes.

"What's there not to get? You take paper tubes, fill them with sawdust, pour old motor oil in them and *whamo* you get easy fire starters. Everyone took all the gas but motor oil is just lying around. Now be a lamb and shred up sheets. I need them to be three inches wide and tied end to end. We'll need at least ninety feet of it."

When the sun went down, they moved the operation outside and worked under the stars. They finished well before they were scheduled to kick off their plan. They ate, each only nibbling. Jenn's stomach was twisting itself into knots and it only got worse as the "Go" time approached.

Finally, at eleven, Jillybean said, "Alright, let's move out." With the dark, she looked small, almost childlike and Jenn was sure that she looked the same. Mike, with his hands stuffed deep into his pockets, had the air of a nervous teen about to launch a prank. Only Stu looked old enough to be taking such a huge risk. He looked like a real adult and that wasn't a good thing.

In Jenn's world adults always seemed to die first.

Chapter 33

Jenn Lockhart

Jillybean had them darken their faces with dirt before they moved out.

Jenn had never done this before and felt like she was putting on make-up, dabbing it on her cheeks with shaking hands. "Here, let me," Mike said. His hands were steady. He wasn't afraid, in fact, he was excited. Jenn knew that if he could bring back a boat larger than the *Calypso*, Gerry the Greek would welcome him home with open arms. She could only hope that if she was able to bring back the girl doctor, the Coven would do the same for her.

Gently, he smeared mud across her forehead, her small nose and her ears. "Huh. I never noticed before but your ears are pointed." He smiled down at her and she felt her chest constrict. They had studiously avoided intimate moments just like this, but just then her guard was down and she smiled back…at first. Then she looked away.

"You shouldn't look at me like that," she whispered. "If anything will break our luck, it'll be us, you and me looking at each other like that. We can't. We have people counting on us."

"You two were *looking* at each other?" Jillybean laughed, a high sound that was almost a cackle. "My, what will the Baptists say?"

"Are the Baptists like the Corsairs?" Jenn asked, turning from Mike. He looked like he wanted to pull her back and even reached out a hand, but stopped as Jillybean really did cackle. It was a shockingly loud sound.

Jillybean was laughing so hard her legs actually buckled and she collapsed, holding her stomach. Stu glared at the spectacle. "Are you trying to sabotage the mission? Jillybean? Is that even you? Mike, can you take a look at her?"

"Don't bother," Jillybean said. "It's me. It's just I… Baptists…Corsairs…" She broke down laughing again.

Jenn dropped down next to her. "Hey, uh, uh could you tell me something about those cranial nerve thingies?"

Jillybean only laughed harder and there was nothing they could do but wait until they began to die off. She wiped away her tears saying, "Thingies? Your grasp of scientific jargon is unparalleled, Jenn Lockhart. And that's all right." They were almost nose-to-nose and, unexpectedly, Jillybean kissed her square on the lips. "Don't ever change and don't die tonight. I wouldn't forgive myself if the world lost such an innocent creature."

This stopped Jenn's hand; she had been about to wipe away the kiss from her lips. "Are you sure you're okay?"

"I took five pills. You guys are stuck with me for as long as my liver holds out." She sighed, chuckled again, this time ruefully. She stood and went to Stu and kissed him as well. It wasn't deep or passionate, it was soft and quick. When she turned around, Mike took a step back and she laughed once more. "Don't worry, I'm not going to kiss you. I just figured that if I was going to die, I wanted his kiss on my lips. Trust me, it's better than sharing a look."

She left the room in stunned silence. Jenn and Mike shared another look. She glanced away first. She wanted to kiss him, but there were too many *what ifs* hanging over them. They didn't have the luxury of living on the edge of insanity like Jillybean.

"We should go," she said, feeling young and cowardly compared to Jillybean who would have laid one on Mike's lips and laughed at anyone who tried to stop her. Laughed or worse, depending on who was running the show in her head.

Jenn stepped outside and felt a sudden chill. The dead were out in force that night. There were hundreds of them roaming along the trashed-out streets and their moans were even more baleful than ever.

The three of them made a slow parade hauling the filled cart to the river, where there were still more of the dead. Even with their ghillie suits and Jillybean's laser pointer, they had trouble getting into position.

When Mike went back with the now empty cart for Stu and the rest of the gear, Jenn and Jillybean crawled from cover to cover down to the chain. "I want you to cut it," Jillybean whispered, handing over a large set of bolt cutters. Jenn took the ungainly tool and just as she lined them up on the bike lock, Jillybean asked, "What's going to happen when you cut the lock?"

Jenn was about to give the obvious answer: *the chain will fall in the water,* but she held off knowing that Jillybean didn't think in terms of the obvious. She thought three steps ahead. And what were those steps? The chain would fall, making a clear splash, alerting both the Corsairs and the dead.

"I need a rope," Jenn said. The words weren't even out of her mouth before Jillybean produced one.

"This life is like a game of chess," Jillybean said, tying off the chain and wrapping the rope twice around the tree.

"Chess with zombies," Jenn said, cutting the lock. As Jillybean slowly let out the rope, the chain sagged into the water, dipping gently below the surface. "You know, it's almost like the dead knew something was about to happen tonight."

Jillybean released the rope. "Why? Because there's so many of them? I brought them here. Our pirate friends will be far less likely to shoot with what could be a significant horde crowding the river."

Jenn wanted to know how she had brought them here, but they had been loud enough and had already attracted a trio of giants that came moaning through the trees. Jillybean gave Jenn a wink and slipped under her ghillie suit. Jenn did the same and watched through the holes as the dead came within spitting distance.

Even before they were gone, Jillybean was moving to the launch point. She didn't like to walk with the camouflage netting over her face so she wore it like a cape draped on her shoulders instead.

290

When they reached the skiff and the stack of dresser drawers, Mike was there, crouched down next to a tree. There was no need for talk. Their plan was simple: head to the thirty-footer, unmoor it and float away, using the skiff's engine to get them mid-channel where the current was strongest.

As always, Jillybean had thought ahead. The car batteries had been recharged and, although they didn't have another ghillie net, she had trimmed some branches and duct-taped them to the skiff. When they pulled away from shore they looked like a hunk of debris—a hunk of debris fighting the current, but a hunk of debris nonetheless.

Jenn lay in the middle of the skiff feeling useless. Mike had the dart gun up front and Jillybean was driving. As far as Jenn knew, her entire job was to keep quiet and out of the way—and not to do anything stupid.

With the dead making so much noise, the skiff's little motor went unheard, but to be on the safe side, Jillybean cut it twenty yards away and allowed them to drift up next to the sailboat which sat high in the water. The name *Saber* was painted in silver lettering on its side.

Mike stood and grabbed the top edge of the *Saber*, stopping the skiff with a little thump. It was a small sound, yet they all froze not daring to breathe.

Jillybean slowly stood, shrugged off her ghillie suit and caught the edge, as well. She nodded at Jenn to climb up first. Jenn had hoped to go last. Dropping her ghillie suit, she grabbed hold of the sailboat and swung a leg up, catching the edge. With an M4 across her back, she wasn't very stealthy. Her boot thudded, the holstered Glock at her hip scraped against the fiberglass and a grunt escaped her before she made it to the deck.

Still, she was quieter than Mike, who knocked a knee against the side of the boat so loudly that it woke someone *inside* the cabin.

"What the hell?"

Jenn's first response was to look to Mike, but he was still struggling to climb onto the bow. Almost too late, she scrambled for her Glock, pulling it just as the cabin opened revealing a shadow of a man. He was indistinct, but the shotgun in his hands was unmistakable.

"S-stop!" she hissed, whipping the Glock up. It wavered and jitterbugged in her hand.

"What is this?" the man growled. He wasn't quiet. They were all of fifty feet away from the guard, sitting behind his machine gun. Jenn couldn't afford any more noise.

She jabbed the gun in his direction to make sure he saw it. "Shut up and, and, and put your hands up."

"No. I'm not doing a damned thing. You come on my boat, point a gun at me and demand that *I* shut up?" As he spoke, he came walking out of the cabin, seeming to grow larger and larger with each step up the short flight of stairs. He towered over Jenn, who was enveloped by the stench of whiskey and body odor.

He was a frightening beast of a man, but Jenn wasn't as frightened of him as he supposed. After all, she had fought and killed Frankenstein, she had ridden a tiny boat into a school of the zombies and saved a man, and she had braved a hurricane on the open ocean.

Yes, she was afraid of the man, but she was even more afraid of making noise. Even more than that, she was afraid that she would make the same mistake Mike had made. She was afraid to let this man turn that shotgun away from her and point it at one of her friends. She would never allow that to happen.

"Put the gun down, now," she said, her voice growing icy as she came closer and closer to pulling the trigger.

"The hell I will." He didn't need to be quiet. In fact, it benefited him to be loud; loud enough to get the guard's attention, but not loud enough to get shot. He knew Jenn couldn't shoot him without alerting the entire town.

What he didn't know was how desperate Jenn was. "Then you don't leave me any choice." He held the shotgun pointed slightly down and away. Jenn saw the track it would have to take before he could pull the trigger: left to right, and just as it began that track, she pulled the trigger.

He was a big man and the 9mm round staggered him as it hit him square in the chest. He was also a vindictive man. He was going to die no matter what and still that shotgun tracked.

Jenn dodged left firing the pistol three more times, blinding herself with the muzzle flashes. The man went down with a sad moan. Suddenly, there were cries all around them. "Cut the lines!" Mike hissed.

Jenn was too frantic to even think about the mooring lines. People were rushing out of the boats all around them. She turned the Glock toward the boat that was next to the *Saber* and started blasting away as someone came on deck. He went down after who knew how many shots.

By then, bullets were going every which way. Jillybean was trading shots with four people on three different boats, all on the north side, so Jenn turned to the south and saw muzzle flashes all down the dock. The air was sighing and hissing with the passage of bullets.

Jenn, standing in full view, fired back until her Glock emptied in what felt like a second. She was reaching for her M4 when Mike pushed his into her hands—it had the lowlight scope and when she put it to her eye, she gasped. Suddenly she could see!

From that moment, the battle changed dramatically. She shot at everything that moved until her ears rang and her hands were numb. She was changing out her magazine when she realized that they were moving. Mike had stuck to the plan and cut away the mooring lines and heaved the *Saber* away from the dock.

"Get us into the channel!" he yelled to Jillybean as he hauled up the mainsail.

There was utter confusion along the docks with people screaming back and forth demanding to know what was going on and it was a full minute before it was decided that either Benny had gone crazy or that someone was stealing Benny's boat. Either way, the guard with the machine gun finally opened up.

They were a hundred yards away and in the dark, the bullets ripped up the river off the port side, sending up a sheet of water. A direct hit would have torn the boat in two. Jenn immediately rattled off a string of bullets, killing the man just as he was correcting his aim.

By then, Jillybean had pushed them into the channel, where they began to pick up speed and pull away from the docks. The firing died away and Jenn changed her aim to the wall, once more taking shots at anyone who poked their head up. Even with the scope she missed every time.

She was changing to another magazine just as bullets ripped through the *Saber* from behind. Splinters filled the air as a scream erupted from *inside* the cabin. That scream, so unexpected, froze Jenn as the air crackled and cracked around her.

A boat was seventy yards back and there were at least eight guns blasting away from its deck. Their only saving grace was that it was a dark night. The black hull and sails of the *Saber* blended so well with the darkness that when Mike heaved the rudder over and they cut to the left, the bullets whipping downriver missed by twenty yards. Jenn held her fire, knowing they would orient on her muzzle blasts.

Mike kept the boat as close to the far bank as possible and only swung back at a bend in the river. It was here that Jillybean had stashed the dresser drawers filled with oil-soaked kindling.

Jenn suddenly saw, with amazement, that Jillybean was still in the skiff, running alongside the *Saber*. Jenn had assumed she was onboard As Jillybean passed them in the skiff, she reached out and grabbed the first and buzzed back out into the river, hauling the chain of them along until they stretched almost from bank to bank.

She lit the first and it burst into flame. The fire traveled quickly along the oil-soaked line of sheets, catching each drawer on fire until they were all burning. The captain of the boat following them panicked and, instead of braving the shallows on either side of the line, he tried to turn around. He heaved the rudder over, fighting against the wind and current which swept him broadside into the line, engulfing him in a flaming hug.

In no time, the forty-foot boat was on fire, lighting up the night. Behind it, more boats could be seen shoving away from the docks. They clogged the river as the first few were hesitant about passing the burning boat. This gave Jillybean time to catch up in the skiff. She thudded its prow into the sailboat's stern adding the power of the little electric motor to the overall thrust.

"Ahoy, *Saber*," she called. "Is everyone all right?"

Jenn glanced down at herself. Everything had been such mayhem and confusion that she honestly didn't know. She was shaking like a leaf, but other than that she was fine. "I-I think I'm okay, but there's someone hurt in the cabin. A girl I think."

"Probably a slave," Jillybean said in a carrying whisper. "Tell her to hold on. Once we get Stu on board, I'll take care of her."

After a deep breath, Jenn swung the cabin door back and looked inside. The *Saber* was actually thirty-two feet from stem to stern and a small kitchenette and crowded "living room" greeted her. Propped against a stiff-looking couch was a woman. In the dark, only her eyes really stood out. The rest of her was a bloody mess.

A bullet had unzipped her cheek from her lip to her ear, while another had punched a hole in her stomach. She looked at Jenn and cried, the tendons of her neck sticking out like pulley wires.

"W-We have a doctor," Jenn told her. "Just give her a few minutes." There was nothing Jenn could do for the woman except watch her die and it was the last thing she wanted to do. "I'll be right back." She fled on deck just as they cleared the mouth of the river. Stu, sitting on the bobbing cart was anchored perfectly along the path of the wind and Mike bore down on him so quickly that they almost crashed.

They slowed down just enough to let Jillybean catch up and for Mike to throw a line to Stu. "Jenn, take the helm," Mike ordered. "Keep us pointed southwest." With the *Saber* plowing on into the dark, Mike pulled the cart in close and Stu began tossing everything up to him. It wasn't easy. The chop in the harbor bucked the sailboat up and down and a few of the jugs of waters and two of the packs fell and had to be left behind.

On the other side of the boat, Jillybean climbed onto the deck just in time to see the second pack fall.

"Get that one!" she screeched. Stu dropped a crate and lunged for the pack, but because of the cast on his leg, he missed. Jillybean ran to the back of the boat, watching the pack sink. "We have to turn around," she said. "That, that, that was my pack. It had my pills in it. You know, the pills that make me, *me*."

"Don't stop!" Mike bellowed as Jenn started to shorten sail. "Our lead is razor slim. We'll get more pills. I'm sure they're everywhere."

Jillybean shook her head. "They aren't and even if they were, they wouldn't have been stored correctly. They'd be useless. I'll use the skiff and I'll be right back."

Mike grabbed her. "No, it's too slow. You'll never catch up. Go below and take a look at that girl. She needs you, *Jillybean*."

Slowly, hesitantly, Jillybean went down into the hold. She seemed even more unsure of herself than Jenn. Mike watched her and cursed, before hissing to Stu, "Hurry!" Stu began throwing items as fast as he could and when the cart was empty, he climbed the rope to the deck where he lay panting.

"You better go check on her," Mike said to Jenn. "I'm worried about her."

Not as much as me, Jenn wanted to say. She went down into hold where Jillybean was kneeling next to the woman. Jillybean had her flashlight set on the floor, pointed into one of the crates. "You okay?" Jenn asked. When Jillybean looked up, one of her eyes went to the woman and the other went to Jenn.

Jenn had never seen anything like it. She couldn't help her reaction: she gasped and leaned back.

"What does this say?" Jillybean asked, holding up a small bottle. "Is it morphine? I can't tell." In one hand was the bottle and in the other was a seven-inch hunting knife.

"First, tell me what the knife's for."

Jillybean's right eye slipped from the bleeding woman and now they were both focused on Jenn. "It's for her. She needs to die."

Chapter 34

Jenn Lockhart

"Eve?" Jenn asked.

The girl rolled Jillybean's huge eyes. "Of course, it's me. Jillybean is too weak for this. She knows this girl ain't gonna live but she's still going to waste supplies on her. Those are supplies we need for your friends, Jenn. So, don't give me that look. I'll make it quick. It'll be a mercy."

She took a step toward the woman and Jenn slid between them. "Please don't. We can figure something out beyond murder, right?"

Eve's eyes flashed. "Murder? Murder? Is that what Jillybean said? But do you know what she's done? Huh? Do you know what she did to the *Believers*? Do you know how many thousands of them she killed? And do you know what she did to the River King and his people? Have you even heard of them? Probably not because *she* killed them all."

Jenn started to shake her head, which only made Eve laugh. "You don't know her like I do. You don't know that the only reason Neil keeps her around is to use her. He needs her genius, but he doesn't care about her and never has. Do you know that the first time he met her, he tried to trade her? He tried to trade her like a slave."

"I-I didn't know that, but, but that was then. We have to deal with right now. Put down the knife and bring Jillybean back. We need her help. And, and besides, you probably don't know the first thing about how to kill mercifully. Do you even know which cranial nerve to cut?"

"Oh, Jenn," Eve said, holding back laughter. "You're a freaking riot. No wonder *she* likes you so much. The cranial nerves are in the head, duh. You can't kill anyone by stabbing them in the head. Not unless you get them right at the base between C1 and, and, the uh." She touched the back of her head, a touch of confusion in her blue eyes.

On a hunch, Jenn said, "It's not C1, it's C4."

"What? No, that would cause a loss of, um, what is it? The diaphragm? Is it the diaphragm that would be impaired?" Jenn had no idea what a diaphragm was, but she shook her head. "Then what is it? A C3 break usually affects breathing and the victim would likely require a ventilator, unless…" She sucked in a breath and her jaw came unhinged so that her mouth came open.

"Jillybean?" Jenn asked.

The girl nodded, then looked at the knife in her hands. "Did I kill her?" she asked, in a strangled voice. Tears were already streaming down, running lines through the mud on her face, making it look as though something had clawed at her. Jenn told her no, and slowly Jillybean turned to look at the bleeding woman. "Okay good."

She knelt and the woman whimpered, holding up bloody, shaking hands. Jillybean took a deep breath and, still dripping tears, said, "It'll be okay. She's gone and I won't hurt you. See?" She tossed aside the knife. "Now let's see what I'm dealing with here."

Jenn had to hold the woman's hand, otherwise she would shake and cry. Her name was Kim Marino and Jenn had no intention of leaving for long, she just wanted to find out what was going on with the Corsairs. Mike was a good captain, perhaps the best alive, and yet his only crew member was Stu whose cast could be heard thumping and scraping along overhead.

It was only when Jillybean hooked an IV up and injected a strong sedative into it that Jenn was able to pop her head out of the cabin. "Where are we? Are we still in the harbor?" She heard a bell off to their right; it had to be a buoy.

"Almost out," Stu said. He was so pale that his eyes looked like a doll's button eyes in his white face.

"Let's switch. You can keep an eye on Jillybean."

He dragged himself down into the kitchenette. Jillybean took one look at him and cleared a spot on one of the stiff couches. "You're overdoing it, Stu Currans." She took his wrist and held it in what to Jenn looked like the least romantic handholding ever. "Yep, your heart rate is over ninety. Let's get you hooked up, as well."

Where Jillybean had been extremely clinical with Kim, she was sweet and gentle with Stu, and Jenn felt it was safe to go on deck. Mike didn't give her a moment to even say hello. He had her rushing about the deck, tying down the skiff that had been hauled up, bundling rope that was strewn all over the deck, and hunting down bullet holes to see if they were drawing water.

She found two below the waterline that she plugged with wads of cloth. When she went back on deck, she found Mike in a sweat working three sails against the wind and trying to slip through the narrow mouth of the harbor. Bells, warning of sandbars, were ringing to the north and south, while behind them to the east the water was crowded with lights. Hundreds of them.

The Corsairs burned candles on deck to keep from running into each other as they tacked back and forth. The closest of the lights were maybe only eighty yards away.

"Use the gun," Mike said, "but wait until I say to fire." She brought the scoped M4 to her shoulder and took aim at the closest of the boats which was on a similar course. She sighted on the helmsman. "Go," he said a moment later. She fired three times, the man fell and complete chaos ensued.

Mike spun the wheel and the *Saber* turned neatly just as dozens of guns opened up, firing in the direction they had been going, ripping up the water behind them. The boat Jenn had shot at yawed away from the wind while at the same time its crew, along with all the other crews doused the candles. In the narrow channel, a crash was inevitable, and Jenn watched through her scope as two boats plowed straight into each other. The two boats became locked and, as the smaller took on water and began to sink, it dragged the other down with it. Between them, they blocked the narrow channel.

Jenn went to high-five Mike but the *Saber* hit a small wave and she fell into him. The high-five became a long embrace that was interrupted by a fast approaching sand-

300

bar. Mike sent the boat on a diagonal course out of the harbor.

"We made it," he grinned. "We're free." Jenn wanted to hug him again, but held off. If they were in fact free, their time together was almost over. She looked to the stars for a sign and saw nothing but pretty lights.

There were no omens save for the wind. As much as Jenn wanted to prolong this last part of their trip, the wind hurtled them along, shooting them down the coast. The weather was beautiful and the *Saber* was the finest boat she'd ever been on. Still, she worried about the future they were speeding towards.

Without her medicine, Jillybean grew edgy, her mind slipping from personality to personality as she struggled to save Kim. The slave woman had been shot in her guts. On that first night, when Jenn went in to check on her, she found Jillybean covered in blood, her hands deep in the woman's bowels, picking through what looked like a mass of giant white worms.

"I can't do this," Jillybean whispered to Stu. "We should let Eve have her."

Stu was as bloody as Jillybean. Under the blood, he was a greenish shade of pale. "No. Never give in to her. Besides, the bleeder's right there. You can get it."

Jenn fled back on deck. By morning the surgery was over. Kim was in a coma, barely holding on. Jillybean, covered in blood and foul-smelling body parts, walked up out of the hold. As though she were sleepwalking, she went to the prow, stripped away her clothes and flung them into the ocean.

"Will you come back for me?" Before anyone could answer, she dove into the water. Mike had been studiously looking away, now he cursed and struggled the boat around.

She went into the water as Jillybean and came out as Sadie. "Did you get a good look, Magoo?" she asked Mike after they had pulled her naked but clean from the cold water. Jenn threw a blanket over her while Mike turned red. This had Sadie laughing. "Magoo, you're a real boy scout, aren't you?"

"Stop calling me Magoo or I'll toss you off my boat!"

Sadie laughed at this, which only had Mike getting even angrier. He held up a balled fist in front of her face. "Scary," she drawled. "Here's something even scarier." Casually, she let the blanket fall away. His eyes went wide for a second before he made a choking sound and looked up at the mast. When he did, Sadie kneed him in the crotch. As he doubled over, she slammed an elbow into his jaw, sending him sprawling.

Stark naked, she leapt on him and grabbed his face with both hands, her sharp thumbnails hovering millimeters above his eyes. "Never raise a fist at me again, Magoo. Never. This will be your only warning. Do you understand?"

"Jillybean," Stu said in a tired voice. He had hobbled up from the cabin. "Let him go."

"Not until he promises me."

When Mike finally made his promise, she jumped up as if nothing had happened. Jillybean didn't reappear for another three hours and when she did, she begged Mike for forgiveness. When he reluctantly forgave her, she turned to look at the cabin door as if it led straight into hell. Stu coaxed her in saying, "She needs you."

On the second day, Mike tried to make landfall. Kim and Jillybean, when she was Jillybean that is, were going downhill. Jillybean desperately needed her meds while Kim was bleeding internally and needed a stable platform so she could be opened up again.

He turned the *Saber* towards the shore and as they got close, the waves built up so that they felt as though they were on a rollercoaster. It was when they were on the peak of one of these waves that Jenn looked north and saw the tips of sails—black sails.

She screamed a warning and Mike flew into action, bringing the boat about and racing her south. "Did they see us?" he asked. Jenn had no idea.

Jillybean was forced to operate on Kim under the same terrible conditions and somehow, she was able to locate the bleeders and stabilize the woman. Kim even woke in the late evening. She was weak and her eyes kept sliding away from Jillybean's face, but she managed to say, "I'm Kim Marino. Don't forget me, please."

Jenn didn't think she would ever forget Kim. Her nose was crooked from an old break, she was missing most of her teeth and her skin was splotchy with partially healed bruises. Her life among the Corsairs had been one long nightmare.

By sunrise of the third day, they saw the hills of Capetown jutting out into the ocean ahead of them, while behind, slowly materializing in the grey light were black sails, looking like bat wings. The Corsairs had almost caught up with them in the night. They were only two miles away.

"God!" Mike cried and ran to let out the foresail. "Jenn! Help me! Point us right at that rock." In the distance was a little spit of a rock called Sugarloaf Island. It rose up out of the water sixty or seventy feet, while studded around it were smaller but no less dangerous spires, any one of which would turn the *Saber* into nothing more than a pile of kindling if they hit them. On a lee coast it was dangerous and stupid to try to thread those needles. It was, however the straightest route home. The Corsairs slowed and swung west to avoid them.

Once clear of the coastal rocks, the wind was almost at their backs and Mike piled on all the canvas he could. They were flying along and still the Corsairs gained on them.

"The math isn't in our favor," Jillybean said. "They'll catch us."

"Tell me," Mike ordered. "Break it down for me."

She looked at him with her head cocked like a dog that had just heard a far-off whistle. "It's me, Jillybean."

"I know!" he snapped. "Just tell me the math."

"Uh, okay. It's not that hard: speed equals distance divided by time. They're covering more distance in the same amount of time. Is that what you want to know? Or do you want to me to tell you about the square footage of their sails in relation to wind and weight? To put it simply, they have bigger ships and thus have bigger sails. This gives them a thrust to weight ratio advantage."

Jenn picked up her rifle and used the scope to get a close-up view of the ships. "The ships in front are much bigger. Fifty-footers at least, and their sails look huge, but they're not going that much faster than we are. Why?"

"That's because they have correspondingly more weight to…" Jillybean stopped and stared at Mike. They wore identical looks. "We have to lighten the load! Mike, tell us what to keep and what goes."

In the next ten minutes they stripped the boat of everything that wasn't needed. Every door in the lower cabins was tossed overboard, as were sheets, carpets, mattresses, clothes that weren't being worn, food and even water. An old engine that was now more or less a hunk of rust was hauled out of the compartment by Jillybean alone, using an ingenious concoction of levers and winches.

The little kitchenette was dismantled piece by piece until not even a fork was left. Then the bathroom was torn apart with only the toilet remaining. The last useless thing left onboard was Kim. They had worked all around her until she was all that was left.

She watched them with dull but knowing eyes. "Am I going to make it?"

Jillybean looked away. Her impossibly large eyes filled with tears. "Possibly," was all she would say.

"What are the odds?" Kim asked.

Jenn was the only other person in the cabin. "You'll make it and really, what do you weigh? A hundred pounds? And what's the bed? Another hundred? That won't make any difference, right Jillybean?"

But Jillybean was no longer there. "Without her, we no longer need the floor, do we? That's going to be another hundred pounds right there."

"Don't be silly," Jenn said with a laugh that was out of place and screamed of terror. "Of course, we need…"

"If you can't handle this, go on deck," Jillybean ordered, kneeling next to Kim. "As usual, I have to clean up the messes." The sound of her knife sliding from its sheath was the same sound a snake made sliding across carpet.

Jenn dropped down next to Jillybean and touched her hesitantly on the arm. "I-I was just out there, and you know what? They weren't gaining on us. We're going to make it home before them. I swear it."

"I believe you," she said. "Mike is a great sailor and we will win. Jillybean has worked out all the factors, but I believed you mentioned living on a hilltop." Jenn was hit by reality; it was like a knife in the guts. Their lead over the Corsairs was measured in minutes. They were never going to get Kim up the hill in time. She would have to be left behind.

"It's okay, Kim," Eve said, smiling at her. "Eve knows what to do. She always knows what to do." Before Jenn could even think to stop her, Eve leaned over Kim and slid her knife quickly and effortlessly between the woman's ribs. She jerked and her mouth came open in an O.

She died nodding her head, whispering, "Iss ah right."

"Get her out of here," Eve said, wiping the blade on the woman's sheet. When Jenn hesitated, Eve growled, "Maybe you should throw yourself overboard if you aren't going to be any help." She wrapped the corpse in the sheet and began dragging her through the empty cabin to the stairs.

There was no way Jenn could stand hearing Kim's head thumping up each step and she ran to help. Once on deck Eve didn't utter any words of loss or prayer. She simply dumped the body. Jenn couldn't look. Eve only snorted as she pushed past, heading back down to tear out the floor.

No one said anything. In fact, the silence on the boat went on and on with the only sound being Eve screaming in fury as she destroyed the flooring. "I'm the only one who cares enough to do the right thing! And who gets called a monster? Eve! It's always Eve and never precious

Jillybean." Muttering to herself, she brought the pieces of flooring up chunk by chunk and heaved them overboard.

Eventually, Stu pointed ahead of them where the land stabbed out across their course. "I think that's the Point Reyes lighthouse. We're almost home."

Mike looked back at the Corsairs. They were two miles back and holding steady. "What? Are we just going to lead them back home?"

Eve had snuck up during the short conversation and startled them by laughing, "You don't have any choice! The only people who can sail like you are the Guardians and they're too goody-goody to ever think about stealing a boat. The Corsairs know exactly where we're going. So, your choices are heading to Alcatraz, where they'll burn your ships at the docks, throw a cordon around the island and starve you guys out, or the hilltop where you might have a very small chance to live."

Chapter 35

Jenn Lockhart

"A small chance?" Stu asked. "How small?"

She shrugged. "I guess that depends on whether your people can fight. Can they?"

Stu shook his head and Jenn was right there with him. In her opinion, compared to Stu and Mike, the few men left on the hilltop were barely men; they were the weak and the cowardly, though they talked big enough. Still, they would defend their home if they were forced to.

"They can shoot," Stu said, "but we don't have much in the way of ammo."

"It won't be enough," Jenn said, her eyes flicking towards Eve. "We're going to need help and a real plan." Eve started to protest but Jenn shook her head. "We need her! Mike, as good of a boat captain as you are, you're not the best on land. Stu, you're hurt and I'm just me. I'm nothing. We need Jillybean."

Eve began laughing so hard that her face went bright red, then in mid-laugh, as though a switch was thrown, she turned mean. "Jenn, you're an idiot. Jillybean may think you're cute and sweet, but the truth is, you're an idiot. Don't you know why I'm even here? It's because poor Jillybean's fragile mind can't handle any of this. You know she's broken, right? You know she's weak and yet you want *her* over me?"

"Yes, I do. You...you're evil."

"You take that back," Eve said, her voice quiet and full of menace. "I'm going to give you one chance, and one chance only, to take that back."

Jenn swallowed hard before standing straight and squaring her shoulders. "No. We need Jillybean. You said it yourself that she killed thousands of people. You said she killed the Azael and they were warriors. The only person you killed was Kim and if you ask me, that was an act of cowardice."

Eve smiled and there was so much hatred in that smile than even Mike leaned back. "Do you really think she's the only person I've killed? If so you're more of an idiot than I thought. I killed a dozen people before I was six years old and that included a bounty hunter, and trust me, he was a badass. I've killed more…"

"Stop it," Stu said, sharply. She turned and if she thought the cold look in her eyes would affect him, she was wrong. Jenn could tell that he honestly liked Jillybean and she liked him as well. When Jillybean was herself she was sweet, though a bit condescending. Unfortunately, she was also terribly vulnerable—and Eve was how she protected herself.

"Stop what?" Eve demanded. "Do you want me to stop being honest?"

Stu kept his face neutral as he said, "I like honesty. Can you honestly tell me what seven times nine is?" She blinked at the question. It had caught her off-guard, but then the cold smile was back. Before she could say anything, he followed the question up with, "How about nine times twelve?"

Her white teeth, looking sharp, showed as she spat out, "That's not going to work. Even if it did, I'd be right back. She can't handle the stress. She…"

"Thirteen times fourteen."

Now, her eyes glazed over for a half-second before she was able to control them again. "Stop!" she screeched so loudly that the word echoed back from the beach.

Stu didn't stop. "Seventeen times seventeen. Twelve times twelve. Forty-one times eight."

Jenn was lost in the numbers, not knowing what they were talking about.

Eve's eyes lost focus with every question until Jillybean finally answered in her normal, soft voice. "328. Forty-one times eight is 328." She ran a shaking hand across her eyes. "I killed…I killed Kim, didn't I?" Stu nodded and Jenn tried to explain and make excuses, but Jillybean only shook her head and gazed back at the Corsair fleet that was strung out in long lines. The setting sun caught her just right, casting half her face in shadow, perfectly capturing her dual nature.

"I can't do anything about Kim now." She let out a long breath and asked "That sure is a lot of boats. How many are after us?"

Stu was quick to answer, "Eighty-two. There's probably an average of about fifteen men per boat, which means we're probably facing twelve hundred men."

"Against seventy?" Jillybean asked. "Isn't that how many people you said were on the hilltop?" When Stu nodded, Jillybean let out a bark of laughter. "Maybe you would have been better off with Eve." She ran a hand through her thicket of brown hair. "Okay, tell me what sort of assets you have."

They had M4s and hunting rifles for each person, but only about a thousand rounds. They had an equal number of crossbow bolts and arrows. When Stu explained this her smile was one of disbelief. "So, you're saying we can't miss with even one shot. Are your people good shots? No? Ooookay. Tell me about the wall."

"It's a cast-iron gate that we've put plywood over," Stu said. She gave him a look that said: *And*? "And there are spears in front. We don't have flamethrowers or bombs or machine guns. We try to keep out of the way and live our lives."

Jillybean looked stunned. "Plywood and a cast-iron gate. Against the dead. Really? The dead must not be much of a menace on your hilltop."

"They were getting bad just before we left," Mike said, easing the wheel to port, the sun glinting in his long hair as he cut the Saber eastward. The Golden Gate Bridge was just visible on the horizon. It would be dark by the time they crossed beneath it. "A big horde had come out of nowhere about nine days ago."

"And displaced all the 'regulars' in the surrounding lands, causing a big stir. Yes, I've seen that happen. It's rarely a good thing."

Mike smirked. "Rarely? How about never?"

"I would advise against using absolutes," Jillybean suggested, "because in this case it doesn't apply. Tell him, Jenn."

At first, she had a *Tell him, what?* look on her face, then she blinked. She was being tested once more. "Um-mmm, it's because, oh right. We're going to use the dead like Jillybean did back at the Corsair place. They'll be our army."

"Exactly," Jillybean said. "It'll be easy as pie. We light fires to attract the dead. Little fires that only burn for a few minutes, but each set closer and closer to the hilltop. If we can time it right, the Corsairs will be trapped between us and the dead. Is that what you were visualizing Jenn?"

Jenn shrugged. "I guess," she lied. She hadn't visualized anything but a cartoon army of giants under Jillybean's absolute command.

"You guess?" Mike asked. "Let's say we can attract the dead, how the hell are we going to get rid of them? And will they show up on time? The Corsairs could overrun the complex in minutes. Have you thought about that?"

"I have," Jillybean replied. "Unfortunately, I don't have answers for you. We have no assets and no chance at survival unless we take chances. Our only other choice is to beach the *Saber*, leave Stu to his fate and run for our lives. Is that what you'd like to do?"

Mike ground his teeth. Jillybean gave him a sympathetic look. "It gets worse. Your job will be to drag Stu up to your complex. You'll use a sail as a sort of stretcher. Jenn and I will be in charge of the fires."

"That's the plan?" He didn't wait for an answer and surprised Jenn by grabbing her hand and dragging her down into the empty space beneath the deck where it was dark and smelled of old blood. "You can't do this." He stood very close and when she looked up they were almost nose to nose. "It's too dangerous."

"Do we have another choice?" she asked. "I'm too small to drag Stu. Even with Jillybean's help, I don't think we could do it. Besides, we'll probably need fires from two directions. She'll have to take the east side…"

He grabbed her with desperate hands. "Jenn, no. It's too dangerous. We'll think of something. Okay? We'll think of something and…and …you'll be safe. That's what's important."

Mike was almost in tears and yet she laughed, feeling a crazy happiness. "I'll never be safe," she told him. "I'm going to die. Maybe not tonight or tomorrow, but I will and I don't want to die like this. Afraid. I've been more afraid of the Coven than I have been of the dead! But not anymore."

She pulled him down to her and kissed him with savage passion, holding him so close that it was almost as if she wanted to pull his heart into hers and join them.

After a moment he kissed her back with equal hunger. Still, he broke away first, his face twisted by fate and love. He held her at arm's-length. "That's why I can't let you sacrifice yourself. I'll light the fires. You…you…figure out a way to get Stu to the top of the hill."

"And if I can't? Do I shove him in some closet or leave him on the street? I won't. Stu is like a brother to me and you *will* respect that! Get him up the hill." She shoved him away and went up on deck where Stu and Jillybean were sitting together staring at her. Mike came up moments later, looking as though he had been kicked square in the groin once again.

He spent an hour desperately trying to come up with a better plan and it was sixty minutes of wasted time. They turned into the bay and now that they faced a headwind, the Corsairs slowly gained on them.

Tension built and soon a new problem arose. Jillybean began to come unglued. Stu tried to help by asking her to explain her theories on zombie migratory patterns. As she spoke her fingers twisted around themselves and she kept looking back over her shoulder at the Corsairs. "It'll be alright. I won't let them get you," he said and Jenn was sure he meant it, but lame as he was, there was no way he'd be able to keep that promise.

It was full dark as they swept past the bell announcing the entrance to Pelican Harbor. Mike had Jenn cut away the jib as they slid right down the length of the dock without slowing. The *Saber* seemed to scream as the paint was ripped from her side.

"Hold on," Mike said without a hint of panic in his voice. As always when he was at the helm, he was a cool operator, completely unruffled. The deck ended at the seawall and if they had hit it, the bow would have been stove in. They fetched up ten feet shy of it as the *Saber* ground against the rocky bottom of the harbor. They were thrown forward; the boat immediately began to list as water gushed in from a gaping wound in her keel.

Mike looked as though it was his child that was dying. "Let's go!" Stu whispered, trying to climb off the boat.

Jillybean, her pack filled with medical supplies, scrambled up onto the dock and with Jenn's help pulled him up and laid him on the silk jib. Mike came up last and started gathering the edges of the sail. "We'll meet you at the top," he said.

His mouth hung open as if he wanted to say more, but when he didn't, Jenn said, "Okay, be careful." He nodded in reply.

"What the hell kind of goodbye was that?" Jillybean demanded. Unexpectedly she shoved Jenn right into Mike's arms. "Make it count, Magoo."

They had no time for awkwardness or fumbling words. They kissed softly as valuable seconds ticked away until Stu cleared his throat. "It's time."

"I'll meet you up there," Mike said. "Don't die."

She wanted to cling to him. "Let them go, Jenn," Jillybean said, pulling her away and pointing at the black ships filling the harbor.

Mike whispered a goodbye, took the ends of the sail that Stu was bundled in and hauled him away.

With a sigh that hurt her heart, Jenn watched them go. When the night hid them, she said, "I know where we can get oil."

It wasn't Jillybean she led through the lower part of the town, it was Sadie. She walked fearlessly along while Jenn went in a crouch, heading for the building where her luck had taken a terrible change for the worse two weeks before. The Jiffy Lube was exactly how she had left it. The only thing that seemed to have changed was the crow-pecked corpse of the first zombie she had ever killed. It seemed deflated and no longer remotely as fearsome as it had been.

Sadie stepped around it and hurried into the one open bay of the Jiffy Lube, shining her flashlight around. "This is perfect. Look they even have sawdust to clean spills." She had the light pointed at a bin, but Jenn only gave it a quick glance. The flashlight was completely freaking her out, and for good reason.

A low groan from down the road was that reason. Sadie turned the light off and the two froze, wasting minutes as a huge shadow crossed in front of the Jiffy Lube. Sadie carried only her laser pointer, while Jenn had her M4. She kept an eye on the beast through the scope until it was out of sight.

When it was gone, they hunted down garbage bags and began filling them with sawdust. Jenn was just setting aside one of the bags when a new and different groan could be heard all through the town and probably up to the top of the hill. One of the old docks had taken the weight of a sixty-foot sailboat against it and had let out a protesting scream. The Corsairs were landing.

"Hurry!" Sadie hissed. They shoveled the sawdust in as fast as they could. Next, they went to a nasty drum that had oil spilled all down its sides. Sadie produced a screwdriver and pried the lid off. Both girls stepped back, gagging as the air fairly shimmered with a harsh chemical smell.

Sadie pulled her shirt over her nose and advanced. "We need a scoop or something to hold the oil."

"What about using fresh oil?" Jenn asked, pointing to a rack that was filled with 10W30.

"That's even better!" Sadie said, slamming the lid back down. "Grab as much as you can carry." Sadie was already loaded down and could only carry four quarts. Jenn grabbed six of them and shoved them on top of the sawdust.

She was about to leave when she had an idea. Taking a handful of sawdust, she poured it on the floor and smoothed it out. Jabbing her thumb down, she said, "This is where we are." Jenn drew a quick series of hills. "If you go up the hill to the top of the ridge, you'll run into a four-lane highway. There's nothing past it. Build your fires along it and you'll get maximum exposure. Head west; the complex will be on your right after a half mile. I'll meet you there."

"Got it. I'll see you at the top."

They stepped from the open bay and both stopped in their tracks, staring as a flood of dark shapes swarmed along the street in front of the harbor, while further back, lit by the starlight, even more ships crowded the docks.

"And that's why Jillybean has been advising the governor to deal with the Corsairs for years," Sadie said. "They multiply like roaches." She gave Jenn one of her unsettlingly intimate winks. "We'll take care of them, right?"

They split up. Sadie went straight up the hill, while Jenn cut through the town only two blocks from the harbor. She snuck along using the lowlight scope to keep away from the dead, many of which were already out in the streets. There was something almost electric in the night air, and the beasts were stirred up and growing aggressive, rushing each other in brief but savage attacks. As soon they realized they were fighting another zombie, their anger would switch to total apathy.

Jenn slipped through all this until she was a hundred yards from the Jiffy Lube. Then she lit her first fire against a wall out of sight from the docks and the Corsairs. "This is crazy!" she hissed, when she lit it.

The dead came rushing at the flame and she had to duck around the building to keep from being eaten. When the dead were completely focused on the light, she was able to scamper a hundred yards further up the road. This time when she lit the fire, beasts came roaring from houses all around her and she was forced to crawl under a hedge.

In minutes, there were thirty of them crowding around and she was only able to escape when a bizarre fight broke out among the dead as they mistook shadows for people and attacked a garage door.

"I have to be like Jillybean. I have to think three steps ahead," Jenn told herself. The problem: she had to light a fire out in the open so the dead could see it, but she also had to be able to get away. She carried the solution in her bag. After preparing the next fire, she ran a line of oil from it to where she hid behind a car.

The slow-burning fuse gave her enough time to slip away and watch as nearly fifty of the creatures congregated.

After two more fires she had a hundred of them and she wore a wicked grin as she beckoned "her army" further up the hill with more fires.

The grin faded when she got close to the apartment complex she had called home for the last nine years. Guiding the dead up the hill had been a slow process and now she saw that the Corsairs had beaten her to the top and were fanning out, surrounding the place.

She started moving to her right, but hadn't gone far before a soft voice said, "How many did you get?"

Jenn jumped, her heart skipping more than a few beats in her shock. It was Sadie or Jillybean, leaning against a tree, looking very relaxed. "I only picked about fifty or so."

"I got a hundred, I think," Jenn said, when she got her breathing under control.

"That's good. The Corsairs are in perfect position. Now, if Mike or Stu can light a fire or make some noise, the dead will move in, and goodbye Corsairs."

They waited in the dark and long minutes passed without either noise or fire. The complex remained quiet and dark.

Finally, even the Corsairs grew tired of waiting for a response and a man with a white sheet tied to a stick went forward. To Sadie's shock, he was let inside. "Are they all complete idiots? Jenn, where's the back entrance?" Jenn shrugged. "You don't have a back entrance? They're idiots!"

"There's not a back entrance, but there is a low point in the fence. It's how we got out. But it's useless, the Corsairs are in the way." Although most were squatting in company-sized formations in front of the complex, a thin band of them had surrounded the complex.

"Just show me," Sadie said.

It wasn't far. As soon as they got close, Sadie unlimbered her dart gun and cleared a path with it. The sentries didn't know what hit them and dropped to the ground senseless.

The two of them crept forward, then crawled beneath the plywood wall. Now that they were out of sight of the Corsairs, Jenn took Sadie's hand and ran for the clubhouse, where a crowd of people stood outside talking in frightened whispers.

"My goodness, they *are* complete idiots," Sadie said so loudly that the crowd turned as one to stare. "I'm risking my life for idiots! Why didn't you tell me, Jenn? Why aren't you morons at your battle stations?" Her eyes were starting to grow wild again.

Eve was on the verge of showing herself, which would have been a disaster. Jenn pulled her close and stared into her eyes. "Don't let Eve out," Jenn said so that only Sadie could hear. "If I have too, I'll light the fires myself. All you have to do is worry about Aaron and the others. They need a doctor. They need Jillybean."

Sadie started nodding uncertainly. Jenn was afraid Eve would slip out in front of everyone. She grabbed Sadie's hand and pushed through the crowd and into the building. Except for a soft murmuring coming from the meeting room, the place was quiet as a church.

Jenn didn't knock or poke her head in timidly. She marched in brazenly, her M4 in one hand. The full Coven sat at their table, looking soft and weak. Off to the side were Mike and Stu.

Stu was pale, while Mike was dripping sweat and exhausted—pulling a hundred-and-seventy pound man uphill for two miles in a zombie-infested environment had left him barely able to stand, yet he and Stu wore matching looks of defiance.

The only person in the room who seemed utterly at ease was the Corsair. He stood directly before the Coven, wrapped in a black cloak and wearing an insolent smirk. He raised a dark eyebrow at Jenn and Sadie.

"This is them!" Miss Shay cried, pointing an accusing finger. She waved back and forth between Mike and Stu, and Jenn and Jillybean. "It was these four. We had nothing to do with any of this. In fact they were banished. You can have them."

"I'm afraid four won't cut it," the Corsair answered. "We lost four ships and over fifty good men."

Miss Shay began to breathe heavier than Mike. "I'm so sorry, but like I said we…"

The man cut her off simply by raising a finger. "While I appreciate the apology, the Corsairs operate on a strict eye for an eye philosophy. We demand proper compensation and we're going to get it. You are surrounded by over two-thousand men and frankly, you have nothing to stop us with. You people are pathetic and weak. Give me fifty warm bodies to go along with these four and we'll leave."

As the council looked at each other in horror, Sadie's eyes changed. Eve was now in charge and her grin was dripping with evil as she started walking forward. She spun the empty dart-gun around as if she were going to hand it to the Corsair, while at the same time her right hand took hold of the hunting knife she had used to kill Kim Marino.

"No!" Jenn said, rushing to get between them. "She was going to kill you." Jenn could see Eve smoldering behind Jillybean's blue eyes. Eve wasn't thinking three steps ahead, she was only thinking in the moment. She had had no idea what another death on Jillybean's conscience would do to the girl, but Jenn saw it all clearly. She finally saw three steps ahead.

It was why she plunged her own knife into the man's chest.

Chapter 36

Jenn Lockhart

For once in her life everything was laid out for her step by step. Someone had to stop the Corsairs and that meant stopping this one man from ever leaving the complex. Just like Jillybean, he had been shocked at their soft defenses and even softer people. If he had been allowed to leave, the Corsairs wouldn't have stopped with fifty people. They would have made slaves of all of them, as well as the people on Alcatraz.

He had to die and if Aaron and the others were going to have any chance, Jillybean couldn't be the one to do it. Someone else had to be the bad guy.

"Jenn, what did you do?" Donna Polston practically screamed, as the man fell, gasping, his eyes locked on the dagger and the blood erupting around it.

The other council members were in hysterics as well. "Shut up!" Jenn yelled. "Everyone just shut up! We have one chance to live through this. Stu, set up some sort of defense. Get everyone on the perimeter. Don't have them shoot unless the Corsairs attack. Mike, I need you to set up a fire on the roof of building four. It's right across the way. Everything you'll need is in the trash bags we left outside the door. The fire has to be big enough to attract the dead, but not so big that we burn down the building."

The two men hesitated and Jenn had to yell, "Go!" before they would move. When Mike helped Stu limp out, Jenn and Eve were alone with the Coven, some of whom glared, some looked like they were on the verge of tears.

"A fire?" Donna asked, her voice high and shrill. "Are you insane? You-you just said the fire will bring the dead. Why on earth…"

"The dead are our army," Jenn explained. This had the women wagging their heads in disbelief. "They'll defeat the Corsairs for us. And this," Jenn pointed at Jillybean, "is the girl doctor."

Jenn turned so the two locked eyes. "Her name is Jillybean," Jenn said very deliberately. "I brought her back from Seattle and yes, she's a real doctor. She saved Stu when he was shot. She operated on him and everything. She had antibiotics, which she made."

"She's just a kid!" Miss Shay cried. "And what's wrong with her eyes? Why are they doing that?"

The stress was beginning to tear Jillybean in half and her eyes were going their separate ways. Jenn grabbed her by the shoulders and whispered, "Stop it, Jillybean, please. You don't need to be scared. You have me." The girl's eyes slowly came to focus on Jenn.

"It's Eve. She's clawing to get out. She knows we won't make it. I-I can't concentrate. I can't think clearly."

"Forget her, and forget them." She gestured toward the Coven. "We don't need their permission to save lives." She took her by the arm and walked her around the Corsair, who was staring up at the ceiling with blank, unseeing eyes. With the Coven trailing, she took Jillybean into the medical wing which was lit only by a few candles. It was plenty of light to see that there were only two occupied beds in the room. Jeff Battaglia was already dead.

William Trafny lay in the closest bed. He was thinner now, his flesh membranous. Jenn could see the blue, spider-like veins clearly beneath it. He was so close to death that in sleep he looked more like a cadaver than a person. Jenn had to touch him to make sure he was still warm.

Watching this from the next bed was Aaron Altman. "He's alive, but not for long," the boy said in a whisper. He was ghostly pale and listless. His face glistened in the candlelight. He was missing most of his left arm. It was cut off at the bicep, and there was a sour smell emanating from the stump.

"Can you do anything for them?" Jenn asked.

Before Jillybean could answer, one of the Coven whispered. "If that really is the girl doctor, they might just take her instead of all of us."

Jenn pulled her Glock. She held it dangling at her side as she said, "Whoever said that leave, or so help me, I will shoot you." The menace in her voice was enough to cause three of the women to leave. When she turned back, she saw that Jillybean's eyes were still focused, but she hadn't moved.

"The smell," she whispered.

"It's gangrene, right?" Jenn said. "Will your antibiotics cure it?" With half the Coven watching and Aaron looking at her with sad, brown eyes, Jillybean astonished Jenn by shrugging.

"Fifty-fifty. He looks like he's half-dead already and the other one is worse. Let's do them a favor." She pulled out the hunting knife, a malicious gleam to her eyes. "I'll take care of these two, you get those three. We don't want witnesses, they can be messy. And weren't these the people who threatened to banish you? I say do it, Jenn. Plug 'em."

Jenn realized that she was still holding her Glock. Donna began shaking her head. "Don't, please." Next to her Miss Shay started making a mewling sound and Lois looked as though she were either going to faint or run away.

"I won't," Jenn said, feeling frantic. Time was slipping away. "No one is dying in here tonight. Do you understand me, *Jillybean*?"

Jillybean wasn't Jillybean. She brought the hunting knife up to her nose and sniffed it. She smiled and sighed as if the smell of Kim's blood was a perfume. "Is that what your silly signs say? If so, I'd roll them old bones again or maybe get some glasses, cuz…" A sudden blaze of gunfire erupted and the girl's smile widened.

Their vague plan was falling apart. "Stop it, Eve! Let me talk to Jillybean."

The girl shook her head. "Why should I?" She suddenly raised her hands to the ceiling and bellowed, "Great and powerful Oz! Give me a sign right now or I'll slice this boy's throat wide open. Hello? Anyone listening? He needs a sign pretty badly." She shrugged. "Did you see a sign because I didn't. Sorry kid."

She turned to Aaron, raising the knife. Jenn cried, "Wait! Listen to me. There are signs. I know I'm not smart enough to pull you out of this. I don't know anything about times tables or cranial nerves or arteries or veineries or…"

"It's just veins. There's no such thing as veineries."

"That's my point. I'm not smart. I don't know nothing about nothing except I know this, all those signs and omens you mock, they brought you right here, right now for one purpose and it isn't to kill Aaron. There's a killer in you *and* a person who can save lives. If you want to kill, go kill the Corsairs. I'll handle this. How hard could it be?"

"How hard?" Eve cried. "Try very hard. No one else can do what she does. No one else even has the guts to try. And do you know why? You don't get a second chance or a do-over. One mistake and Aaron's dead and you know who gets blamed?" She pointed the knife at herself. "They'll say: he would have lived if she hadn't been so crazy, or better or smarter. I know it because I say the same thing every time. I try to be better, it's why I practice so much and I try to be smarter, it's why I read all the time. But what can I do about being crazy?"

Somewhere in there Jillybean had come back, only now she was crying. Jenn hugged her in a fierce embrace. "I'll help you with the crazy. You know that. And Stu and Mike will help you as well." Saying their names caused her chest to spike with pain. They were out there in the thick of the fighting, which was turning savage by the sound of it. The screams and the gunfire were now all around them.

"Do you believe me?" Jenn asked.

"I do believe you," she answered, "but pretty soon it won't matter for these two or for any of us. You have to help Mike and Stu. I would help but I don't think these two will last even an hour. I'll be good, don't worry. I have these three fine ladies to assist me." At this Lois broke for the door in a sprint.

"I'll help," Miss Shay said, taking one step closer.

322

"Me too," Donna added. "Just tell me what to do."

Jillybean appraised them. She pointed to Donna. "You, get my bag from the hall. And you, start boiling water." When they scurried from the room, the girl turned to Jenn. "The battle can go one of two ways: either the dead wins or the Corsairs do. We know what happens if the Corsairs win, we become slaves. But if the dead win…"

Jenn knew. "We die."

"Maybe not. The same thing that brought them here can lead them away. Do you understand?"

A flash of goosebumps swept her. She understood. Someone would have to go outside the walls in the middle of a war and she already knew who that someone was.

Feeling dizzy, Jenn said, "I gotta go." She hugged Jillybean and ran out of the room, pausing to grab the garbage bag with the last of the oil and sawdust, as well as her M4. Rushing out into the night, the noise struck her full force. It was an assault on the ears that was like having nails driven into her eardrums.

The fight was chaos. The Corsairs were winning and losing at the same time. On one side of the complex they had managed to scale the wall and were battling around one of the buildings, while on the other side of the complex, they were being overrun by the dead, whose numbers kept increasing as more and more were drawn to the bonfire Mike had lit.

She found Stu pulling people from one side of the complex and sending them to the other. He had taken a hammer to his cast and was now hobbling about, issuing orders at the top of his lungs.

"Where's Mike?" she yelled over the din. She had used her scope to check out the top of building four, and he wasn't there.

"Where do you think? In the thick of it. I don't think he can help himself. Some…Hey!"

Jenn left him in mid-sentence, sprinting towards where the gunfire was heaviest. The firing was almost all one-sided. The hill people weren't fighters and the only reason they still existed was that no one had yet tested their feeble defenses. For the most part, they hid or fired from windows and balconies when they felt it was safe.

Only the forest of spears kept the full Corsair army at bay, but in the one spot where they were able to get past it, the hill people had simply fled. Only Mike still fought.

Using the lowlight scope, Jenn could see him pinned down on a ground-floor porch hunkered in a corner, using a stout grill as cover. When bullets ricocheted off it, they looked like fireworks. The Corsairs had a great advantage in training and ammo. They were shooting like mad, but only when they were shot at. They were looking for captives, not kills. Mike was the one exception.

Jenn quickly became the second. With her lowlight scope, she became a terror. Three shots and three kills. In greyscale, the deaths looked like movie deaths. When she went aimed at the fourth, all she saw was a blaze of light while all around her the air hissed.

Acting on instinct, she rolled and kept rolling as the bullets tracked her, kicking up dirt and whining off cement. She rolled into one of the little personal farms that sat between the buildings and dropped into a ten-inch trench. It was just deep enough that the bullets blistered the air above her head, but left her unhurt.

When the gunner shifted his aim, Jenn lifted up just enough to aim. Two more Corsairs died before she ducked down and began low-crawling forward. Fifteen seconds later she popped up again and killed another man. She was about to shoot again when two men ran up from behind her.

She screamed and kicked as they reached down and lifted her off the ground as if she were a child. "Shut up!" Mike whispered, as he and Stu ran for the cover of the porch. They set her down and both fired at the fence where one of the Corsairs twisted with the impact of their bullets and fell as he was trying to climb over.

"What are you doing here?" Mike asked.

"I, uh, wanted to give you, or rather Stu, this," she lied, presenting the M4 to Stu. Although she wouldn't need the gun where she was going, the real reason she had come was that she *needed* to see Mike. She would be going out-side the fence as soon as the Corsairs realized how terrible their position was, and that time was coming quickly. There were screams from all over the perimeter and cries of retreat echoed over the gunfire.

At the same time, there was a great cracking sound as the dead began to tear down the plywood boards on the west side of the complex.

Mike looked confused. "What are you talking about? Stu can barely limp around. Keep the rifle, Jenn. You're more effective…"

Stu tried to hand back the rifle. "We can get someone else. Or I can do it."

"Do what?" Mike demanded.

Angrily, Jenn pushed the gun back, saying, "Someone has to be ready to put out the fire, and I can't climb up there. Someone else has to clear out the last of the Corsairs and then button this place up. That'll be Stu's job, because frankly, we can't trust anyone else to do it."

Mike glanced back and forth from Jenn to Stu. "And?"

"And someone has to go outside the fence to distract the dead," she said in a whisper. "Or they'll get in the perimeter."

"I'll go," Mike said, standing up. "We'll get someone else to go up onto the roof. One of the men." He looked around, ignoring two of the Corsairs as they climbed up the wall and disappeared. Other than the few Corsairs left, there were no men in evidence.

Stu stood, wagging his head, his mouth hanging open in disbelief. "Maybe I could get them away. I don't have to go far. Just far enough…"

Jenn punched his hurt leg and he crumpled. "No. This has to be done, now! The fire has to be put out, now! The complex has to be shut down, now! Three jobs for three of us." She stood, staring up at Mike and swallowed hard. "Stu, look away."

He turned to the wall of the porch and punched a hole in the siding. Jenn ignored him. She brushed away one of Mike's tears. "Maybe…maybe, I'll make it," she said.

"Wait! I could…" She shut him up, kissing him for the third and final time. Midway through the kiss, his shoulders slumped as he realized their fates were set.

He looked broken as she pulled away from him. His face was a mask of misery and his green eyes were tortured with the knowledge that she would never get away from so many of the dead.

She left him, knowing that another kiss would only doom them all. She ran away, her vision blurred by tears. Savagely, she ripped them away with the back of her hand. Tears were wasted now. They all had their jobs, and hers was the most important.

This was what she told herself as she ran up to her apartment, stopping only long enough to grab her broom and wrap it loosely in a pair of sheets. Then she sped to the gate and looked back at building four, where she saw Mike's silhouette as he smothered the fire. At the same time, the last of the gunshots rang out in the complex and people began to hush each other into silence.

The only sound were the dead tearing the wall and the running feet of the Corsairs.

It was time for her to go. After dousing the sheets with oil, and lighting them, she ran through the gate, a scream of anger and fear erupting out of her. The dead turned to Jenn Lockhart and converged on her by the hundreds.

She was a beacon. Every eye, dead or alive fixated on her and her, fear was visible for all to see as she ran zigzagging all over the hilltop. The dead seemed to appear before her out of nowhere. She dodged back and forth, panic gripping her just as surely as she gripped the Glock. It was her insurance policy against the inevitable. It was only a matter of time before she would need to use it on herself; there were just too many of them and they were fast and strong and their arms seemed to stretch farther and farther so that their claws were always inches away.

Almost mindlessly, she ran from one, only to blunder into the next, and more and more her thoughts turned to the gun. Jillybean would have been disappointed: Jenn was thinking only one step ahead and that step was suicide.

What would a second step ahead even be? she wondered.

A gunshot from down the hill gave her an idea. If she was going to die, she could at least take a few Corsairs with her. Holding the burning sheet above her head, she ran down the hill, dodging the dead, tripping over branches and crashing through bushes.

The hill was covered in black shadows and the flames only made them deeper. She fell and fell again, sometimes rolling uncontrollably, sometimes going down and popping up almost without losing her stride. She couldn't spare a second even to look back. There was an avalanche of giant grey bodies pouring down the hill after her. Not only could she hear them crushing everything in their way, she could feel the hill itself tremble.

Cut and bruised and muddy, she raced down onto the streets just up from the harbor. Up until that moment she had been running with panic driving her, but suddenly she knew exactly where she was and, what was more, an actual plan came to her.

With an insane laugh, she tossed the broom to her left and cut right, racing through the front door of the Jiffy Lube and slamming it behind her.

At least a hundred of the dead charged after the broom and the burning sheets, stomping them out. An equal number attacked the Jiffy Lube. The metal door was bent in and torn down in seconds, while the front window was smashed in even faster. That was just fine with Jenn who needed only seconds to put her plan in motion. As the creatures swept around the building and bashed their way inside, she threw down the barrel of used oil and set her lighter to it. Before the first of the dead charged into the bay, the barrel was covered in flames. She kicked it out into the street and then ducked down into one of the black pits.

She had visions of the barrel rolling like a ball of fire all the way down to the docks, where it would smash into the flagship of the Corsairs and burn it down to its waterline.

Nothing so spectacular happened. The barrel rolled with a side spin halfway down one block before it veered off the street, bounced over a curb and struck a fire hydrant. This knocked the barrel back on course, but the spin sent it into the curb again where it burst open. Burning oil poured down the gutter for another fifty feet or so before emptying into the sewer where it set fire to a dozen years of moldering leaves that burned with such a dense cloud of black smoke that the flames were hidden and the dead turned away.

It wasn't a complete bust, however. The grey wave of zombies that had followed the barrel now moved on to the closest noise which happened to be the Corsairs attempting to get their boats away from the harbor as fast as they could in complete darkness.

It was pure chaos. They had docked haphazardly with the larger ships in close and crowded by the smaller ones. Men ran around trying to find their ships, not knowing which dock was which. Some boats were overloaded with so many men that they fell over each other trying to get them moving, while other boats sat empty and in the way.

When two ships collided and became locked together, shouts erupted and flashlights beamed back and forth. The dead went crazy and rushed full onto the docks, or waded out to grab the boats and hold them fast. The strength of the dead was fantastic. Boats were overturned and the men either drowned or were eaten alive.

Gunshots began to ring out, which only had more of the dead rushing in. Desperation turned to panic and in the mad scramble to get away a third of the fleet was abandoned. Over a hundred men ran north with the dead racing after.

Jenn watched this, sitting with her back against the Jiffy Lube. It played out in shadows but she saw enough to know that they had won an amazing victory. Although she was exhausted and drained, the reason she sat there for over half an hour was that victory or not, there would be casualties and she would be blamed.

She was still sitting there when she heard twigs snap and pebbles kicked. A smile spread across her face. Even before she saw *his* shadow she knew. On the ocean he was a king, on land…well, he tried. "Mike. I'm over here."

He had the M4. The little red battery light gave away the fact that he was sizing her up. "Are you alright?"

The best way to answer that was not to answer it at all. "Sit," she said, patting the cement next to her. When he eased down, groaning like an old man, she asked, "How bad is it?"

His eyes were red and swollen, but his smile lit up the night. "Not bad at all. Two hurt, well three if you count Stu. He had a stitch come undone and is bleeding like a stuck pig. I was coming out to find you anyway, but Jilly-bean rushed out and stopped me at the gate. She said she wants you to assist her. She said you need to learn the fine art of surgeoning."

"Huh. She wants me to be a doctor? What else did she say?"

He hesitated before answering, "She said that there's only time for me to kiss you for one minute." Jenn was sure he was blushing; she could practically hear it in his voice.

"Only one minute?" she asked. "Well, that's a bit disappointing. Jillybean must not have believed I would make it. She should have known that there's no way I'm going to stop at a minute."

And she didn't.

THE END

***

Author's Note

Thank you so much for reading Generation Z. I sincerely hope that you enjoyed it. If so, I would greatly appreciate it if you would, please, take the time to write a kind review on Amazon and your Facebook page. I will choose my favorite reviews and send the reviewers a signed copy of the book as a thank you.

For my new readers, Generation Z is a spinoff of my highly successful 10-book series: The Undead World. While you eagerly wait for Generation Z Book 2, please check out The Apocalypse to discover what true desperation and inhumanity lies within all of us.

Peter Meredith

PS If you are interested in autographed copies of my books, souvenir posters of the covers, Apocalypse T-shirts and other awesome swag, please visit my website at https://www.petemeredith1.com

The Apocalypse:
Greed, terrorism, and simple bad luck conspire to bring mankind to its knees as a viral infection spreads out of control, reducing those infected to undead horrors that feed upon the rest.

It's a time of misery and death for most, however there are some who are lucky, some who are ruthless, and some who are just too damned tough to go down without a fight. This is their story.

What the readers say about The Apocalypse:
"No frills, just raw and earnest fear."
"Fun and scary, it will have you turning the pages right to the end..."
"This has everything I love in a good story: interesting characters, vivid details, fast pacing, and a shocker at the end."

Fictional works by Peter Meredith:

Printed in Poland
by Amazon Fulfillment
Poland Sp. z o.o., Wrocław